HALF A CENTURY OF DARING PASSIONS . . .
HALF A CENTURY OF AUDACIOUS
DREAMS. . . .

CORDELIA DORFMAN LOVEJOY—Her courage would carry her through the dark hours of war and tragedy. . . . Her passions would propel her into a dazzling world of wealth, elegance, and power.

MARY—The Irish servant girl. She left Shanty Town, risked losing the only man she could ever love, to become Cordelia's friend and confidante on Society Row.

JOHN SPEER—The publishing genius who ignited the spark of Cordelia's passion, filled her with longing, and showed her the world that could be hers.

STEVE—He would forsake his mother's empire for another woman's outrageous dream.

AL—He began life as Cordelia's greatest hope and lived to become her greatest enemy.

CATHY—The quiet child who would fulfill a family's hope and share the final triumph.

THEY ALL BEGAN IN . . .

MURRAY HILL

MURRAY HILL

Charles Mercer

A DELL BOOK

TO
ALMA
WITH LOVE

Published by
Dell Publishing Co., Inc.
1 Dag Hammarskjold Plaza
New York, New York 10017

Dell ® TM 681510, Dell Publishing Co., Inc.

ISBN: 0-440-16124-X

Reprinted by arrangement with Delacorte Press

Printed in Canada
First Dell printing—June 1981

BOOK ONE

1

Mrs. Stuyvesant Fish is generally credited with the remark. But Mrs. Fish never was above stealing the lines of others in trying to maintain her reputation as the leading wit and sage in society. It was not Mrs. Fish but Mrs. Augustus Peyster who first said: "Do what you want to in life, but make sure you do it better than anyone else."

Mrs. Peyster uttered those words to Cordelia Dorfman when she was fourteen years old. That was in 1884. Years later, when Cordelia was twenty-eight, Mrs. Fish told her precisely the same thing. After repeating Miriam Peyster's words in the guise of an original thought, Mamie Fish peered at Cordelia through the lorgnette she sometimes affected and added, "My pet, you have all the raw material. It's only a matter of improving your manufacture and putting your product in the right marketplace."

It was no wonder Cordelia at twenty-eight radiated self-assurance even in her time of greatest trial. Her face and body had exquisite beauty, her hair the sheen of a chestnut. Eyes and lips were the most striking features of her lovely face.

"Believe me, dear," Mrs. Fish told her, "you are still young enough to be the belle of Newport society next year because I can show you how to do it better than anyone else. The right men will fall at your feet like rose petals at the end of June."

"But suppose," Cordelia said, "it's not my goal to be popular in society?"

"God's teeth," said Mrs. Fish, "what else is there for

a woman to try for except to excel in society and collect men?"

The sagacious Mrs. Fish knew that Cordelia had an excellent mind, but failed to realize that she wanted to use it. Cordelia did not attempt to explain. She was weary with people setting her goals to which she did not aspire. An expression that her mother used to call "your stubborn look" came over Cordelia's face.

That expression is preserved today in a photograph taken of Cordelia Dorfman in 1880 when she was ten years old. One sees in its faded details a thin, intense child wearing black stockings and a scowl. She is carrying a pail which appears heavily weighted down. Behind her there seems to be a forested mountain.

When one of her grandchildren came across the picture several years before Cordelia died and asked for an explanation, Cordelia had a ready one:

"That was taken by a photographer named Clarke who used to wander around New York. He'd worked for Mathew Brady. My bucket there in that picture is full of blackberries. I look mad because Mr. Clarke, a friend of my father's, has stopped me to take my picture. I wanted to get the berries home. Or more likely there was something else I was in a hurry to get to. But there's Mr. Clarke setting up his tripod and wanting to take my picture. He knew my father would buy it. So I had to be polite. . . . Mountain? That's no mountain. That's East Sixty-fourth Street. Yes, East Sixty-fourth in Manhattan. It was no street at all then. Just a deep, twisting gully—and, oh my, the best blackberries anywhere growing on its banks."

When it came to old New York families, none was older than the Dorfmans. By the 1880s many families were better known because no Dorfman had accomplished anything much in more than a century. But if "old" had any importance in society, the Dorfmans were in a group with the Bayards and Beekmans, the Schuylers and Livingstons, the Roosevelts, Rutherfords, and a few others. They were descendants of a Netherlander who had arrived in New York when it still was Nieuw Amsterdam, an inhabitant so early that he was reputed to have fitted Peter Stuyvesant with a wooden leg.

The Dorfmans had been royalist in the Revolution, viewing families like the Jays and Clintons as radical upstarts. Despite their guessing wrong about which side would win that war, they had managed to cling to some of their land in Manhattan and up the Hudson after the American victory. The family fortune, such as it was, consisted of land. If the menfolk of succeeding generations had tried a little harder, they might have become very wealthy simply by holding the Manhattan real estate. But the Dorfmans enjoyed leisure, and they sold off parcel after parcel to support themselves. While the house on Forty-eighth Street near Madison Avenue where Cordelia and her older brother Nicholas were born was not pretentious, their father Loren and mother Marie found it "comfortable." They would have liked one more servant in addition to the two who worked for them, but that would have entailed giving up their box in the sacred circle of old families who were members of the Academy of Music, quitting membership in the exclusive old Coaching Club, and making other sacrifices.

Their financial situation began to shape toward a crisis after Nicholas, seven years older than Cordelia, went off to Harvard and the price of everything suddenly seemed to soar. At last Loren Dorfman came to a decision he had long put off. He, who never had worked a day in his life, would "retire" to the farm he owned in Dutchess County where there was a rambling old house known as Dorfman Manor in which the family spent the summers. Cordelia, who had just turned fourteen, was delighted with the plan. She was bored with study at the St. Thomas's School for Young Ladies and had recently decided that horses made better companions than human beings.

But she had not reckoned on her mother's cousin, Miriam Peyster. Miriam, like Marie Dorfman, had been born an Applegate—an English family that had arrived late in New York, around 1760 or so. She had married Augustus Peyster, whose family was almost, though not quite, as old as the Dorfmans. Their marriage had not been blessed with children, a fact that gave Miriam much free time to engage in good works. In Cordelia the restless Miriam Peyster saw a grand opportunity for her best work ever.

"How," she demanded of her cousin Marie, "can you bear to bury such a bright, pretty child off in the wild hills back of Poughkeepsie? You're cutting her off from all opportunities. It's simply dreadful!"

Marie and Loren, knowing they could not offer Cordelia the opportunities that Miriam and Augustus could, did not raise much resistance. Cordelia herself had no say in the matter. To her vast disappointment she would live with the Peysters in their Fifth Avenue house near Thirty-ninth Street on Murray Hill and stay with her parents at Dorfman Manor during vacation periods.

Miriam was a large, restless woman while her husband was large and sedentary. Each tried to smile occasionally, but found the effort difficult. Six days a week Augustus walked to his office in the Grand Central Depot where he was a vice-president of the New York Central Railroad under Mr. Cornelius Vanderbilt II. He also had extensive market investments that often took him downtown and kept him up late nearly every night at his study desk on Fifth Avenue. Not knowing what to make of Cordelia, he made nothing much at all—and this she found satisfactory.

It was Cousin Miriam who was troublesome. The very first day Cordelia went to live with them, Miriam made her not really immortal remark, "Do what you want to in life, but make sure you do it better than anyone else." Cordelia paid no attention to it until she discovered with alarm that it meant she must do what Miriam wanted her to do and must be better at it than anyone else.

The Dorfmans were members of St. Thomas's Episcopal Church, second most fashionable in New York, while the Peysters were members of the most fashionable, St. Bartholomew's. They carried Cordelia off there at once, for membership in St. Bartholomew's would facilitate her being admitted to Miss Troy's School. The chief aim of Miss Troy's was to teach a girl to be a lady. A lady, as differentiated from a woman, was one who displayed perfect breeding always, who wore silk stockings and silk gloves, and who *never* turned a hand to menial tasks. Of course there was more to it than that, as students at the day school discovered. Miss Troy herself was dead, but her work was carried on by a stern martinet appropriately named Miss Grimsby and a staff of strict women teachers who prepared the daughters of wealthy, socially prominent New Yorkers to carry on the traditions of their mothers.

Cordelia, at her previous school, had struggled with Latin, French, mathematics, English literature. No Latin or math was taught at Miss Troy's. English literature had been Cordelia's favorite subject, but "English" at her new school had none of the pleasures of literature; it consisted mainly of how to converse properly without offending anyone by purging one's language of all slang and colloquialisms. French was entirely "conversational." The dancing lessons were thorough and a delight. But "geography" was strange: The teacher never mentioned interesting places like Africa or Haiti, but informed her students of the best hotels and points of interest in such cities as London, Paris, Rome, Nice, Lucerne, Baden-Baden. In "art appreciation" the students were taught to recognize the works of Van Dyck, Constable, Millet, Corot, and many others and to memorize appropriate comments they should make about each.

Yet that was only the beginning of the many things a girl must learn in order to become a competent wife and hostess who would be a credit to her husband. While a lady never cooked herself, she must know all about the purchase, preparation, and serving of food, as well as the appropriate wines, so that she could direct her servants properly. Two solid weeks at Miss Troy's were spent on table settings—which dishes remained and which disappeared during a complete seven-course dinner. (It sounded easy, but the intricacies often tripped up even the best students.) Then there was the study of furnishings—how to recognize a Louis XVI *boiserie*, a Gobelin tapestry, a Savonnerie carpet, to say nothing of qualities of petit point, linens, and laces. Floral arrangement was an art which required a separate course. And always there was clothing, clothing, clothing—style, style, style.

Looking back on this training later, Cordelia was surprised she hadn't run away from the Peysters and hidden in the country. Actually, however, she enjoyed some of it. But she never thought she'd put it to much practical use because she did not expect to marry a wealthy man: The wealthy boys she knew were bores. Being very fond of romantic literature, she thought marriage to a pirate or highwayman would be far more satisfying. The problem, of course, was to meet one.

Hard as Cordelia tried during those growing-up years, she could not become fond of Miriam and Augustus Peyster. Several times, when she felt she was accepting their generosity under false pretenses, she asked to withdraw from Miss Troy's and go home to Dorfman Manor.

"But dear," Miriam would say, "that would be *giving up*. And who likes a quitter?"

Cordelia tried vainly to explain. Then Miriam would pout and say, "But you know how fond Augustus and I are of you."

Cordelia did not know, yet feared that if she said so she would sound overly demanding of affection.

"Think what Augustus is doing for you," Miriam would say. "All of us know your father just doesn't have the money to give you such an education. But Augustus can afford it and we both take pleasure in your continuing success."

If, at that juncture, Miriam ever had made a gesture of affection or told her she was like the daughter they never had had, Cordelia might have become fond of them. But Miriam always made affection seem to be a weakness and ended their colloquies with a remark like:

"Remember, child, Augustus *can't stand a quitter*."

Cordelia finally figured out for herself what no one ever tried to explain to her. Personal vanity made the Peysters desire her social success. Augustus was backing her the way other rich men bred racehorses or sailed racing yachts or outbid others for European objects of art. The point was to win at something. Never having enjoyed much social success themselves, Miriam and Augustus would find pride of their own if Cordelia made a hit in society.

Extraordinary success came to her before she was eighteen. When Augustus heard the news, he lumbered up from his chair with an animal cry that was meant for joy. Miriam, fairly dancing around the room, announced that Cordelia had been invited to Mrs. Astor's next Patriarch Ball and that Augustus and she were to be included among the guests. That very afternoon a footman wearing the blue livery of the House of Astor had left Mrs. Astor's card with the Peysters' butler and the invitations had followed an hour later.

The Patriarch Ball, held annually, had been organized by Mrs. Astor with the help of Ward McAllister, who had set himself up as a promoter of social occasions. The ball was the most exclusive and best-run of any in New York. Each year Mrs. Astor and McAllister carefully selected twenty-five "patriarchs" of New York society who could invite four ladies and five gentlemen to the gala ball. Each patriarch was personally responsible for the social acceptability of his guests. The patriarch who had arranged for Cordelia and the Peysters to be invited was Morris Beekman, who knew that their bloodlines were impeccable but had barely met them socially. Morris acted at the behest of his son Marshal, who was known to his contemporaries as Marshmallow—not because of any particular softness in his character but because he looked as round and malleable as one of those confections. Marshal, nineteen and a sophomore at Yale, had met Cordelia at one of Miss Troy's dances and fallen hopelessly in love with her. She appreciated his emotion, but found it hard to reciprocate since Marshal, besides his confectionary appearance, had myopic vision and a bad stammer. The Beekmans were devoted parents who wanted their son to be happy; they thought Cordelia's family most acceptable and took note of the wealth in her Peyster connection; but once they saw her in person they were realistic enough to believe Marshal was doomed to disappointment.

Cordelia's and the Peysters' preparations for the ball consumed days. Rather late everyone suddenly realized she had not one decent item of jewelry. Augustus himself dashed (insofar as his large bulk was capable of it) to Cartier's and selected a suitable strand of pearls. These Cordelia wore with her white chiffon ball-dress, which was modestly décolleté and intricately embroidered with appliquéd flowers of white satin. By her own wish the only other decoration on the white purity of her costume was a little ivory fan, which her paternal grandfather had bought on a voyage to China, suspended from her belt by a simple gold chain, which was a gift from her mother for this occasion. Thus attired and with her makeup consisting mainly of her ecstatic expression at participating in such a momentous celebration, she and the Peysters, attended by two maids, rode up Fifth Avenue in their carriage to the Astor mansion.

Never after was Cordelia very coherent about the scene at Mrs. Astor's. Such a blaze of glory! Four immense bronze outdoor candelabra flooded the darkness with torchlight as white-wigged footmen assisted guests from their carriages. A huge and noisy crowd that had gathered early to witness the spectacle kept up a cataract of comment beyond restraining lines of policemen wearing egg-shaped helmets. Heavy wrought iron, great oaken doors, and then a glare of marble stretching everywhere. It was marble honed so white that it hurt Cordelia's eyes: huge floor expanses of it, with walls arching whitely into pure celestial domes of light, and then a marble staircase that seemed to climb toward infinity.

The bustle of a woman climbing the stairs ahead of Cordelia swayed provocatively. She must remember to wriggle her bustle. But what if it came loose from its moorings? There was a snatch of orchestra music—a waltz. Was it by Waldteufel? She was not sure. She was in a forest of roses. For this ball Mrs. Astor had decided to decorate her mansion with Gloire de Paris and Baronne de Rothschild long-stemmed roses by the thousands at the incredible price of two dollars a rose. (The *Times* had reported that morning that the florist Klopper would submit a bill for twelve thousand dollars.) The heavy scent of the roses made her feel dizzy. What if she fainted? *Cousin Augustus would kill me!* Onward and upward with Miriam, their two maids attending behind, until they came to the maze of upper rooms where lady guests were undergoing the final ministrations of their maidservants. All the maids wore gray and made cooing sounds. As each lady completed her final processing and departed for the rigors of the ball, her maid sank on a bench. There were rows and rows of maids cooing softly to one another like doves in a cote. Cordelia's maid Hattie suddenly cast her a look of such envy that she wondered what would happen if they exchanged places.

Miriam looked deathly pale, and Augustus, when they joined him, had the look of a man about to charge into a cannon firestorm. At the entrance to the grand salon the Beekmans and others waited. Cordelia, just for the fun of it, curtsied so low to them that anyone less lithe would have tumbled on her head.

Marshal, who appeared laced into a straitjacket for the occasion, bowed bumpily and worked his lips: "S-s-say, Cordelia, you c-c-curtsy like that to Mrs. As-As-Astor, she'll think you're ri-hi-ri-hi-diculin'."

Waves of waltz music washing out of the grand salon inundated them. At the entrance the butler, holding a guest list in a white-gloved hand, announced their names as they went in. The scene within was breathtaking—like a child's imagined fairyland. Young couples swooped and turned to the music of two orchestras in the ballroom which reminded Cordelia of a great gold-and-white cavern. Around its sides sat watchful dowagers who literally glittered with jewels while their plumes waved as in a turbulence. There were men, of course, all wearing white ties and tails, and there were young women disconsolate at not dancing on the floor, but the scene was dominated by the dowagers.

On a slightly raised dais before a huge white marble

fireplace sat the chief dowager, Mrs. Astor. As befitting a queen, she sat on a chair which was more like a throne, all gold and blue. On a lesser throne to her right sat her companion of the moment, Mrs. Ogden Reid. And at her left stood the clever lord chamberlain who had made her the doyenne of American society, Ward McAllister. Cordelia felt herself quailing before his piercing gaze.

"Dorfman," he said to Mrs. Astor. "Beekman. Peyster."

If these old names bore magic, it did not show on Mrs. Astor's face. Despite all the attention that had been lavished on her face and hair, she really was quite plain. She wore a white silk gown with a sage-green silk bodice and drapery on the front, the entire costume festooned with diamonds like fly netting on a horse in summer. Cordelia never had seen a general, but somehow she thought of Mrs. Astor as more a general than a woman. Maybe it was her shrewd, hard face that looked to be plotting a war. She stared, nodded, stared, nodded as the women curtsied, the men bowed.

Mrs. Reid thrust her old campaigner's face toward her friend and said something. Mrs. Reid was much to be feared; she had said true New York society was confined to only twenty families. She didn't name them, and that left a hundred families wondering if they were beyond the pale.

"What?" Mrs. Astor's failure to hear made her seem almost human.

"Dorfman," said Mrs. Reid.

"Come here, child." Mrs. Astor beckoned Cordelia and waved the others on.

Surprisingly, Cordelia was not frightened. Approaching, she curtsied again.

"No need for that," Mrs. Astor said.

"At least it's well bred," said Mrs. Reid, "and the young show a woeful lack of breeding these days.

Young Miss Dorfman, how are your mother and father?"

"They are well, thank you, ma'am."

"Remember me to them. Tell them Mrs. Reid was asking after them. Why did they leave town for the wilderness? Has your father fallen on hard times?"

"Not that I know of, ma'am." Cordelia didn't know why she went on as she did, except that her father's finances were none of Mrs. Reid's business. "I think it's because of his philosophy. He's working out a whole new philosophy and needs the peace of the country for it. Father feels too many men are wasting their time at business. He wants to be like a—uh—balance."

Mrs. Astor looked almost interested. "Now what do you think of that, Mr. McAllister? You bring me only businessmen. Can't you produce me a philosopher?" He had no chance to reply. "You're a pretty child. What are you going to marry when you grow up? A philosopher or a businessman?"

"I guess a businessman, ma'am." Cordelia suddenly thought of something. "I've heard there's some kind of philosopher's stone, but I reckon it's not diamonds."

Mrs. Astor and Mrs. Reid were still laughing as McAllister moved Cordelia on to make way for others to pass the throne.

Augustus Peyster never completely recovered from attending Mrs. Astor's Patriarch Ball. When they returned home about five o'clock the next morning he sat in his shirtsleeves drinking champagne and gloating like a stuffed toad in a puddle. Not a single Vanderbilt, those parvenus, ever had darkened Mrs. Astor's door. But *he* had been there! Cornelius Vanderbilt's deputy general, Chauncey Depew, had been so jealous at learning of the Peysters' invitation that he had fairly ground his teeth.

"Money," declared Augustus in that gray dawning of

another day, "is for spending and enjoying. Miriam, I've been too niggardly with it."

"That is true," she agreed.

His pleasure at having visited Mrs. Astor's was to cost him a considerable sum. First he paid out four times the amount of money Loren Dorfman could raise to make sure that Cordelia's presentation to society, under their combined sponsorship, was a great success. It was accomplished at Sherry's and was highly successful because both Mrs. Astor and Mrs. Reid honored the occasion by stopping by for a while.

On the wings of that, Miriam had little trouble convincing him she should take Cordelia to Europe for the summer "to broaden her out." The prospect excited Cordelia, but the trip itself began to bore her as they did predictable things in England, France, Germany, and Italy. When they returned home she admitted to herself that she had more fun during one week at Dorfman Manor, where she put on an old pair of her father's pants and rode bareback every day, than she'd had in all her twelve weeks in Europe.

Still Augustus continued to spend money. At Miriam's urging he bought a villa on fasionable Bellevue Avenue in Newport, which offered Miriam new worlds to conquer. Besides making herself socially acceptable in New York, she now must find acceptance in the summer world of Newport, too.

Cordelia did not like Newport. At eighteen she was more reflective than anyone gave her credit for being. Though not deeply unhappy, she never was as happy as she pretended. She was bored by many of the things she did, especially by the rigorous routine of Newport, but she felt she would be ungrateful to show it. Always she was happiest in the days she spent with her parents, who enjoyed life at the Manor far more than they ever had in the city; indeed her father, after a life of unemployment, was delighted to find that retirement enabled him to become a day laborer on the farm. But what, Cordelia asked herself, was she to do? It would be pointless to throw over all the opportunities offered her and spend the rest of her life on the farm performing the menial tasks she enjoyed whenever she went home.

Her brother Nicholas became furious with her when he came to the Manor one holiday and found her milking a cow in the stable. "For Lord's sake, Cordelia, this is no way for a lady to act!" Nicholas was a supercilious snob who grew worse with each passing year. He made a living as an investment salesman for Lewis and Lewis on the Bowling Green, but life evolved for him in society. He never would get over the fact that Cordelia had been invited to a Patriarch Ball before he had. He had been carping at her for social shortcomings for as long as she could remember. Most of the time she tolerated him patiently, telling herself he was the only brother she had, but once in a while she would fly at him in a screaming rage. Then Nicholas would stop picking at her for as long as a fortnight.

However, she had to credit Nicholas with one thing: It was he who introduced her to Jay Spencer at Newport. Maybe Jay was the highwayman she had been longing to meet. Tall, dark, handsome, he was two years out of Yale and already a noted yachtsman. Surprisingly for one who acted like a gallant highwayman, Jay was incredibly wealthy—or would be some day. For he was the only son of John "Jocko" Spencer, the timber and mining king who had locked horns at various times with most of the biggest bulls—Carnegie, Frick, Vanderbilt, Gould. Though as rich as Croesus, Jocko was reported to be as vulgar as old Commodore Vanderbilt had been. In fact, Mrs. Ogden Reid had said of him, "That man should not be allowed in the same room with children."

Of course Jay was a complete gentleman and not at all like Jocko, except in one respect: Though still tender in years, he already was operating some of his father's interests, in which he was said to be every bit as hard-driving and ruthless as the old man. At Newport the Vanderbilts, Goulds, and Wilsons repeated a bit of gossip about him to the Peysters that Cordelia thought was caused by jealousy. Before his senior year at Yale, when Jay had spent the summer working for J. P. Morgan, he had been observed kissing an actress one evening in the upstairs public room at Sherry's. When Mr. Morgan upbraided him for such conduct, Jay had replied, "Well, sir, at least I wasn't doing it behind closed doors." "Why not?" Mr. Morgan had said. "That's what doors are for."

But Mr. Morgan thought highly of Jay, for he told Augustus, "Anytime that young man doesn't want to tend to his own fortune, he can help me tend to mine." Augustus like Jay and defended him when Miriam entered a demurrer about his lack of good family. Then they started one of their increasingly frequent quarrels. Augustus said he was growing weary with talk of family, family, family. And Miriam said she was weary with his talk of money, money, money. But Cordelia saw it was family that advanced the Peysters in Newport and that the Vanderbilts used them to advance their own social standing by paying Augustus a much bigger salary at the New York Central, besides offering golden investment tips.

All this came about after Cordelia fell in love with Jay. That happened one summer afternoon when she was nineteen and watching a dinghy race in Narragansett Bay from Cornelius Vanderbilt's yacht. Jay won the race, as usual, then turned his boat over to his companion and came aboard the yacht for sherry. Cordelia had danced and talked with Jay at social occasions before that afternoon, but she never had really *seen* him until then. As he vaulted over the rail, someone said, "Welcome aboard, Captain Kidd." Maybe it was the rhetorical line that did it for Cordelia. Or maybe it was the way Jay's handsome white teeth flashed a grin in his tanned face. Whatever the reason, she suddenly was in love with Jay Spencer.

This love was different from the passing crushes she'd had on other men. It was not more tender, but fiercer. This time Cordelia had to admit to carnal feelings she never had experienced before. It was at once exciting and frightening. There was something about Jay—as her friend Nancy Crown whispered to her: "He's dynamite, Corey. Pure Dynamite! You be awful careful."

Although not wanting to think about it, she found herself concentrating on it. Her young women friends were forever discussing the unmentionable subject with an indirection that had an explicit language all its own. Indeed, at Miss Troy's pious school it had been the chief subject of discussion among most of the students, rating far ahead of floral arrangement. If Cordelia had been required to write a brief essay on the subject, she would have generalized in some such way as this:

Every properly reared young lady is a virgin until she marries. Only ninnies and hypocrites pretend not to understand where babies come from, though hardly anybody's mother and nobody's father brings up the unmentionable subject. You just find out these things yourself somehow. Men are said to be lustful devils, and after you're married all you can do is submit to your husband. Some say from second- or third-hand knowledge that there's really nothing at all to the act. Just a couple of seconds, and then it's as if nothing ever had happened. Anybody who understands horsebreeding understands that. But what does horse-breeding have to do with the feeling of love that starts somewhere between your heart and stomach, then extends all the way to your extremities with a tingling sensation?

That, at least, was approximately the way Cordelia

felt the first time Jay took her in his arms and kissed her. He did that in the garden of the Wilsons' house the day after he climbed aboard the Vanderbilt yacht. She pretended to be very angry with him, but he knew she was not. Young ladies and gentlemen were not supposed to kiss each other unless they were engaged—but they did it all the time. She tried to disguise the fact that she had fallen for him, but he was too perceptive not to see it. As Cordelia later reconstructed the situation, he knew she cared nothing about his money and was touched that she had fallen in love with *him*. She couldn't be sure he was in love with her, but he gave signs that he was. Since she was not vain, it did not occur to her that he was attracted by her beauty. But it did occur to her that possibly he was, more than he let on, attracted to her long American lineage: He had a disdainful remark for his father after the *Tribune* reported Jocko as saying from his financial citadel in Chicago that *his* father had been chased out of Northern Ireland as a horse thief.

"If it's really so, is the old bandit *proud* of it?" Jay demanded.

"Possibly so," Cordelia replied. "I guess there's a certain distinction to having a horse thief for a father when nobody else's father will admit to stealing horses."

Jay simply cast her a sour look.

Conversation was not his forte in what she hoped was their courtship. But he did enjoy rebellious remarks and attitudes, of which she had many.

One day when they were looking out at a Gould yacht, he said, "There the damn thing sits, costing two million Yankee doll-air and not goin' nowhar."

"It's the sailors of these big expensive yachts I feel sorry for," Cordelia said. "Do you know they make only ten dollars a month?"

He looked at her with mock horror. "Corey, what you said! You're a *radical*!"

"No, I am not. I just think the sailors deserve better pay."

In some perverse way he was amused by what she said and would not let up on her. When little Alfred Vanderbilt came along, Jay said, "Alfred, Corey says your father is a mean old skinflint."

Alfred looked at her gravely, "In so many words?"

"No!" Cordelia exclaimed. "I said—"

"And I quote," Jay interrupted her, " 'Cornelius Vanderbilt is a mean old skinflint because he pays his sailors only ten dollars a month.' "

"I rather think she has a point," Alfred said. "Corey, I'd be honored to go with you to Father while you tell him so to his face."

Of course she would not do such a thing. Nevertheless, none of her friends—not even she herself—realized how rebellious she could be.

Like many courtships, hers and Jay's (if such it really was) seemed to involve more pain than pleasure. One worry was always piling on another for her. Had anybody seen them kissing? Was he at all serious about her? What was that fantastic melting feeling he started in her simply by touching her hand? Was she in danger of going beyond the bounds of propriety? Didn't he drink too much?

Yes, he drank a lot, but appeared to handle it well. So, on the last big social event of the Newport season, a ball at the Vanderbilts' to which Jay took her, she did not realize he had been drinking more than usual.

It was one of those splendid September nights that made up for much foul Rhode Island weather. Cordelia rode to the ball with Jay, facing him in his new vis-à-vis victoria. She was a froth of white chiffon and tulle, her hair done in the most elaborate coiffure she yet had tried, a great bouquet of violets and white jasmine cradled in her left arm like an infant. A bright moon hanging over the Atlantic and shining down on Narragansett Avenue lighted the big *caléches* rolling in a procession toward the Vanderbilts'. The procession made a wonderful music: the purring of rubber-tired wheels, the rhythmic thump of horses' hoofs on the gravel avenue, the sharp crack of the coachmen's whips. Cornelius Vanderbilt's great mansion, The Breakers, still was only an idea in his mind and would not be completed for another five years, but the house where the carriages turned into the drive was impressively large.

The ball was the last in a series of grand affairs Cordelia had attended that summer. She and Jay danced several dances, then somebody cut in, and Jay disappeared, and somebody else cut in. After not seeing Jay for a long time, she excused herself from a partner and went looking for him. As she searched from room to room, her curiosity grew into panic. Had he gone off somewhere with a woman? Should she search the gardens? She did not want to know the answer to her jealous question, yet she could not stop herself from continuing to hunt for him.

"Jay?" a youth said in answer to her question. "I just saw him in the north billiards room with a bunch of the Yalies."

She should have turned back then. Let boys be boys and men be men while women waited patiently. But she went on toward a strong smell of cigar smoke and sounds of ribald masculine laughter rising above the click of billiard balls. A white-wigged footman wearing the maroon silk knee-breeches of the House of Vanderbilt came out of the billiards room bearing a tray of empty whisky glasses. He looked at Cordelia, obviously trying to tell her something. She was forever looking into the faces of footmen under their white wigs and discovering human beings. This one was a nice middle-aged man who probably went home and complained to his wife about the rigors of his job. He was trying to tell her what he dared not say: "Don't go into that room, miss." Understanding, she halted as he hurried away.

She was about to turn back when from inside the room a man's voice rang out drunkenly: "You mean that, Jay?"

Jay's voice, sounding drunken, too: "Sure I mean it."

"Bet you won't tell Harry and Bob what you just said to me."

"Sure I will."

"Hey, Bob—Harry! Listen to Jay. I said to him that Corey Dorfman looks to be a passionate wench. And he said . . ."

Jay's voice: "I said she is."

"Go on, Jay, finish what you said."

"I said before I break it off with her we're going to have it three ways in a single session."

Cordelia felt stricken physically. She wanted to flee, but could not stir. What did "three ways" mean? She supposed it meant three times, though what difference did it make? Tears started from her eyes and she turned and started to run away. The little ivory fan, heirloom from her grandmother, pattered against her thigh. She halted, seized the fan and the gold chain by which it hung from her belt, and then, with a powerful wrench, she broke it off.

Hurrying back, she flung the fan through the billiards-room doorway. As it clattered on the floor, there ensued a silence from the men in there such as might never lift. Then Cordelia really ran.

It could have been nothing—a stupid, drunken remark that simply proved its author a hopeless boor. Jayo son of Jocko. It could have been nothing, but Cordelia turned it into everything. When her fan clattered on that floor, it was like the flung gauntlet of some knight of old declaring war on an enemy. But her enemy was not merely Jay Spencer. It was the Peysters, Newport, New York society, Miss Tory's, the entire empty, inane charade that had consumed the years of her youth like a devastating disease. She was finished with it all.

Without a good night to anyone at the Vanderbilts', she summoned up the Peysters' coachman, who had driven Miriam and Augustus to the ball. His name was Harold McCrory, and he was a very nice man. He took Cordelia home without asking a single question. She did not go to bed—did not even think of sleep. The war had been joined, the sides declared. Changing into a simple traveling suit, she spent the remaining hours until daylight going through her wardrobe. After eliminating all the things she considered frivolous, she found that her clothing could fit into two valises. At some hour of dark morning she heard Miriam and Augustus in the hall outside her door, Miriam saying there had been "a lovers' quarrel," Augustus saying, "Forget it." They went to bed, but Cordelia did not.

Around six o'clock, in the bright dawn of a new day, she went down to the kitchen. The cook was there, drinking coffee with Harold, who was having a snort of bourbon. She said her parents wanted her to come home and asked Harold if he could take her to the Jamestown Ferry.

He stared at her. "Miss Cordelia, you sure you want to do this?"

"Harold, do you question me?"

He gave her an odd smile. "No, ma'am, I never really have since I used to drive you to Miss Troy's on bad days and you'd comment on the state of society. Miss Cordelia, what you going to do once you get off the Jamestown Ferry on t'other side?"

"Take the stage to Kingston and board the train for New York."

Harold had the best victoria and a pair ready in fifteen minutes. But he did not leave her at the ferry. He drove the victoria aboard, and then, as the ferry chugged for the mainland, she stood up in the carriage and looked back at the browns and blues of lovely Newport, a bit of paradise at the tip of the Island of Rhode Island which must have been a wonderful place before it was fouled by human society. To her left the morning sun dazzled the blue and heaving Atlantic.

Harold spoke to her from the box: "Pretty, ain't it, Miss Cordelia?"

"It's beautiful, Harold. But I won't be seeing it ever again."

"Miss Cordelia, don't never say never. Nobody never-ever knows 'bout that."

After they left the ferry, Harold drove her all the way to the Kingston railroad depot. When she reached in her purse for a couple of dollars to tip him, she found to her dismay that she did not have a cent. Fortunately she had the railroad pass which Augustus renewed for her each month; it was good for coach fare, but not for a parlor car. The nine-fifteen from Boston's South Station for New York was coming into Kingston twenty-two minutes late as Harold seized her suitcases. He could not understand why she didn't want to ride parlor car, but found her a vacant seat in a coach which smelled of hard-boiled eggs, bananas, and people. As he was stowing her valises overhead, she triumphantly found a stray quarter in the bottom of her bag and insisted that he take it.

Harold looked so forlorn standing alone on the little platform as the train jerked ahead that Cordelia started to cry. She certainly had planned this departure badly: no money, neglecting even to drink a cup of coffee before leaving Newport. Now she was famished and New York was seven hours distant; but even there everyone she knew would be absent for the summer. What a life to be raised in such pampered luxury yet not know a soul from whom she could borrow fifty cents for a meal. She began to cry harder.

Through her tears she made out the shape of a man in the aisle looking down at her. Thinking he was the conductor, she dug out her pass.

"No, miss." His voice was kind. "The conductor will be along in a minute. I was sitting here and got off at Kingston for a paper cup of ice cream."

"Sorry," she quavered, and sharnk closer to the window to give him ample room.

He was not an old man, but he was somewhat *older*. An interesting-looking brown sort of man with a handsome round face, brown eyes, brown mustache, a serviceable brown worsted suit, and, when he took off his brown derby, the most beautiful curling brown hair she ever had seen. But by far the most surprising thing about him was the fact he was eating a large cup of chocolate-brown ice cream.

She stopped crying and watched him, lips parted, and swallowed just in time to prevent herself from drooling.

He smiled at her. "Seems awfully early in the day to be eating ice cream."

"Yes it does," she said.

"Basically," he said, "when you stop to think about it, ice cream is a perfect breakfast food. Here you have sugar, cream, something cooling for the heat of the day to come. It's no wonder George Washington always had ice cream for breakfast when he wasn't out with the troops."

Cordelia gaped. "He did?"

"Oh, yes. I'm quite a student of Washington. Miss, would you like to sample my ice cream?"

Cordelia did something she thought herself incapable of: She took the ice cream from the nice brown man and ate all of it, then licked her fingers and said, "Thank you very much."

"You're welcome," he said. "When we get to Westerly I'll hop off at the station and get us *two* cups. What's your favorite flavor?"

"I rather fancy strawberry. I should think, sir, that strawberry is especially suitable to breakfast. I mean, that way you get some fruit with your—your other things."

She had been reared never to talk to strangers, but it was hard to think of one whose ice cream she had just shared as a stranger. He introduced himself as Edward Lovejoy and explained he was in the book-publishing business in New York. Of course she was too well bred to give him her name; she simply said she had been visiting relatives in Rhode Island and was returning to her home and family in Dutchess County.

Book publishing was an interesting-sounding business she never had thought about. Mr. Lovejoy was so caught up in telling her what happened between the author's setting down his pen and that woman across the car aisle reading a book that he almost forgot to leap off at Westerly and buy them ice cream.

"I'm keeping a strict account of everything you're spending on me," she said. "My father will send you a check for every penny of it."

He cast her a thoughtful look. "You're traveling without any money, Miss—uh—?"

"Dorfman." There, it had slipped out, and she hadn't intended to reveal her name. "Oh, I have money, Mr. Lovejoy. But it's in a stupid large denomination. Fifty dollars."

"My oh my. It's so long since I've seen a fifty-dollar bill I can't even remember whose picture is on it."

Did he think she was going to show him the money she did not have? She grinned wickedly at him and said, "Grant. General Ulysses Simpson Grant is on a fifty-dollar bill, Mr. Lovejoy."

The diner was put on the train at New London, and he asked if she would like something more substantial than ice cream for lunch. She said she wouldn't mind provided they continued to keep strict account of what he was spending on her. They went into the diner where they had a nice table for two and an attentive waiter who served her a dozen oysters on the half shell, lobster bisque, a half a fried chicken with vegetables, apple pie à la mode, and coffee. Mr. Lovejoy ate somewhat less than she.

He didn't ask her direct questions about herself, but she found herself divulging more than she intended. She was delighted that he had lived most of his life in New York and had never heard of Miss Troy's School.

"What is it?" he asked. "A sort of finishing school?"

"Yes," she said, "when you graduate from there, you're really finished."

He didn't laugh much, but when he did, his voice made the pealing sound of a bell. It sounded so good to her that she wished she could think of other things to say that would make him laugh. By the time they had passed New Haven and the train was bearing down on Stamford, Cordelia found herself thinking that the woman who was married to him was very lucky.

"Do you and your family live right in the city, Mr. Lovejoy?"

"I don't have a family, Miss Dorfman. I have a father. We work together, but we don't live together. I'm not married."

"I think you're wise," she said. "I plan never to marry myself."

He gave her a kind of a peering look. "Why is that?"

"I've known many men," Cordelia said, "but I've never known one whose company I could tolerate for more than an hour or two."

"Well," he said, "I guess that takes care of us men."

She wanted to add, "Present company excepted," but did not have the nerve. Instead, she asked for his card so that her father could send him the money. He took one from his wallet.

EDWARD LOVEJOY
Vice-President

LOVEJOY & SON
Publishers & Booksellers
36 West 23rd Street, New York City

He was such a pleasant, easy man to meet, she wondered how he could be the vice-president of anything. It was a bit disappointing. She had believed he was a friendly salesman, a pursuit that must be altogether more interesting than being in an office acting like a vice-president.

After a porter had trundled their luggage into the cavern of the Grand Central Depot, Mr. Lovejoy asked what she was going to do now.

His question surprised her. "I told you, take a train to Poughkeepsie."

"But how are you going to get from there to your family's farm?"

"Take a hack. They meet all the trains in Poughkeepsie."

"But the driver won't be able to break your fifty, either. May I loan you a couple of dollars for the hack?"

As he reached for his wallet, she drew herself up and said haughtily, "Mr. Lovejoy, sir, I cannot accept cash. My father has an arrangement with the hack drivers." Suddenly she hated herself for sounding like another little prig from Miss Troy's. Reaching out, she grasped his hand warmly. "Thank you, Mr. Lovejoy, for all your kindness and for what must be the most pleasant trip ever made between Kingston and New York City." Then she snatched up her valises and marched off in search of a train to Poughkeepsie.

* * *

Loren and Marie Dorfman understood perfectly Cordelia's wanting to come home. They never had had any real liking for the course Miriam and Augustus had set for her in society.

Nicholas was the first to come in pursuit of her. He arrived at the Manor the day after she did, absolutely livid at the way she had fled from Newport. He brought no apology from Jay. What had happened was entirely her fault because she had overreacted like a child.

When their shouts at each other reached a crescendo, their father came into the room.

"Nicholas!" Cordelia never had heard his gentle voice so sharp. "Leave your sister alone. It's time you go back to your job in the city and mind your own business."

"But Father—"

"Nicholas, *go!*"

He went at once because his father's will was stronger than his.

Miriam and Augustus came in search of her the following week. Cordelia refused to face them. Leaving her parents to deal with them, she went to her room. Hours seemed to pass as voices rose and fell downstairs.

At last she heard Miriam cry, "Where *is* she?"

"Wherever she is," Loren Dorfman said, "she's where she wants to be."

2

It would have been easier to take a train from Poughkeepsie, but Colonel Bob, who was called a master
planner, said they must take the boat which sailed for
the city at four P.M.

Rather, it was supposed to sail for New York at that
hour. On this day it was twenty minutes late in leaving
because the bridal party was twenty minutes late in ar-
riving at the pier. Fortunately Colonel Bob, who had
put himself in charge of arrangements, had sent one of
the Dorfman servants ahead on horseback with a five-
dollar gold piece for the captain of the steamer and
written orders to wait for the bride and groom at peril
of losing his job. The roads from Dorfman Manor to
Poughkeepsie were a terror that afternoon, part mud
and part glazing ice while sleet rattled out of the northeast, making carriage travel very hazardous and
prompting one wedding guest to wonder aloud why anyone would want to get married on February twenty-
first.

"Because," the groom, Edward Lovejoy, replied
cheerfully, "we didn't want to wait till Washington's
Birthday."

The carriage came slipping, sliding, careening down
the slopes of Dutchess County; miraculously all arrived
safely at the Poughkeepsie pier where the steamboat
waited. In vain Cordelia had tried to dissuade Loren
and Marie from making the unpleasant carriage trip to
the boat: They had only one daughter to give away in
marriage, and they would not do it halfheartedly. Similar sentiment prevailed among others in the procession,

which included several county relatives and friends. Among those who had sent regrets, and not even a wedding gift, were Miriam and Augustus Peyster.

As everyone climbed from carriages and buggies and shrank before the gale that lashed the pier, Cordelia had a desperate feeling she might burst into tears. Not because of the absence of the many, for whom she cared not a thing, but because of Edward, whom she loved passionately, and because of her wonderful parents.

"Oh, goodness!" She made a strange, gulping sound and started to run for the gangplank, Edward jogging beside her. But then she paused to kiss her mother and father good-bye. What with the sleet and the tears, it became a thoroughly sodden occasion. Even the rice the guests flung descended in lumps, as if it had been soaking overnight.

At last she and Edward stood at the top of the gangway, waving and calling out and weeping. Edward weeping, too? Through her tears Cordelia looked at him with astonishment and said something silly: "Why are you crying? Your father's going with you."

"It's such a wonderful family." His voice broke. "I can't bear to leave them."

She kissed him, he was such a love. That brought a cheer from relatives and friends on the pier. Meantime Edward's father Robert, who was widely known as Colonel Bob for services rendered to the Republic in a now distant war, directed the loading of Cordelia's four trunks. The whistle blared, hands hauled back the gangway and cast off the lines while the people ashore waved frantically and shouted above the storm.

Cordelia felt that a sense of peace would be appropriate after so much excitement. Instead, trouble seemed to be brewing as the steamboat backed into the Hudson. A red-faced man, the captain apparently, had lowered a window of the pilot house and was roaring imprecations at someone. The object of his wrath appeared to be Colonel Bob, who seemed to think it must be someone else by the way he looked about and shrugged.

Colonel Bob came off the deck into the forward cabin where Cordelia, Edward, and Nicholas, who was traveling to New York with them, were standing, and said, "There's always method to my madness. You'll learn that, Cordelia. We're taking the boat instead of the train because we dock one block from Vestry Street where you two are taking your boat for Norfolk tonight. If we took the train from here to Grand Central, the fastest hansom cab in the city couldn't—"

"You!" The red-faced man (he must indeed have been the captain since there was so much braid on his cap) had left the wheel to other hands and now advanced into the cabin. He pointed directly at Colonel Bob, who glanced over a shoulder as if to discover who was being pointed at. "I mean *you!* You're no more Cornelius Vanderbilt than I'm a pig's ass."

Colonel Bob was not tall, but he was bayonet straight and his lustrous leather boots seemed to possess springs that made him taller when angered; his white mustache began to quiver and his plump face turned as pink as the captain's. "There's no question about you being a pig's ass, my man," he replied shrilly, "but who says I'm Cornelius Vanderbilt?"

"*You* do!" the captain shouted. "You've been pointed out to me as the author of a note ordering me to delay my sailing schedule. You're—"

"Did you receive and accept a five-dollar gold piece?"

"That has nothing to do with it," the captain said.

"That has everything to do with it. Do you know the penalty in this state to the operator of a public carrier who accepts a bribe? Let me see that note."

The captain, handing it to him, stormed, "Anytime I delay I have to answer to the board of directors."

Colonel Bob studied the note. "It's as plain as that red nose on that red face of yours, my man. This signature is mine—Robert Lovejoy." The captain uttered a whinnying sound. "Look at this, Edward. What do you make of the signature?"

Edward looked at it gravely. "It's your signature, Father—Robert Lovejoy."

Cordelia, standing on tiptoe and looking wide-eyed over Edward's shoulder, sympathized with the captain's confusion. The R looked remarkably like a C to her, and surely the L was a V, so that she herself would have believed it the signature of the great multimillionaire and railroad magnate at whose home she used to dance.

"The trouble with you, my man," said Colonel Bob, "is not just that you're a pig's ass, you're an *illiterate* pig's ass."

The captain demanded the note back, but Edward folded and put it in the watch pocket of his waistcoat. "We'll keep this for evidence, sir." His voice had grown deeper as his father's went higher, and now it seemed to Cordelia that he towered over everyone in the cabin. This masterful man was a different person from the gentle Edward she had married; it was thrilling to know he was her husband. "You listen to me," Edward went on measuredly to the captain, "I'm tired of your obscenities in the presence of my wife. I warn you, sir, that my father has a very short temper and an unfortunate habit of carrying a derringer in that right pocket of his. There have been some unhappy incidents with it. Go back and run your boat and leave us alone."

The captain hesitated, then left the cabin while Colonel Bob looked at Edward with conspiratorial triumph. "You'll restrain me from going after the rogue?"

"Yes, Father," Edward said dryly. "He's had his comeuppance."

Cordelia, thinking they were more like brothers than father and son, envied Edward. She never had enjoyed such a relationship with anyone older—certainly not with Nicholas, who stood there regarding the Lovejoys with undisguised superiority. She told herself she must not hate Nicholas. Considering his behavior on her wedding day, though, it was awfully hard not to.

Colonel Bob invited Edward to go with him to the smoking salon for a cigar; Cordelia understood, of course, that they were going to the bar for a drink. She expected Edward to accept his father's invitation to join him. And she knew Nicholas would refuse the invitation—which he did.

Edward told her he'd be gone for just a few minutes and followed his father aft. Nicholas, looking after them with disdain, said, "He forged Mr. Vanderbilt's name to that note. Despicable!"

"I'd just say his signature was careless, Nick. Forgery is a strong word."

"Not when applied to Robert Lovejoy," Nicholas said. "He has no fortune to speak of. But what money he did make came mainly from piracy. Yes, piracy, Cordelia. In the days when he could get away with it he stole the works of English authors. That, my dear sister, is known as *piracy*." His long face grew more dour. "With your looks and our family breeding you could have had your pick of husbands. You might have married a real Vanderbilt. But no, you had to marry a man forty-two years old—"

"Forty-one!"

"He's in his forty-second year and you're a silly girl not yet twenty-one. But you had to marry him against everyone's advice. A bookseller! A mere low *publisher*!"

* * *

It had been an odd courtship. After returning home, Cordelia had obtained a check for one dollar and eighty-five cents from her father—the amount Edward had spent on her lunch, tips, and ice cream—and mailed it to him with a friendly note of thanks. He had immediately replied with a friendly note of his own, inviting her and her mother to visit the Lovejoy bookstore and publishing offices and have lunch with him when they came to the city on a shopping trip. Cordelia had convinced Mama that they must go shopping right away.

There was nothing very exciting to see on the premises of Lovejoy and Son except Edward himself. It had been a disturbing experience for Cordelia. She realized that she felt the same about Edward as she had about Jay—only more so. What ailed her? If she kept on being this way over every man she met she'd end up one of those loose women who haunted the millionaires' cottages at Saratoga. But she could not help how she felt. To her delight Mama found Edward a very fine gentleman. In a couple of weeks Coredlia saw to it that he was invited to the Manor for a weekend to meet Papa.

It got off to an unfortunate start. Horsemanship counted a lot with Loren Dorfman, and Edward was an abominable rider. First thing he fell off a gentle old mare when she started to trot. He lay there laughing so hard at himself that Loren and Cordelia had difficulty in lifting him off the ground. She was sure he had put himself in Papa's bad graces.

But that was not so. Loren liked Edward very much. True, he respected good horsemanship. Yet Nicholas was an excellent rider and Loren had come to the point where he could barely tolerate his firstborn. What counted about Edward's horsemanship with Loren was the fact he had laughed at himself when he fell off the mare. Not many men could do that. Certainly Nick could not have.

Something else interested Loren about Edward. Like himself, and unlike Nick, Edward had not attended college. He had, in fact, gone to work as an apprentice in his father's bookshop and printing business when thirteen years old. Edward had in effect been an orphan at the time. His mother had died in 1861 when he was twelve, and his father, in a paroxysm of grief that the passage of time had translated into a sense of patriotism, had answered President Lincoln's first call to the colors and marched away from his young son and his business. None of this desertion and deprivation had caused bitterness in Edward, Loren observed. Edward loved his father and the business, being so successful in his relationships with both that the publishing house now was incorporated as Lovejoy and Son.

The more Nick raged to the family against Edward's age, the way he made a living, and his lack of distinguished forebears, the more Loren defended him.

"Pay no mind to Nick," Loren told Cordelia. "Since you and Edward want to get married, just go ahead and do it. I'll tell you one thing. Nick himself will never marry, and for just one reason. He bores every living woman to extinction. Speaking of marriage, why didn't Edward ever want to get married before?"

"I asked him that," Cordelia said. "He told me there were two reasons. He's kept awfully busy at work he enjoys. And he never fell in love before."

Now, looking out at the northeaster from the steamer cabin and seeing how rough the Hudson had become, Cordelia could not even count the many reasons why she loved Edward. She paid no attention to Nick, who was carrying on about the scant number and low social quality of the Lovejoy guests at the wedding—one actually had been a *printer*! He fell silent when Edward returned and sat down.

As they entered the wide stretch of the Tappan Zee the boat began to rock more violently. The half-dozen passengers in the cabin fled, one after another. Nick, looking ashen, was last to go.

"Good riddance," Cordelia said to Edward. "I'm glad you're a good sailor, darling."

"We're the two best sailors alive." He took her in his arms and kissed her so deeply that she actually thought she was going to swoon like one of those silly heroines in romances.

The Poughkeepsie boat was due to dock at six-fifteen and the *Queen of Norfolk* to depart at seven-thirty. But it was five after seven by Edward's big gold watch before the riverboat gave off her arrival-whistle blast and began to warp into her pier.

"Plenty of time," Edward said. "I'll get a drayman and we'll be over to the next pier in minutes. I confess now I never saw it as rough on the Atlantic on my two trips to Europe as it was just now up in old man Tappan's sea."

The vessel grew still, then bumping sounds began. Colonel Bob, looking wretched, darted into the cabin. *"Bon voyage!"* He fled. Nick came next, looking worse. "Hope you'll be very happy," he muttered through clenched teeth, and ran.

Edward found a drayman to take their luggage one block to the Vestry Street pier, but there was not a cab anywhere. Never mind, Cordelia told him, they'd run for it. Heavy snow was mixing with the sleet driving out of the northeast as they scampered down West Street.

Cordelia was proud of her satin going-away outfit, and the storm seemed determined to destroy it as she ran, holding onto her wide-brimmed hat with one hand and clutching up the folds of her gored skirt in the other. The sleet and snow pierced her cloth overcoat with icy needles, and by the time they came panting into the covered Vestry Street pier she felt wet through.

A heart voice echoed in the gloom of the pier, which was curiously empty: "Avast there! Where you bound?" A whiskered man appeared, and Edward explained they had passage on the *Queen of Norfolk*. The man, fond of rhetoric, replied that no one had passage on her tonight, that nothing was sailing from New York—not the Fall River Line, the Providence Line, the Newport Line, the Stonington Line, and certainly not the Coney Island Line; even the faithful Hoboken, Jersey City, and Staten Island ferries were shut down. "Friends, I doubt you can find so much as a railroad train can take you far as Stamford. Mark my words, this'll be remembered as the Blizzard of Ninety-one."

For the first time since Cordelia had known him, Edward appeared rattled. He babbled about their having dinner on the *Queen*, then occupying their stateroom and sailing whenever possible. Impossible, the man said; service was suspended, the *Queen* locked tight as a drum. However, he took pity enough on them to check Cordelia's trunks and help them find a hansom.

Edward told the driver to take them to the Astor House on lower Broadway opposite the post office. The Irish driver told Edward he was being a fool: the Astor was solid with people held in town by the storm. He took them, instead, to the Cosmopolitan on Chambers Street, but it was also booked full. So were Smith and McNeil's on Washington Street and Earle's on Canal.

The howling wind enveloped them in a permeating stench of soft-coal smoke that Cordelia thought must come from a big fire somewhere. But Edward explained that was the characteristic smell of the city in any season: "It gets into your eyes, your nose, your lungs. It gets into your blood and finally your brain, and then you can't bear to leave New York. You feel it's a waste of time even to go to the country for a few days." He spoke as if New York were new to her, as if he did not know she had grown up in the city, too.

She recalled that Colonel Bob lived in a suite at the Brevoort House; maybe he had connections to get them a room there for the night. But Edward did not want to go there. Too far uptown. The driver, who had opened the rear panel and was joining in the discussion from his box, said there was nowhere to go but uptown. Edward suggested that they first go to a restaurant and eat something warming, but Cordelia maintained she still was so full from the reception luncheon at home that she might never eat again. An edginess had crept into their tones, but as no cross word ever had passed between them, it was unthinkable they should start to quarrel now.

How about the Martin Hotel on University Place where Edward had lived for years? She was only trying to be helpful, but he sounded a note of umbrage at her suggestion, saying vehemently that the Martin was a *residential* hotel.

"Easy, easy," the cabman counseled, "we'll think of *somethin'* any minute now."

"I have one more suggestion"—Cordelia's voice sounded as haughty as Nicholas's when she was peeved—"but I won't venture to offer it."

"Please tell me, dear," Edward said. "Driver, close that damn hole over our heads, it's snowing in here."

"In a minute, sir," the driver replied. "I want to hear what the lady's suggestin'."

"What about the house you've rented?" Cordelia asked Edward.

"Oh, Lord save us!" the driver cried. "Us drivin' round in the blizzard and all the time ye have a *house!*"

"But it's not a quarter furnished," Edward said. "I thought you liked my idea that you pick most of the furniture. I did hire a biddy to clean the place and her husband is supposed to keep the furnace going so as not to freeze the pipes. But—"

"Oh, dear God, dear God," the cabman said, "where is this heaven of a house?"

"Foot of Murray Hill," Edward told him. "On East Thirty-second between Fourth and Lexington. A small brownstone. Number one hundred twelve."

"To paraphrase our friendly cabman," Cordelia said, "why the hell don't we go there?"

Her remark silenced both men as the driver touched his horse up Broadway through the snow. At last Edward ventured, "Are you angry, dear?"

"Not at all, dear. I just think that since you've paid for a roof over our heads, we might as well enjoy it on a snowy evening."

"I hope you understand it's not in the condition you expect."

"Of course," she said. "You've mentioned that a dozen times. Don't worry. Tell me again about Murray Hill."

"It's the best residential section in the city," Edward said. "It's not much of a hill anymore. Maybe it was back in the Revolution when it was the Murray family farm. Since then it's been smoothed down a lot. It covers roughly the area from Thirty-second to Forty-second Streets and from Third Avenue over to Fifth. Cordelia, I'll tell you something. I intend to make enough money that someday you and I will have a mansion on Murray Hill. Somewhere near the top."

"Just where is the top?" Cordelia asked.

"It's hard to say. Some claim it has no permanent top. J. P. Morgan thought he'd bought the top, but then it turned out one of the Vanderbilts had a higher elevation. In a curious way the top of Murray Hill seems to keep changing."

The snow fell more heavily and the wind rapidly piled the drifts higher as the hansom plodded up Broadway. By the time they reached Thirtieth Street they were creeping. Cordelia worried about the horse, and Edward worried about Cordelia while the driver became a silent snowman. When he turned them up Fourth Avenue, the horse began to flounder and could go no farther.

"We'll walk the rest of the way," Cordelia announced. "You get that horse of yours into shelter and rub him down. Have you a place to take him?"

"Relay livery over by Herald Square," the snowman replied in muffled tones.

Edward paid him generously, grasped their two valises, and led the way into the storm while Cordelia followed, trying to hop in his footsteps.

"It's a narrow house," he called back to her, "not like you're used to. But it's long and has three floors above the basement, top floor half-finished. . . ."

She didn't understand why he wasted his breath in this storm to keep fretting about the house. On Thirty-second Street the gaslights had gone out and it was like trying to find one's way in the dark season at the North Pole. When Edward stopped suddenly, she bumped into him.

"This is our number," he shouted into the wind, "but there must be some mistake because it's lighted."

Against a light from inside, the number 112 showed plainly on the glass above the door. Cordelia, grasping the iron rail and stumbling up the snow-clogged steps, yanked the bellpull. The resulting sound was like milk cans being hurled down stairs. When no one answered, Edward began to struggle for his key. At last the door was opened a crack and a woman asked, "Who is it?"

"This is Mr. Lovejoy." He couldn't remember the name of the cleaning woman he had hired. "Let us in, for heaven's sake."

The door swung back slowly; in the gaslight glow a pale, haggard woman stared at them with stark terror.

"Ah. . . . Ah! . . ." Edward made an awful strangling sound before he finally remembered her name. "Mrs. Culligan! This is—ah—Mrs. Lovejoy." One of his feet slipped and he might have plunged back down the steps if Cordelia hadn't grabbed him and pulled him inside.

"Ah! Mrs. Culligan, you said your husband would keep the furnace going. Glad to see he has."

Mrs. Culligan shrank back, speechless with fright, and then ran from them.

"What in thunderation ails that woman?" Edward demanded.

"I don't know," Cordelia said. "Could you have the wrong house?"

"Of course not." He led the way along a narrow hall past a narrow staircase that ascended into darkness, and suddenly they came face-to-face with a bald man in shirtsleeves who gaped at them.

"Ah," Edward said, "you must be Culligan."

The man nodded.

"Well, Culligan, glad to see you have the furnace going. This is Mrs. Lovejoy, absolutely horrible night out. Cordelia, this is the dining room. I mean it *will* be." Culligan seemed to evaporate as Edward pushed a door open farther.

Glancing past him, Cordelia let out a gasp. There were fifteen, maybe twenty people sitting or standing in the room, all as immobile as figures in a waxworks.

Culligan materialized again, trying to button a celluloid collar onto his shirt and saying, "I can explain everything, Mr. Lovejoy, sir." In his nervousness his brogue came as thick as porridge in the mouth. "These are relatives and friends of the wife and me that've come to help us tidy up the house."

Cordelia saw that several were sitting on boxes since there was only one chair. All were shabbily dressed, and nearly every one looked half starved. They had put a bowl of punch, a cake, bread, and the cheap sausages known as sawdust-fillers on a box top. At first Cordelia thought how sad it was that they lacked a table, but then she saw there was a small one in a corner. Apparently they were not using it for fear of damaging its finish.

"Yes, yes," Edward said vaguely. "How d'you do, this is—ah—my wife—ah—Mrs. Lovejoy."

All eyes shifted to her. "Well—ah"—she heard herself sounding like Edward—"nice to meet you, sorry to barge in like this, but our boat didn't sail as planned."

"Mrs. Lovejoy, ma'am!" Culligan bowed awkwardly. "Welcome to your home. A little housewarming, you might say. A pause in our labors by the cleaning staff. Ma'am—sir—would you care for a nip—a bite o' refreshment?"

"Oh, no, thank you very much," Cordelia said. "Sorry we aren't properly furnished yet. You folks go right ahead. We're just looking around. Dear"—Edward turned a glazed expression on her—"I'd like to see the kitchen."

They passed into it like sleepwalkers, and he muttered something about the cookstove and the cabinets. Then, circumventing the dining room where silence prevailed, they went along the hall and looked at what would be a windowless little library behind the larger front living room.

"Edward," she whispered, "I'm very proud of you for not being cross with these people."

Drawing her to him and kissing her lips, he said he was the one more pleased: "I'll never forget how kind you are. Their embarrassment is just awful, isn't it?"

As they started up the stairs, Culligan burst suddenly into the hall, crying, "Mr. Lovejoy!—Mrs. Lovejoy! Please sir—ma'am!" His voice and face reflected great pain.

"Enjoy yourselves, Culligan," Edward said jovially, "while we do the grand tour." Cordelia followed him to the head of the stairs; when he turned up a gaslight, she saw that this second-floor hall was even narrower than that below. He said, "The bathroom is here between the front and back bedrooms. I had the four-poster I bought put in the front room because it's larger and the light is better. What we're really short of is closet space. I'll show you."

He opened the door to the front bedroom, and both froze as a man's and a woman's voices joined in a low, releasing cry of passion. The gaslight in the hall cast only enough glow for them to glimpse two heads close together on the pillows of the four-poster where theirs should lie. Cordelia had one other memorable impression: how quickly and quietly Edward closed the door on the lovers. It made her believe—or hope, at least—that in their intensity the two did not realize they had been observed.

She and Edward went quickly along the hall. She found herself shaking as with a chill, and that reminded her they had not taken off their overcoats. Edward quietly opened the door to the empty back bedroom and gestured without a word. Then they climbed to the third floor where he made further gestures. There was a furnished room where a maid might live if they could afford her and an adjoining attic space that could serve for storage. Edward was doing everything in pantomime, as if he had lost his voice.

Slowly, quietly, they went downstairs, almost a step at a time. Hearing people leaving, they paused long enough to avoid them. Then they went all the way to the basement where Edward consumed time gesturing at furnace, coal bin, mysteriously winding pipes. By the time they returned to the first floor the house was quiet and they believed everyone had gone.

But suddenly Culligan came at them from the kitchen, as if intending assault. His look of rage dissolved in tears and he cried, *"Sorry!"*

They shrank from him. They didn't blame him for anything, so what had he to be sorry about?

"We live worse than pigs in the shacks down there!" he cried. "Me daughter Mary got married today to a good young man name of Tim McMahon. It come over the old woman and me"—his face seemed to open somehow, as if slashed by a knife, and anguish poured like blood from the wound—"goddamn you bloody rich bastards!" He ran from the house into the blizzard.

Edward locked the door slowly after Culligan had gone. Looking round at Cordelia, he said, "You might as well take off your coat and stay awhile. I'll bank down the furnace for the night."

She walked numbly into the dining room and said, "Are you hungry? They left some things to eat. I guess this must be their wedding cake." And then she broke into tears.

3

She had thought a great deal about this moment. Instinctively she felt there was more fire in Edward than ever would exist in Jay Spencer. But had she spoiled everything by bursting into tears? He might think she wept for herself and fail to understand her tears were only for the Culligans of the world, folk less fortunate than she. Being of such a gentle nature, he might decide not to disturb her innocence at this time. And if not now, when would he?

"It's been a hard day," Edward told her. "Nothing has gone right. The wedding itself and the reception were wonderful. But since then—the storm, the canceled sailing—"

"Nonsense!" The possibility he was starting a retreat from the strong advances he had made to her a couple of times in the past made her dissolve her tears as quickly as they had started. "I think it's fine we came to our own home tonight. Aren't you going to fix the furnace?"

She hastened upstairs with their valises while he went to the cellar. When she turned up the light in the front bedroom she saw that the young McMahons had evacuated the four-poster in such haste they had left its covers and pillows in disarray. It was unthinkable that she and Edward not have clean sheets for the night. A kind of panic seized her. There were no sheets in the drawers of the dresser Edward had bought along with the bed. That and a chair were the only other articles of furniture on the entire second floor. In the bathroom she found clean towels, apparently Mrs. Culligan's contribution to her daughter's wedding-night accommodations, but Cordelia could not find clean sheets anywhere.

She returned to the four-poster with dread. Doubtless its sheets and pillowcases would smell bad, for these recent Irish immigrants were said to be dirty. To her surprise there was no bad odor; in fact there was a pleasant clean smell of lilac, one of her favorite scents. So— the McMahons having made the bed, the Lovejoys would lie in it. She remembered a line of her father's when he was faced with something not precisely to his liking: "Well, what the hell!" Somehow that made everything all right.

Undressing quickly, she folded and put her clothing in a dresser drawer since there was no place to hang anything. The bare floor was very cold to her feet as she pulled on her nightdress. She sprang into the bed and lay there, shivering and wondering what would happen next. Her wildest imaginings had not prepared her for what did happen.

Edward strolled in, sat down on the side of the bed, began to wind his watch slowly, and said to her, "There's a plumber named Powers down on Fourteenth Street has developed a new hot-water heating system. I want to get that installed just as soon as the winter's over. This hot-air system we have is no good. Can't you smell the coal gas? I had anthracite put in, of course, but still. . . ." On and on he went about the heating system till she feared she might start to cry again. At last he loosened his tie, picked up his valise, and left the room.

When the ensuing silence finally became unbearable to her, she yelled, "Where *are* you?"

In a moment his voice came patiently from the hall: "I'm undressing in the bathroom. Where did you think I was?"

"I thought maybe you'd gone to the cellar to sleep with your damn furnace."

His tone sounded amused: "Do you know, sweetheart, I find it very attractive the way you drop cuss words now and then. Don't worry, I have no passionate attachment to furnaces."

A couple of minutes later he came in wearing a nightshirt. He looked adorable in it. She hoped he didn't cover his beautiful hair with a nightcap and, wanting to know immediately, she asked, "You don't wear a nightcap?"

He stared at her in astonishment. "Nobody has worn a nightcap in a hundred years."

"My *father* does."

"Excuse me. I mean nobody of our generation has— Jesus, this floor is cold!" Turning off the light, he climbed in beside her.

For what seemed a century to Cordelia they lay there, silent, not touching, scarcely seeming to breathe. The storm made mute sounds beyond the windows: a low moaning, a sibilant whisper of driving snow. Then their hands touched.

"Corey," he whispered.

"Yes, Edward."

"I love you, Corey."

She turned to him. "I love you, Edward."

"I know you must be very tired."

Slipping out of her nightgown, she put her arms around him and drew him to her. "I'm not at all tired, dear."

"I want it to be perfect—"

She put a finger over his lips and pressed his head down to her breast. He uttered a moan of pleasure as his hands felt the soft roundness of her naked body. When he closed his mouth on her nipple, a torrent of warmth began to flow through her and she almost cried out. She climaxed even before Edward was inside her.

* * *

A cow had kicked over her milking bucket, which went clang-clang-clanging along the stable floor. Of course it was only a dream. She and Edward were sound asleep, arms wrapped about each other. Even in sleep his breath smelled as sweet as honey.

There it came again: *ka-lung-a-lung-a-lung*. It was the cursed bellpull, Cordelia thought. Edward slept on; there must be no trace of guilt on his blessed conscience for him to sleep so soundly. She would join him in sleep because nobody they knew could realize that they were there. The wind had died, the storm had passed, good night all.

"Help!" It was a woman's voice shrieking. *"Help!"* And then another *ka-lung-a-lung*. Cordelia started. In response, Edward suddenly leaped up with a shout, propelled by strange dream forces that sent him careening into the dresser. His shout of fright became a howl of pain that died away in eloquent cursing.

"Help!" The woman's cry was bloodcurdling.

"My God, did you hear that?" Edward hobbled to a window and wrenched it open violently. Cordelia stepped beside him as packed snow tumbled onto their feet. The street gaslights had come on again, revealing a snowy white waste.

Edward, leaning out, shouted, "Who is that down there?"

"Mr. Lovejoy?"

"Yes, yes."

"Mr. Edward Lovejoy?"

"Yes!"

"Maude Mudge here. I'm almost dead. Need shelter quick!"

"Oh, shit," Edward said. Then, to Cordelia: "Excuse me, dear."

"Some old girl friend of yours?"

"I don't have any old girl friends." He slammed the window shut. "She's just an author."

Cordelia moved quickly from the piled snow. "Just an author? Does that mean we can go back to bed?"

"I can't leave her there. Don't you see the headlines in the *Tribune*? AUTHOR FREEZES TO DEATH AT PUBLISHER'S DOOR. What I can't figure out is how the hell she knew we were here. I wrote her a couple of weeks ago saying—"

"You know something, Edward?" Cordelia began to pull clothing from the dresser as he turned on the light. "You're going to have to watch your language. All these months I never heard you be profane. But now that we're married it's almost straight cussing from you all the way."

It was one-fifty A. M. as they made their way downstairs. When Maude Mudge gave another impatient yank on the bell, Edward shouted that they were coming.

"Does she drink a lot?" asked Cordelia. "I understand George Sand drank a lot. Do you find a lot of your women authors are heavy drinkers?"

"Maude Mudge is no George Sand," Edward said. "She comes from a hamlet called Caesar's Corners upstate and she never had a drink in her life. She never had a Chopin, either."

He opened the door and caught Maude as she tumbled in, while Cordelia took her valise. She was a small woman who looked almost square under a mantle of snow. Unwinding layers of scarf, they came to a small, square, cheerful face that had a few moles on its cheeks.

"Death hath an icy sting!" gasped Maude. "Edward, may I please sit down? A pleasure to meet you, Mrs. Lovejoy."

They half carried her into the dining room and sat her on the only chair. Cordelia found a box of tea in the kitchen; she shook up the dying range fire and started water to boil.

"Oooo," Maude kept saying. "I didn't plan to come to the city for a couple of weeks. But I finished *Christian Love* early. Here it is." Moving stiffly, she took a thick folder from her valise and handed it to Edward. "Lucky you sent me your new residence address. There's not a hotel room available in the city. The storm, you know. I walked here all the way from Grand Terminal. My train was six hours late."

Cordelia was impressed to meet Maude. She never had met an author—and now a *woman* author! When Edward came into the kitchen to see if the tea water was boiling, she asked in an undertone if Maude was famous.

"She's famous with Lovejoy's," Edward said. "I'm the one got her to write *The Making of the Master*. You've heard of that, I'm sure."

She had not, but said of course she had.

"I mean," Edward said, "I saw possibilities in her and brought her all the way up from Sunday-school tracts. Her first book—it was my idea—was *Up from Calvary*. I know you never heard of it, I'm sure no Episcopalian would read it."

They served Maude tea and fed her the remnants of the Culligan wedding cake and sausages, which she consumed to the last crumb. When she asked if they could spare a bed for the rest of the night, Edward started to explain their circumstances. But Cordelia interrupted, saying that of course they could. So they escorted her upstairs to the only bed in the house—the four-poster.

Their attempt to sleep on the living-room floor, wrapped in overcoats, was unsuccessful. Cordelia gave up the attempt first. She wandered quietly between dining room and kitchen, cleaning up the Culligans' litter and thinking about Edward: how wonderful marriage to him was; wondering how she could have lived so long without him.

At last, noticing Maude's manuscript and having nothing left to do, she picked it up. *Christian Love* was concerned precisely with the subject posited in its title: How much happiness you could find in caring for others. Employing an easy vocabulary and writing in simple declarative sentences, Maude cited one homely illustration after another of people who had found abiding happiness by helping neighbors and chance strangers.

Cordelia's favorite reading was novels, her favorite novelist Charles Dickens. As one skeptical of religion, despite her Episcopal affiliation, she was prepared to scoff at Maude's simple homilies. She found, instead, that Maude carried her along quite pleasantly. She cared about the people and situations described because Maude cared herself. Simpleminded though it was, Maude offered a program for happiness; and Cordelia, wanting, like everyone, to be happy, felt willing to follow the program.

Edward came from the living room, stiff, sleepy, cross.

"I'm reading Maude's manuscript," she told him. "It's quite interesting. If people in Caesar's Corners act like these she describes, maybe we should move there."

He yawned. "I'm sure they don't. Maude wouldn't tell a lie at gunpoint, but she has a scribbler's natural talent for fibbing. I think writers make up things the way they do because they just can't stand the world as it really is."

"Let's have some tea. There's not a bite to eat in the house. Maude ate everything. It's Washington's Birthday. Are shops open in the city on a holiday?"

"I don't know. I never paid any attention. Almost as

long as I can remember I've been eating in restaurants. I know how we'll get rid of Maude. She'll move on when we tell her we're out of food. She's always saying she eats like a bird, but I'll tell you something. I have to take her to dinner whenever she comes to the city, and I know from personal experience that the bird she eats most like is the vulture."

Cordelia poured them tea and said, "A thing I think about Maude—the way she puts her illustrations together, I think she could easily write novels."

Edward shook his head with a trace of a Nicholaslike deprecating smile. "Sorry, dear, but you're wrong about that. You haven't had the experience in the field I have. It takes more than ability to tell an anecdote to be a novelist. It takes—well—" He waved vaguely.

"But I think she has more than anecdotal ability," Cordelia said. "You know what Maude has? She has *passion*."

Edward made a hooting sound. "I can't wait to tell Hal Wiggins at the office what you said. He can't stand her and—"

"You and Mr. Wiggins don't have to have a passion for Maude in order for her to be passionate about people and ideas."

Their argument dragged on until Cordelia yielded goodnaturedly. Even when she started arguing she had known that she would have to yield. Her mother, as well as Miss Troy's, had taught her that. While Marie Dorfman had failed to instruct Cordelia in certain unmentionable subjects, she had trained her thoroughly in something basic: A woman must never try to win an argument with a man. Otherwise she would become known as a shrew and her marriage would be an unhappy failure.

The sound of shovels in the street made them realize it was almost six A.M. The scraping drew nearer until it seemed to be on their own steps. Cordelia went to the front windows and saw that a woman wearing a scant old overcoat was cleaning the steps. Opening the door, she looked at a small, thin-faced girl who stared back at her fixedly.

"Thanks for doing our steps and walk," Cordelia said. "But I wonder if you have the wrong house. We didn't request it, you know."

"No mistake, Mrs. Lovejoy," the girl replied. " 'Tis our pleasure. I'm Mary Culligan. Mary McMahon, I mean. My husband Tim's down there doin' the walk. Mrs. Lovejoy, I thank ye for bein' so good. We're awful sorry what happened last night."

"It's nice to meet you, Mary. There's nothing to be sorry about. You and Tim come in and have a cup of tea. There's not a bite in the house, but we do have tea."

"Thank you, ma'am. In a minute, soon as we finish here. I'll come in, but Tim won't. I'll ask him, but he won't. He's that shy."

Edward was upstairs shaving when Mary came in. "My husband is so hungry," Cordelia told her as she poured tea and they sat down on boxes, "that he's beginning to sound cross. Are there shops around here where I can get bacon and eggs and other things for breakfast?"

"There's places round on Lexington will be open by seven," Mary said. "I'll fetch anything you want." She breathed deeply and her face took on a determined look. "Mrs. Lovejoy, I ask you something. I want to work for you. I'll work for two dollars a week and keep."

Cordelia knew that, however inexperienced Mary might be, she never would find a better servant. But she and Edward had not discussed employing one. "Two dollars sounds ridiculous to me, Mary. What's the going wage in the city for a maid?"

"Five a week, ma'am, and keep if experienced. I had almost six months with Mrs. Mott on Sixteenth Street, but she went sudden and I can't get a 'commendation from her. But you can get 'em cheaper than five a week fresh off the boat, Mrs. Lovejoy."

"I'd like you to be my helper, Mary," Cordelia said. "And I'd want to pay you the going wage. But I have to discuss it with my husband. I know you were married yesterday, too, like us. Would you want to live in?"

"All the more reason, Mrs. Lovejoy. That third-floor room you have'd suit me good. If I could have Sunday off an' Tim could have visit privilege 'twould be the greatest blessing a couple ever had. Tim has a job at the carbarn and is off Sundays and'd live with his family. We don't have money for a place of our own. The way our families live"—she raised her hands—"it's like the cattle in the West Side slaughterhouses. We don't want to live with family, but—"

When Edward came downstairs, he gave Mary a quarter, which she did not want to accept, for their shoveling. Cordelia suggested he go for groceries with the McMahons, saying that now he was a married man it was time he got acquainted with the shops. Watching them plunge off through the snow, she hoped he would like Mary well enough to agree to their hiring her. Cordelia did not feel a great need for a servant to perform chores she could do herself. But she would enjoy a good companion while Edward was absent six days a week, and she was certain Mary would be the best.

They had been gone only a few minutes when Maude appeared. "Do I smell bacon and eggs?" she asked. "Do I smell flapjacks swimming in syrup? Usually I eat little as a bird, but that long walk in the storm gave me an appetite."

Cordelia explained she would have to subsist on tea until Edward returned. Serving Maude a cup, she said she had enjoyed reading a part of the manuscript of

Christian Love. "Miss Mudge, do you object to novels?"

"Not if they're moral ones," Maude replied. "I think a good story is the best way there is to make a moral point. Have you read *Esther at the Cross*?" Cordelia had not. "That's a good story about a good girl who becomes a *better* girl."

"Miss Mudge, I'll bet you could write a very good novel if you tried."

"Oooo!" Maude put down her cup quickly as if she had scalded her tongue. "Oooo! Cordelia, never let your husband hear you say that. I'm sure I could write a good novel. I've told Edward so many times, but it makes him cross with me. The one I want to write is called *Janet of the Rockies*."

"Have you been to the Rockies?"

"No. But in a surprising way it's a great advantage to an author not to have been to the place she's writing about. I found that true in writing *Reflections on the Holy Land*, where I've never been."

She described in detail the plot of her unwritten *Janet of the Rockies*. It was not a story Cordelia would have stayed awake all night to finish. But she could visualize it having appeal to many—especially women.

"Why not go ahead and write it?" Cordelia asked.

"And not let him know?" Maude looked at Cordelia with conspiratorial delight.

"I'll not tell if you won't."

"Never!" A sound of pleasure bubbled from Maude. "I'll just present him with the manuscript when it's finished. He'll *have* to accept it when I tell him Yarborough Brothers are interested in it. You're a very clever woman for being so young, Cordelia. You understand how we have to work *around* men. And it's only for their own good. Why, if Edward and that rough-spoken editor of his, Harold Wiggins, were left to their own devices, they'd publish nought but biographies of Arctic explorers. And who cares about *them*? All those explorers do is bumble around in blizzards and never find anything."

4

The morning after Maude went back to Caesar's Corners Edward dawdled over a third cup of coffee at the breakfast table and said, "Corey, dear, next time you're shopping, please order us a bathroom scale. I think I'm putting on weight, and I'm going to start a physical-fitness program."

"Are Mary's and my meals too hearty?" Cordelia asked.

"I could have done without the flapjacks this morning," Edward said. "But I do believe in a healthy breakfast. In winter I think oatmeal and cream is a good start to the day. And then I like about six slices of crisp bacon, two fried eggs turned, maybe some fried potatoes. And of course some muffins or biscuits or toast. Preserves with that are nice. And I always have two cups of coffee with just cream. The sugar that slips into your coffee can be awfully fattening."

Cordelia, staring at him solemnly, saw that he was not joking.

"Is Mary in the kitchen?" he asked.

"No, she ran down to the store."

"Corey, honey, I want to compliment you on how thrifty you are. All the furniture and things we've been buying—you're very sensible. You know a bargain. But I will say this about Mary McMahon. You could have got her for less than five dollars a week and keep. You could have got her for four—maybe three a week."

"But dear," Cordelia said, "we must pay her five because that's the sum I promised. And my word must be good to Mary if Mary is ever to be of any good to us."

"Well—" Edward could not quite meet her challenging gaze.

"What surprises me about Mary," Cordelia went on, "is that she can bear to be separated from Tim six days a week right after their marriage."

"I can understand it," Edward said. "Those poor Irish immigrant families live like rabbits in warrens on both the East and West sides of town. She and Tim would have no privacy, since they can't afford their own place and must live with family. Besides, I suppose as Catholics it's an acceptable way for them to manage the births of their children. Continence, I mean."

Cordelia's interest livened. "Is there any way but continence?"

Edward stared at her. "Well, yes." Then he went on to explain. He acted so unabashed by the discussion that she decided not to be embarrassed either.

"So it's possible," she said, "that we can plan our family."

"It's possible, my dear Corey, that we can *try* to plan a family. My own brothers and sisters died before I was ten and I grew up an only child. I didn't like that. I think it would be pleasant if we had three sons."

Cordelia agreed enthusiastically. "Boys are so much more interesting than girls. And they could follow you in publishing. You could rename the company Lovejoy and Sons."

Edward beamed. "Yes! Or Lovejoy's Sons." Then he looked sad. "But no matter how hard you plan, there's no way you can prevent boys from turning out to be girls."

"I suppose not. I guess the main thing is always to make love a lot."

"Yes," he agreed. "There's no point in planning if we don't make love."

"Edward, what are you going to do this morning?"

"Well, I don't exactly know." He looked out a window. "It's raining."

"Nothing out there but rain," she said. "Let's go back to bed and make love."

His expression brightened. "Right after breakfast?"

Her smile was bold, not coy. "Why not? I didn't marry you so we could eat breakfast together."

It was wonderful, absolutely wonderful. She was still trembling from the power of their emotions after he grew still.

"Something happened," he said.

"Yes, the roof fell in and buried us alive." Her arms tightened around him. "My love, I need you so. Don't ever leave me."

"I never will. I'm not ever going back to the office. *I* am the one who needs *you*." He placed a finger on the tip of her nose.

He wished for the eloquence to tell her how he felt. His initial attraction to her had been completely sensual. But then he had quickly come to love her mind, her energy, the very way she walked: a lovely body that flowed along without self-consciousness in friendly give-and-take with earth.

There was no end of joy in their lovemaking because she was naturally so passionate, so unstinting in her desire to satisfy both him and herself.

A few mornings later, fortified by a hearty breakfast, Edward went back to work reluctantly. In the little hallway he gathered Cordelia to him tightly and kissed her good-bye.

"I can't wait to get home," he told her. "Let's go to bed early this evening."

"Yes!"

He felt sad at parting as he looked back at her waving to him from the stoop of the brownstone, and then he trudged on through dirty slush toward Fourth Avenue. If he had not resolved to walk everywhere in his new plan of physical fitness he would have hopped into a hansom cab upon turning onto Fourth. The horse-cars were lined on the avenue below the tunnel which went underground from Thirty-third to Fortieth Street—thus removing the unsightly cars and their skeletal horses from the eyes of the rich on the fashionable stretch of Park Avenue, which was the name given to Fourth Avenue beginning at Thirty-third Street. Ah, someday he would buy Cordelia a mansion on that height of Murray Hill.

But today, alas, he must go to work. He could board a horsecar, but that too would be cheating in his program of physical fitness. The worst thing about walking in New York was the traffic, the noise, the aggressive pedestrians. To the clash of iron hoofs and iron wheels on cobbles was added the shrieking of dry axles. Or maybe worse than the noise was the stench of uncollected garbage in this filthy city. Or the permeating smoke that set everyone to coughing. No wonder walking was such a bore. Yet all walking was boring. The boredom of marching had made him quit the National Guard a decade ago. If it weren't for the marching, he would have liked to be a soldier. How he envied his father that Civil War experience.

At Twenty-sixth Street Edward cut west to Madison Avenue where the old Leonard Jerome house still stood on the corner. Now Jerome was gone, with all his beautiful mistresses and handsome horses, but the mansion would forever fascinate Edward: the ground-floor stables fitted out with rich carpets and walnut paneling; above that a ballroom and theater with tapestried walls that could accommodate six hundred guests; and on the top floors, living quarters for the much-neglected Mrs. Jerome and her daughters. Edward hurried on across Madison Square Park, surrounded by hostelries like Delmonico's and the Fifth Avenue Hotel, gambling clubs which pretended to be political clubs, and several old mansions. The big money was moving uptown, and not a penny of it ever had rubbed off on Edward Lovejoy. He gazed at his favorite New York statue as he strode along: Saint-Gaudens's likeness of bluff old Admiral Farragut with feet planted wide on a heaving deck while a blustery wind tugged at his jacket.

Lovejoy and Son was located at that time on the south side of West Twenty-third Street between Fifth and Sixth Avenues. The bookstore was on the ground floor, the editorial offices on the second, and the third and fourth floors were crammed with Lovejoy books which had not yet been—and might never be—sold. The printing plant of which Robert Lovejoy had acquired full ownership in 1839 had long since gone at a profit; now the books which the firm published were jobbed out to printers and binderies on bid. The company's location in the heart of what was then one of the best shopping areas in the city was excellent for the store, but the rent was high—too high, Edward reasoned, for the editorial and storage facilities. In vain he had tried to convince his father they should maintain the store in the high-class shopping area, but move office and warehouse to less expensive quarters. However, Colonel Bob always had grouped his enterprise within a single physical entity, and—as with several other things—he was not about to change.

As Edward charged up the stairs to the office, Hal Wiggins, the editor-in-chief, greeted him on the landing. "Behold, the bridegroom cometh. Welcome, Mr. Vice President. How goes it, Viscount?"

"What d'you mean, Viscount?"

"Of course you've been in the Southland and not seen the papers."

"We never got to Norfolk," Edward said. "That storm changed everything. But why do you call me Viscount?"

Hal, who had been a wedding guest with his wife, handed Edward a newspaper clipping. "From the *Times* a week ago."

The story announced the marriage of Cordelia and Edward and described the reception at the Dorfman ancestral estate. On this news peg was hung the story of the distinguished Dorfman family that had been descending for two and one half American centuries from one Hans Dorfman. Edward was surprised that Cordelia never had chosen to explain to him that he was marrying into American aristocracy. Then he was more astonished to read that the groom was scion to the publishing enterprises of Colonel Robert Lovejoy, a decorated hero of the War Between the States, and that the Lovejoys were descended from Viscount Lovejoy of Ardsley in Northumberland.

"Should we call you Ardsley?"

Hal was a short, plump, genial man with golden fuzz on his head and a passion for good writing in his heart. He and Edward were the best of friends and lapsed into a formal employee-employer relationship only when Hal asked for a raise.

"This mystifies me, Hal. How did the old man take it?"

"Crowingly. Lapped it up. Said he never liked to brag about the Viscount himself. Could your wife Cordelia have pulled this trick?"

"Never. Must have been planted by her brother. He's an awful snob. She can't stand him. Hal, what's new around here?"

"A sales problem. Not my problem, thank God. Max will tell you."

Edward turned toward his office and almost trampled Granger Cantwell, Hal's assistant editor. Granger made a gesture of obeisance and a civil remark about Edward's marriage. Edward did not like him, but Hal insisted he had editorial talent. Granger was twenty-five, thin and tallish with a droopy mustache and darkly prurient good looks. He was the only man Edward ever had known to wear a smoking jacket to the office; Edward recognized it was a courageous gesture, but felt that was the limit of Granger's courage. Granger had taken his master's degree at Harvard, and Edward thought he should be teaching literature on a New England campus. But here he was at Lovejoy's, somewhat underfoot and often looking pained by the dearth of excellence.

Edward said hello to old Sidney Barlowe, accountant extraordinary and treasurer of the company, who ran his office like an old-fashioned counting room. A devout Christian of the Methodist variety, Sidney kept two young wretches employed on high stools at high desks, barely allowing them time to go to the toilet, and might have insisted that they do their columns of figures with quill pens if quills had still been available. The names of these slaves of Sidney's changed frequently, always after a payday; but the shiny elbows of their alpaca jackets remained the same, as did their expressions of barely restrained outrage.

"Oh, Edward!" Sidney rolled his eyes. "You heard of the scandal?"

"Which one?"

"It's Jason Beauchamp—"

"I'm on my way to discuss it with him." Max Gurland, manager of the company's small sales force, came behind Edward. "Welcome back, Edward. How is Cordelia?" He and his wife, like the Wiginses, had been wedding guests. He followed into Edward's office and shut the door.

"What's the scandal about Jason?"

Max sighed deeply and sat down. "Jason overdid it on the expense account and Sidney caught him on a false voucher." Jason was Lovejoy's star traveler who covered the territory west and south of Philadelphia to

Cincinnati and Washington; he also was Max's brother-in-law.

"So," Edward said, "it's a well-known fact of life that people cheat on their expense accounts. We allow ten percent cheating, as everyone knows. If Jason went over ten this month, he'll have to even it off next month and the next."

Max grimaced. "Trouble is he went *away* over. I know the trouble. It's his wife. Her uterus. The doctors are into him—her uterus, I mean. Why is there suddenly all this concern about women's uteruses? When I was young nobody would *mention* such a thing. I *told* Jason to talk to you about it, that you'd be sympathetic. A doctor's bill of over four hundred, that is. But no, Jason had to be pigheaded proud and try to work it out of his expense account. And Sidney caught him."

"Well," Edward said, "you'd better write Jason to come up and talk to me about it. We'll work something out."

"I *told* Sidney to wait till you got back. But he had to go running to Colonel Bob. And the Colonel has decided to make an *example* of him. He won't accept my explanation about Jason's wife being sick."

"Oh goddamn it!" Edward said.

"Right, Edward, goddamn it."

It was a serious problem. Edward knew they never would find as able a salesman as Jason to cover that highly competitive territory. Worse, Jason and Max were close. If Jason went, Max wouldn't be far behind him. Max was an extraordinarily talented salesman who covered the New York area and served as manager over the company's five other traveling salesmen around the country. Only last month Lipscomb Brothers had offered him a fifty-percent raise to come work for them.

"I'll talk to Father as soon as he gets here."

Everyone in the company knew about it; word even

had penetrated to the clerks in the main-floor bookstore. There were ten men employed at Lovejoy's above the store, ranging from Robert himself to little Abe Schneider, the lowliest stock-room inventory clerk, and all were waiting to see if anything more would happen after the president overruled the vice-president and fired Jason Beauchamp.

Colonel Bob arrived at precisely nine o'clock and came to Edward's office for an affectionate reunion. He was surprised to learn they never had got to Norfolk on a honeymoon trip and was pleased to be asked to dinner at the Thirty-second Street house next week as soon as Cordelia could get her silver down from Dorfman Manor.

Colonel Bob beamed at him. "Oh, say now—did you see the piece in the *Times* about the wedding?"

"Hal showed it to me. I just glanced at it."

Colonel Bob took a well-fingered clipping from a waistcoat pocket and handed it to him. "Marvelous piece. Why didn't you tell me what a distinguished family you were marrying into?"

Edward weighed his father's words carefully. "Father, why didn't you ever tell me about Viscount Lovejoy of Northumberland?"

"Well—well—" Colonel Bob made a huffing sound. "I've told you my pa was just a plain old Maine dirt farmer. But I'll tell you something, Edward, I heard tales of *his* father amounting to something."

"Nicky paid a call on us yesterday afternoon," Edward lied. "He's great on genealogy and researched the Lovejoys thoroughly. The story he told about Viscount Lovejoy! Father, the Viscount was your great-grandfather! What a splendid tale of *noblesse oblige*."

"My God, my God!" Colonel Bob sounded close to babbling as he led the way into his office. "I confess, Edward, *noblesse oblige* is one of those fancy phrases that has always confused me."

"It means not just the obligation but the wish of the well-born to be generous in their behavior to those less fortunate. Nicky told us one example of this is Viscount Lovejoy's experience. Said it was characteristic of the man."

It had been in one of the English wars against the French in the last century, Edward explained. Viscount Lovejoy had been in command of the Northumberland Lancers. One of his able sergeants was found to have stolen money from the headquarters company mess-fund. It made no difference he had taken it to buy. medicine for his sick wife. Under the rules of the time the sergeant was to be hanged by the neck till dead. But Viscount Lovejoy intervened, remarking on what a good and faithful soldier the sergeant had been. He made up the missing money out of his own pocket and restored the sergeant to active duty. After the war when he returned to Northumberland, the sergeant quit the service and became the Viscount's best and most loyal servant till the day he died.

"Remarkable, remarkable," mumbled Colonel Bob. "*Noblesse oblige*, eh? I finally understand that phrase. Edward, you tap Nick for some more of those Viscount Lovejoy stories."

Edward rose. "Yes, Father. Are you lunching with anyone?"

"Yes, there's a meeting of the Credentials Committee."

As Edward returned to his office, Max came prowling through the hall and asked, "Any final decision?"

"Not yet."

"It's my turn to buy you lunch at Sullivan's."

"All right. Mind if Hal comes along?"

Sullivan's, near the corner of Sixth Avenue, had a bar that looked a mile long. By purchasing as little as a five-cent beer a man could eat free all he wanted from enormous serving tables of hot and cold foods (ladies were not admitted). When Edward, Hal, and Max arrived there at half past twelve, the long, high-ceilinged room was crowded and you had to raise your voice to be heard in the lively din.

Edward usually drank nothing stronger than a beer at lunch, but today he said he was having a boilermaker and the round was on him. Neither Max nor Hal objected. Hennesey, their customary waiter, found them a table and served each a four-ounce glass of whisky and a mug of draft beer.

Edward raised his shot glass, said, "Here's to Jason," and drank off precisely half of his whisky, following it with a swallow of beer. The others followed suit, and Max said, "I never could really figure whether it's good or bad when the old man goes to a luncheon meeting of the Credentials Committee."

"Is there really a Credentials Committee?" Hal asked.

"There really is," Edward said. "It's composed of veterans of the Grand Army of the Republic, the Jack Hand Post on Eighth Street, and they get together to pass on the fitness of applicants—if there are any. Incidentally they have the opportunity to drink together. I've found over the years that a meeting of the Credentials Committee generally makes my father look on company business more benignly in the afternoon. But in the present instance I promise nothing."

They had another round of boilermakers, ate rather less than usual, and returned to the office.

It was after three o'clock when Colonel Bob, somewhat flushed from Credentials Committee business, appeared in Edward's doorway.

"About this Jason Beauchamp affair," he said, coming in and closing the door. "He has acted most—er—his action has been"—Colonel Bob had a bit of difficulty with the words—"reprehensible. But there were"—more difficulty—"extenuating circumstances.

Sick wife, you know. I'm going to order Jason up here to New York and ad—admonish him myself. Know it never will happen again. The poor chap must be worried sick about losing his job."

"Father"—Edward rose and shook Colonel Bob's hand solemnly—"that's what I call true *noblesse oblige.*"

When Edward told Cordelia about the incident at dinner that evening, she asked, "Does your father really believe that story Nicky must have made up about the Viscount?"

"I doubt it," Edward said. "Father has shortcomings, but naiveté is not one of them. I imagine that ever since he announced his intention of making an *example* of Jason, he's been looking for a way to get out of it. The story I made up offered him a way out. It's the sort of situation that always secretly amuses him. Father never minds lying if it's ingenious enough. He just hates clumsy lying where people have to pay the penalty after they're caught."

Cordelia envied Edward his day at the office. Her own day of household tasks with Mary had seemed endless, utterly boring. Did she face a whole lifetime of it? For hours she had been wondering how she could coax Edward to let her do something useful at Lovejoy's. She loved to read and felt that her judgments of what she read were sound. A job in book publishing would be the most exciting experience in the world. But she must not frighten Edward by appearing to want to abandon their home and move into a man's world. She must approach the matter cautiously, show great finesse.

Ever since she had begun looking askance at some of the ninny ways of Miss Troy's School, she had often wished she were a man. Not physically, but in the sense of having important responsibilities and making significant decisions as contrasted to the relatively unimportant role of women. After she'd come home from Newport in disgust it had occurred to her that managing a farm was one thing a woman could do that would bring her the joys of a man's responsibilities. Before she fell in love with Edward she'd thought she might learn farm management from her father and take over direction of Dorfman Manor when he grew too old to be active. Loren always had been glad to encourage her opinions and answer her many questions. Now she hoped Edward would be the same, for book publishing sounded infinitely more interesting than farming.

Thus she questioned Edward at length about the workings of Lovejoy's and other book publishing houses. At the time there were dozens of American publishers, almost all in New York, Boston, or Philadelphia, competing with one another for a rather modest audience of readers. Among these Lovejoy's was about average in size, financially stronger than most but weaker than a few. Like most houses, it was an outgrowth of the printing industry.

Robert Lovejoy, born in 1820, had escaped his father's tyranny at the age of twelve and made his way to New York, where he became a printer's apprentice. Through hard work, luck, and shrewd business sense, he owned his own small printing shop when nineteen. (The line of the company's letterhead, "Publishers since 1839," was not precisely correct.) In order to keep his flatbed presses busy, Robert took to stealing the works of English authors in the early 1840s, binding the pages cheaply, and selling the books thus made wherever he could. His later defense of this practice was that everyone was doing it. That was not so. Many were doing it, but not all publishers were.

When Colonel Bob came to dinner, Cordelia led him into reminiscing about earlier days: "What I want most in a writer is a good storyteller. And they're always hard to find to be sure, to be sure. In the old days good storytellers like Washington Irving and Fenimore Cooper were the exception rather than the rule. And even their best efforts weren't very well rewarded by us publishers and our readers. No wonder so many promising young American writers give up and disappear— or take to writing books that nobody wants to read. One that comes to mind was a chap named Herman Melville. You probably never heard of him, Cordelia. He wrote a couple of entertaining tales about the South Seas, then turned to absolute aberrations. One manuscript I read was a long book called *Moby Dick* about a bunch of crazy whalermen. It told more about the whaling industry than anybody could possibly want to know. Of course I turned it down. Forget who finally published it. Didn't sell worth a damn. . . ."

Edward explained to Cordelia that most of the publishing companies that had survived and prospered were those that owned stores to market their books. In 1852 Robert had opened a bookstore on lower Broadway to sell the products of his own presses as well as those of other publishers. He had good merchandising sense, and the store prospered. It was, in truth, the store that enabled the business to survive his absence in the Civil War when he was off pursuing paths of glory and earning the sobriquet of Colonel Bob as commander of a New York regiment. After returning from the war he moved the store and the office away uptown to Twenty-third. As his interest in publishing books began to wane, he would have kept the store and sold the rest of the business if Edward had not intervened.

In 1870 Edward had left his father's business for a couple of years and gone to work as a traveler for a Boston publisher. He covered various areas from Portland, Maine, as far west as the Ohio and the Mississippi. These had become the frontiers of culture since the North had just about destroyed the South, which before the war had been one of the most literate book markets in the nation. In his years of travel Edward learned much about what Americans of the time wanted to read.

He returned to New York and a job as what Colonel Bob called "my chief of staff." It was Edward who hired a small group of travelers and sent them out to sell Lovejoy books. "Always see what's beyond the Hudson, gentlemen," he told them wryly. "Remember that you don't go as missionaries to the great unwashed but as humble learners of a mysterious trade." It was Edward who, in a serious confrontation with his father, prevailed on him to stop publishing a flow of Civil War memoirs: "Father, the war is over and people want to forget it and they don't give a damn about old soldiers' memories. I'm sorry to put it so bluntly, Father, but they simply do not give a damn." Above all it was Edward who gave Lovejoy and Son an increasing aura of respectability through his belief that publishing good literature was the way for a house to be successful.

"Dear," Cordelia asked him, "what do you mean by good?"

He looked surprised. "Just what I say. Good as compared to evil. I admit I don't attend church. I'm a freethinker. But I do know the difference between good and evil."

"Of course I understand," Cordelia said. "I was just trying to think of an evil book."

Edward frowned. "The French have published some." He forced a smile. "Well, of course I don't mean *Candide*. But by good, Corey, I mean books that stress the moral perfectibility of man."

"How about woman?" She could have bitten her tongue. Was he going to become cross?

But Edward maintained an air of sweet reasonableness. "I mean what you know I mean. The perfectibility of all humans. The perfectibility of our society. Surely you must believe in that."

"Oh, I do!" Cordelia spoke with some fervor. "Only I think it could become more perfect if women had a greater role in it. Just last night when I was asking about publishing practices, you said there are no women in it."

Once more he looked surprised. "But there are no women in *anything*. How many women doctors do you know? Not one because there are none. Why should publishing be any different?"

"Oh, I think publishing is the most natural field in the world for women," Cordelia said. "It's as natural as—uh—cooking. Because women are far greater readers of books than men."

"You can't prove that!"

"Well, next time you ride on a train or a horsecar take a look at who is reading what. The women are reading books, but it's a rare man you see reading one. They're nearly all reading newspapers or magazines."

"That," Edward said, "is because men are concerned with politics and finance."

"You're proving my point," Cordelia said. "Night before last you were saying how distressed you and other publishers are that most books on politics don't sell well. I think they don't sell well because men don't read books and women don't give a pig's whistle about politics. Why should we? We don't even have the right to vote. Why should we care who's President of the United States?"

"Oh, Corey!" Edward's voice reverberated with surprise and alarm. "You really go too far when you say you don't care who is President. Really! What a dreadful thing for a patriotic citizen to say!"

"Well, anyway, going back to my main point," Cordelia said, "it would be the most sensible and natural thing in the world for publishing houses to have women editors because women naturally know better than men what women like to read."

"Your fallacies fall one on another. You're speaking emotionally rather than logically. How can there be a woman editor when there are no women in *any* part of publishing? I know this business thoroughly. Here and there you'll find ladies selling in bookstores and there are a few lady librarians. But I don't know of as much as one lady *clerk* in any publishing house in this country or England. Did you ever hear of a woman printer or a woman traveler covering a territory? Oh, Corey!"

Edward's air of consternation with her was so great that she realized it would take all her efforts and considerably more time before she began to realize her ambition.

5

A great thing about being married to a man who owned a bookstore, Cordelia found, was that she could borrow and read all she wanted without charge. The Lovejoy store became a gold mine where she dug two and three times a week. Her omnivorous reading of contemporary books led her to past and foreign writers she had missed during her years at Miss Troy's. She discovered such writers as Victor Hugo, Tolstoy, Shakespeare, Tennyson, Browning.

As soon as she found to her surprise that Mary could neither read nor write, Coredlia set out to teach her. Three o'clock each weekday afternoon was the hour set aside for Mary's lessons. She was an apt student, avid to learn, and three o'clock became a most precious time of day to them both.

One afternoon Cordelia saw that she had lingered too long browsing in Lovejoy's and that she must put a sprint into her step to make the three o'clock lesson. As she swung along toward home, a male voice cried, "Miss Cordelia!" Out in the clotted traffic of Fifth Avenue, Harold McCrory was standing up in his coachman's box and doffing his hat to her.

"Harold!" She waved to him. "How are you?"

He was unable to respond, for Miriam Peyster's face came into view in the enclosed coach and she obviously was reprimanding him for indecorum. And then Miriam cast Cordelia a look of total contempt. Harold sank down with a chastened expression, and the river of traffic carried them away.

There was something ghostly about the experience to

Cordelia, as if she had glimpsed a former friend stirring beyond the grave. It was clear that Cousin Miriam, in snubbing her, felt emotion that she did not. Cousin Miriam had looked at her as at a certificate of stock that had become worthless. Cordelia, far from hating her, felt a twinge of sympathy. The Peysters *had* invested heavily in her, and she had not responded with increased social value.

She must take care that she never acted toward Mary in such a proprietary way. Since she herself wanted mightily to be her own woman, she must make sure that Mary had equivalent opportunity to grow and become what she pleased.

When she hurried into the house, the clock was striking three. "I made it in time!" she called. There was no answer. "Mary?"

The kitchen door into the hall squeaked open slowly, and Cordelia almost cried out at what she saw. A man about four feet tall stood in the doorway. He was hairless, and a scar, dividing his forehead symmetrically and descending to his flat nose, separated an empty socket from an eye that glared with rage.

Cordelia, thinking rape and murder, shrank back. But he gestured to her—peacefully, she thought—and spoke. A cleft palate made his words incoherent at first. Then she understood he was speaking of Mary; there was trouble of some kind; it had been necessary for her to go somewhere. And suddenly Cordelia realized that Mary, who had not yet learned to write well enough to leave her a note of explanation, had asked this messenger of bad news to explain. The dwarf kept bowing civilly as he tried to make Cordelia understand what had happened; the look of rage in his single eye was not at her, but at a fate that had made him what he was.

"Where did Mary go?" Cordelia demanded.

The man pointed south: a whole hemisphere in that direction.

"She's in trouble? Is it Tim?"

His gesture indicated it might be a lot more than Tim.

"Maybe I can help her. Can you take me to her?"

He hesitated, at last nodded doubtfully.

Cordelia put down the books she had brought from the store and led the way out of the house. Though the day was cold, the man did not wear an overcoat; she saw then that his patched jacket and pants, his bald head and scarred face, were covered with a fine dust like talcum.

Cordelia's concern over Mary grew as the little man trotted ahead of her to the Third Avenue elevated line where he climbed the stairs of the Thirty-fourth Street station. She paid the nickel fare for each as a steam train, showering them with smoke and cinders, clattered to a halt at the platform. Where Mary's and Tim's families lived she did not know—only that it was somewhere in the Lower East Side slums. It struck her as odd that during all the years she had lived in New York she never had visited the slums. Once, when she had expressed a wish to do so, Cousin Miriam had replied angrily, "If you ever say such a nasty thing again, I'll punish you."

As the train rattled and jerked down Third toward the Bowery, Cordelia looked out the windows curiously. Quite suddenly they passed into a different world. Cordelia's first glimpse of it came through the upper windows of the buildings on either side. Many windows were without panes, and the people inside were dressed heavily against the March cold. Most were working—at sewing machines, at dipping candles, polishing furniture. In one long block all the activity involved doing something with brass bedsteads. Through one window she saw a half-clothed man and woman doing something unspeakably obscene.

Everyone wore peasant black, that uniform of poverty. Now the people boarding and leaving the train at each station looked different from most of the people one saw farther uptown. In their black clothing they looked either grotesquely thin or fat with pallid skin that reminded Cordelia of tallow. No one spoke English; even the Irish brogue seemed to become more incomprehensible the farther they journeyed into the slums. Italian, Yiddish, Lithuanian, Russian, Greek—it was a babble of tongues that seemed not to belong in America. Gradually the car became permeated with unpleasant smells: sweat and rancid grease and strong garlic.

She was glad to leave the train when the dwarf beckoned. They descended rickety wooden stairs into bedlam. Cordelia had no idea where she was. A mass of humanity simply rose from the street to smite her. Ragged, barefoot boys screamed the headlines of the *World*, the *Post*, and a dozen foreign-language newspapers she never had heard of. The conflux of traffic at two streets was like the torrents of spring creating a flood. Wagons and rigs and masses of pedestrians struggled against one another and swirled around shrieking pushcart vendors at the curbs. The din, the odors, were awful. Dominating all was a stench like dead fish, as if some giant whale had become stranded here in the city and was slowly rotting away. Black, black everywhere—only faces were pallid white.

While these people were foreign to Cordelia, she looked equally strange to them, because she was a fashionably dressed beauty. Among the women of the slums, poor food and bad air contributed to unsightly skin; poverty made a scowl more natural than a smile. By contrast, Cordelia's skin was like alabaster, her hair lustrous, a slight smile of confidence almost habitual. Her clothing possessed color and style that set off her slender, well-formed body. She was a beauty, as Edward had told her so often that she was not unmindful of the fact. She carried herself with pride, as well she might.

A leering youth addressed her. His language was foreign, but his suggestion universal. The dwarf confronted him and said something she did not understand. Then he reached out with exceeding gentleness to take her handbag from her.

"Oh, no you don't!" she cried. "So that's your game! Getting me here to steal my purse! *Where is Mary?*"

His single eye eloquently expressed a hopelessness. Once more he tried to make her understand that he would carry her bag.

"No!" she shrieked. "I want a policeman!" She looked around wildly, but there was not a policeman in sight. There was only the crowd pressing in, watching with amusement now this confrontation between the uptown lady and the dwarf thief.

He stopped trying to take her handbag, but somehow made her feel she should continue to follow him. They had not taken twenty steps when her handbag simply evaporated from her arm. She had been carrying it carefully with its leather strap hung over her right arm when there was a flash of a razor-sharp knife and the bag was gone. She screamed, the dwarf whirled, and someone disappeared in the crowd like a stone sinking in deep water. The dwarf went after him.

Cordelia screamed again, and a large policeman materialized from nowhere. Gazing down at her balefully, he demanded, "Wot the hell ye doin' in this neighborhood, lady?"

"My handbag!" she cried. "I—"

Far off came the shrill and tinny sound of a policeman's whistle, and her savior galloped toward it. She, not knowing what else to do, ran after him.

At the entrance to a dead-end alley down the street the policeman and a fellow officer held back a throng of the curious.

".'Tis the Culligans aginst the Wops agin," one said. "An' yon's Timmy McMahon wiv 'em. Gi' the lady a ringside look. 'Tis her bag the Wops stole."

Cordelia watched wide-eyed as the dwarf and three other men, including Mary's Tim, moved warily with clubs toward three youths who had drawn knives.

"Dwarfy," yelled one policeman, "be ye needin' help?"

"Nah!" snarled the dwarf without looking round.

"Wops!" called the other policeman. "Touch the hair of a Culligan er McMahon head an' ye're in jail. Now drop thim knives an' gi' the lady back her bag."

Reluctantly the youths let their knives fall to the ground and one tossed Cordelia's handbag to the dwarf. Then they scuttled out of the alley and disappeared.

"My God, Miz Cordelia, wot ye doin' here?" cried Tim McMahon when she saw her.

She explained, and he told her that the dwarf was Sean Culligan, a cousin of Mary's father. " 'Tis sad news fetched Mary an' me home this afternoon. Her father—Jim Culligan—he's passed away. He was doin' mason's work wid Sean on Lafayette Street an' the scaffold give way. Fell four floors to his death, he did. Sean fell, too, but just got up an' walked away. Ye can't kill Sean. Was on my way to the undertaker's wid these here Culligans when we come on Sean after the Wop thieves."

Cordelia expressed sorrow over Jim Culligan's death. "Since I'm close now, Tim, may I stop by and pay my respects to the family?"

He hesitated. "The Culligans be not livin' so good, Miz Cordelia. Ye might mind goin' there."

"I don't mind at all," Cordelia said. "Anyplace Mary's family lives is—" She could not think how to finish the sentence. "Lead on, Tim."

He led the way reluctantly to another street teeming

with people where the rows of six-story tenements were indistinguishable one from another. As Cordelia learned later, they were "old law" tenements built with a dumbbell-shaped floor plan in order to accommodate air shafts. The law had been passed in 1879 with the best of intentions to give air and light to those who dwelled in the buildings; but these had become the worst of tenements because the air shafts, inaccessible from the ground, became vertical refuse pits which bred germs and rats.

When Tim led Cordelia into the Culligans' tenement building, she felt assaulted physically by an indescribable stench. It took willpower for her to go on—up narrow, fetid stairs and along dark, cluttered halls where the screaming of infants and children and a quarrelsome clamor of older voices seemed unending. Cordelia felt she was suffocating. But she perservered up another flight, and at last Tim opened a door.

The light in the small room was dim, the air vile, for the single window onto the air shaft had been nailed closed to try to shut out the stink. An indistinguishable number of people stirred and whsipered like shadowy creatures. Then Mary emerged, bringing her face close to Cordelia's, like someone viewed in a dream. But she was real enough when Cordelia hugged her thin body and said, "I'm so sorry, Mary."

Dry eyed until then, Mary started to cry. "Ye shouldn't have, Miz Cordelia. Come here, I mean."

"But I wanted to pay my respects to the Culligans."

They gathered round her, murmuring appreciation. Someone lighted a candle. There was one comfortable chair, and they begged her to sit in it, but she refused. There was no bed, only pallets on the floor. (How wonderful that wedding bed on Thirty-second Street must have seemed to Mary and Tim, Cordelia thought.) By the light of the candle she made out Jim Culligan's body on one of the pallets, covered with something. His boots stuck out grotesquely—and by the feeble candle-light Cordelia saw that his boots were dusty.

She must say something. But what words could she utter? Mary was right; she should not have come here. She heard herself babbling, "God bless Mr. Culligan. God bless everyone here."

But why mention God? If God were what He was supposed to be, why did He allow these devoted humans of His to live like animals?

"What can I do?" she demanded of Mary. "What will help the most to—to make people feel better?"

"We want a High Mass for Papa." Mary had stopped crying; her tone was brisk.

"Well—fine. What can I do?"

"Ye can take it out of me wages, Miz Cordelia— three dollars a week out of me wages. 'Twill cost fifteen dollars."

"Your priests *charge* you for Masses?"

"Didn't say that!" Mary sounded angry. "Priests don't charge nothin' never. 'Tis the other parts—the undertaker an' all."

"He will have a High Mass."

"Thankee, Miz Cordelia." Mary's body slumped and she started to cry again.

Cordelia and Edward contributed the fifteen dollars necessary for Jim Culligan's High Mass and also sent a wreath which was vociferously admired by all of his relatives. Cordelia attended the services, but Edward pleaded pressing business. Cordelia was glad that Mary and Tim, once they had expressed sincere gratitude for what the Lovejoys had done, stopped talking about it. A significant aspect of life in the slums, she thought, was how everyone accepted the inevitable.

The day after Jim Culligan's funeral a servant deliv-ered a note to Cordelia's door.

Dear Corey,

Remember me? I hope you do. I admired you
so much when you were a year ahead of me at
Miss Troy's. And I was so impressed to read of
your marriage to the noted publisher Edward
Lovejoy. Having great literary interests myself, I
think that the publishing of good books is a calling
as noble as that of the clergy or medicine. Your
own distinguished family has been joined to another equally distinguished. Personally, I was married a year ago to my beloved Gilbert Bancroft.
Though Gilbert's career is in investment banking,
he is a most literate graduate of Harvard who
reads books!

I hope that you can join me for lunch here at
my home Thursday a week, the twenty-third. A
few other dear friends will be here. We all of us
get together not just to reminisce about the past
but to study the future and see how we can improve it. The interest of all of us is to try to improve conditions in the New York slums, and I
hope you can share our interest. I do look forward
to hearing from you.

Your old friend,
Gloria Renssalaer Bancroft

Cordelia remembered Gloria as a coltish girl who'd
had some discipline problems at Miss Troy's but who
never was bounced out of school because she was of
that notable old Renssalaer family. Of course she was
pleased to go to the luncheon. When she told Mary of
the women's concern over the slum life, Mary replied:

" 'Tis only one thing the ladies can do. Have 'em
make sure their husbins don't invist in no tenement
property. 'Tis the landlord money makes the slums."

It was true, Cordelia knew, that tenements provided
lucrative investments for the wealthy. "But the trouble

is," she told Mary, "there's not a living woman can tell her husband what he should do with his money."

Mary sighed. " 'Tis trouble any way ye looks at tenements. Me ol' man said best thing is all in the slums make a big march into the country. But Tim says do that an' some'll stay behind an' rob blind everything the marchers don't take wiv 'em."

The Bancrofts lived in a Park Avenue mansion on Murray Hill where Cordelia appeared promptly at half past twelve on Thursday. A dozen women, most of them young matrons, crowded into a drawing room which was so stuffed with furniture, in the mode of the time, that there seemed barely room for them to fit in. Cordelia quickly found that all accepted her as an equal. Happily, new social views prevailed among the younger generation, who did not scorn a book-publishing career as the Peysters did. If a woman was well bred, it didn't matter as much as it used to what her husband did for a living.

All professed interest in literature, and most said they read her husband's books—as if he wrote them himself instead of publishing them. But Cordelia's joy at discovering how well known was the Lovejoy imprint vanished after one guest referred to her as "Mrs. Scribner" and another addressed her as "Mrs. Harper."

When they sat down to luncheon in the dining room a maid and footman served each a clear soup. Then the two servants together carried in a monumental salad. It consisted of boiled and marinated scallops mixed with celery and mayonnaise and formed into a mountain on whose sides were designs, outlined in capers and filled with red and white garnishings of chopped beets and egg whites. A forest of bright spinach leaves crowned the top and the base was surrounded by rosetted radishes and flower-shaped cuts of celery. The guests admired the creation while the servants excavated it. Ladyfingers with whipped cream preceded the coffee.

After they adjourned to the drawing room, Gloria addressed them: "I wonder how many of you have visited the slums."

Cordelia started to raise her hand, then thought better of it when no other hand went up.

There was a bit of triumph in Gloria's smile. "Well, I won't say that I was *privileged* to, but I *did* go down to the Lower East Side week before last." There was a stirring of interest and one small gasp of surprise. "Oh, I was well protected." Gloria smiled again. "There was an agent of my husband's and two policemen with me all the way. But I did prepare a report of what I saw there—my inspection report, you might say." Oh Gloria, Gloria, read us your report, several called out. She beamed. "You'd really like to hear it?"

Cordelia found the report dull compared to her own vivid impressions; Gloria had missed a great deal and apparently had not ever actually entered a tenement flat. After a while Cordelia stopped listening and didn't become attentive until all started applauding. Wonderful, Gloria! Simply wonderful!

"I think," Gloria said, "it would be helpful now if each of us made some comment. We'll sort of go around the circle starting with Cordelia."

"Well," Cordelia said, "first of all I want to congratulate you, Gloria, on a beautifully written and intellectually incisive report. It's important that you've brought to our attention such an unspeakable blight on our city. These conditions should not exist!"

"Hear! Hear!" someone said. The women continued to deplore the slums as they went around the circle till they came to young Hattie Fisher, who said, "Of course these conditions shouldn't exist. But what are we going to do about it?"

There was profound silence.

At last Cordelia spoke up: "Well, Hattie, what do you suggest?"

Hattie smiled across at her faintly. "We should start nagging our husbands not to invest a penny or recommend that anybody else invest a penny in slum real estate. As long as it remains such an enticing investment there will be a slum."

"I agree," Cordelia said. There were murmurs that did not convey much conviction. "If we're going to nag our husbands, remember that there's strength in numbers. Let's adopt a resolution. Then we can cite the opinion of many when we go to nag our husbands."

"That makes sense," someone said.

However, the way they had passed three afternoon hours did not seem very sensible to Cordelia on her way home. It was pleasant to know she still was accepted in society and nice to have friends. Yet there had been no stimulation in the occasion; it would have been far more stimulating to read an interesting book.

No question about it, Cordelia thought, she was unlike Gloria and most of those women. She was not at all interested in the life of the typical New York matron whose habitat was a protective cocoon from which she hoped to burst as a beautiful social butterfly on special occasions. Those women wished the world to rotate around them, she thought, while she personally wanted to rotate round the world. She wanted to see and learn and travel and *do*, discovering other ways of life than her own. Yet, considering how tightly laced social customs were, would she ever be able to?

One afternoon early in May, Cordelia visited young Dr. Prettyman on East Thirty-fourth Street and learned that she was pregnant. She almost ran home and literally danced through the little hall to tell Mary the good news.

"Congratulations, Miz Cordelia." But Mary did not sound happy.

"Well now, young lady," Cordelia said, "do I detect a note of disappointment?"

"Well," Mary said, "thought I'd be the first. Ye're not even Catholic."

"What does that have to do with it?"

"Lots. But honest, I'm happy for you."

Edward was ecstatic. Of course he knew—as did Cordelia—that the baby would be a boy. So did Colonel Bob, who made plans to change the name of the company to Lovejoy and Sons. Edward bought some Standard Oil stock, predicting it would rise—and it did. He predicted a large advance sale for a new romance from Lovejoy's entitled *For Love of a Magnolia*—and there was.

"Suddenly," he told Cordelia, "everything is perfectly predictable."

But it was not.

For Memorial Day of 1891 the Grand Army of the Republic planned a massive celebration in New York City to commemorate the thirtieth anniversary of the outbreak of the greatest, indeed the *only* war in history. Veterans' posts from towns for miles around were invited to join with the city's veterans in the great festivities that began at nine A.M. At that hour a huge parade of thousands of veterans, military units, bands, and floats started from Washington Square and marched up Fifth Avenue to Twenty-third Street. There the route turned west to Seventh Avenue, and then by way of Broadway, Seventy-second Street and Riverside Drive, it terminated at the tomb of the greatest veteran of all, General Ulysses Simpson Grant.

But that was only the beginning of the celebration. At the tomb the assembled veterans were to be prayed over by preachers and harangued by politicians before being released to a series of noonday dinners held at scores of hotels and other places in Manhattan. Following that, all were to assemble at the Battery for more speeches and a vast picnic that would end with the largest display of fireworks ever seen in New York. Nothing in the city's history, not even the dedication ceremonies for the Statue of Liberty on October 28, 1886, could match the grandiosity of the Grand Army's plans for this Memorial Day.

As the *World* reported, "The day dawned as bright and hot as on that long ago morning when the Boys in Blue marched forth to meet the enemy at First Manassas." Some members of the Grand Army objected vehemently to the *World* bringing up the memory of one of their worst defeats, but everybody—including the anonymous writer for the *World*—was trying awfully hard to celebrate a memorable occasion. That it turned into a debacle was a fact tactfully unreported by the press.

First of all, the eight-mile route of march was too long for veterans whose girths had increased much since the days when they boasted of thirty-mile marches. Also, there were too many refreshment points offering free beer along the route; indeed any veteran, either in or out of uniform, could have all the free drinks he wanted at every public bar in the city. So what started out at Washington Square as rather sprightly-looking military formations ended up a drunken rabble at Grant's Tomb. The Grand Army collapsed into itself, like an old building long in need of repair on which too much strain had been placed. Few ever made it back to the Battery, and two who did fell into the harbor and drowned.

But early in the planned festivities, when the long column turned from Fifth Avenue onto Twenty-third Street, the Grand Army looked somewhat like its name. Drums rolled, brass blared, men swung along in time to "Marching through Georgia" and "The Battle Hymn of the Republic" and "We Are Coming, Father Abraham." Lovejoy and Son, like most buildings on the line of march, was festooned with bunting and decked with flags. Although the company was closed for the holiday, all employees understood they had to be hanging out the windows and cheering their president when he passed at the head of the Jack Hand Post; employees were, in fact, encouraged to bring along their families to make the cheering louder. After the parade had passed, everyone was invited to the young Lovejoys' house for a buffet luncheon. The suggestion had been Cordelia's, and Edward was delighted she cared that much about company morale. She and he sat at an open window of Colonel Bob's office with others to watch the parade.

It had a splendid beginning as it wheeled onto Twenty-third Street. General Nelson Miles, resplendent in dress uniform and weighting down a small bay mare, was the grand marshal. Behind him, flanked by mounted policemen and riding in a victoria, was a more ancient relic of the war—a white-haired, mean-faced old man with stars on his shoulders to signify he was a general. Everyone applauded and asked who he was. Next came a massed band whose brass, winking in the sunlight and blaring triumphantly, made patriots shiver.

While we go march-ing through Geor-gia!

Edward's foot tapped and Cordelia's eyes welled with tears. Patriotic airs always made her forget that women lacked the right to vote.

Little Abe Schneider was first to see the Jack Hand Post and announced its approach with a terrifying shriek. There came Colonel Bob, ramrod straight in his immaculate blue uniform, dress sword bared on his right shoulder, mustachio seeming to quiver in time to the drums. All employees, relatives, and friends set up an unearthly din of yelling, whistling, and applause that the president ignored until he came directly opposite his place of business. Then, with startling suddenness, he did a graceful whirl and two-step like a Highlander dancer and gave all a beautiful sword salute, hilt to chin, and then a bow while the men of Jack Hand Post, most of them marching in step to the music, solemnly performed a smart eyes left. The cheers of the loyal claque at the publishing house were picked up by the crowds along the street.

"My God," exclaimed Max Gurland, "the Colonel must have been practicing that!"

He had, actually, in front of a full-length mirror in his room, falling down a couple of times in the process and badly bruising a hip.

On marched Colonel Bob and his comrades, slowly fading from view. Toward noon, as the torrent of the parade continued to flow along unabated, the Lovejoy group made their way to the house on Thirty-second Street. There Cordelia had brought in two extra girls to help Mary dispense cold meats, salads, pastries, watermelon, beer, and iced tea to the more than fifty people who crowded into the little house and overflowed onto the front steps.

Later it seemed highly appropriate that all the members of the company should have been assembled when a man came running and panting along the street with the news. While marching through Columbus Circle, Colonel Robert Lovejoy had pitched over dead of a heart attack.

6

Edward's grief over his father's death was deep and abiding. Nick, of all people, came to pay his respects on the Saturday following the funeral and was so decent that Cordelia invited him to stay to dinner.

"I wish I could care as much about my father as you do about yours," he told Edward.

Edward did not know what to say; one of his few illusions was that all sons loved their fathers.

"I'm sorry," Nick said, "that I did that stupid thing about your father's family. As Corey knows, I've suffered for years from a terrible case of snobbery. Frankly, I've been—uh—reconstructing myself. I see how well you and Corey do. I see how badly I do."

Cordelia gaped at him. Edward could think of nothing but to say, "Let's have another glass of wine. Nick, my father adored that fictitious story. I can't tell you how much I appreciate your thinking it up."

"I'll tell you something," Nick said, "I'd like to get married."

"Well—ah—" Edward poured wine with his right hand while making circular motions with his left. "Why not try it?"

"I can't find the right woman. They all think I'm boring."

"Well, dear Nicky," Cordelia said, "we'll just start a program to make you more interesting."

"That would be very nice," Nick said. "I'll do my best to cooperate."

Cordelia was delighted with the idea that Nick actually was going to reform himself. She must try to find a woman with whom there might develop a mutual attraction, she told Edward the following Monday evening.

"Well," he said, "don't look among any of those independent-minded friends of yours such as adopted the resolution on the slums. Nick needs somebody *dependent*." He smiled. "I was looking at a manuscript in the office today which contained a quote from a trustee of Columbia Law School in 1886. Three bold young women had applied for entrance to the law school, and the trustee said: 'No woman shall degrade herself by practicing law, especially in New York, if I can save her.'"

Cordelia frowned. "You find that funny, dear?"

"Yes, I do."

"To you is it funny that the women applied for law school or that the trustee said what he did?"

"Somehow it's the trustee who sounds funny," Edward said. "To me, I mean. He sounded so pompous."

"There's hope for you," Cordelia smiled at him, "as for Nick."

"Among manuscripts received today was one from Maude Mudge."

"She wrote me last week it was on the way. How is it?"

"I just glanced at the first few pages. It's awful. I don't see why she thinks she can be a novelist."

"Please, Edward, bring it home and let me read it."

"I assure you, sweetheart, it's just dreadful."

"Edward, are you trying to tell me that no woman shall degrade herself by practicing editing, especially in New York, if you can save her?"

He brought Maude's manuscript home next evening. It was entitled *Janet of the Rockies*, and Cordelia sat up half the night reading it. The following morning she discussed it with Edward at breakfast.

"I don't think it's dreadful," she told him. "I'd call it only pretty bad."

"In Maude's covering letter," he said, "she claimed Yarborough Brothers is interested in this novel. I figure she's fibbing. Hal took a look at a few pages and says it's drivel."

"The main drivel in it," Cordelia said, "is at the crisis where Janet is rescued from that mountain torrent by the trapper. Up till then I think it's pretty much the sort of story lots of women like to read. But at the crisis Maude is trying so hard not to sound circumstantial that she turns ridiculous. It should be the hero—Bob—interesting she named her hero Robert—anyway, in a story like this it's the hero who *has* to rescue the heroine." She went on to suggest how Maude, by slight changes earlier in the story, could make it perfectly credible that hero and heroine were together at the crisis.

"Interesting," Edward said. "That would take *some* of the drivel out of it."

"But I have an even better suggestion," Cordelia went on. "Women don't want to read about life in the Rockies. Only men do. Probably it's the sort of place they want to go to get away from women. What I want Maude to do is keep her basic story but change her locale. Women like to read about cities. Especially right now I think slums are popular with women. I want Maude to call her novel *Janet of the Slums*."

Edward stared at her. "But Maude has never seen a slum."

"Neither has she ever seen a Rocky Mountain. I'll send her a few pages of description of the Lower East Side and she can sift it into her story like—like baking powder in biscuits."

Next day a messenger brought Cordelia a note from Hal Wiggins saying he'd like to talk with her about

Maude's manuscript. She was in his office the following afternoon at three o'clock.

"Edward says you have a sincere wish to do some editorial work. I think it's a good idea, and I'll be glad to help you all I can. Edward says you'll be spending the hottest weeks at your family's farm in Dutchess and he'll go up there weekends. You might function for us as a reader. He could take up a couple of manuscripts each weekend and bring back a couple with your opinions."

"I would like that!" She sounded childlike with elation.

"Fine. Now let's go over this novel of Maude Mudge's together and I'll give you some of my impressions and opinions. First, did you at any time encourage Maude to write this—uh—what's-her-name of the Rockies?"

"Mmmm, yesss—in a way."

"Maybe that's the first thing to learn about being an editor, Cordelia. Whenever you encourage a writer to develop an idea, you have, in a sense, entered into a contract with him—her. As a result of your encouragement, Maude has worked how many hours, days, weeks, for no compensation? Now Edward says you suggest her dropping the Rocky Mountain milieu and transferring the background to the slums. I believe you said something about sifting the new background in like baking powder into biscuits. Cordelia, isn't that thought rather *blithe*?"

"Wellll—maybe."

"I think there's a fine novel—many fine novels—about the human horrors of the slums. But I don't think Maude is going to write one because she has no experience with the subject. I think your notion of changing the background, as if it's merely a matter of pasting on new wallpaper, is unfair to Maude and—if you follow me—to the integrity of the novel, any novel, as a craft or art form."

"I follow you," Cordelia said. "I just hadn't thought of it that way."

"You *are* right about Maude being a natural storyteller—and I was wrong a while back when I said she wasn't. Another attribute of Maude's is that her syntax is excellent. Sometimes a natural storyteller can't write a decent sentence—and then an editor has his—her work cut out for her. But what I'm trying to say is that you and Maude already have established a *rapport*—an understanding such as should exist between an author and editor. One time Edward quoted to me—proudly, I emphasize—what you said when he wondered if you hadn't offered a maid too much money. You said, according to him, that was the amount you had promised. Then you said, 'And my word must be good to Mary if Mary is ever to be of any good to us.' That typifies the ideal relationship between author and editor as much as between mistress and servant."

Then Hal began going through Maude's manuscript page by page and reading from notes he had scrawled on a yellow pad. Cordelia was surprised by the number of problems he found in her flowing script. Most involved some character saying or doing something that did not ring true to one's personal experience with actual people. Also Maude had a tendency to "overstuff the sofa," as Hal put it, with lengthy descriptions unrelated to the development of the story. Wherever he found problems he offered solutions whose simplicity fascinated Cordelia. His work, his methods were so absorbing and meticulous that she lost track of time.

Next she knew it was quarter to six and Edward was standing in Hal's doorway saying, "Is my wife going to make me work overtime?"

"Edward," Hal said, "you don't just have a wife. Now you have an editor on your hands." He held out the manuscript to Cordelia. "You're the editor of *Janet of the Rockies*. I won't see this again. My final remark is that I hope you and the author can think of a better title. But from here on you deal with her. I suggest you offer her a three-hundred-dollar advance against standard royalties. When you feel the manuscript is in the best possible shape, give it to Mr. Pribbles, the copy editor, who will find enough faults to exasperate you thoroughly. But fight for what you want the author to say. As a working editor you outrank the copy editor. Give me a note when you hand the manuscript to Pribbles."

"I think," Edward said, "Corey would be interested in seeing the book all the way from that manuscript to bound volume. I'll guide her after the manuscript goes to copy."

"Oh, thank you!" Cordelia hugged Maude's manuscript to her breast. "Thank you both more than I can ever say." Tears welled in her eyes, causing both men embarrassment.

When she and Edward started walking home she exclaimed, "Hal Wiggins is a great editor!"

"Yes, he really is," Edward said.

"What I just learned about a great editor's relationship to her authors, it's like—well, like a fine doctor's to his patients or a good lawyer's to his clients. Being a good editor is the highest calling in the world."

"Don't ever tell Hal that," Edward said, "or he'll sound hostile. But between us, honey, what you say is absolutely true."

Maude accepted Cordelia's suggested revisions in her novel without a whimper, and they agreed by mail to change the title to *Where the Stars Fell*.

From mid-July until Labor Day Cordelia stayed with her parents at Dorfman Manor to escape the city heat. She had Mary come to spend two weeks, and Tim, who got no vacation in his job at the horsecar barns, came for the Sundays Mary was there. Nick also visited for a week. He actually seemed to be struggling against his snobbery and to still want to fall in love with and marry someone; the trouble was, as his father pointed out, he had only complaints about every woman he knew.

Edward took the train up every Friday evening and returned to the city on Monday morning. He always brought two or three manuscripts from the pile that poured steadily into Lovejoy's from would-be authors, and he took back those Cordelia had read and criticized in the preceding week. The reading and the writing of critiques was sheer joy to her, never a chore.

A few days after she returned to New York, Maude mailed her the new draft of *Where the Stars Fell*. After going through it carefully she turned it over to Mr. Pribbles, Lovejoy's one and only copy editor. A white-haired, wasted-looking man who wore thick glasses, Pribbles was a retired teacher of high-school English who warred religiously against bad grammar and syntax. ("But keep an eye on him," Hal warned everyone, "or the old bastard will turn everything into the subjunctive.")

Four days later Edward brought Maude's manuscript home to Cordelia. In a covering note written in a prim hand Pribbles admonished her own and the author's weakness for dangling participles. The manuscript was festooned with green bits of paper pinned neatly to the margins.

"What are these things?" Cordelia demanded.

"Those, my dear, are called flags," Edward said. "Each designates some place in your manuscript that Pribbles questions for one reason or another."

"There are ninety or a hundred of the goddamn things!" Cordelia cried.

"Easy, easy, don't let Mary hear you cursing. Remember the joys of being an editor."

"Listen to this very first one." Cordelia's voice rose in exasperation. "He says, 'The past participle is preferable here.' What the hell is a past participle?"

"I have no idea. Thought you knew. You're supposed to be better educated than me—than I am. Wherever you disagree with Pribbles, just unpin the flag and throw it away. But save the pin. Once a week Pribbles comes around and collects pins from editors. As a publisher I have to commend his thrifty ways. One time, before Pribbles came with us, old Sidney Barlowe gave Father a report on pins. Said we could save twenty dollars a year if the editors would stop throwing them away."

After Cordelia brought her exasperation with Pribbles under control she had to admit that many of his questions were sound and helpful.

"What happens now that I've endured the hell of Pribbles?" she asked Edward.

"Now," he said, "you begin to learn what book publishing is all about."

There was a production assistant who took care of the routine, but Edward functioned as his own production manager. He would hire one, he said, as soon as he found a man who knew more about producing books than he did.

Now something called an estimate would be prepared for *Where the Stars Fell*. After the assistant had done a castoff of the manuscript to determine its exact number of words, Edward would know how many pages there would be in the book. Then he would figure costs of printing, paper, binding, jacket, advertising, royalties; he would allow for something called overhead in order that some of the cost of operating the company be deducted from each book; he would decide how many copies of the book there should be in a first printing; and he would determine what the price of the book should be in light of all these factors.

To his surprise Cordelia was fascinated by the intricacies of planning estimates. Once he saw that she had aptitude for it, he enjoyed spending Sunday afternoons teaching her what he knew.

"I didn't realize you had a head for figures," he said. "You're only the third person in the company, including me, who knows how to do estimates. And you're not even in the company. But if it entertains you, honey, I guess you might as well be doing this as knitting."

For *Where the Stars Fell,* a book of two hundred fifty-six pages, Edward decided to try a different pricing. The usual price for a book of that length at the time was $1.25. But this one he would price at $1.19. "That sounds a lot farther below a dollar and a quarter than it really is," he told Cordelia. That was, of course, the retail price which the bookseller charged the customer. But at the time, the publisher sold his book to the merchant at a twenty-five-percent discount. A copy of *Where the Stars Fell,* for which a purchaser would pay $1.19, would cost the merchant who sold it to him $.90. Thus Edward had to figure Lovejoy's costs and profits on the basis of $.90 per unit book rather than $1.19.

"By this time you know," Edward instructed Cordelia, "that we plan an eight-percent profit on each book in order for the company to make a profit and survive. So you begin to see how tight the costing and pricing becomes. That's why I take the managers of printing and bindery companies to lunch—or they take me. Differences of fractions of pennies away up on a ledger can make a tremendous difference on the bottom line, the line that counts."

"Why," asked Cordelia, "isn't the public ever told about these things?"

"Because the public doesn't give a damn, my dear. It wants a book or it doesn't, the way it will buy some brand of beer or not buy it. The details of success or failure are the problem of the merchandiser. And so, much as you admire the works of Robert Browning, you have to remember that the merchandising of his works is a business venture. I know I sound crass. But a publisher who makes a success of selling books is not a great deal different from one who makes a success of selling sausages. The entire story is not based on the quality of the product but on the shrewdness of the one who sells it."

On a Monday early in December, Cordelia sent Mary in a hurry for Dr. Prettyman. He arrived in time to be of little assistance in the birth of the Lovejoys' child.

To the consternation of everyone except the doctor, Robert Lovejoy II turned out to be a girl. And in the sense of confusion that overtook everyone they gave her the unlikely name of Eunice.

Cordelia's becoming a mother, far from diverting her interest in publishing, made her wish more than ever for an editorial career. Of course she loved Eunice, but there was something so boring about nursing and tending to an infant that she wished she could turn the duties over to Mary until her baby began to be interesting.

Edward understood that she needed something more than motherhood. So he encouraged her to continue the production of Maude's book. After a printer set Maude's manuscript, long type galleys of the novel were sent to the author and Pribbles for corrections. Meanwhile Edward helped Cordelia pick an appropriate display type for chapter titles and a jacket design.

"But it's still not a book," he told her. "Now we come to the phase where the editor plays merchant."

Very few publishers other than Edward made such careful cost estimates of their books. (It was mainly those who used such methods who survived and prospered; most who priced books carelessly with little regard for costs went bankrupt.) But no publisher was ahead of Edward in the discipline and encouragement he showed his small sales force. Now that Colonel Bob was dead, Edward was finally able to offer the travelers, as salesmen then were called, the incentive of a percentage bonus above specified sales figures.

Edward divided Lovejoy's average annual production of forty books into two lists—one for fall, the other for spring. Every April and December he sent galleys of all books to each traveler, who was directed to read them. Then, in May and January, the travelers were brought to New York, where Edward and Hal grilled them mercilessly on the contents of the books. Woe betide the traveler who had not studied his galleys: Those who flunked were dismissed.

"If you're illiterate," Edward told them at each conference, "go sell washing machines." The salesmen's knowledge of their books paid off. "Booksellers haven't the time to read everything that comes into their stores," Edward said. "If you can offer a bookseller a simple statement of what a book is about, the seller can pass it along to his customers."

Edward was a pioneer in his merchandising methods. Not until many years later did publishers universally adopt the custom of seasonal lists of books. And Edward's innovation of bringing his traveling salesmen to the home office twice a year for discussion was laughed at by many publishers. (He said he had got the idea from a company which was continually revising its manufacture of farm machinery.)

He put Maude's novel on Lovejoy's fall list for 1892, which meant that he, Hal, Granger, and the salesmen would discuss the book at the New York conference in the preceding May.

"I'd give my soul to listen in and hear what's said about the book," Cordelia told him.

"It's all right to give your soul," Edward said. "Just make sure you don't give away your precious body. I'll see what can be arranged."

She realized she could not mingle with the men, who crowded into Edward's office for the sessions and turned the air blue and foul with smoke from the cigars he dispensed liberally. The presence of a woman, she understood, would throw everyone into consternation. So she was highly pleased when Edward let Li'l Abe in on the secret and had him put the door ajar and have a chair in the hallway for Cordelia when it came time to discuss *Where the Stars Fell*.

She was sitting there, quietly, when Edward began: "The next book for discussion on our agenda is *Where the Stars Fell* by Maude Mudge. You've all done a pretty good job of selling Miss Mudge's inspirational works. Now she has done a very interesting job in her first novel. Jason"—he addressed Jason Beauchamp—"it's your turn. Would you please summarize the plot for us."

"Sure," Jason said, "but before I begin, Edward, I've got to say I think this novel is a big piece of shit."

"Aaaah!" Edward had a strangling fit of coughing. "Somebody close that door! There's a terrible draft."

Cordelia felt as if a spear had pierced her and riveted her to the chair.

"Don't close the door," someone else said. "You're coughing, Edward, from the goddamn smoke from these goddamn cheap cigars you've been handing out."

Jason said, "The trouble with this book is—"

"Never mind," Max cut in. "You want to be an editor, Jason? Just tell us the plot. The way you're talking I think you didn't read it and are just bluffing."

Cordelia felt physically ill. How dreadful if she should throw up right here in the hall. Or might she be going to have a heart attack? Imagine the *Tribune* headline:

FIRST LADY EDITOR SUCCUMBS IN PUBLISHING HOUSE.

But Jason *had* read the novel; he recited its plot perfectly.

"Now," Edward said loudly after he had finished, "I think that's a very entertaining story that will have great appeal to our many women readers. . . ."

Cordelia listened carefully, but there were no more derogatory remarks. She told herself she must not let a bit of adverse criticism spoil the great thrill she had felt when Maude's work finally had completed its development from manuscript to book. But worry over it kept her awake after she went to bed that night. She still was awake when Edward came home after midnight, having spent the evening out with the travelers. As he crept into the room he reeked of cigar smoke and whisky and made a snuffling sound like a hound suffering from a cold. She pretended to be asleep as he sank, groaning softly, into bed.

Next morning, when Edward stumbled down to breakfast and sat staring at his oatmeal with bloodshot eyes she did not mention the terrible thing Jason had said at the conference.

A couple of days later he told her, "The travelers are putting thousands of copies of Maude's novel in the stores."

"How many thousand?" she asked.

"Uh—hmmm—over four. Nearly five."

"Is that all?" Suddenly Cordelia realized she never had felt as deeply about anything (except Edward) as she did about this book. It actually seemed more important to her than Eunice did.

She began pestering Edward to bring home reviews of the book. When he failed to do so, she dropped into his office one day and *demanded* to see a review. He said the only one he had at the moment was unfavorable—all the good ones were in someplace he was vague about. It was a very bad review, and she became depressed after reading it.

Edward kept insisting the reviews were "mixed," which was his euphemism for bad. However, Maude sent her a review from a weekly newspaper in Oneonta, New York, which called the novel "clever" and "charming." Loyally Edward refused to say that Maude's novel had "crashed," the word he always used to describe a book that flopped, and neither of them mentioned how Jason had spoken of it.

But then, one evening the week after New Year's, Edward bounded home joyfully and announced a reorder of three hundred copies of *Where the Stars Fell* in Philadelphia. Then other reorders began to arrive, to Cordelia's intense joy. Finally, when the New York store restocked it a second time, she said to Edward:

"You know, dear, this book isn't doing badly for a big piece of shit."

"Ah," he said. "Mmmm." And that was all he said.

Though he did not suggest to Cordelia that she cease being a housewife and become an editor at the office, he was more pleased by the sales of Maude's novel than if it had been the result of his own genius.

Maude came to New York to discuss an idea for another novel with Cordelia. Cordelia was not enthusiastic about it, but Maude went home to Caesar's Corners insisting that she was going ahead with the book anyway. Before she had got far into it, however, events transpired that made novel writing seem trivial.

7

In February 1893, Edward came across a man who knew more about producing books than he did—and promptly hired him. His name was John Speer, and he was only twenty-four when he became production manager of Lovejoy's.

John had a love of books such as often is most passionately felt by one with little formal education. A native of western Tennessee, he had quit school at ten to become a typesetter's apprentice and had been involved in publishing ever since. At seventeen he was in Nashville, designing and setting Sunday-school tracts which were so greatly more attractive than the usual dreary format that they pleased even non-Christian eyes. Next he went to Philadelphia, where he designed Balway Brothers' famous Classical Series and other beautiful books until he quarreled with old man Balway over binding cloth. Easygoing in manner and often loquacious, John made friends readily. He had remarkable mental control, as evidenced by the way he could turn a Tennessee accent off and on at will.

When Edward invited him home for dinner, Cordelia immediately saw what Edward did not: John was extraordinarily handsome, with an angel's fair skin and blue eyes, a devil's curling black hair. He was small—and Edward took a typical masculine view that a man wasn't handsome unless he was almost as big as a horse.

Prophetically John and Edward talked about a business recession the April evening John came to dinner.

Edward was complaining about a slow but steady decline in book sales. "No matter how hard we try."

"Nationwide," John said, "in the past twenty years there's been more of depression than prosperity. You can always see signs of recession, but what can you do about 'em? We work in a precarious industry. The profits never have been large and the rate of business failure—measured by bookstores, printing establishments, and publishing houses—is one of the highest in the country. If someone offered you a good price for the company tomorrow, what would you do?"

Edward raised his brows and spread his hands. "Just squat there, I guess. Where would I invest the money? I don't know any business but publishing. More to the point, I *like* publishing."

On May 3, 1893, there was a sudden drop on the New York Stock Exchange. Stocks really crashed late in June. By the end of the year nearly five hundred banks and more than fifteen thousand commercial institutions had failed in what became known as the Panic of Ninety-three.

The crash of stock values did not precipitate sudden lower book sales. That accelerated in following months as middle-class people found that beef—milk—the rent—a new pair of pants—must take financial precedence over a new book to read. Stores which for years had done a thriving business in Lovejoy books simply could not meet their bills to the house. By early 1894 about the only customers in the Lovejoy store, apart from furtive browsers, were the very rich. All but the store manager and one clerk were laid off.

Yet book publishing was only one of many industries badly hit by the depression. If one had started at the Battery on a rambling walk up the spine of Manhattan its effects on New York would have been seen. But it was not safe to take such a walk after dark because the rate of crime, especially robberies and muggings, soared.

Inevitably the dwellers of the slums were the worst hit because many proprietors of sweat shops making clothing, bedding, mattresses, and the like, simply locked up and decided to stay home until things got better. The unemployed went hungry and some starved to death without help from government. Except in the Wall Street area and the residential streets of the well-off above Madison Square, garbage accumulated in great piles for complex reasons that the rulers of City Hall didn't seem to understand. The so-called middle class suffered, too. Clerks and others who had been thrown out of work thronged the parks and idled in the streets. Everyone said the price of food would come down, but it did not.

Meanwhile the very rich enjoyed their Golden Age as if there were no economic depression. William K. Vanderbilt's new Fifth Avenue mansion was one of the great sights of the city; the unemployed could dawdle and envy but were kept at a respectful distance by continuous guards of city policemen. In order to keep the unemployed further entertained the *World* ran illustrated story after story about Marble House, Mrs. William K.'s magnificent "cottage" in Newport which was so opulent that she was made a fellow of the American Institute of Architects.

Above Twenty-third Street there was no sign of a depression. Below it, the existence of nearly everyone was in upheaval.

Layoffs were a nightmare to Edward, yet they were essential. He knew he no longer needed a production manager, that he could do the job himself; but John adapted himself so well to all kinds of chores and Edward liked him so much that he kept him on at a reduced salary. The others who remained at cut salaries

were Hal Wiggins, Granger Cantwell, Max, Sidney, and
Abe Schneider (who became no bigger as he grew older
and forever was known as Li'l Abe). Edward wanted to
get rid of Granger, whose family was said to be well-off
on Boston's Beacon Hill, but when Granger begged
hard to stay and accepted a fifty-percent pay cut, Edward relented. Everyone else went.

Cordelia pitched in as an unpaid manuscript reader.
Everyone tried his hardest, and Lovejoy and Son remained in business while some other houses were closing their doors. Edward had given up his plan for moving the offices and storage space away from the store;
now the main thing was to survive. Though the spring
list for 1894 was only half the usual length, there *was* a
list, the books *were* being shipped, and there remained
three travelers out in the far places who were trying to
sell them.

Early in the crisis Edward cut his own salary from
three thousand to fifteen hundred dollars a year. He
had imagined, without checking the facts, that the cost
of living was declining in pace with the devalued dollar.
He had forgotten that economics does not work so logically.

"Corey, honey," he said, "we've got to cut back,"
and thought *that* somehow would take care of *that*. Of
course it did not. Cordelia tried to act brave, but
learned that no amount of bravery could face down an
unpaid butcher's bill.

The trouble was not that the Lovejoys were short of
money; it was that they had no money at all except for
Edward's suddenly reduced salary. His stocks had
stopped paying dividends, and from his father he had
inherited less than five hundred dollars. With consternation he'd found in the settling of the estate that Colonel Bob had had so little in savings left that for years he
had drawn what amounted to a modest living allowance
and plowed all profits back into the firm. Edward's

chief inheritance was a company approaching insolvency.

Desperate to find a means of paying household bills, Cordelia approached her father. To her dismay he confessed that he was as hard up as Edward and having to sell good land at ridiculous prices in order to keep going. Nick was no help, either. Unemployed, like nearly all investment salesmen at the time, he was living moodily at the Manor and darkly prophesying a bloody revolution by the newly formed populist People's Party.

Cordelia knew she should dismiss Mary, but with servant jobs impossible to find she feared that Mary might starve to death, as the newspapers reported actually had happened to an entire immigrant family in Hell's Kitchen. So she reduced her wages to three dollars a week.

One morning she found Mary weeping in the kitchen. Putting an arm around her, she asked what was wrong.

" 'Tis Tim. He was laid off at the horsecar barns last week. I didn't want to tell ye. He can't find nothin'. Now his family's havin' to give up their room an' go separate ways. He ain't even got a piece of a floor to sleep on. Last night he says to me he says he don't seen nothin' fer him to do but take to the road as a hobo. Oh, I can't stand that! He'll die off in a ditch somewheres!"

"No, he won't," Cordelia said. "He's moving into your room with you. I don't know why I never thought of that before anyway."

Mary cried harder. "We can't go on foriver livin' off you an' Mr. Edward's charity, Miz Cordelia."

"Look at it another way," Cordelia said. "Look at it that we're living off yours."

In emotional gratitude for food and lodging Tim offered to work nights for no wages cleaning Edward's store and offices.

"That's very sweet of you, Tim," Cordelia said. "But a clerk Edward had to let go already is doing that at half his former wages. I've been meaning to ask Mary and you, how is Sean faring in these hard times?"

"Didn't Mary tell ye? The dwarf is doin' better'n anybody in the whole family. When the Quarles Brothers Circus come to town Sean took a job at a dollar a week shovelin' up after the elephants an' such. Then they wanted a dwarf in one of the acts. Now Sean has become a clown! Think on it! Saddest man ever lived a clown! He's earnin' five a week, eats the best for free, an' travels to far-off places like Hartford an' Springfield. Miz Cordelia, when the circus comes back to town, say the word an' Sean'll give ye all the free passes ye an' Mr. Edward wants."

Soon after New Year's of 1894 John came into Edward's office with a peculiar proposition. The leather market was glutted, he said, and gold leaf couldn't find customers. He had worked out an estimate which he handed to Edward showing that at a cost of ten dollars in the current market one could produce just about the most handsome book ever published in America or Britain.

"But," Edward said, "figuring on our eight-percent profit, who in these times is going to pay ten dollars and eighty cents for the handsomest book every published?"

"Nobody will pay that price," John said. "But they'll pay a hundred dollars. Or, to be more precise, they'll pay ninety-seven dollars and fifty cents when it's presented to them as a special offer for a limited time."

Edward stared at him. "What the hell has come over you, John? You know we're in the midst of a terrible depression."

"All that's come over me is a very good idea," John replied. "Mr. Dickens put it shrewdly about a previous time. You know—while the poor get poorer, the rich get richer. The other day I went down in the store and watched the rich ladies from Fifth Avenue and Murray Hill. They haven't heard about the depression. They're looking for more expensive things to buy than the store is offering them."

Edward started up from his chair and sat down again. "But what book do we have currently or back-listed that could command such a price?"

John smiled slowly. "Any book, almost. Depends on how we present it to 'em. But there's one book we must start with, because this has to be a series. And the name of it is the John Jacob Astor Edition. Remember that biography of him you published a couple of years ago?"

"That crashed. Completely. Nobody wants to read that book."

"Nobody will," John said. "Except for J. P. Morgan, there's scarcely a rich person in the city ever looks into the contents of a book. Or so they tell me downstairs in the store. What counts in our scheme is the binding and the magic name of Astor. The very rich will put our very handsome volumes on the shelves and mention vaguely to their friends something about an Astor connection."

"You're insane." Edward walked all the way around his office agitatedly. "It'll never work."

John smiled drolly. "But our offer is for a limited time only."

"I'm shocked, John. You're a rogue."

"Why do you think I'm attracted to book publishing?"

"I should have fired you before Christmas."

"If this doesn't work, I'll consider myself fired."

"You're practically gone. Do you think we should take out ads in the *Times* or the *Tribune*?"

"In both. Very small, special, exclusive ads. I already have a type design for them. Let me show you. . . ."

It worked.

The John Jacob Astor Edition of books published by Lovejoy and Son eventually ran to fifteen volumes. Sumptuously bound and illustrated, they were routinely-written treatments of uncontroversial subjects which had been published and forgotten years previously. It was doubtful if anyone but a copy reader ever read one of them from beginning to end. As editor of the series, Hal had little to do but make sure that nothing dangerous like politics or religion infiltrated those beautiful pages for the very rich.

On the initial volume Edward had hoped for a sale of forty or fifty copies in New York. To his astonishment, nearly two hundred were quickly sold in the city, and then sales spread to other places. All told, the series netted the company almost a half million dollars. John's genius in conceiving the bold plan carried Lovejoy and Son through the worst times and enabled it to face the improved days with a better financial balance than the great majority of New York publishing houses.

A second child was born to the Lovejoys in October 1894—another daughter. Edward chose the name Penelope and would not yield to Cordelia's plea to name her something serviceable like Mary or Martha. Cordelia, finding her own name awkward and pretentious, wished she could have done better by her daughters than calling them Eunice and Penelope. However, Edward was fond of the names.

Penelope, forever called Penny, was different from Eunice. Once born, she began a squirming and screaming that Coredlia thought never would end while Eunice lay or sat passively and watched her baby sister with a look of consternation.

Having two babies, Cordelia found, was vastly more complicated than having only one. While Mary did everything possible to help, Cordelia kept constantly busy with the children. Mary said they were the best-aired babies in New York City. It was true that Cordelia liked to push them in a double carriage up, down, and around Murray Hill. Much to her own surprise, she was enjoying being a mother.

For a while she still talked about being an editor, too. But as the company fortunes improved and Edward began hiring employees again, there were practically no manuscripts for her to read. And then, in answer to a letter, Maude said she had fallen ill of an obscure writer's disease called despair and announced her intention never to write again. In letter after letter Cordelia urged her to keep trying, send something for criticism, take heart. But Maude's final answer was *Never!* How could Cordelia be an editor when she lacked even one writer? Besides, being a mother and housewife had more predictable satisfactions, she thought, than could be found among the uncertainties of publishing.

To the astonishment of everyone the third Lovejoy daughter, born a week before Christmas in 1895, turned out to be a boy. When Edward heard the news he fell the bottom six steps down the stairs, but picked himself up uninjured. The plan, which no one had mentioned in a few years, had been to name a son Robert II. But now Edward, sounding somewhat embarrassed, told Cordelia that maybe it would be good to name him something different in order to give him a fresh start in life. How about Steven? Cordelia said fine, and she made Edward's joy complete by suggesting that they name their son Steven Edward Lovejoy.

From the very beginning, Steven looked the way Cordelia felt a child should. Instead of appearing to be a dried-up apple, he was stunningly handsome in her eyes. He laughed a lot and walked and talked much earlier than his sisters. Altogether he changed Cordelia from a devoted into a doting mother. His advent in her life made her think that Edward should run the company while she stayed home and took care of the family.

One raw afternoon in January 1896, a victoria stopped in front of the Lovejoys' and a liveried footman delivered a note to Mary. Cordelia, opening it, was astonished to read that Mrs. Stuyvesant Fish requested the pleasure of her company at tea next Wednesday.

She vaguely remembered having met Mrs. Fish at Newport long ago, but never had encountered her since. However, she had read much about her in the newspapers. As a member of an old and wealthy family, Mamie Fish had decided to liven up the crusty old ways of society in both Newport and New York by inviting all sorts of celebrities to her home. "Anybody who can hold a fork is welcome," she reputedly had said, "provided they've done something more interesting than hold forks." Mrs. Astor had dropped the social bars low enough for Isadora Duncan to step into her mansion, but Mamie Fish was even more daring: She had invited the notorious John L. Sullivan to dinner.

"Why should she invite me to tea?" Cordelia asked Mary.

"I don't know, Miz Cordelia, but you should decline. I don't trust the woman."

After Cordelia had taught Mary to read, Mary's chief pleasure was to follow society events as imaginatively reported in the *World* and the *Journal*. She considered herself an authority on the subject.

"What's wrong with Mrs. Fish?" asked Cordelia.

"Her family's money is tied up with slum tenements."

"If society ruled out everybody who's invested in tenements there'd be no society."

Of course she intended to go. She and Edward had become social friends of the Bancrofts and of Hattie and Gerald Fisher after she, Gloria, and Hattie began serving as volunteer aides at New York Hospital in their spare time. While Cordelia had no wish to be a shining light in the even higher society Mrs. Fish represented, she was interested in a closer look at its glitter. The question that nagged her curiosity, of course, was what could Mrs. Fish want of her?

Tim had found employment as a doorman in Hart's Department Store and continued to make his home with Mary at the Lovejoys'. He loved his job because he wore white gloves and a gold-brocaded coat as he turned the revolving door for customers at Hart's. When he came in from work that evening, Cordelia had him keep on his uniform and deliver her note of acceptance to Mrs. Fish.

If there was a top to Murray Hill, the Stuyvesant Fishes appeared to inhabit it. The mansards and elaborate chimneys of their mansion on the northeast corner of Fortieth and Fifth towered above the Peysters' house across the Avenue and all other nearby houses. When Cordelia alighted from a hansom cab at precisely ten minutes past four the following Wednesday, the door to the house swung open before she could pull the bell. A footman, without glancing at the card she presented, said, "Mrs. Fish is expecting you, Mrs. Lovejoy. This way, please."

He gestured her into a small gilt cage beside the marble stairs, and, having enclosed her in it, began to turn a large wheel as fast as he could. She rose as on wings, the wires of the lift making a humming sound, passing floor after floor until she wondered if she was in the tallest building in the city. Suddenly the lift stopped and another footman, wearing brown livery, opened the cage door and bowed to her.

She found herself in a Turkish sultan's harem as large as a ballroom. If someone would clear away the clutter, you could waltz for miles in this space. But the

Turkish motif in the vast room provided an excuse for
a surfeit of pillows and an endless echoing of the curvi-
linear designs of the art nouveau. The vast Oriental carpeting was like a reflection of the papered design on the
ceiling. And between ceiling and floor were archipel-
agos of divans, footstools, huge chairs, small and large
tables inlaid with agate and mother of pearl. There on
Fifth Avenue the Ottoman Empire had been reconstructed.

Somewhere out in this Eastern continent of one thousand pillows rose the nasal Western voice of Mrs. Fish:
"Good afternoon, Mrs. Lovejoy." The blue and gold
Oriental design of Mamie Fish's gown detached itself
from the effulgence of the Ottoman Empire and Cordelia made out her plain old Western face.

"Good afternoon. I appreciate your invitation." Cordelia made her way toward Mrs. Fish, almost tripping
over an ottoman despite extreme caution. She sat down
on a pillowed chair which almost smothered her and
wondered if she ever could struggle free of this silken
quicksand.

Mrs. Fish, shrewdly avoiding entanglement with her
Ottoman furnishings, perched on a straight-backed
wooden chair so that she could rise and attack anything
without floundering. "Did you enjoy your ride up in my
new lift? I'm collecting comments about it."

"Yes, I enjoyed the ride. I had a thought. The footman who winds and unwinds the thing—suppose midway between floors the man decides he wants a raise in
wages and leaves you there till you promise him one."

Mrs. Fish stared at her. "My footmen never act that
way. They wouldn't *dare*. Come tour my new decor before we have tea." Cordelia struggled out of the chair to
her feet. "You know how interested I am in overturning
stodgy old ways," Mrs. Fish continued. "I'm doing it
here, too. My servants live in the cellar. Why should
they have the privilege of such splendid views from the

top floor? This is the ballroom for formal entertaining at the proper times. This week I'm having the servants practice clearing out these furnishings and putting them back. I have them down to three hours for a transformation."

Cordelia feigned appreciation of the furnishings Mrs. Fish pointed out, but enjoyed more the views out the large windows. In the bright afternoon light shone the waters of the reservoir, located across Fifth where the Public Library and Bryant Park later would stand. Beyond the reservoir stretched the slums, the vast area that had been known as the Tenderloin since a corrupt policeman, upon being named its precinct captain, announced he'd never again eat anything but tenderloin.

"My word!" Cordelia exclaimed. "I hadn't noticed till now. The Peysters' house is boarded up. Are they away for the winter?"

"They're away for good, I understand. Know they're related to you, but understand you're no longer close. Augustus got wiped out in the Panic. You'd wonder how it could happen, but it did to several. I understand they've gone into hiding in Cape May, New Jersey. Somebody said Miriam is taking in boarders to make ends meet."

Cordelia was aghast. "I—I really don't see how it could have happened."

"Anything can happen," Mrs. Fish said. "And usually does. So many of our best old families giving up the whirl. How are your dear father and mother?" Without pause for Cordelia to reply: "A lot of new money coming in." She gestured north disdainfully; up Fifth Avenue, past Sherry's new restaurant at Forty-sixth Street, rose the gray of St. Patrick's and the brown of St. Thomas's. "Did you know, my dear, there literally is a dollar sign over the Bridal Door in St. Thomas's? Vanderbilts everywhere you look up yonder. That new family proliferates faster than the Dunegans of County Galway. Goulds, too. I heard last week Charles Harkness of Standard Oil is taking over a Vanderbilt vacancy." Mrs. Fish rolled her eyes. "And near him Benjamin *Altman*, some *Guggenheims,* and their lawyer Samuel *Untermeyer.* Change, change, but oh, Lord *what* change! How is your brother Nicholas?"

"Well. He retired to the country during the worst of the Panic, but now he's back at the investment business."

"I don't understand why he hasn't married."

"None of us do. He doesn't himself, but feels it's the result of his being such a snob."

Mrs. Fish nodded. "That's the most admirable thing about Nicholas. There aren't enough snobs left. Everybody's trying to act democratic. He's a very handsome chap, you know. Could just about have his pick if he didn't act so haughty. It frightens the young ladies, who never are very sure of themselves anyway. Mrs. Lovejoy—Cordelia—I see you're no ninny, so I'll just out with it in my forthright way. I've asked you here today to meet a young lady who is quite taken with your brother. I hear her rising in the lift this very minute."

"What's her name?"

"Suzanna Neiswander. A family of new money. She's much taken with both Nicholas's person and old family."

"What's her failing?"

Mrs. Fish grimaced. "I hoped you wouldn't ask me that. She's—well, shy. Well, you'll see for yourself. She's coming off the lift now." Mrs. Fish advanced with an air of determination. "Ah, Miss Neiswander— Suzanna."

It was Suzanna Neiswander's failing to be hugely fat. Within her jowls, however, there was a pretty young face with brown eyes and a look of such eloquent mute appeal to be accepted that Cordelia would gladly have given her a reassuring embrace. As soon as she began to talk it was evident she was no fool. And Cordelia observed she must know that her problem was weight by the way she rejected all the sandwiches and rich pastries the footman passed.

"How many lumps of sugar?" Mrs. Fish asked her as she poured tea.

Suzanna answered with disarming candor: "None, thank you. You can see yourself where the sugar goes."

Cordelia liked her so much that she resolved to undertake two things: thin down Suzanna, and convince Nick she would make a perfect wife.

Neither project was easy. After Cordelia introduced them over tea at her home she feared it never would work. But she was determined to persevere.

"The trouble with me," Suzanna told her privately, "is that I eat when I'm bored. And the other part of the trouble is that I'm bored most of the time."

The only child of a wealthy railroad director, she had been transplanted from Pittsburgh to New York, where she did not root readily because she had no friends and didn't know how to make them. With her parents she had attended one of Mrs. Fish's dances where she had become smitten with Nick, and so—

Privately Nick told Cordelia, "I like Suzanna as a *person*. It's true I'd like my wife to be rich because you know yourself there's nothing coming to you or me from Papa and Mama. But I insist on marrying a *thin* rich woman."

"Suzanna has begun a program to thin down," Cordelia said. "Please be patient and continue to see her from time to time."

"Gladly," Nick said. "I have all the time in the world."

For a time she thought that such things as trying to bring Nick and Suzanna together and loving Edward and caring for the children made her life complete. Let

Edward run the company and let them be lovers and companions for every possible moment. Gradually, however, Cordelia felt the need for something more in her life. She did not want to cut herself off from the world of books.

It was Hal who found something for her to do. Edward recognized that Hal was not trying to butter up his wife; he knew that Hal was right in saying Cordelia had genuine talent as an editor and worked well with a writer. While her only author, Maude, had sunk into creative silence, Cordelia could work effectively with a couple of other woman writers Hal mentioned. Cordelia was delighted to try it. Soon after she'd thought there was no hope of her ever having a career as an editor, she believed that it might be just beginning.

8

John Speer was of a restless nature that kept him looking for personal challenges—"something interesting to do," as he put it. When Bacon's in Boston offered him the opportunity to serve as production manager and also develop a new line of reference works, he couldn't resist it.

Edward, sorrowing over his departure, began to look around for another production manager but could not find one who suited him. Once more he took over the preparation of estimates himself. Then, because Edward had so many other things to do and both Hal and Granger claimed they were too busy editing to learn the intricacies of production, Cordelia began to help him out by working on estimates at home.

"Sometimes I'd like to *force* Granger to learn how to do an estimate," Edward said. "He acts so damn superior to everything he doesn't like."

"But he's a very good editor," Cordelia said.

"So they tell me," Edward grumbled.

Edward was beginning to take an interest in international politics such as he'd never displayed before. He became wrathful over the Venezuelan boundary dispute in which Britain rejected the validity of the Monroe Doctrine. Only a couple of days after Steven was born, Edward's joy over a male heir was interrupted by his reading in the *Tribune* the content and manner of Lord Salisbury's reply to the United States Government.

"Just listen to this prime minister!" he cried passionately to Cordelia. "The same old English way of patient condescension! Smugly pointing out the error of their ways to all who disagree with 'em. It's been the same throughout history. No wonder they turn even their friends rabid with indignation against 'em!"

Cordelia was all for passion, but in those days she invariably was startled when passion was applied to politics.

Hal implied that Edward was an "expansionist." Edward was not, but had difficulty making it clear to Hal and others. He was one of the first book publishers to espouse the cause of Cuban freedom from Spain (or, as he always put it, "the yoke of Spain") by publishing books on the subject which scarcely anyone bought. Cordelia imagined that Edward's anger at Spain must result from something business-connected which he had not explained to her.

Edward's devotion to Cuban freedom seemed just a natural part of him, like the brown of his eyes. When William Randolph Hearst bought the *Morning Journal* and began to build its circulation, Edward denounced the newspaper as "a sensation sheet supplying cheap fictions to entertain the masses." But when the *Journal* began to publish sensational stories about Cuba, he became credulous about every word of them. He never had had any use for Joseph Pulitzer's *World* until its owner decided to engage in a circulation battle with the *Journal*; then Edward read the fictions in the *World* about Cuba as avidly and believingly as he did those in its Hearst rival. He had been a lukewarm supporter of Mr. McKinley until the President saw it was not expedient to be a stubborn pacifist in the Cuban situation, and then Edward praised him lavishly as a great leader.

Somehow, as the nation drifted toward war with Spain, Edward showed less enthusiasm for business than he previously had. He involved himself with a couple of mysterious propaganda committees and twice broke luncheon appointments with Tranch Claverlay, Lovejoy's best-selling historical novelist, in order to have lunch with an aged military relic with whom he enjoyed discussing strategy. Several times he traveled to Washington on matters that he did not discuss with Cordelia but that obviously had nothing to do with company business. Yet he was as concerned as ever for her and the children's welfare.

One day in April 1897 he told Cordelia, "Next month we're moving—not a mansion yet, but closer to the top of Murray Hill."

"Fifth Avenue?" she asked dryly. "Park Avenue?"

"Some day, yes." He meant that. "We truly will, sweetheart. Just wait and see. But not next month. Just a little higher up the hill this time."

He took her to see a new four-story brownstone at 127 East Thirty-sixth Street between Park Avenue and Lexington. It was a quiet, pleasant, tree-lined street, kept freshly graveled at the behest of one of the Vanderbilts, who had stables off Thirty-sixth near Third Avenue. Though the house was unpretentious compared to the mansions around the corner on Park or Mr. Morgan's mansion and library a block farther west on Madison, Cordelia thought it delightful.

"But can we afford it?" she asked.

"Probably not," he said. "But if you wait till you can afford something, you'll probably never buy it. Business is slackening again. However, I can get this house for a small down payment and a large mortgage."

The house was large enough for each child to have a personal room on the third floor, and on the top floor was pleasant dwelling space for Mary and Tim. At the front of the second floor was a commodious master bedroom for Cordelia and Edward; at the rear of that floor she arranged a small den for them. On the main floor they had two smaller rooms enlarged into a handsome drawing room, with the dining room behind it. The kitchen was in the basement, and food was lifted up to the dining room by dumbwaiter. A narrow walkway ran along the side of the house to a small back-yard.

Not long after they moved in, Edward began to talk about selling the store and finding less expensive office space.

"The store simply is not turning a decent profit," he told Cordelia. "Hotchkiss is getting old and doesn't understand modern merchandising methods. I'm not a retail man myself, and I can't find one so far to put in charge of the store. But I know that now is the time to get rid of it while I still can get something worthwhile for it. In a couple of years everybody will catch on that the neighborhood is changing and I won't get nearly as much for it."

"What would you do with the money?" Cordelia asked.

"Invest some of it for our old age and the children's education. I want the girls to go to college as well as Stevey."

"I want that, too," Cordelia said. "They must be better educated than I was."

"Some of the money from selling the store should go toward buying some good authors," Edward said. "We're approaching great changes in the company. Sidney, that relic from the Buchanan Administration, has to go. His bookkeeping methods are antiquated. I dread firing him, but I have to."

"When?" Cordelia asked. "When are all these changes coming about?"

Edward hesitated. "After the war."

"What war, dear?"

"The war with Spain," he said. "It's inevitable. There's no avoiding it. But it will last only a few weeks. What would you think if I got into it?"

"I'd think you had lost your mind. Edward, you'll be forty-eight your next birthday."

He looked troubled. "Women don't understand how

a man feels. Here I've been talking and talking against the Spanish oppression in Cuba. What sort of man would I be if I didn't *do* something about it when the time for action comes?"

"You'd be a sensible man, as you have been all your life, to mind your own business."

"Corey"—he reached out and clutched her hand— "suppose I felt I *had* to go?"

It was the only frightening thing he ever had said to her. Withdrawing her hand from his, she said, "I believe your reason will prevail—and I believe our country is led by reasonable men." She hoped that was so, and then she wanted to stop thinking about it.

She loved the house and its backyard. She and Edward often sat there on summer evenings and watched the flight of swallows and the soaring of gulls off the East River while the Third Avenue elevated trains raised a distant clatter that was comforting somehow.

They had not lived there quite a year and Cordelia was in the backyard preparing a petunia bed when Edward appeared unexpectedly on the afternoon of April 25, 1898.

"I guess you've heard the news, Corey."

She scarcely looked up from the flower bed where she was kneeling. "What now?" At all hours of day and night for the past week boys had been hawking extra editions of the newspapers through the streets, crying out the stages that brought the United States and Spain closer to formal declaration of war.

"It's official." Edward's voice sounded strained. "A few hours ago in Washington—retroactive to April twenty-first."

Suddenly aware that he did not sound happy, as he should have, considering his views, she looked up at him. He looked wretched.

She got to her feet. "Dear, do you feel ill?"

"Yes—no, of course not." His effort to smile was like an expression of pain. "There's something I've been working at I haven't told you about. Didn't want you to worry. It was approved just this afternoon. I— Corey, I've *got* to do it. I have a first lieutenant's commission in the army. Next week I go to Washington for further assignment."

She uttered an incredulous sound, then blinked back tears.

Cordelia saved Edward's "war letters," as she called them, all her life. Her own to him she thought dull. In the weeks after he went away she sometimes felt she was living in a trance. The children were not the comfort he had said they would be in his absence; they were peevish and had summer colds and did not miss their father as they should have. Friends were kind and tried to entertain her, but they were not the solace they wished to be.

To her surprise the greatest comfort Cordelia found in Edward's absence was reading manuscripts and preparing book estimates for Lovejoy's. She worked at home, going to and from the office two or three times a week. Every Friday she accepted from Hal the check Edward had stipulated she receive; apparently the two men corresponded directly about company business. Since Edward had asked her to keep an eye on things at the office, she always inquired of Hal if there were any important developments, and he always replied there were none.

Gradually Cordelia began to feel that Hal was trying to hide something from her. What did he know that she did not? Like other friends, Hal and his wife Caroline occasionally entertained her at dinner—and she detected a growing reserve in Caroline's manner.

At last Hal asked her to sit down and shut his office door one Friday when she came to pick up her check.

He looked grim. "Cordelia, I have some news. Oh, it's not about Edward, don't look frightened! It's about me. I wrote him yesterday about it. David and Smith have been after me for a long time to move over there as editor-in-chief. I've resisted it. I really have. The idea has made me feel guilty because I know I'm supposed to hold the fort here till Edward gets back. Now they've come back with a final offer I simply can't resist. I have to think of my own future."

"Could we—I mean could Edward match their offer, Hal?"

"No, I wouldn't want you to—and I don't think Edward could afford it the way things are going here just now."

He meant that things were going better at David and Smith and he had a more promising career there. Was Lovejoy's heading into trouble?

"So I'll be leaving at the end of the month, Cordelia. Everybody agrees this Spanish thing will be over in a few weeks, and then Edward will be back. Meanwhile I suggest that Granger take over, at least temporarily, as editor-in-chief. He's very capable and familiar with everything going on. I hope you understand, Cordelia."

"Of course." But she could not overcome the feeling that Hal was deserting the responsibility Edward had counted on him to bear while he was away. Apparently such a thing did not matter, even with as fine a person as Hal, when there was ambition to be served and more money to be made.

She did not tell Edward how she felt when she wrote him about Hal that afternoon.

Edward's letters to her were the most important events in her life. During the hot months she did not take the children to the farm, as she had planned, because her father was feeling poorly and her mother wrote that they'd had to cut their servant help again and the children might be a trial to Loren. Cordelia decided she was just as glad to stay in the city since mail delivery, twice every day but Sunday, assured her of receiving Edward's letters more promptly than she would have at the Manor.

Though Edward had not yet seen action against the Spanish, his letters began to sound like those of a veteran in his railing at the army's stupid way of doing things. He was something called an adjutant with the 71st New York Volunteers. She asked him what an adjutant did, but he didn't make it plain, if he even knew himself in his struggle to make the army stop dallying and start fighting the enemy.

He was in Tampa, Florida, awaiting shipment to Cuba. He described Tampa as a steaming hot sandy waste where the water was bad and the mosquitoes swarmed at the end of a single line railroad track. A real-estate speculator named Plant had built the railroad to the miserable place, and there among the shacks and sand he had built a magnificent hotel which the army had turned into a pleasure dome for its officers. The hotel had miles of piazzas and acres of ornamental minarets and gingerbread outside, while inside were enough sofas and statuary to stuff the Grand Central Depot. Every day from reveille to taps hundreds of officers rocked on the piazzas of the hotel, consuming vats of lemonade and bourbon while swatting at mosquitoes, talking about times past, and viewing enlisted men who performed close-order drill under the direction of their sergeants at a distance from the hotel.

The U.S. Army, Edward wrote, had fallen into such deplorable shape in recent years that he had come across a captain sixty-three years old with a white beard that stretched to his belt who sat all day in Plant's Hotel, rocking and drinking and talking about good old Lookout Mountain in the Civil War. The commander of the badly fouled-up situation at Tampa was Major General William R. Shafter, who weighed three hundred pounds and had had two horses faint under his weight and who—among other shortcomings—could not get along with the newspaper correspondents who were trying to run the war. Shafter was supposed to be gathering a siege train to invest the enemy in Santiago or Havana or someplace in Cuba, but the guns and ammunition were lost on railroad sidings all over Florida, Georgia, and Alabama. The only officer Edward could locate who made much sense was Lieutenant Colonel Theodore Roosevelt of the Rough Riders, with whom he had been slightly acquainted for several years. He had asked Roosevelt for a transfer to the Rough Riders, but Roosevelt simply had laughed—apparently Edward's reputation as an inept rider had preceded him even to Tampa.

Cordelia felt so desperately sorry for him that she begged him to resign his commission and come home. He replied that he could not do that even if he wanted to—which he did not. All he wanted was to get to Cuba and fight. His letter stating that determination was dated June fourth. Then to it was appended a scrawl: "Hurray I sail for Cuba in the morning!"

Weeks of silence followed while she tried to interpret from the newspaper stories how Edward and the 71st were faring. Neither Granger nor anyone at the office had heard from him. Frantic with worry, she wrote him daily.

At last, on July thirtieth, the postman brought a letter with an indecipherable postmark. She tore it open and saw it was from an officer, a Captain James Briggs, whom Edward had mentioned as a good friend. Briefly and sadly Briggs informed her that Edward had died at sea on June twenty-ninth of yellow fever. She did not receive official notification from the War Department until weeks later.

BOOK TWO

BOOK TWO

9

At first Cordelia's grief was so acute that she became ill and took to her bed. Dr. Prettyman administered a sedative. Mary brought chicken broth and comfort. The children, wearied by companionable weeping with her, came and stared wide eyed at the sight of Mama lying in bed at midday.

Her bed, she kept thinking, had been *their* bed. Edward and she had lain here and made love wonderfully. Why had he left her? Everyone called his death "tragic," though she did not see in it the tradition of heroic Greek literature. To her mind Edward had not died for a cause he believed in, but simply had perished of fever while traveling pointlessly on a ship from noplace to nowhere.

Awakening in the middle of one night, Cordelia found that she had stopped grieving for Edward and become angry with him for acting stupidly. Suddenly deciding to wash her hair, she rose quietly from bed. Faithful Mary, sleeping fitfully on a cot she had placed in a corner of Cordelia's bedroom, started up and cried out as at sight of a ghost. Then, hurrying after Cordelia to the bathroom, Mary seized her in a viselike grip and uttered strangled sounds. They fought like vixens. It took Cordelia a while to understand that Mary thought she was so wild with grief that she intended to slash her throat with one of Edward's old razors. By the time Cordelia did understand, she had with her greater physical strength hurled Mary out of the bathroom, shouted that she was fired, and slammed and locked the door.

She was beginning the soothing task of washing her

hair when Tim, roused from sleep on the top floor by Mary's screams, fetched the kitchen ax and began to smash down the bathroom door. Like an anvil chorus, the screams of the awakened children joined the cries of Mary. Cordelia, having forgotten grief and even the wish to wash her hair, thinking only of the damage being done to the door, hastily unlocked and opened it. Stepping back nimbly to avoid another swing of the ax, she demanded:

"What are you doing, Tim McMahon?"

He gaped at her, then cried: "Goddamn you, Mrs. Lovejoy, I might've busted open your head with this goddamn ax!"

His profanity shocked him and everyone else so deeply that all went quietly to bed.

Cordelia did not find solace from expectable sources. Religion was no help. She never had been devout, but after Eunice was born she'd had her baptized in the Episcopal Church of the Incarnation at Madison Avenue and Thirty-fifth Street and had begun to think of herself as a communicant there. (Edward, staunch agnostic, had not been highly pleased when she attended services and had the children properly baptized. It would have amused him to know that a memorial service was held for him there.) But neither the words of the kindly rector nor Cordelia's attempts at prayer within that architecturally beautiful church assuaged the loss of her staunch agnostic.

The children were not much help, either. They did not realize how vital their father had been to their happiness and failed to miss him the way they should have. Would they ever cease being little animals who wanted only food and play?

She appreciated the sympathy of friends, but sympathy could not restore her to a feeling of life. Hal and Caroline rushed to the house the moment they heard the news, but Cordelia believed that the chief emotion Hal exuded was guilt over having deserted the company where Edward had left him in charge. The Renssalaers and Bancrofts and many others asked her to luncheons, dinners, late suppers, early teas—everything but breakfast.

Mrs. Fish and her husband had her and three aged widows to the most dramatically funereal dinner conceivable. Everyone wore black and the Fishes invited in a Salvation Army band to serenade them between courses with sad hymns and marches for the dead. All of the women wept and Mr. Fish finally claimed illness and was assisted off to bed by two footmen.

Suzanna Neiswander, who had lost several pounds and was seen occasionally with Nick at the theater or Sherry's, wanted Cordelia and the children to be her guest for a week at her family's home in Newport. But Newport was the last place Cordelia wanted to go.

Immediately after the memorial service for Edward, Cordelia took the children up to Dorfman Manor with the thought of spending a week. But she saw she could not last more than a couple of days there. The place was going to rack. Everywhere she turned in the house or the farm buildings she found the need of repair. She'd had a notion of galloping across the fields, but there was not a horse left that was worth riding. One of her first thoughts had been to get rid of the mortgaged house and move to the country, but that clearly was impossible. Her parents were so taken up with their own troubles that they had little time for hers. Her father was ill, her mother dazed and confused. It was necessary for her to be a comfort to them rather than they to her.

Probably it was no surprise that Mary was the greatest comfort of anyone. As soon as Cordelia and the children returned from the country, Mary said:

"My Grandma Culligan used to say there's nothing like a good housecleaning to get over a funeral."

"When we first got together," Cordelia said, "I used to want to scrub the floor, but you always objected it was beneath me."

"As the judge said to the prisoner, Miz Cordelia, objection is removed."

And so that year they worked together at a grand housecleaning of 127 in August. Each night Cordelia fell into exhausted sleep without requiring any sedative from Dr. Prettyman.

Nick had rushed to the house as soon as he got word of Edward's death.

"I'm so sorry," he babbled. "What made him tip over? Why should a grown man with a wife and children want to run off to a stupid war?"

Cordelia closed her eyes and controlled her temper. "Nicky, did you come to comfort the bereaved or criticize the deceased?"

"Sorry, sorry. . . ."

The evening at the end of August after she and Mary finished housecleaning, Nick again came bounding in. "Good news, Corey! Good news! I have a customer wants to buy Lovejoy's!"

"Who says it's for sale?"

He made a face. "It *has* to be for sale."

Edward had told her once that if he died she would inherit the company, and if he died before Steve was of age, she should sell the company at the best possible price. Although the War Department had not yet officially confirmed Edward's death, Davidson Murch, the company lawyer who also had been Edward's personal attorney, had told her informally that she was heir to everything: the company, the mortgaged house, cash amounting to less than one thousand.

Now she asked Nick, "Why, dear brother, does the company have to be for sale?"

"Because it's a business organization," he replied, "and no woman can run a business."

As so often in her dealings with Nicky, she was determined to remain cool. But she could not stop herself from saying, "You try my patience just as I thought we were getting along better."

Of course he had no idea why she should be irritated. "My customer offers seventy thousand. You can't hope to do better. Follow my advice on what stocks to buy and you'll be worth a hundred thousand before you know it."

"We'll see, Nicky, we'll see. Thanks for your interest."

Following confirmation of Edward's death from the War Department, Davidson Murch came to see her. He made it sound as if she had inherited a fortune and he acted so suave that Cordelia did not trust him.

"How much should the company bring?" she asked.

Murch tipped his fingers together. "For your sake—for the sake of our dear Edward—I'll try for fifty, maybe sixty thousand."

Yet Nick's prospective buyer offered seventy. Why hadn't Edward ever told her what he thought the company was worth?

"What would be your commission on the sale, Mr. Murch?"

"Less than the standard ten percent. A mere five."

Suppose he received another five or ten percent from a purchaser for whom he arranged a knockdown price? She said, "There must be an accounting of assets before we decide on an asking price."

Murch acted surprised. "But I'm already seeing to that."

Then it was time, she thought, that she had an accounting done by someone other than the aging Davidson Murch.

A couple of days later Granger sent a note by an

office boy inviting her to lunch with him at the Harvard Club Ladies' Dining Room the following Friday. She accepted gladly. While they ate an almost indigestible lunch of limp apple salad, bleeding roast beef, and leaden Yorkshire pudding, he introduced a subject so delicately that it took her a while to understand what he was talking about. It was this: He had found financial backers who wanted him to be their spokesman and publisher. Would she consider their offer?

"Of course, Granger."

"Mrs. Lovejoy—"

"Please!" Just for the fun of it she fluttered her eyelids at him. "After all these years, Granger, it's time you called me Cordelia."

He actually blushed. Now what did that mean, a man in his thirties blushing at such a remark? Why had he never married? What did he do about sex? Did he have an attractive woman tucked away somewhere? Or didn't he like women at all?

"Then, Cordelia, you'd entertain an offer from my supporters?"

"Entertain?" There was a fundamental difference of semantics between them—and to him nothing was more important than language. To her, "entertain" meant what P.T. Barnum offered the public; to him, it meant considering an idea. "What's your proposition, Granger?"

"I think my backers would come in for maybe sixty-five thousand."

"I'll think about it. Thanks for a pleasant lunch."

There must, she thought, be some hidden value in Lovejoy and Son that so many people wanted to offer such various low prices for it.

When she got home she found a note from Mrs. Fish inviting her to tea the very next day. Its tone was so beseeching that she accepted.

Mrs. Fish was not quite as self-possessed as usual

when she introduced Cordelia to a heavy, balding man with a large nose, small dark eyes, and a trim mustache. "May I present Mr. Morgan."

"Charmed." He bowed stiffly. "Most charming." Though he did not smile, she sensed that his little eyes were beaming approval of her. She realized he was J. P. Morgan, Jr., son of the famous financier.

"Pierpont is back from a long stay in London," Mrs. Fish told her. "Pierpy, you're still staying with your father? Is he well?"

"Yes and no, Mamie. Yes, I'm still staying with him and the family. And no, he imagines he's not well at the moment. So I'm going to look for other diggings till he turns more cheerful. Mrs. Lovejoy, I believe we're neighbors on Murray Hill."

"Well," she replied, "there's a certain geographic proximity."

"I recall seeing you walking on Park Avenue."

"I walk a lot, Mr. Morgan. I enjoy it."

When he smiled his red lips gave her an impression of sensuality.

"Mamie, Father heard you claim the highest vantage point on the Hill. He wonders should he add another story to his house to recover his advantage."

"Won't do him any good," said Mrs. Fish. "After you accepted today, I decided to settle that old question with your father. Charles!" A footman turned to her. "Bring that thing." He hastened back bearing a small telescope mounted on a tripod which he set up at a southeast window.

"We're going to study the stars by daylight?" asked Morgan.

"No," said Mrs. Fish, "Charles is focusing this thing across the rooftops to your father's house at Thirty-seventh and Madison. You can see Charles has it dead level. And when you look through it, Pierpy, you're going to see that not even two additional stories would raise your father's house as high as mine. You can so report it to him."

Morgan peered through the glass for a long time. At last he said, "The old man is hard to beat. His property still rises higher than yours, Mamie. Take a look."

She looked through the glass for a moment, then cried, "Damnation!" Cordelia looked too and saw that J. P. Morgan, Sr., had erected a tall new flagpole on the roof of his house which rose higher than anything existing on Murray Hill.

When Cordelia felt it time to go, Morgan excused himself, too. His coach was waiting at the curb, and he offered her a ride home. The coachman touched his horses into a trot up Fifth instead of down the avenue, however, and she finally said, "But I live on East Thirty-Sixth."

"I know," said Morgan, "but let's take the long way home with a turn through Central Park."

She did not like his failure to ask her and his boldly taking the matter into his own hands. "That's a very long way home, Mr. Morgan."

He glanced at her. "Do you feel I'm compromising you in any way?"

"It's very difficult to compromise a widow with three young children."

"So I'm discovering, Mrs. Lovejoy. If that were indeed my intent. But if you feel I'm abducting you, I'll tell my man to turn around."

"I accept your dare, Mr. Morgan. Central Park holds no terrors for me."

"I observed your wit, and now I see your bravery matches it. I haven't met many young widows with three young children, but those I have always ask financial advice."

"So you dare me again. And again I'll accept your dare. My husband owned a publishing house, and I'm uncertain whether to sell it."

"They're not offering you enough for it."

She stared at him in amazement, refusing to ask the obvious.

"I made it my business to find out," he said. "I told you I had observed you walking on Murray Hill."

"Because I walk the streets," she said, "doesn't make me a streetwalker."

He gave a loud laugh and reached a hand toward her, but stopped himself before he touched her. "I like your company—may I call you Cordelia?"

"If you insist. Personally I dislike the name."

"No worse than—dear God—Pierpont or Pierpy. I like an intimate friend to call me Jack."

"Yes, Mr. Morgan."

He sighed deeply. "Anyway, Cordelia, the people wanting to buy Lovejoy and Son are trying to cheat you. That business—if you can find the right person to run it for you—is worth a hundred twenty or thirty thousand."

"Suppose I ran it myself?"

He looked full at her. "Brave, brave Cordelia. But a woman can't do that." He raised a hand. "Now wait, don't say it. Not because a woman lacks the experience. Not because a woman is more stupid than a man. But because it would put her in a man's world that is so incredibly stupid she will inevitably be destroyed. Ninety-nine percent of all businessmen are massive fools."

"What are the other one percent?"

"Massively lucky. They're the ones inhabit these handsome houses we're passing on Fifth. Nearly all the others go broke."

They talked on as they turned into the evening shadows of Central Park, and she finally asked if his investigation of Lovejoy and Son had revealed glaring weaknesses in its workings.

"I know little about publishing," he said. "It doesn't

interest me. Nearly all the books published are so silly. And most publishers must be pretty silly people themselves to publish 'em. Anyhow, my agent mentioned that your company's accounting system is totally antiquated. You have an old head bookkeeper there—"

"I know," Cordelia said. "Edward—my husband—knew he should be let go. But he'd been at it so long that Edward figured he would let him stay on till he got back from the war."

"That's what I mean about publishing." Morgan sounded bitter. "That's what I mean about businessmen. Fools, nearly every one of them. Now, politicians are different. Successful politicians, that is. I'm not talking about the amateur reformers, who never last more than a term or two. Every last successful politician is dishonest—and that goes for honest-sounding Roosevelt, too. But they're very smart, seeing precisely the structure of society and manipulating it to their own ends while businessmen go bumbling along not knowing anything about anything. . . ."

Darkness had fallen by the time they clopped out of the Park and turned down Fifth.

"Stop at Sherry's with me for an early dinner," he said.

"Thank you, but I must get home. Remember I have three children expecting me."

"Three children." His tone was wondering. "Do you know I dislike children? I think they should be put away somewhere until they grow up and turn interesting."

"There are days," Cordelia said, "when I heartily agree with you."

"I dislike children so much," he went on, "that I intend never to marry. Next to children I most dislike wives. Marriage can turn a delightful, perfectly ravishing companion—like yourself, Cordelia—into a tedious harridan who drives her poor husband off to the ends of

the earth. Marriage' and having children are the two
most vicious habits of our society."

That was being candid, she thought, and said, "I like
your integrity, Mr. Morgan."

"Jack," he said.

"I repeat that I like your integrity, Mr. Morgan, but
don't agree with you about marriage and children."

He did not speak again till he handed her down at
her door.

Cordelia did not mention her encounter with John
Pierpont Morgan, Jr., to Mary or anyone. Although it
had been a fascinating experience, she did not expect to
see him again. She liked his thorough, direct manner,
but was not in the least attracted to him. He was only
three years older than she, yet he seemed aged compared to Edward's youthfulness. If ever she were to
marry again, which she was pretty certain she would
not, it would not be to one like J. P. Morgan, Jr. But of
course, in his forthright way he had offered far less than
marriage. How long did it take a man like him to ex-
haust his interest in a woman and pursue another?
Probably a few months, maybe a year at most.

However, the information Morgan had given her was
invaluable. The important thing was how she should act
on the basis of it. She was pondering that question the
next day when a letter arrived from John Speer in Boston. He had just learned of Edward's death from a mutual acquaintance and sent condolences. Somehow his
letter was more comforting than any other she had received.

She was reading John's letter a third time when up
trotted one of Mamie Fish's carriages with a message
delivered by a footman: Could she please reply by return messenger if able to receive Mrs. Fish that very
afternoon?

Of course she could. She changed clothing and made
sure of a scrupulously clean drawing room in which a

properly uniformed Mary would serve tea, cookies, and little sandwiches.

Mamie Fish arrived ten minutes before the four o'clock hour. In her socially overturning way she entered with a dramatic announcement: "I'm sure you know, my dear, that I am no procurer. I'll match my morality against the best."

Cordelia said of course she knew that.

"Pierpy said you saw clean through his design. Believe me, Mrs. Lovejoy, so did I. But among my good works is my dedicated plan to bring that most eligible man to the marriage altar. And from the way he talks about you, I think you're the one can manage it." Then she made her memorable speech, possibly stolen from Miriam Peyster, about "Do what you want to in life. . . ."

That stubborn look came over Cordelia's face after Mrs. Fish asked what else was there for a woman to try for except to excel in society and collect men. For Cordelia's plans had nothing to do with such goals. She was going to call a meeting of all employees of the company next Monday when she would announce her intention of doing what Jack Morgan said a woman should not—could not do.

10

Like all gamblers, Cordelia was sometimes supersti-
tious. On that Monday morning she put on a flowered
hat which she believed always had brought her good
luck. Deciding to walk to the office, she had almost
reached Park Avenue before she realized that—as
when a child—she was taking care not to step on any
cracks in the sidewalk. She turned down Madison Avenue and was approaching Twenty-ninth Street when
disaster loomed.

Across Madison, halting carriages and wagons in
both directions, strolled a magnificent black tomcat. He
was on a course bound to cross her own path even if
she broke into a run. Unhesitatingly she veered to her
left and threaded her way across the avenue in the
opposite direction from the tom. She soiled a shoe in
horse manure, but at least no black cat crossed her
path. Now, she thought, if only I don't walk under a
ladder.

Sure enough, there was a ladder raised from the sidewalk to an upper story of a vacant row house on the
east side of Madison. Cordelia paused, circumspectly
preparing to skirt the ladder, when she noticed a sign in
a window of the house: For Rent. A man in the doorway, thinking she was about to climb the steps, called
down to her, "The agency sent you?"

"Well," Cordelia replied, "what's the monthly
rental?"

"Thirty-five."

"Awful high," she said.

"You could get it for twenty-five on a five-year lease."

A sudden sense of excitement possessed Cordelia. Some primitive instinct within her cried, A sign! A sign! Through such signs the ancients knew where to build another mound, the tribe trekked into a different valley. Black cat, raised ladder, step on a crack and you'll break your back!

That part of Madison no longer was completely residential. Some lawyers' and insurers' offices had moved in, ever a sign of low rents in an area declining into rooming houses, and at the corner of Twenty-ninth a tearoom flaunted lace curtains. There would be no zoning problem—and, anyway, Edward had said you could circumvent almost any zoning regulation by a judicious payment of fifty bucks at City Hall.

Cordelia was appalled by how little she knew about the workings of Lovejoy and Son. But one thing she did know: The monthly rent on the Twenty-third Street premises was three hundred and twenty-five a month and no doubt would go higher when the lease ran out in three more months. That included the store, of course, but the employees had a surprise awaiting them.

Cordelia was going to sell the store. It had come to her in a dream on Saturday night and a visit by Nick on Sunday afternoon had confirmed her dream notions: Potential purchasers of the company were more interested in the store than in the publishing house; they could understand the workings of a store, but publishing was a mystery.

"What are you going to use the place for?" the man asked as he showed her the three floors.

"Why," she answered, "are you looking for a five-year lease?"

"I'm not. It ain't mine. If it was, I'd turn it into a rooming house. Taxes on the place are only about seventy a year. The old lady who owns it, the one I'm agenting for, don't want to bother with roomers herself. She's cuckoo. Lives in a two-dollar-a-week room she likes and says she has just five years to live. Twenty-five a month for the next five years is her idea of heaven."

The three-story building would house the company offices comfortably, but Cordelia said it wasn't right. "I want a real big storage-space handy."

"Then you come to the right place, ma'm."

Beyond a tiny backyard cluttered with junk was a large brick building fronting on Fourth Avenue which was renting storage space. Cordelia went around there and found ideal accommodations for book storage at a low price. The owner would knock open a door in the back of his building so that there would be communication with the row house on Madison. Thus Cordelia could rehouse the company for about eighty dollars a month.

It was almost ten o'clock when she arrived at the office, and Granger fussed over her being late. "I was about to send the St. Bernard out for you." He gestured to a large young man of cheerful, rugged countenance. "Cordelia, this is my new assistant, Runyon Fiske. He came out of Princeton last June and thinks he'd like to go into publishing." For some reason Granger's assistants never stayed longer than a few months.

A dark young man appeared in the doorway. "Excuse me, Mr. Cantwell. I—"

"Goldman, how often must I tell you not to barge in? Can't you see I'm occupied?"

"Sorry, sir, it's just that—"

"Whatever it is, you know that I deal only with Mr. Barlowe in business matters. Now spin off!"

"Sir!" Goldman's tone was desperate, his look pleading. "It's that Mr. Barlowe is wrong about this."

"Goldman, I've had enough of your impertinence. You are fired."

"Oh, come now, Granger." Cordelia spoke very softly. "What a way to greet the new owner of the company. I haven't been here five minutes and somebody's fired. What do you do here, Mr. Goldman?"

He made an awkward effort to bow to her. "I work for Mr. Barlowe in accounting, Mrs. Lovejoy."

"I know what a trial that can be. Have you had formal training in accounting?"

"Yes, ma'am, I earned my degree at City College night school."

Granger said, "Sidney Barlowe was doing accounting before you were born."

"Maybe that's just the trouble with old Sidney," Cordelia said. "Mr. Goldman, I've heard on good authority that our accounting system is totally antiquated. Do you find that true?"

Goldman swallowed; his eyes grew large and his hands clenched spasmodically. Cordelia could feel Runyon Fiske willing Goldman not to quail. Goldman stared from Cordelia to Granger and back again, then whispered, "Yes, ma'am."

"I value your opinion," she said. "You'll be interested to know that Mr. Barlowe is resigning today and you're not fired."

"Cordelia!" cried Granger as Goldman and Fiske fled. "I've never heard of anything as high-handed as your overruling me! Sidney has been like a father to me. He's taken the full burden of thinking about finances off my shoulders. If you fire him, you fire me!"

"Suit yourself, Granger. I think what you mean is that you don't *want* to think about the financial aspects of the business. But as editor-in-chief I think you *have* to know almost as much as the accountant about the way the business is run. Sidney is going. You're welcome to stay if you want to."

She went out, closing the door behind her. There

were only thirteen employees in the publishing home-office, but they seemed more numerous as they gathered in whispering, gesticulating knots as she went along the hall toward accounting. Davidson Murch had not been invited to the meeting, but he must have got wind of it, for there he was, rushing toward her with sycophantic gestures. She brushed past him and into accounting, which was a long and narrow room with light coming from high windows, as in a prison cell.

Old Sidney, seated at his rolltop desk, blinked around at her over his spectacles. He smiled wanly and looked so vulnerable that she thought she could not possibly go through with what she must do.

"Ah, Mrs. Lovejoy, good morning."

"Good morning, Mr. Barlowe."

A large, ancient, eight-day Waltham clock above his desk loudly tick-tocked life away. How had he endured its noisy ticking all these years? Perhaps he had taught himself not listen to it, and thus it accounted for his being somewhat deaf.

He frowned. "Where's everybody gone? Ah, yes, the meeting. Is it time I went to it?"

"In a few minutes, Mr. Barlowe, but first I want to confide something. Edward told me before he went away how much you've longed for years to retire, but bore your sense of duty to the company with the fortitude of a good soldier. Edward said—and I quite agree—that you must be relased from your arduous toil just as soon as possible. That time has finally come. Mr. Barlowe. You must have some days to enjoy. . . ." She found herself carried away by her rhetoric until she seemed to watch herself take one step toward Sidney, put a hand on his shoulder, and hear herself say, "You know whereof I quote" (though she could not remember precisely whereof) "when I say, 'Well done, thou good and faithful servant.'"

Tears sprang to Sidney's eyes and his voice came tremulously: "It's so kind of you, Mrs. Lovejoy, to recognize my deep and I thought secret desire these many years to retire. Are you sure I shouldn't linger a bit longer to break in a successor?"

"Thank you, thank you, Mr. Barlowe, but absolutely not. That's so typical of your sweet and generous nature to offer to stay on awhile. But Edward was right. No, much as I appreciate it, I won't hear of it. Let us remember that old Christian sentiment of the sooner the better. . . ."

A few minutes later all assembled in L'il Abe's stockroom, which was the only place with enough space for the thirteen men and boys—fourteen, including Murch—and Cordelia to crowd in. Some stood, others sat on piles of books as Abe wheeled around a squeaky old chair for her. For an instant she wanted to smile at being the female president of this all-male club, then she welcomed them gravely and said:

"I have a couple of announcements. There has been some talk about the company being sold. It will not be. It will continue under the Lovejoy family."

Murch made a strange sound and spoke: "Mrs. Lovejoy!"

"Sir?"

He got to his feet, face flushed. "Mrs. Lovejoy, it's perfectly apparent to me and everyone here that you are not competent to run this company. You—"

"It's not apparent to me, Mr. Murch, and I happen to own the company."

"But I object."

"To what can you possibly object, sir?"

"I—I—" He made a fizzling sound and was at a loss for words.

"I inform you, Mr. Murch, that you no longer are legal counsel for Lovejoy and Son. I ask you to leave this meeting."

He stood fast and made more strange sounds.

"Mr. Goldman? Mr. Fiske? The flight of stairs is long, Mr. Murch, and our young men are strong."

Murch left quickly.

Then Cordelia announced the resignation of Sidney Barlowe and praised him lavishly. When he responded with heartfelt thanks for being allowed his dream to retire, there were loud cheers.

"Two other announcements," Cordelia said. "I am selling the downstairs bookstore."

There were murmurs and gasps.

"Might as well let everybody in on it," she went on. "If you know anybody wants to own a bookstore, you can tell them ours is for sale. My other announcement. We are moving from these premises within three months. I'll reveal our destination once I've signed the lease. No sense in having our rent kited by premature announcements. I guess that's about all. Oh, yes, one other thing. I've accepted Sidney's resignation with deep regret. I'm willing to accept the resignation of anyone else who feels he won't be happy here under the— new management. But I emphasize that I'm not seeking the resignation of anyone."

She looked at Granger, but he was staring at the floor.

Cordelia did not expect to hear any more from Jack Morgan. It must be apparent to him, she thought, that she was not available for the sort of arrangement he had in mind. She saw him once, on Sunday afternoon following her first week at the office when she took the children out for a walk. He came sailing down Park Avenue in a huge victoria, surrounded by his mother and three sisters, all holding their broad-brimmed hats in the wind. His derby was jammed low on his head and he had the desperate look of a man smothering in a flutter of family lace. No wonder he hated marriage and children. If he saw her, he gave no sign as he stared fixedly ahead.

Next day upon returning from the office she was surprised to find a note which had been delivered from him. He requested the honor of her company at dinner the following Thursday at Sherry's and would be pleased to call for her at seven P.M. Without hesitating she sat down and penned acceptance. Because she did not wish to become a kept woman didn't mean she was ready for a nunnery.

He was precisely on time. She had put the children in an upper room and waited at the top of the stairs till Mary had seated him in the parlor. When she appeared, he bowed and made some compliment about her dress.

"Your children," he said. "I expected to—uh—see your children."

"Crawling all over you?" she replied. "Nothing doing. I lock them up at night. And if they make a sound, I go in at them with a whip. You are so kind to invite me out."

The children's current cat, a calico named Nancy, strolled in at that moment and, sensing that Morgan feared cats, made straight for him. Morgan took up a defensive position. Nancy paused, realizing that if she advanced one more step, the fearful man might seize a chair to protect himself. However, before she could create that interesting scene, Cordelia swooped down on her and tossed her, protesting, into the hall. Then Cordelia got Morgan and herself out of the house as quickly as possible.

"Why did you do it?" Morgan asked after his hansom wheeled off.

"Why did I do what?"

"Put your store up for sale. It's your biggest asset."

"Intuition. I had a dream."

"Oh, dear God!" Morgan would have clapped a hand to his head if his hatbrim hadn't got in the way. "I told you businessmen are idiots. So it applies to businesswomen, too. Intuition!"

"This one worked pretty good," Cordelia said. "I've already had an offer of forty-two thousand, and I think I can get them up to forty-five."

"My dear lady, what do you intend to do with forty-five thousand dollars?"

"Buy Blackwell Brothers. They're up for sale. Sort of secretly."

"Who, pray, are Blackwell Brothers?"

"There's only one left—Jerome. He's old and sickly and tired of the business. They have only one line, it's all they've had for years and years. School readers. You know, little books that give students readings stolen from uncopyrighted classics and make them feel cultured. Or it makes the teachers feel they're dispensing culture."

"Sounds awfully thin," Morgain said.

"It's fat, really. Teachers swear by Blackwells, as they call 'em. Of course old Jerome won't give it all away for forty-five thousand, but I'll let him get a percentage of the profits and I think I can persude him he's better off not having to bother with the business. Edward—my husband—my late husband—would have leaped at the opportunity if he could have raised the initial payment. He always coveted Blackwell Brothers, but never could touch 'em. A couple of weeks ago I heard one of the salesmen say that Blackwell is about ready to sell."

"I'm relieved to hear," Morgan said, "it wasn't intuition alone made you get rid of the store. You did act on information."

"Well, yes. But that dream helped me make a decision."

Jack Morgan drew attention wherever he went. His father was not the richest man in the world, but he was known as the wisest rich man. Cordelia, as Jack Morgan's companion that evening, drew as much attention. It amused her that no one there knew who she was; years ago, when a debutante, it would have been unthinkable to her to be unrecognized at Sherry's.

Morgan was a great trencherman. He worked his way methodically through courses that Cordelia skipped. Oysters were followed by *consommé de tortue*. Hors d'oeuvres preceded striped bass with cream sauce and cucumbers. Next came saddle of lamb with green peas and hothouse new potatoes. Then he urged her to try just a slice of the terrapin, but she wanted only a bite of the salad. Still the hovering waiters brought food. Sherry offered one of his fabulous desserts: hot sponge cake heaped with orange ice cream and topped with rum sauce. "Try one of the delicious petits fours with your coffee," Morgan urged her. Then came champagne.

Cordelia said she no longer was up to date on society, and he replied that society was a bore. He was pleased that she was more interested in hearing him talk about what absorbed him most: business.

"Tell me," he said, "what other intuitions you've had since becoming active in publishing."

When she described the black cat that had crossed Madison Avenue and her renting of the new premises, he laughed heartily.

"But publishing doesn't involve just business," she said. "It concerns art."

"Do you mean art or artifice?" he asked. "By 'artifice' I mean something contrived. What would you call an editor—artist or artificer? What is an editor?"

"I think an editor is a person who draws things together—gives them balance—makes them work."

Morgan's fork paused. "By your definition an editor is an artificer who may not recognize an artist when he sees one. *Art*? Now there's area in which my father has tried to train me as thoroughly as at business. Probably not as successfully. Art is a daring venture by a free human spirit to express itself in a work that tries to communicate something fundamental about life. I don't see anything much connected with art in current American writing, painting, theater. Do you?"

A sense of inadequacy overwhelmed Cordelia. Would she ever recognize *art* if confronted by it? She had not been properly trained to scale the heights to which she aspired. It had nothing to do with being a woman. The men she knew—Edward, for one—had not been trained to it, either. Maybe it was an American failing, maybe almost universal.

She started to speak of something else, but Morgan went off in another direction: "I have to go to London and Paris. I'm sailing day after tomorrow on the *Savoy*. Cordelia, can you imagine you might leave your children in good care and take a few weeks' vacation in Europe?"

"I can imagine it, but I could not manage it."

He delivered her to her door a few minutes after eleven.

Jerome Blackwell lived away up in the country on East Ninety-seventh Street. An aged bachelor, he had two passions remaining: playing Bach fugues on a concert grand which almost filled his parlor, and raising exotic plants and flowers in a large greenhouse behind his home. Cordelia went to call on him and lingered for an entire afternoon, admiring his plants, about which she knew little, and listening to him play Bach, about whose music she knew less. They became friends, and after considerable discussion over a number of weeks, Jerome agreed to sell his firm to the Lovejoy imprint for a down payment of fifty thousand and a ten-percent royalty on the future sales of all Blackwell readers until his death.

Cordelia negotiated the terms with Jerome entirely

on her own. The details were carefully worked over by Marty Goldman, whom she had put in Sidney's job, and young Bill Paisley, the new lawyer she had hired on Max Gurland's recommendation. Taking into account the costs of additional storage space required for the books and the special Blackwell sales force of four men, they conservatively estimated that the deal meant a net income to Lovejoy of about three hundred thousand annually—a profit figure undreamed of in the company's history.

Jerome came to the signing at the company's new Madison Avenue offices in a disreputable old coach driven by a drunken coachman. And there he met Granger for the first time. Something must have been said between them—what, Cordelia did not hear. Or maybe, it was only a look. Whatever it was, there suddenly stood Granger and Jerome hating each other. By that time, fortunately, Bill Paisley was blotting the signatures on the agreement.

Cordelia had invited Jerome, Granger, Marty, Max and his wife, and Bill and his vivacious young wife to her home for dinner after the signing. Now, beckoning Granger out of the office, she told him, "I don't want you to come to dinner. It'll be a disaster between you and Jerome."

Granger looked crushed. "I didn't start it." Then angry. "That old Blackwell is an ass."

"I don't think so. But you are not coming to dinner."

He flushed. "Are you *ordering* me around, *Mrs*. Lovejoy?"

"I'm not ordering you, *Mr*. Cantwell. I'm just *telling* you. I will not let you spoil a pleasant, profitable situation. I'm taking Runyon in your place. He never loses his temper no matter what happens."

They shook awake the drunken coachman and made their way to Thirty-sixth Street, Cordelia, Max, and Bill riding with Jerome while Marty and Runyon trotted behind to pick up the coachman if he fell off the box.

At dinner Cordelia raised a matter she had not mentioned before. In her study of the Blackwell readers it had occurred to her that in the future the publisher might offer teachers a special guide, not available to students, that would give the teachers more information than their pupils could obtain from their reading books.

"You know," she said, "how teachers like to be superior to their students. I guess they have to be if they're going to inspire the trust they must have in order to teach effectively. So I thought that if the teachers can be supplied with *extra* information, it might promote the sale of the students' readers."

Jerome stared at her until his bright blue eyes began to shine humorously. "Clever, clever Mrs. Lovejoy! You're going to be very successful some day. Too bad I didn't make connection with you sooner. I'd have had more leisure to enjoy life—and both of us would have made more money. But no matter, I'll enjoy the proceeds of your efforts for the rest of my life."

Max, who had great aversion to Granger and growing fondness for Cordelia, told her that Granger was making snide remarks about the Blackwell deal. "Let me be the first to report to you on the bastard. Granger is telling everybody that those Blackwell readers do not constitute *publishing*. He says they're only *merchandising*."

Cordelia was crestfallen. "I'm sorry to hear it. Really, the material in the readers is designed to interest young people in the best in literature."

"Of course it is!" Max was amazed by her reaction. "When I told you this, I hoped you'd get your back up at Granger. Seriously, Cordelia, the sooner you get rid of that character as editor-in-chief the better for the company."

"But then who?" She felt depressed. "Nobody knows

better than I that I'm not an experienced editor—that I'm an amateur at business."

"You're doing wonderfully for an amateur," Max said. "I didn't tell you this to put your spirits down. I hoped you'd act like Teddy Roosevelt and give your enemies hell."

"But who can I get in Granger's place?"

"Editors are a dime a dozen. But somebody who sees the—*entirety* of a publishing house is hard to find. Next to Edward there never was a better man worked here than John Speer."

She gazed at him. "Everybody seems to agree on that. Jerome Blackwell has dealt with him and says John is the best. Max, I'm not very comfortable going to work every day and trying to run things. There's too much gunfire. I'm going to write John and invite him to become managing director of the house with control over Granger and everybody else. Maybe I should take a lesson from Mr. Blackwell. He said he's going to enjoy the results of others' efforts for the rest of his life."

It turned out, however, that Jerome Blackwell was not a profound prophet. He died six months later, and then Lovejoy's no longer had to pay him royalties.

11

John Speer replied promptly to Cordelia's offer to become managing director of Lovejoy's.

> I'm deeply honored by your asking me to take on such responsibility. There's challenge in a job that would give me responsibility over all the workings of the company and have me report only to you. I would indeed enjoy working with you, Cordelia, but I must say no. Your salary offer of six thousand is perfectly fair and generous, so don't take this as my trying to bargain for a higher amount. But I've just signed a two-year contract with Bacon's and been made a vice-president. Also, I was married last month and my wife, Veronica, is so greatly attached to Boston that she can't bear the thought of leaving it. . . .

Cordelia's disappointment was profound. She felt somehow that John had betrayed her, as she had felt betrayed when Hal left Lovejoy's. So a woman finally had captured John Speer. Good luck to them. Personally, she would forget him.

Going to the office was not the pleasure she had thought it would be. She had good friends there—Max, Marty, Runyon, Li'l Abe. But she realized that others who worked there or came on business resented her female invasion of the male preserve. She kept very busy with a multitude of duties that others did not or would not perform, but she assumed no title and made herself as inconspicuous as possible. Thus she took the smallest, most obscure office space—a middle room on the top floor where the only light was from a gas lamp and the heating was so weak that in winter she had to keep on her greatcoat.

With her connivance Granger spread the fiction among authors and other callers that she only dropped by occasionally. Once, when she was creeping down the stairs for a solitary luncheon sandwich at the corner tearoom, she heard Granger tell a visitor as she passed his large, second-floor front office: "Yes, Mrs. Lovejoy comes by once in a while. I try to teach her a little about the editorial art."

At first the remark stung her. But then she told herself that Granger was only being tactful, that tact was one of his finest qualities. Both realized how deeply men hated to have a woman in any position of control over them. For this reason she went to great pains to make Granger feel he had complete control over the editorial functions of the company. What he had told the visitor was true: She *was* trying to learn all she could from him about being an editor. Whenever she had time from her work at book production and dealing with advertising and other chores that bored Granger, she read manuscripts and sought his criticism of her opinions. Sometimes they disagreed, but she studiously accepted his thinking as authoritative.

Occasionally he invited her to the Harvard Club Ladies' Dining Room for lunch, and once in a while she had him to a dinner party at home—though she took care never to ask him when she had the Gurlands. He could be a gay, witty companion, and indubitably he was handsome. Granger could make her laugh, he could bore her, he could make her angry, but he never could make her cry; that is, she did not have any romantic feelings about him.

"But you must have," said Mrs. Fish when Cordelia explained that to her, under pressure. "He's as handsome as Byron. As witty as—well, I've caught him stealing some remarks by Mark Twain. However, I know how longheaded you are, my dear. By all means hold out for a man with money."

Mary discussed Granger with Cordelia somewhat differently:

" 'Tis true he's handsome. Ye know, there's lots o' handsome Irish lads like that. Mainly they goes into the Church. Being priests they don't have to bear the consequences of their handsomeness."

"Now what do you mean by that?" Cordelia demanded.

"Just what I says." And that was all Mary would say.

Granger lived on Washington Square North, but was too proper ever to invite her there. Or was it, she wondered, that he was ashamed of her as too unintellectual to mingle with the literati who were reputed to gather sometimes in his flat? Runyon had been there. He told Cordelia that all the rooms were lined with books, and he let her in on a secret. Granger was fond of making peppermint fudge which he served to his friends during evenings of poetry readings.

"I've never known him to bring any to the office," Cordelia said. "Is it good fudge?"

"Well—" Runyon did not sound enthusiastic. "It's sort of grainy, but then I'm not keen on peppermint."

Granger was an acknowledged authority on poetry, and under his influence Lovejoy's published some American editions of the works of distinguished English poets such as Algernon Charles Swinburne, Christina Rossetti, Gerard Manley Hopkins, and a version of *The Yellow Book*. By far Granger's favorite poet was Swinburne, the subject of his master's thesis at Harvard. Whenever he was upset by something at the office, Cordelia could divert and soothe him by asking some innocent question about Swinburne.

"Ah, yes, ah, yes, is it any wonder that Tennyson

said of him, 'Swinburne is a reed through which all things blow into music'? Have you ever heard that, Cordelia?" Granger had said it a dozen times. "I can only call the new freedom he brought to poetry polyphonic. What he did with *form*! The way he freed verse from the prim domesticity of the Victorians by way of *ideas*! Can you imagine Walter Scott embraced in the passionate arms of Dolores, Faustine, Félise, Fragoletta?" Granger extended his own arms passionately.

Cordelia refused to sound gauche by reminding him that Lovejoy's had had little success in selling the imported works of any English poet since the Victorians.

Granger, admiring Swinburne and the poets known as Pre-Raphaelites who had rebelled against Victorian convention, found nothing comparable in America as the nineteenth century ended and the twentieth began. Cordelia herself discerned signs of healthy rebellion in American poetry and prose that Granger did not. Oddly, she saw the predominant gross materialism of the age more clearly than he. When she first read Edwin Markham's "The Man with the Hoe," for instance, she found it "ringing with conscience, utterly thrilling." But Granger dismissed Markham's verse as "mere rhetoric." Though Cordelia was not sure how American society could be restructured, she need look no farther than a few blocks downtown or across town to see how badly imbalanced it was. But Granger was totally oblivious to slum life in the City of New York.

In November 1901 Steve fell ill with something mysterious. It started with the symptoms of a cold, and then he developed a high fever that made him delirious. Dr. Prettyman came two and three times a day. He arranged for nurses round the clock, though they were not really necessary since either Cordelia or Mary was constantly at his bedside. Cordelia stopped going to the office; frantic with worry over him, she did not realize the extent of her exhaustion.

Dr. Prettyman established that Steve had none of the well-known childhood diseases. At last he brought in a colleague who believed that he had meningitis. The opinion struck Cordelia with terror, for she had heard there was no recovery from that dread disease.

"I'm not sure of that," Dr. Prettyman said. "Whatever he has, he's fighting it. He has a strong little body and a will as powerful as your own, Mrs. Lovejoy. I may be wrong, but I'm betting on him to make a full recovery."

By nightfall Steve's fever had abated somewhat.

That was the night a Western Union messenger brought a telegram from Marie Dorfman. Loren had died of the cancer from which he had been suffering for six months and she begged Cordelia to come to the Manor.

"I will not go," she told Mary. "I cannot go. Please send Tim to Nick's flat down on Gramercy with the news."

As she continued to sit in Steve's room and watch him, she thought about her father and how much she had loved him. She had been going up to the Manor every week or two during the final months of his illness even though there had seemed nothing she could do to comfort him or her mother. If only she could weep, it might relieve this awful depression that weighted her down. But she could not cry. She only could sit and think of Steve and Edward and her father and how pointless it seemed to struggle to achieve and be happy while the tragedy of death lay in wait for everyone.

Nick came back with Tim on his way to catch a train for Poughkeepsie. "Of course you can't leave Stevey," he told Cordelia. "Mama wouldn't want you to—and neither would Papa have. I'll take care of things. I'll postpone the funeral as long as I can. Maybe you can attend, maybe not. Don't think about it. I'll be in touch."

At last, thank God, Nick was acting with the understanding and responsibility she always had wished to find in him.

By next morning Steve's temperature had lowered further.

"We're not out of the woods yet," Dr. Prettyman said. "But I see light through the trees. I'm going to give you a sedative, Mrs. Lovejoy. You have to get some rest."

The following morning Steve's temperature was almost normal, though he was weak and spent. Dr. Prettyman said that he would recover and that she could attend her father's funeral the next afternoon.

She found with dismay when she reached the Manor that her mother was close to collapse and she would have to take her back to New York with her. Following the funeral service the Dorfmans' aged lawyer had more bad news for Cordelia and Nick: "There'll be probate, of course, but I can tell you right now that what's left of the farm is mortgaged way over its eyes. Your mother has nothing, absolutely nothing, left, but I guess you're well enough off to take care of her."

"Shall I take her in with me?" Nick asked. "I'm glad to."

"Thanks, no, Nicky, she'll come with me. I have a spare bedroom and"—Cordelia tried to joke, though it sounded feeble—"we're having enough trouble marrying you off. An aged, widowed mother on your hands will finish your chances forever."

She brought her mother home, eager to get there so that she could check on Steve. His languor worried her. She discussed his health with Dr. Prettyman, who said she was inclined to be impatient. After a few days, however, Dr. Prettyman admitted that Steve was not showing a wish to get out of bed, as he should.

"I don't know why Stevey's so listless," he told Cordelia. "What entertains him? Does he have favorite toys or games that might stimulate his interest?"

Cordelia, Eunice, Penny, Mary, Tim—all tried everything they could think of, but to no avail. Steve did not even pay any attention to several exquisite old Dutch figurines which he used to admire at the Manor and which his Grandma Dorfman had brought to New York.

"Stevey," Cordelia coaxed, "what is it, honey? You can't still be too tired to try to get out of bed."

He shrugged. "Why should I? What's the fun in getting up?"

After Dr. Prettyman took away his bedpan, he would go to the bathroom—then come straight back to his bed.

Tim had an idea. "Sean's in town with the circus. Remember how Stevey loved the circus last year? Sean'll gi' us all the passes we wants. Let's try to tease him into gettin' up an' goin'."

But Steve would not be enticed. "Who cares about an old circus?"

"Remember," Cordelia urged him, "how you enjoyed your friend Sean the Clown?"

"Who cares, Mama?"

Next morning when Cordelia went downstairs to the kitchen she was surprised to find Sean eating breakfast. His successful career had not changed him much; he looked as ugly and angry as ever and his speech was still incomprehensible. Tim had left for work, and Mary explained their plan. Cordelia was dubious at first, but then agreed and offered to pay Sean for his role. However, he vehemently refused to take money.

"He says the debt's all ours to the Lovejoys," Mary said. "He has to do it this mornin' 'cause he works in the ring this afternoon an' evenin'."

Cordelia explained the plan to her mother, Eunice,

and Penny, who promised to cooperate. Then she carried Steve's breakfast up to his room. "Suppose," she told him, "I stop this room service of yours. Then you'll have to come down to the dining room for meals like everybody else."

He cast her a fey look. "But I'm too weak." He realized that she did not yet have the will to starve him out of bed.

"I don't know what you're trying to prove, Steve, by acting like a baby this way."

He paid no attention to her as he sat up in bed and ate hungrily while she opened a book and pretended to read.

"Mama!" Steve stopped eating, and his voice came in a startled whisper.

Sean had appeared silently in the doorway. His makeup and clown's costume, disguising his ugliness and angry look, made him totally different. Here was a person of charm, bubbling with happiness.

"Sean!" Steve cried, upsetting his tray and starting out of bed.

Sean laughed silently and waved to him, then did a handstand.

"*Look,* Mama!"

She glanced up from her book. "Now why did you upset your tray?"

Sean had disappeared. But from the head of the stairs, while Penny and Eunice watched him with hands clapped over mouths to stifle their giggling, he whistled—three sweet and haunting notes.

"*Hear* him, Mama?"

"Hear what?"

Steve bounded from the room as Sean disappeared down the stairs. In the second floor hall he whistled again, and Steve raced after him. Sean kept ahead of him all the way to the front door while Cordelia and the girls hurried behind.

"Sean! Sean!" Steve cried as he chased him.

Sean turned into the living room. When everyone else got there, Sean was whistling and he and Steve were doing a jig. Mary, up from the basement, joined in. Then so did Penny, Eunice, Cordelia, and even Grandma Dorfman, who only yesterday had been complaining of being too stiff to walk.

They laughed and danced together for almost five minutes, and Steve never again tried to malinger in bed.

One evening early in December, after Steve was completely recovered, the doorbell rang and Mary answered it. Coming into the den, she told Cordelia, "A creature at the door, Miss Mudge, claims to be doing battle with Giant Despair. Meself, I'd say she's already been conquered by Demon Rum."

Cordelia, hurrying to the door, pulled in Maude and an old valise held together with rope. She smelled of whisky and looked ill-kempt. Clasping Cordelia to her, Maude said, "Heard about Edward a long time ago, but couldn't bring myself to write. Oh, God help us all! I'm destitute, though not yet prostitute. It's my battle with Giant Despair."

"'Tis an Irish disease she's got," Mary said behind Cordelia. "Ye've got to call it by the right name to beat it. Whisky—not Despair."

Marie had taken over the spare bedroom, so Cordelia, refusing to disturb the privacy of the children or that of Mary and Tim in their top-floor apartment, gave Maude her own room and began sleeping on a cot in the half-finished cellar room.

The whole family worked hard to prevent Maude from getting possession of a bottle. She was good company for Marie, who was pleased to find a woman having worse luck than herself, and the children adored her. They decided that she looked like Queen Victoria; in fact, they made up a game in which she *was* Victoria.

The game pleased Maude, who began to pretend that she actually was the Queen come to America in disguise to start a new life instead of having died earlier that year, as had been widely reported and mourned.

Cordelia and Eunice came upon her one day looking at herself in a mirror. "It shocks me to the core," she told them, "but I do look more like Victoria than Victoria herself. I understand the Queen sometimes enjoyed a little nip of brandy."

"No sir, ma'm," Eunice said. "Never a sip of the bad stuff. Not by a *Queen!*"

Tim was the greatest of help to Maude because he could tell the most graphic tales of the evils of the bottle. Soon he was laid off from the department store for two weeks without pay, a common practice of Mr. Hart's short of outright firing when an employee had been involved in some minor infraction of his strict rules. Tim had been accused by a customer named Mrs. Harold Bennison Brown of turning the revolving door at the entrance to Hart's too fast and causing her almost to fall. Hart's motto was "The customer is always right," and so Tim had been put in economic limbo until his case was settled.

Old man Hart, a penurious Scotsman who had assuaged his anger at failing to be accepted by the New York socially elect by building one of the finest mansions on Murray Hill and filling it with vulgar works of art, became the focus of Tim's hatred.

He did not curse Hart to Cordelia, but she helped his feelings considerably by telling him, "Tim, that old man is a genuine son of a bitch."

Tim grinned at her. "Ye're so right, Miz Cordelia. But don't let Mary hear ye cursing. Me point is that when I begin to think o' Mr. Hart, I finds meself thinkin' o' turnin' socialist."

"Oh Tim, I know so well how you feel. There've been times in the past few years when I've thought of turning to socialism myself. But I'll tell you what I decided. I thought, instead of turning socialist, I'll become a *super* capitalist. That way I'll trample down all ordinary capitalists who cross me. Don't think anymore about old Hart. The work gets heavier here all the time for Mary with my mother and Maude moving in. Any time I'll match your Hart's salary if you want to work here."

Tim, pleased, told her, "I'll see Maude through the vale."

Then—unknown to Cordelia in advance—Mary paid a visit to Dr. Prettyman and came home with her hat on cockeyed, shrieking that she was pregnant. In his ecstasy Tim trotted down Lexington Avenue for a quart of Irish whisky so that he could quietly celebrate his founding of a new McMahon dynasty. When Maude stole his bottle for a couple of nips, Tim almost hit her.

Cordelia summoned everyone to a temperance lecture. Maude wept, Tim sulked, Mary beamed over the expectation of motherhood.

"Oh, Cordelia," Maude begged, "what can I do about my drunkenness besides stop drinking?"

Cordelia answered, "Write another novel better than the first."

Maude stopped weeping and stared at her. "About *what*?"

"Something that's important to you. Not just something you make up in a hurry for a royalty check. Have you read *Madame Bovary*?"

Maude had not, so Cordelia gave her an English translation of Flaubert's novel. "Don't think of writing anything till you've finished reading it."

Of course she didn't expect Maude to become a Flaubert. Her initial purpose was for Maude to occupy herself so thoroughly that she'd stop thinking about whisky, and at least in that respect the plan seemed to be successful.

"At first," Maude told her, "I had it in mind to write a story about a young countrywoman who comes to the city and wants to rise in society. She's loved by a good man and a bad man. She's inclined to love the bad man, but the good man wins her and—well—she rises in society. Now that I've read *Madame Bovary*, I see what nonsense a story like mine would be. Cordelia, do you think the bad should be punished?"

"I think they should, but they really seldom are."

Maude nodded. "And the good should be rewarded, but seldom are. That's the trouble with what I've been writing all my life. I make things what they should be instead of what they *are*. Lying awake last night I got to thinking of two young women. One not as bad as she seems to be and one not as good as she thinks she is. And how neither gets what she seems to deserve."

"Go on," Cordelia said.

"I want the story to be in the city, but I don't really know anything about the city. I'm going to get a job clerking in a store. It'll support me. And just as important it'll give me the chance to learn things I've never observed. How people dress. How they act. What interests them. Things like that. This afternoon I'm going looking for a job. It shouldn't be too hard to find in the pre-Christmas shopping rush. And after one week I'm going to find a boardinghouse where I can start writing my novel nights and Sundays."

While Cordelia admired Maude's goal, she knew how admirable ideas had a way of falling flat.

"Wouldn't you like to stay with us till after Christmas?"

"I'd like to, but I've got to start on my own just as soon as I can if I'm ever going to do it alone. I've lived off your kindness long enough, Cordelia. I must stop playing silly games like Queen Victoria and get on with the hard things. But I'd certainly love to come to Christmas dinner."

To Cordelia's surprise Maude found a job as a ribbon clerk on Fourth Avenue that very afternoon, and a week later she moved into a boardinghouse at the foot of Murray Hill.

That Christmas season seemed more hectic than usual to Cordelia. Tim, having been punished, was restored to full employment in Mr. Hart's Christmas amnesty to a dozen of his workers. Cordelia stayed home from the office to help Mary in preparations, since Marie was not feeling well enough to be of much aid.

On the afternoon of Christmas Eve all of Lovejoy's employees, a multitude of friends, and almost a score of McMahons and Culligans were invited in for refreshments and carols. At one point in the afternoon more than fifty people were milling through the house.

After all the guests had left, the children hung large stockings from the mantel and Tim extinguished the flames in the fireplace so that Santa would not burn himself when he came down the chimney—observing the myth they had long ago ceased to believe. After midnight Cordelia still was putting up decorations and wrapping gifts.

The children awakened her before six o'clock, and a couple of hours after that she and Mary were hard at work in the kitchen. Tim's task was to shuck and ice a keg of oysters, and there were moments when Cordelia wondered if he'd ever finish the job as he frequently slipped upstairs, returning with an ever more cheerful smile and smelling strongly of what he had forbidden Maude to taste. Besides oysters there was to be a delicious pumpkin soup made from an old Dutch recipe; there were two geese weighing twelve pounds each and stuffed with chestnut dressing; gravy, white and sweet potatoes, turnips, creamed onions, cranberry sauce, and preserves rounded out the main course. Then came mince and pumpkin pie and steamed pudding with hard sauce.

"The Dorfmans," Marie kept saying, "have been having dinner at two o'clock on Christmas since 1639." She was not so much offering historical information as mildly rebuking Cordelia for setting the dinner hour at *one* o'clock. And since 1639 Dorfmans had been inviting their servants to sit down at table with them on Christmas. It was a custom Cordelia had continued with Mary and Tim. Today two hired girls would serve dinner.

Besides Mary and Tim, there were four Lovejoys, Grandma Dorfman, Nick, his friend Suzanna, and Maude. Cordelia also had invited Granger, whose only living relatives were two maiden aunts in Boston whom he wished to avoid. These added up to eleven.

At half past nine a runny-nosed boy rang the bell and came in from the cold, gray morning with a message from Granger. Regretfully he would not be able to attend because Lovejoy's most distinguished novelist, Tranch Claverlay, was in town from Maryland unexpectedly and Granger felt it would be uncivilized to leave him in solitude on Christmas. Cordelia, agreeing, sent back a note by the messenger saying that he must by all means bring along Mr. Claverlay to dinner. So there would be twelve at table.

Cordelia never had met Tranch Claverlay, whose name sounded like a pseudonym, though she had read all of his historical novels. She found that they told rather more than she wanted to know about past wars and leaders, but Edward and Hal had thought so highly of him that she had never breathed a dissenting word about his work. Obviously hers was a minority opinion because his books sold very well to the praise of knowledgeable reviewers—at least they had sold well until his most recent novel from Lovejoy's. *Dark Pageant of Triumph*, about Cortez's conquest of Mexico, had "crashed," as Edward would have put it. Cordelia had not been able to drag herself beyond the first chapter: all that Aztec mumbo-jumbo and not a single character to interest her.

Tranch Claverlay was not at all what Cordelia had expected when he came in with Granger. Though forty-five, he looked much younger—tall and fit, with blond hair and merry blue eyes. His manner was so affable that Cordelia would have thought he was a salesman rather than a writer.

"Mrs. Lovejoy!" He took her hand in both of his, then let it go and raised his arms, as if to embrace her, all the time warming her so with his gaze that she almost wished he would embrace. "I've heard wonderful things about you. But I'd no idea you were so young—so beautiful!"

Mary sighed deeply, and Maude murmured, "Well, my word and honor!"

Granger got Cordelia aside quickly. He was in a sweat, brow beaded despite the cold day. "Cordelia"—speaking in an agonized whisper—"Tranch arrived last night in a rage. He blamed Lovejoy's for not even trying to sell *Dark Pageant*. Threatens to move to Hal at David and Smith."

"I expect he'd have done that already if he really wanted to," Cordelia said. "But when Hal left, he had the decency not to pressure him to change publishers. If he wants to go, don't try to keep him."

Granger squared his shoulders. "But my reputation as an editor is at stake. He blames *me* because his book won't sell."

"Why should you care? Edward used to say that all publishers know all authors blame everybody but themselves when their books don't sell."

"Of course there are extenuating circumstances in the way he feels. He's upset in his personal life. Says he's divorcing his wife."

"Really? Now that's interesting. In all my life I've never known a couple to get divorced. How's he arranging it?"

"How should I know, for God's sake?"

When they joined the others, Suzanna was asking Tranch, "How could you bear to leave your family on Christmas Eve?"

"How could I bear not to?" he replied.

Suzanna had recently lost ten pounds (though Nick had told Cordelia she must lose twenty before he'd consider marrying her), but the way her jaw sagged at his reply endowed her with an extra chin.

"Miss Neiswander," he went on, "you'd have to know my wife to understand how impossible she is. It's why I'm getting a divorce—because she's so impossible, I mean."

No one could think what to say till Cordelia finally spoke: "We New Yorkers are basically provincial, Mr. Claverlay. I don't think any of us knows anyone who has obtained a divorce. Conditions must be more—more advanced in your state of Maryland. How do you go about it?"

Tranch waved a hand airily. "Oh, I'm leaving that up to my lawyer. That's why one has a lawyer, you know. Janet—my wife—is all for it."

"Then she didn't mind your leaving home on Christmas Eve?" Maude asked.

"She was *de*-lighted," Tranch said. "She's prone to vulgar language, and I won't repeat all she said. But just to give you a notion, since the children have run out of the room at the moment, Janet said, 'I'll be so goddamn glad not to have to attend another goddamn Christmas family gathering I'll celebrate by sleeping till noon.' Go, she kept urging me. 'Go to New York and never come back!' "

"Such blasphemy!" Mary exclaimed.

"The disloyalty of the woman amounts to downright

infidelity," he went on. "Do you know what I discovered about her? I presented her with a copy of my last novel, *Dark Pageant of Triumph*, six weeks ago and—"

He paused to accept their words of praise for the book, though no one present except Granger, who was paid to do such things, had read it from beginning to end.

"Well, night before last I discovered that Janet *had not read more than two chapters of the novel*!"

"Incredible," said Cordelia, thinking that Janet sounded like a bright, interesting woman.

"Isn't it, though?" Tranch responded. "How's that for loyalty? And she said some remarkably unkind things about the book, too. *How dared she*?" He turned to Granger. "You remember how Mr. Howells praised it in the *Atlantic*?"

"Mr. Claverlay," asked Tim, "how be ye're children takin' this divorce?"

"Oh, they haven't heard about it yet. But they won't care. We have two sons aged—let me see—nineteen, no twenty, and twenty-two now. They couldn't take college. Most troublesome children ever born. It really was a relief when they left home. Neither has been back in almost a year. They're at sea. Literally, I mean, as sailors. Good for 'em to get the wanderlust out of their systems. Went through the same thing myself. But I've carried on too much about my own selfish concerns. Mrs. Lovejoy, it's so kind of you to invite me here today with all these good people. . . ."

Once he got off the subjects of his wife and his novel, he was the most delightful guest Cordelia ever had entertained. He had traveled nearly everywhere and, when lubricated by the glass after glass of wine which Nick poured for him throughout dinner, told dozens of fascinating anecdotes.

Somehow Cordelia felt he was talking only to her.

He was lavish in his praise of her dinner and gallant in all his remarks. But perhaps what she liked most about Tranch Claverlay was how well he got along with the children and how much they obviously liked him. How strange that he'd had trouble with his own sons. And as for his wife—she sounded like a harridan he would be well rid of when he got his divorce.

As he and Granger were leaving late in the afternoon he said, "Mrs. Lovejoy, publishers are forever entertaining authors. So good of you, Granger, to be putting me up at the Astor House."

"Well," Granger said in the preoccupied tone of one computing entertainment expenses.

"So for a change," Tranch said, "an author is going to entertain a publisher. Mrs. Lovejoy, *you* are going to by *my* guest at the Astor for lunch tomorrow."

"Well," Granger said.

"Not you, Granger," Tranch said. "I'm entertaining you another time. Mrs. Lovejoy, would half past twelve be convenient in the main dining room?"

"I'd be delighted." She meant it. Tranch Claverlay struck her as the most interesting man she'd met since Edward Lovejoy let her have a bite of his ice cream.

Cordelia was on hand at the Astor five minutes before the appointed hour. A maitre d' seated her, and then she waited—and waited. At twenty minutes to one a bellhop came in paging her.

"Mr. Clavercal"—that was how the hop pronounced the name—"asks you to telephone his suite, ma'am."

As she went to the lobby she thought, *suite*? Did all Lovejoy authors have suites rather than rooms at company expense? However, Tranch was their very best-selling author.

The Astor House had recently connected telephones in suites with the reception desk. Cordelia, who had never had the opportunity to use a telephone before, approached it gingerly. "Don't touch it till I tell you to," a clerk warned her. Then he began shouting into it: "Mr. Caverslay? Mr. Caverslay?" He whirled to her. "Now!"

Putting the receiver to her ear, she shrieked into the mouthpiece: "Yes! Yes! What is it?"

"Bu-da-ber-derp-ah-hoot-du-ber," replied the telephone. At least she thought that was what she heard. She spoke indignantly to the clerk: "I can't understand what this thing is saying."

"Let me try." The clerk negotiated patiently with the innovation and at last told Cordelia: "Mr. Coverstill regrets to inform you he is ill, ma'm, and requests the honor of your coming to his suite."

"Honor?" asked Cordelia.

"That's what the gentleman said, ma'm."

"Oh, I couldn't do that." Then, recalling Tranch's best-selling status and thinking he might be gravely ill: "What is the number?"

When she knocked on his door, his voice came faintly: "Come in."

He was not in the living room of the suite, but spoke from the bedroom, whose door was open. "I'm in here, Cordelia dear."

She stepped to the doorway and looked in at him. He lay on his back, eyes closed and chin pointed at the ceiling, like an unreconstructed corpse.

"What's wrong?" she asked him.

"I feel wan." He kept his eyes closed.

Thinking that he looked mainly Don Juan, she said, "I'm sorry. Shall I call a doctor?"

"No," he said, "I'm a Christian Scientist."

"A what?"

"Haven't you heard of Mary Baker Eddy?"

"Oh, yes."

"No doctor. My religion forbids it. I'll feel better soon. Been working very hard. At my new novel. When I got up this morning and went back to work at it, I felt faint and had to return to bed."

She observed that, faint though he had been, he had found strength to shave and put on a lotion that smelled pleasantly of lilies of the valley.

"Sit down," he said, "and I'll tell you about my new novel."

She looked around for a chair, but he patted his bed and said, "Sit here. Don't you care about my new novel? Don't you want to be the editor of it?"

"Of course I do, Tranch. I'm so deeply honored you'd—"

"Then please take off that goddamn overcoat and sit *down*." She complied, and he said, "For the new book I'm going quite modern. There's a lot of research involved and I'll need a bigger advance." He took both her hands in both of his. "Is that all right with you, Cordelia?"

She was trying to remember what had been the advance on his last novel and forgot to remove her hands.

"Well, Tranch—"

He was handsome in a virile way that Granger was not, but of course that had nothing to do with the amount of his advance on the next novel.

"What is the theme?"

"Love!" He squeezed her hands. "A more passionate romance than I've yet wrote—written. Do you think I write love scenes well?"

She thought they were only mediocre, but she said, "Very well indeed. But what is the—uh—background of this love story?"

"The Spanish-American War. Is that going to be too personal for you to take, dear Cordelia?"

"No, why should it be?"

"I was thinking of Edward. He was a great and good friend of mine and I'll never forget him."

Neither would she, but he had receded now into history. She never would try to explain that to anyone, however.

"Oh, Cordelia, life is such a lonely business. We pass each other like horsemen in a dense morning mist. It would be so much better if we paused in our passages and said, 'How are you? Let us be friends.' "

She recognized that he had stolen that line from his novel before last—at the moment she couldn't think of the title. It had not seemed very effective to her then, but somehow it sounded a bit better now.

Tranch let a hand fall upon her thigh and began to caress it slowly. Nothing as pleasant had happened to her since Edward went away, and she knew she was in danger of being a damn fool. Clasping a big hand around her neck, Tranch drew her head down to his and kissed her. She found herself responding.

"Oh, lovely, lovely Cordelia," he murmured, "what a wonderful editor you're going to be. The best I've ever had. Does it seem warm to you in here?"

Frankly it felt hot as hell, but she did not say so.

"Take off some of that warm clothing," he told her.

"Oh, I couldn't do that," she said. "What do you take me for?"

"A wonderful editor. A beautiful, lonely woman as I am a terribly lonely and badly misunderstood man." His naked arms drew her to him.

She found herself writhing, less from a desire to escape his hold than a wish to be more comfortable in it. Suddenly she realized that her big bush of a hat was pinned firmly on her head. It struck her as so absurd to be seduced with her hat on that it amounted almost to an obscenity—whereas seduction should be beautiful instead of obscene.

Fighting free of Tranch's arms, she found the pin and yanked it loose, sending it flying in one direction and the hat in the other. He, thinking she intended to escape from him, floundered out of bed, uttering plaintive, birdlike sounds. But the astonishing thing about their confrontation was that he was stark naked and his erect penis was aimed at her as irresistibly as a pistol aimed at one bent on suicide.

"Oh, I'm so sorry!" he gasped. "But my need for you, Cordelia, is like—like—" He was fresh out of similes. "I *need* you, my dear!"

"That's all right. These things happen."

"Of course they do. Quite against our plans or our wishes they happen."

She surrendered herself to a pleasure she had not quite forgotten.

* * *

Later, while she was dressing, the altogether surprising thing was that she felt no guilt, no shame. Instead, she had a sense of joy and peace such as must come to one released from prison.

"You're wonderful, just wonderful." Tranch sat up in bed, looking as self-satisfied as a cock robin that had just swallowed the fattest worm. "Do you think I'm a good lover?"

Now why, she wondered, did he have to spoil it by saying a thing like that? "Oh, yes," she murmured. As a matter of fact, he was not nearly as good as Edward had been—too quick, too concerned with his own satisfaction, too insensitive to hers.

"Then you really think I'm a great lover?" he asked again, goddamn him.

She gave a short answer: "Yes, I said yes."

"I'll have room service bring us up a meal," he said, "and we'll talk about the new novel. There's one thing I must ask for. I need a bigger advance this time, my dear."

"How much did you get last time?"

"Thirty-five hundred."

"How much do you want this time?"

"Forty-five hundred."

"Why are you worth a thousand more this time?"

"Well." He took on a smug look.

Did he really believe, she thought, that his phallus was worth a thousand?

"Why are you putting on your hat?" he asked.

"Because I have to go home now."

"But we haven't had lunch yet and it will soon be time for dinner. May I see you this evening?"

"No, I'm occupied with my children this evening." Now she could not wait to get out of there. She had recovered everything that belonged to her except her goddamn hatpin, which she could not find anywhere.

"What about after the children go to bed? Could you slip back here and—"

"No!" She would stop looking for the hatpin, because if she found it she might stab Lovejoy's leading author with it. "Goodbye, Tranch."

"How about a little kiss?"

"I'm in a hurry." Someone more astute than he, she thought, would have realized she never would kiss him again. On the other hand, someone more astute than she never would have kissed him in the first place.

She must not look as composed as she wished to, for the elevator operator gazed at her twice—three times. And then, as she stepped from the elevator into the lobby, she came face to face with Jack Morgan.

"Cordelia!" he exclaimed. "How are you? It's been a long time." He was flanked by two young men who must be assistants of some kind by the way they hovered protectively and frowned at her, as if she had accosted the Great Man when in reality she would have given a lot to escape from him.

She said something trite while his face took on a slightly amused look and his searching gaze seemed to read all her secrets. Her stupid hat must be slipping and her hair must be disheveled, she thought. No detail was too small to escape J. P. Morgan: not even a woman emerging from a hotel elevator in mid-afternoon with her hatpin missing.

Glad to escape his scrutiny, she hastened to the ladies' room and searched her reflection in a mirror. After arranging her hair and giving the woman attendant a nickel for a cheap hatpin, she left the hotel and started downtown through light snow.

She did not want to go home or to the office; she was not hungry or tired or happy or unhappy; she did not want to see anyone she knew. Under different social conditions she would have gone someplace and bought herself a drink, but it was impossible for a lady to do that. She was simply floating among the currents of holiday-season pedestrians.

It was a raw, unpleasant winter afternoon and a bad smell pervaded the city. There had been a fire the night before which had burned out nearly two blocks of Hell's Kitchen before firemen brought it under control. Eight had died and scores were homeless. A hardy band of the homeless had marched to the old Bible House in search of help, but all they'd got there was coffee and doughnuts. So they'd gone on to the Labor Temple, where they'd got nothing. Undaunted, several had made their way to the First Presbyterian Church parish house where the assistant minister, mistaking their mood as ugly and frightened by them, had given them ten dollars. Since all of them were Roman Catholics anyway, they'd gone next to the prosperous Church of St. Alphonsus on Fifth Avenue and asked a priest if they could sleep there. "Git on wid ye," the Irish priest had replied. "A Catholic church is not a place for sleeping. The Blessed Sacrament is here. And we've had to git rid of half the cleanin' help. Don't ye know there's a business recession agin?"

Cordelia, still not wanting to go home, went into the tearoom of the Fifth Avenue Hotel where a woman could decently sit alone. There was a rack of magazines and newspapers from which a woman could make a selection so that she did not have to stare vacantly at other lonely women. Cordelia selected the *Century Magazine* to scan while she sipped coffee and ate a pastry. In it she came across the strangest coincidence of this strange day. A Boston lawyer named Louis D. Brandeis warned that "neither our intelligence nor our characters can long stand the strain of unrestricted power." And then he bemused Cordelia by giving this example of how money and power were held in a very few hands:

J. P. Morgan (or a partner), a director of the New York, New Haven & Hartford Railroad, causes that company to sell J. P. Morgan & Co. an issue of bonds; J. P. Morgan & Co. borrow the money with which to pay for the bonds from the Guaranty Trust Company, of which Mr. Morgan (or a partner) is a director. J. P. Morgan & Co. sells the bonds to the Penn Mutual Life Insurance Company of which Mr. Morgan (or a partner) is a director. The New Haven spends the proceeds of the bonds in purchasing steel rails from the United States Steel Corporation, of which Mr. Morgan (or a partner) is a director. The United States Steel Corporation spends the proceeds of the rails in purchasing electrical supplies from the General Electric Company of which Mr. Morgan (or a partner) is a director. . . .

Cordelia stayed away from the office again next day. Late in the afternoon a messenger brought her a note from Tranch written on Lovejoy's stationery. Its tone was a mixture of apology and longing. "With great melancholy I'm returning to my hermitage on the Eastern Shore after waiting about the office nearly all day in the vain hope you would return and I could see you. . . . I continue to pray that you will be my editor, as I have told Granger, and that we will see each other again when I come back to New York in the spring. Do write me at my personal postal box. . . ."

She did not write him. She never wanted to see him again.

When she returned to the office the following day, Granger did not appear and sent no word by messenger, as he usually did when confined at home with one of his numerous colds. The day after that, when there still was no word from him by ten o'clock, she sent Runyon to investigate. He reported back that Granger would not open up in response to his bell-ringing, but had spoken through the door in a weak, depressed voice, saying he was very ill. Cordelia clapped on her hat and rushed off to Washington Square by hansom. Suppose Granger died? She admitted that her next thought was selfish: She needed an editor-in-chief and didn't know where to turn for one as knowledgeable.

Bolting up the stairs to his second-floor flat, she rang and rang the bell. No answer. Feeling that she somehow would lose all dignity if she pounded on his door, she rang the bell once more. At last his voice came faintly: "Yes? Who is it?"

"Messenger." She made her voice pipe like a boy's.

"Slip it under the door," Granger said.

"It won't fit, sir. Too big. And I need a receipt."

The door was unlocked and pulled open; Granger, unshaven and looking wretched, gaped at her.

"Granger," she demanded, "why aren't you at work?"

"There's no message?" His voice quavered somewhat.

"No, I just made that up."

"You Jezebel!" he cried suddenly. "You Delilah! You've made me ill." He backed away from her across the room.

"Halt!" she shouted. "Halt, you—you damn editor!"

But he kept backing along a little hall while she followed slowly. "You have no right to invade my house this way!" Tears started to his eyes. "You've no idea what it's like having to work for you! You—strip a person of all dignity. Cordelia, you're just *awful!*"

She felt stricken by his criticism. She hoped he would explain what she specifically could do to be better.

"Please!" His voice rose suddenly in a kind of shriek. "Look at you! You've followed me into my very bedroom!"

Well, by God, so she had. What was this new custom of hers of wandering into men's bedrooms? Yet somehow there didn't seem anything improper about it this time. Maybe it was because the walls of this bedroom were lined with books. It was as if she had walked into a man's library instead of his bedroom. Granger slept with books. As Runyon had reported, the entire flat was filled with books which gave off a musty odor. If decadence had a smell, this would be it—like old chamber pots in a derelict country house. Maybe that ancient canard was true after all: that Italian bookbinders really did treat their calfskin with urine.

"Why do you call me Jezebel?" she asked. "Why Delilah?"

"Because you *betrayed* me!" he cried. "You want to be Tranch's editor. You're taking him from me!"

She let herself slump. "Oh, Jesus Christ, Granger. I'm sorry, I know you don't like cursing, but as Edward used to say—Jesus *H*. Christ! I didn't ask to be Tranch's editor. He asked *me*."

"What did he say against me?" Granger demanded.

"He didn't say anything against you. He just—for Lord's sake, take back Tranch and welcome to him."

Granger brightened. "You mean it?"

"Why would I say it if I didn't mean it?"

"Because people seldom mean what they say."

"All right, Granger." Cordelia suddenly felt very tired. "Please stop this pouting and come back to work as soon as you can."

He returned next morning, acting as if nothing unusual had happened. That afternoon he invited her to dinner and a lecture by a noted Egyptologist at the Harvard Club the following Monday.

It was the dullest lecture ever; she dozed off in the midst of it, but did not make a display of herself as did the president of the Harvard Club, an eminent banker, who, while dozing, fell out of his chair with a frightening crash.

In the hansom on the way home Granger asked to come in. "I have a very important question to ask you."

She was very sleepy, but braced herself in a chair while he paced back and forth before the fireplace. At last he spoke:

"I would be deeply honored, Cordelia, if you'd consent to be my wife."

Suddenly she was wide awake. "Granger, this is very sudden."

"Oh, I don't want to rush you. One must think carefully about such an important step, and I've been thinking about it a long time."

She made a little face. "You disguise passion well."

"Passion?" He looked around at her with some surprise. "Ah, yes. But I offer some good reasons. I think I get along well with your children."

Actually, they were indifferent to him because he never said or did anything that interested them.

"Then there's the social aspect," Granger said. "You would lead a more active social life if escorted by a husband."

"That's true."

"Concerning that," he went on, "there's a special problem involved. Socially you're avoided sometimes, Cordelia, not because of any fault in your person, but because publishers and editors don't know what to make of a woman being the president of a house. I guess you can understand that."

"I guess so."

"Now if a man like myself were the president of Lovejoy and Son, if your *husband* were—"

So he wanted to marry her so that *he* could be the president.

She got to her feet, prepared to dismiss him angrily. But he mistook her action for an affirmative gesture.

He turned, and his arms went about her awkwardly. They were like brittle sticks. She felt alarm in realizing she was physically stronger than he. She extricated herself from his awkwardness in a manner which could not be construed as passionate.

"You must give me time to think about this, Granger."

"Yes, yes, I don't mean to rush you into a decision."

After a decent interval of several days she told him that she must regretfully say no, she could not marry again. Rather than being hurt, Granger seemed to be somewhat relieved.

In March, Marie Dorfman fell ill with some malady that neither Dr. Prettyman nor the consultants he called in could diagnose satisfactorily. She lingered into April, then died.

Meantime Cordelia worried about Mary. Her pregnancy was difficult, and when it seemed that she must lose her child Dr. Prettyman ordered her to bed. Cordelia kept the household going with a series of indifferent servants until Dr. Prettyman delivered Mary of a baby girl on July 14, 1902.

"A daughter," Mary said weakly in gray morning light after Dr. Prettyman had left and the nurse was bathing the child. " 'Tis a son we wanted."

"Na, na," Tim said. "A b'y next time, a girl this. An' her name is Cordelia."

"No," Cordelia said.

"Yes," Mary said. "We planned it so."

Cordelia was highly pleased, but said, "It'll lead to confusion with two Cordelias in the house."

"Cordelia it is!" Tim crowed.

He went down Lexington to buy talcum powder, but friends diverted him to a saloon on Third Avenue to celebrate fatherhood. The celebration, meant to be brief, grew long, and Tim forgot to go to work. Friends carried him home at eleven o'clock in the morning, and Cordelia, who did not go to the office so that she could be with Mary, had them hide Tim's body in the cellar out of Mary's sight. A few minutes later Mr. Hart, as was his custom when an employee failed to appear, sent a messenger with word that Tim was fired.

Cordelia marched down to the store. Her manner was so forceful that she was quickly brought before the great man himself, as she demanded.

"What," she began, "is the meaning of your firing a poor man who early this morning saved two young children from death in a burning building and still lies unconscious from inhaling smoke?" It was a long sentence, but Cordelia shot it off without pausing for breath.

Before she left she had so cowed Mr. Hart that he granted Tim two days off at full pay.

She was crossing Park Avenue on her way home when a coach stopped and Mamie Fish hailed her out the window: "Cordelia, how you do stride along."

"How are you, Mamie?"

"I'm fine, but Stuyvesant has been suffering the tortures with kidney stones. He's feeling better now. Guess the doctors managed to melt them or something. While recuperating he's been enjoying the historical novels of one of your authors—the chap with the ridiculous name I never can remember."

"Tranch Claverlay?"

"That's the one. Do you know him well?"

"We've met."

"I plan a small dinner next Wednesday in honor of Stuyvesant's recovery. Is there any chance you could come and bring along this Tranch fellow? Stuyvesant would love to meet him."

"I'm afraid not, Mamie. He has a hermitage in Maryland and practically never comes to the city. And he's a dreadful social bore."

"How too bad," Mrs. Fish said. "Stuyvesant will be interested to hear that. He had the notion from reading his work that the man must be something of a gay and witty blade."

"Sorry to disappoint Stuyvesant," Cordelia said.

Cordelia managed never to see Tranch Claverlay again.

13

There was a Russian Jewish immigrant who worked Murray Hill with a pushcart collecting junk which the rich people threw out. He was a big, tough man named Ipl, but since no American could exist with a name like that and since this junkman wanted very much to be a regular American, he took the name of Israel Epstein. His wife was dead and he had one son, likewise named Israel, who lived with him in a Hester Street basement on the Lower East Side and helped him on Murray Hill.

In June of 1903 the son was eleven years old, big for his age, tough like his father. They had to be tough in order to hold onto their beat. Murray Hill was an area coveted by junkmen who often fought one another for the loot. The two Izzys, as they were called, had some magnificent fist and knee fights with competitors who tried to invade the territory they had staked out for themselves. Because they were fearless and tougher, the Epsteins always won, providing great entertainment for the goys who watched the fights out their windows.

Young Izzy was something of a showman. Once he'd helped his father push the cart up the steepest slant of Lexington Avenue, he usually would walk ahead as the cart clattered through the side streets, noisily beating an iron triangle and shouting, "Any rags, any bones, any bottles today? There's a big Jew ragpicker comin' this way!" His cries were effective—maybe because people liked the fact that the Epsteins admitted to being exactly what they were: Jew ragpickers. Nearly all directed their servants to give old newspapers, bedsteads, carpeting, and the like only to "the Izzys."

Everybody on Murray Hill knew who they were, yet no one but Penny tried to strike up intimate friendship. Penny had been a wanderer from the time she learned to walk; Mary or someone had to keep constant watch lest she follow some wagon or stranger to the ends of the earth. Why the Izzys took her fancy that summer she was eight she was not at first certain. But they did: Maybe it was the cavalcade, the wagon train, winding into the land of child's dreams. One day she just started following the Izzys. Children sometimes did that, but old Izzy always turned them back, fiercely, if necessary. Their mothers or nurses appreciated his doing so, for nothing was more nerve-wracking than a missing child, and old Izzy knew that a pack of children following his cart involved a waste of time that was bad for business.

Never, however, had he had such a persistent follower as Penny started out to be. She was not at all frightened by his fiercest noises, faces, and gesticulations. At last he had to have young Izzy take her by the hand and lead her back to 127 (more lost time, old Izzy grumbled). He spoke about her to Mary, who promised to lock her in the house, if necessary, when the Izzys passed. But a couple of days later Penny contrived to escape. She followed the Izzys along Thirty-sixth to Park, and then up Park to Thirty-seventh, where old Izzy angrily ordered his son to take that child home again.

Cordelia, returning home early that afternoon, came upon them at the corner of Thirty-sixth Street as Izzy led Penny along by the hand. "She broke out again, Mrs. Lovejoy." When he grinned a gap appeared where he had lost two teeth in a fight. "Here she is. G'bye, Penny."

"Why do you keep doing that?" Cordelia asked crossly as she and Penny walked on toward home.

"You're eight years old and you shouldn't be acting like a four-year-old."

Penny began to weep silently.

"What's the matter?" Cordelia asked.

"But I love him, Mama."

"You love who?"

"Izzy."

Cordelia was startled. "Why?"

"I dunno why, I just love him. He has those missing teeth and people call him the Jew boy and when he takes my hand and leads me home his hand has watchamacallits—"

"Calluses," Cordelia said. "Well, Penny, I can see what you mean, but there's something you've got to understand. You're getting along toward becoming a young lady soon. You know that."

Penny stopped weeping and nodded.

"And the point about being a young lady such as you want to be is that you don't show how you feel. It's all right to love Izzy if you want to, but just keep it to yourself."

Penny gave a deep sigh. "But I wonder if it's as much fun being a young lady as everyone pretends."

The following week Cordelia rented a house on Long Island where she and the children would stay until their public-school classes reopened after Labor Day. Mary and little Cora (as they called young Cordelia) would go with them, and Tim could visit on his Sundays off.

The house she rented for fifty dollars a month was on the Long Island north shore near a village called Hastings and only a mile from the railroad line which ran out from Brooklyn. It turned out to be an extraordinary old clapboard house of fourteen rooms with a huge verandah around two sides, the entirety scalloped and gingerbreaded with fretwork. The house and its large stable were set in one hundred sixty acres, with untilled fields divided by stone walls rolling back from a small beach and marshlands to pine woods. Cordelia loved it the instant she saw it, and the children were ecstatic. Even the closets of the old house were permeated with wonderful smells of saltwater and bayberry and pine and woodrot.

Steve, who could not say "Hastings," called the place "Hasty's," and his sisters began to call it that, too. At the end of summer Cordelia would buy house and land for three thousand dollars, and always after, the Lovejoys never referred to it as the farm or the summer place or the north shore house but as Hasty's.

The day before they began their complicated trek to the country (a dog, a cat, a canary, and four goldfish had to be transported along with numerous trunks and other things), Cordelia received a three-word note from Maude:

IT IS DONE!

Maude referred, Cordelia knew, to the novel at which she'd been toiling for a year and a half. All that time she had continued working as a store clerk. Except on holidays, when Cordelia usually invited her to dinner, they saw each other rarely.

There was a great change in Maude. She admitted to a tremendous struggle, but she appeared to have won the battle against Demon Rum. In the course of it she had lost weight and improved her hair and dress. Though forty-nine that summer, she looked younger and no longer was garrulous, as she once had been.

"Conquest of the bottle is the greatest thing in the world to improve a woman's character," Mary declaimed.

"Don't say that," Cordelia replied. "It means a woman must take to the bottle in order to conquer the bottle."

None of this was of as much consequence in Maude's mind as the answer to the burning question: What kind of novel had she written?

Cordelia sent Steve to Maude's boardinghouse, giving her directions on how to get to the country place and inviting her there the following Sunday: "Be sure and bring the novel and plan to leave it so that I can read it."

When Maude walked up the dusty road from the station that Sunday morning, she lugged a loaded, ancient portmanteau, as if intending to spend a fortnight. It contained little except her manuscript—more than fifteen hundred pages of carefully written script. Cordelia looked at it with dismay.

"But I like the title," she said. "*Side Street.*"

She began reading it that very morning and did not want to put it down when Mary summoned everybody to one o'clock Sunday dinner. The story of two different women struggling for survival and success in New York at the turn of the century was not Flaubert—yet neither was it the former Maude Mudge of the Sunday School tracts.

Around three o'clock in the afternoon the children began fretting at Cordelia to take them to the beach so they could go swimming.

"Maude, you take them," Cordelia said.

"What do you think?" Maude asked anxiously, staring at the manuscript.

"I think you must be careful not to let any of my children drown."

When Maude herded the reluctant children back from the beach a couple of hours later, Cordelia told her:

"You've written a wonderful novel. It's much too long, but together we can cut it. Your store-clerking days are over, Maude. Lovejoy's is publishing this book on its next spring list. Go to New York on the morning train and check out of your job and boardinghouse and come back here as fast as you can. You and I have a lot of work to do on this book."

Maude wept.

Just one week after she returned to spend the rest of the summer, the man who delivered milk, groceries, and necessities every day pulled up in a victoria instead of his customary buggy.

"Looks like you've started a boardinghouse for ladies," he said to Cordelia. "See what I brung ya."

His passenger was Suzanna Neiswander. She was fatter than ever, and the moment she saw Cordelia she burst into tears.

"Can you take me in, dear Cordelia? I'll pay you anything."

"This 'pears like an expensive boarder," the driver said, looking Suzanna over.

Suzanna cried harder. "I've run away."

"From where?" asked the driver.

"Newport."

"Come in, Suzanna." Cordelia embraced her. "You, sir," she told the driver, "hand down my friend's luggage and stop your gratuitous comments. Then take those groceries round to the back door."

Suzanna explained that she'd learned where Cordelia was from Tim at 127. "I came here because Daddy's New York house is closed for the summer and I can't think of anywhere else to go."

"Do your parents know where you are?"

"They think I'm at the Newport house. But they don't care anyway. They're in Europe for the summer and weren't at all keen I go with 'em. I just *had* to leave Newport."

After Cordelia had settled Suzanna into one of the many bedrooms, she said, "Several years ago I felt *I* had to leave Newport—and I've never regretted it."

"Why did you have to get out of there?"

Cordelia pondered a while, planning her lie. "I never told you because—well, I guess the reason will be apparent. Suzanna, when I was young I was terribly fat."

"*You* fat? You're the sveltest woman I know. As fat as me?"

Cordelia nodded. "At Newport I thought I was in love with a boy—a young man—and then I overheard him say, 'Who wants to be seen with that fat-ass?' It killed me."

Suzanna clapped a hand to her fat cheek. "You, *too?* You heard almost the same thing I did?"

Cordelia nodded gravely.

"But what did you do? How did you get yourself to look like you are now?"

"*I stopped eating.*"

"Didn't you get faint and giddy?"

"Whenever I did I'd drink a glass of water and have a bite of fresh fruit or green vegetable."

"But what did you do at mealtimes when everybody sat down at the table?"

"I'd go for a long walk and not come back till mealtime was over."

Suzanna breathed deeply. "I'll try. This time I'll really try because if I don't I might as well die."

And she did try.

Maude and Cordelia worked mornings at cutting and making some revisions in *Side Street*. In the afternoons Cordelia hiked with Suzanna and bathed and gardened. Then, deciding to resume her favorite sport of riding, she rented a couple of geldings and stabled them on the farm. Suzanna became an enthusiastic rider, and together they taught the children the basics of riding. At this sport Eunice was the best, Steve the worst.

Although Cordelia did not know how to sail, she wanted her children to learn, and so she found a young man with a little sloop who was glad to make some money teaching them the sailor's art. At sailing Steve was the best, Eunice the worst, while Penny was indifferent to both riding and sailing.

That summer Cordelia began to pay closer attention to the directions in which the children appeared to be heading. To her annoyance, Eunice was in danger of becoming a snob. Hard as Cordelia tried, she could not make her overcome her superior ways. Eunice did not care enough about people; she cared only how they dressed and performed, as if they were merely dolls on a puppet stage. Already Eunice was nagging at her about entering Miss Troy's when she became fourteen. Miserable though Cordelia thought that education was, it seemed the only thing that Eunice wanted.

Penny, on the other hand, was such a democratic spirit that she was forever getting herself into scrapes that a trace of Eunice's snobbery could have avoided. Cordelia hoped that Penny would attend a good women's college, though she could not tell if that was what Penny wanted.

Neither could she tell yet where Steve's greatest interests lay. Thank heavens he was bright—the brightest of the three, she thought—and could handle the best possible education. That was very important, for Steve was the one destined to guide Lovejoy and Son someday.

Maude completed her revision of *Side Street* on Sunday, August twentieth. It was the day Suzanna brought her weight down another pound on the scale to which she acted as devotedly as a devout Catholic to the Cross.

"One nineteen!" she crowed at dinner while picking at a small salad. "Down fifty-four pounds in thirty-six days. How much is that a day?"

"Precisely one and a half pounds," said Nick, who had come to visit them for the third consecutive weekend. "Eunice, dear, please pass the butter."

"Why don't you congratulate Suzanna on the marvelous way she's lost weight?" Cordelia said to him.

"I have," Nick said. "I've congratulated her every weekend on her—recovery. Just sorry I won't be here next weekend." He was leaving the following day for Chicago, where he was helping to open a branch office of the brokerage house. "But I'll be back in five, six weeks and—" He smiled benevolently on Suzanna.

After Suzanna left next morning to take Nick to the station in a livery rig, Cordelia remarked how lovely she had become.

"If Nick really means to marry her," Maude said, "he'd better stop acting so smug, or some other man will marry her off right from under his nose."

Later Cordelia said she hadn't realized Maude was a prophet. For, when Suzanna returned from the station in the livery rig an hour later, she had another passenger. His name was Jim Farnol and he was on his way to visit an uncle who lived farther east along the shore. He was ten years younger than Nick and (Cordelia thought) ten times as handsome and, most important of all, he treated Suzanna as if she were the most beautiful woman in the world.

Suzanna drove Jim on to his uncle's, but in a couple of hours he was back driving another rig and he and Suzanna went sailing. He stayed for dinner, and then he and Suzanna went sailing again. Long after darkness had fallen his infectious laugh and his playing of "Dixie" on his harmonica drifted up to the house where Maude and Cordelia rocked on the side porch.

"Good-bye, Nick," Maude said.

"Never count out a Dorfman," Cordelia said, but her tone lacked conviction.

She didn't want to return to town. Now that she had decided to buy Hasty's she wished she never had to leave it. But the children must go back to school, and there were affairs to attend to at Lovejoy's—or were there? She had not made a trip to the city all summer, and presumably Lovejoy's was getting along perfectly well without her.

Maude's novel was what impelled her to start back to New York. So often Granger did not share her enthusiasm for a manuscript, but this time she believed he would. He must read it before he left at the end of September on his annual six-weeks' pilgrimage to London in order to buy titles for Lovejoy's. Cordelia agreed with Maude that the manuscript should be submitted to him under an assumed name since he never had liked Maude's work. Hope Traymore was the pseudonym Maude had chosen.

The day after they returned to the city Cordelia presented the manuscript to Granger with an eloquent endorsement. Indeed she was so convinced of its success that, unknown to Granger, she arranged with Marty to put Maude on a "drawing account." This would support her with a regular monthly income while she wrote her next novel and the money would be deducted from her later royalties. With this assurance Maude moved into a better boardinghouse higher on Murray Hill.

More than a week later Granger strolled into Cordelia's office one afternoon, placed the manuscript of *Side Street* on a corner of her desk, and said, "I don't share your enthusiasm for this."

"Oh?" She stared at him.

"This sort of naturalism falls awfully flat with me—and with the reading public. I know there are people who lead such drab, struggling lives, but—well, Cordelia, there's no poetry in these lives."

"No *poetry*?" she exclaimed. "What kind of *poetry* would you expect in the lives of people at the edge of the slums who are striving to move up to a better side street?"

Granger smiled airily. "I wouldn't know. And this

author, Hope Traymore—who is she?—can't make me
care. She has some narrative talent, but she should apply it to a story which has more—well, optimism. No,
my dear, this one is not for us."

He walked out while Cordelia gritted her teeth and
gripped the arm of her chair. She went home seething
and scarcely slept that night. In the morning she took
the manuscript back to the office and called in young
Jerry Newcomb, a new reader. He was glad to do her a
favor and knew she must have her own good reason for
not wanting Granger to know she had asked him to
read this manuscript.

Jerry must have stayed up all night finishing it because he looked somewhat bleary the following morning
when he brought Cordelia his reader's report. It was a
rave.

"But I can see a problem," he told her. "This just
isn't a Granger book."

"What *is* a Granger book?"

"Well"—Jerry made vague waving motions—"you
know."

"Yes, I know," Cordelia said. "Swinburne in the sub-
urbs."

This time there was no question about her overruling
Granger. The only question was how to do it. She could
wait until he sailed for England, then put the book into
production, and break the news to him gently after he
came back. (Maybe his ship would sink!) Of course
that would be cowardly, but she truly was a coward
when it came to confronting Granger. She had accepted
his judgments for so long that she had convinced herself
he could not be wrong about anything. She was dependent on him, and thus she was afraid to cross him. She
must overcome her fear.

Fearfully she went into his office and said in a faint,
squeaky voice, "I think we should publish *Side Street*."

"*Side Street*? Oh yes, I remember. By what's-her-name." He gave his most-jovial smile. "No, my dear Cordelia, this time I must overrule you."

She smiled bravely in reply. "Wrong, my dear Granger. This time *I* must overrule *you*."

The color drained from his face as he got slowly to his feet. "Do you want my resignation?" he cried.

"If necessary, yes." At last she felt fully in control of herself.

"Do you know what you're doing, Mrs. Lovejoy?"

"I think so, *Mr*. Cantwell. But I'm not sure that you do."

He made a sound like steam escaping from an engine. Then he walked around his desk with odd, jerky steps, picked his hat off the tree in the corner, and went out, slamming the door behind him.

She thought he might not return. But he was back next day, pale and grim and avoiding her. Cordelia put *Side Street* into production, and he did not mention the book again.

14

That fall Cordelia did not go to the pier to see Granger off to England, as she had in previous years. Before his ship had passed the Statue of Liberty she was hard at work with Marty in the most thorough sales survey the company ever had undertaken.

She knew that she was prospering, that personal profits had enabled her to pay off the mortgage of 127, buy Hasty's outright, purchase stock in Standard Oil and other big corporations, and do things she used to think she never could afford. Where was all this money coming from? Marty's and her analysis of the years since Edward died revealed that all of it came from sales of Blackwell Readers—the project which had been entirely her own doing.

Regular trade sales had been declining steadily for four years, and a study of sales by titles showed definite trends. Books imported from England generally did not sell as well as they had a decade ago with the exception of certain popular novels; especially a "literary" book of verse or essays, in which Granger took his greatest interest, had a much smaller market in the United States than it used to. What sold best were frothy light American novels that taxed no one's intelligence.

"It's too bad in a way," Max Gurland said. "I never want to agree with anything Granger believes. But it is true I liked book-selling best the way it used to be—the way Granger wants it to stay. A small, elitist business. But it's changing. The book business has growing pains. There are more people who can read, though they're not as literate in the old-fashioned sense. They don't *know* anything except their daily jobs. All they want from a book is entertainment."

Cordelia did not agree altogether. Another trend she observed in this study of sales was strong public interest in books that explained how to do practical things—books on sewing and knitting and crocheting, even one on "gentleman farming." But the problem was that Lovejoy's published very few such books because Granger had no interest in them.

She discussed the matter with Runyon, who had become an assistant editor but was so discouraged with his lack of progress that he was thinking of quitting publishing. In Granger's absence she gave Runyon a raise and sent his spirits soaring by assigning him the task of searching out, buying, and producing "informational" books in this overlooked category.

Max said, "When Granger comes back, he won't be happy about your throwing your weight around."

"I don't care what he thinks," Cordelia replied.

"Two and a half cheers," Max said. "I'll give you the other half cheer when you stick to your guns."

No one reckoned on what happened after Granger came off the *Berengaria* in mid-November. He strode jauntily from the Cunard pier onto West Street and into the path of a Franklin motorcar. It was being driven at five miles per hour by a young woman who was appropriately dressed for the occasion: visored cap, chiffon veil, leather gauntlets, a flashy bolero. Twice she squeezed the rubber bulb of the horn forward of her steering wheel: *wah! wah!* Granger, who detested motorcars, whirled to defend himself. The young woman lunged a foot at the brake, but hit the accelerator instead. Granger was carted off to the New York Infirmary with a fractured skull, two broken legs, a torn liver, besides numerous abrasions and contusions.

It was the following June before he was able to come

into the office for a half day of work two or three times a week. By that time Cordelia had decided that his tastes and instincts were too outmoded for the best interests of Lovejoy and Son. But she could not bring herself to fire a half-crippled man who hobbled about on a cane. She thought she must wait until he became whole and arrogant again.

Meanwhile he was blessedly absent for the launching and promotion of *Side Street* by Hope Traymore early in May. Maude had decided that the book would be better served if she did not reveal her true identity, and Cordelia went along with her decision. Reviews of the book were excellent; Cordelia gave it more advertising than any Lovejoy book since the last Tranch Claverlay novel. Until the reviews began to come in she had not wanted to admit how important they were to her. If they had been unfavorable, she'd have felt that Granger was right and she wrong in judging *Side Street*. The fact she had a large majority of critical opinion on her side gave her a greater boost of self-confidence than anything that had happened since she began an active role at Lovejoy's.

The book sold briskly. Reviews and sales encouraged Maude, who was having difficulty with her next novel.

"Tranch says the second is the hardest for a novelist," Cordelia said.

"But it's more than my second book," Maude replied.

"But it's Hope Traymore's second. Whatever became of Maude Mudge?"

"She died. The other day at the boardinghouse old Mrs. Barclay asked me why I don't go by my true name of Hope Traymore. She says it's ridiculous for me to go around pretending I'm somebody named Maude Mudge. I explained to her that I feel I have to protect my privacy from my reading public."

Their conversation occurred on a Saturday in June as they rode up Park Avenue to St. Bartholomew's for the noon marriage ceremony of Suzanna Blaine Neiswander to James Henry Farnol.

"Is Nick really not attending?" Maude asked.

"He sent his regrets—and a beautiful silver bowl. He claims to me he's heartbroken."

"But there he is now," Maude said, looking out of the hansom. "Walking to St. Bartholomew's in striped morning pants."

"It can't be. He's heartbroken." Cordelia looked out, too. "But it is. Slow down, driver." She leaned out. "Yoo-hoo, Nicky, want a lift to the church?"

Nick smiled at her. Then, remembering he was heartbroken, he changed to a look of deep gloom. "No, thanks. I'll see you there. But not at the reception."

When they alighted in a crowd at the foot of the church steps that was waiting to see the bride arrive, Cordelia came face-to-face with Miriam and Augustus Peyster. She suppressed a wince as she waited for them to cut her dead, but to her amazement Miriam smiled and extended her hand while Augustus took off his top hat and bowed.

"Cousin Miriam! Cousin Augustus! You both look very well." They did indeed look happy, prosperous, and very well-preserved for a couple of old derelicts from Cape May, New Jersey. "Are you enjoying life at Cape May?"

"Mamie Fish started that story," Augustus said. "Heaven knows why. We own a hotel in Asbury Park and live there very happily."

"Right on the boardwalk," Miriam said. "The Peyster House. You must visit us sometime. I hear you have three lovely children. . . ."

Cordelia was pleased to find they no longer bore a grudge. What had changed them? If there were a school someplace that trained people to overcome snobbish pride, it should be attended by thousands. Maybe, however, the best training in a democratic spirit was a cruel course in bankruptcy.

She introduced Maude, and then Nick came up and the Peysters exchanged warm greetings with him. "Nicky," Miriam asked, "when are we getting you to the altar?"

He looked at her bravely. "I almost made it this time with Suzanna. But then my friend Jim betrayed me. Frankly, I'm heartbroken. But I felt it was only decent to attend the service."

The Peysters had been invited by Suzanna's parents, whom they had known before their social life was abruptly transferred from Newport to Asbury Park. All of them went in together and sat on the bride's side of the church. Suzanna looked so slender and lovely in her bridal gown that Cordelia thought Nick might weep with regret and envy. But he maintained his bravery throughout the service, and afterwards was prevailed on to attend the reception at the Neiswander mansion even though he had sent his regrets.

Nick was waltzing with Suzanna at the reception when Maude observed to Cordelia, "I've never seen a heartbroken man smiling so gaily."

"What I think we are seeing," Cordelia said, "is the relieved look of a born bachelor."

Some said that Granger never fully recovered from his accident. Cordelia thought, however, that he never recovered from her overruling him in publishing *Side Street*.

"Every couple of days," Marty told her, "he comes into accounting to check on the sales of that novel. Gets real gloomy about it."

Of course Marty never forgot that Granger had fired him before Cordelia intervened. Detesting Granger, he looked to Cordelia as the responsible head of the company. He supplied her with all sorts of important information: authors' royalty and drawing-account reports, what were the current conflicts among key employees, why someone was soldiering on the job, the possibility that a production assistant was receiving kickbacks from a printer. If Granger had known about it, he would have thought they were engaging in idle gossip. But that was not so: Cordelia and Marty realized that the health of a company depended on its leadership being informed of signs of illness and trying to do something about it.

To Cordelia's great regret she did not feel free to leave town and spend the entire summer of 1904 at Hasty's. She had utter faith in Marty, Max, and Runyon, but she no longer trusted Granger's judgments. So, throughout the summer, she would spend one week at Hasty's and the next week stay in New York and go to the office every day. It was a good thing she did. The publication of *Side Street* brought Lovejoy's a letter of inquiry that summer from a talented young writer of the naturalistic school. Granger would have turned him down, but Cordelia asked to read the manuscript of his next novel and bought it at the end of July. In August she bought a second excellent novel by an acquaintance of the first author. Later that month Jerry Newcomb recommended a novel from the "slush-pile" of unsolicited manuscripts that constantly came to the house. He said Granger would have rejected it, but Cordelia agreed it should be accepted and published.

"It's getting to be like there are two lists," Max said. "There's Cordelia's, and then there's Granger's."

"And never the twain shall meet," Runyon said.

Granger proceeded as if nothing unusual were happening. He was always firmly polite with Cordelia, but he pretended that the manuscripts she bought did not exist.

She, in turn, began to needle him occasionally.

Once: "Stop being penny-wise and pound-foolish." Again: "This company is supposed to be a group effort. You increasingly view it as designed mainly for your personal accomplishment and benefit."

Granger went right on doing things as he had more than a decade ago. His chief interest was to acquire manuscripts and edit them for the typesetters; he did not seem to care how they grew into books—what was their display type, how they were designed and jacketed, how promoted and sold.

When she tried to discuss this failing with him, he became angry.

"Nobody appreciates a handsome volume more than I! I've collected hundreds in my flat. Nobody is happier about a good seller. But we have production and sales people to tend to these details. Why do you carry on so?"

"Because, as an editor, you should know as much as they—even more. You know what a turnover of employees there is in all publishing houses. Able people forever leaving and being replaced by novices. These novices can do considerable damage before they become well trained."

"Cordelia, that's just the nature of book publishing."

Perhaps, she thought, it was the nature of every skilled industry in which the ranks of workers were poorly paid. But she didn't say it. Lovejoy's paid wages like those of other publishers. Book publishing, as a result of its intellectual aura and air of gentility, commanded an extraordinary labor market. No other industry attracted so many bright young graduates of Harvard, Yale, Princeton, and similar colleges for wages no better than the seven a week Mr. Carnegie paid illiterates in his steel mills. Yet Cordelia was not about to pioneer a new wage pattern; Lovejoy's would revise its salary scale when other publishers changed theirs. (And, of course, other publishers were thinking the same.)

Sales showed a considerable upswing in the spring of 1905, encouraging Cordelia to move the company to larger, more comfortable quarters farther up Madison Avenue. She decided a housewarming should be held, with the families of all employees invited. Steve, Penny, and Eunice were among the first to arrive, immediately after their release from school on a mellow spring afternoon. All the office windows were opened wide and people drifted about with nothing much to look at and not much to talk about.

Steve, like the other children, stuffed himself with cake and lemonade, then became bored. Wandering into Granger's office with a couple of other boys, he leaned out the third-floor window. Autos, though still a novelty, already were increasing the congestion of the city streets. Steve was fascinated by them and took delight in identifying every motor-driven vehicle he saw.

"See that old, old open-seated four wheeler down there?" He pointed, and the boys with him leaned forward to look. "That's a Ford built in nineteen three."

Granger bustled in, saying, "Good afternoon, boys, would you like to look at some books?"

"Nah," Steve said over one shoulder, and the other boys said, "Nah," over their shoulders, too. A boy said to Steve, "There's another Ford," but Steve said, "Nah, it only looks like one. That's a Haynes eighteen ninety-eight. Now look down the street. There's somethin' interesting. See the eighteen ninety-six Olds. Well, it sort of looks like that eighteen ninety-eight Winton, but there's a difference. The Winton is covered like a buggy."

Granger came behind them. "Those dreadful cars. You can smell them way up here!"

Steve looked around at him. "How you feelin' now, Mr. Cantwell?"

"All right," Granger said. "Why?"

"It was a Franklin hit you, wasn't it? Did you make out the year before you went down?"

Granger fled, and Steve went on identifying cars: Locomobile, Knox, electric brougham, White steamer, Packard, Pierce-Arrow, Cadillac, Packard, Knox . . .

Everyone knew how much Granger hated the advent of the automotive age, but no one thought he would try to fight it so hard until he cajoled Max into going to lunch with him one day in June. As Max described it afterwards, they were crossing Madison Avenue at Thirty-fourth Street when the policeman directing traffic at the corner waved on an Olds auto driven by a bearded man who wore goggles and a duster. But Granger felt that the traffic directions did not apply to him.

"A pedestrian *always* has the right of way over a motor-propelled vehicle," he informed Max, who wisely hung back as Granger stepped boldly into the path of the oncoming Olds. At the last moment Max tried to drag him back, but Granger shook off his grasp. Since his accident, Granger had taken to carrying a cane, not for support but as a kind of weapon; now he shook his cane fiercely at the Olds bearing down on him.

As Max described it: "The driver tried to stop the damn auto, but I guess the brakes didn't grip in time. Anyhow, the auto hit Granger and he just went ass over teakettle. For a second he was way up there in the air with a shocked look on his face. Then, wham, he was on the pavement with his pantlegs somehow up to his knees and his long underwear showing."

Mercifully Granger was not killed or even seriously injured, but sustained only a sprained right ankle. In his wrath he wanted to sue the driver of the Olds, who was so stunned by what had happened that he vowed never to drive again. However, Bill Paisley talked Granger out of court action: said he had violated traffic directions and didn't have a case.

After Granger recovered from his sprain, he continued to carry his cane and sometimes shook it menacingly at autos which he felt were threatening him. When Cordelia occasionally walked someplace with him she was frightened to see that he had learned nothing from his accidents. Formerly a timid pedestrian who shied from horse-drawn carriages, Granger had turned into an aggressive one who waded into a stream of traffic like Richard the Lion-Hearted into a courtyard filled with armed enemies.

"Look out!" she shrieked at him one day on Madison Avenue, and covered her eyes as he lashed his cane furiously at the nose of a Packard which was trying to intimidate him.

Turning back safely from the fray, Granger vented his wrath on her. "Pick-pick-pick!" he cried. "Pick-pick-pick-pick! When are you goddamn women going to stop *shrewing* me?"

For a moment Cordelia was speechless, then she flared, "When you start *screwing* us!"

Granger blanched. A well-dressed matron standing on the curb nearby cast them a look of contempt, then clutched her long skirt closer, as if to avoid horse manure, and strode off. Granger, making babbling sounds, galloped in the opposite direction from the offended matron. Cordelia felt paralyzed. Whatever had made her say such a dreadful, incredible thing?

When she and Granger met again, she apologized profusely and tried to make amends. But he cared not so much for what she had said as for whether the woman on the curb had recognized him. Hadn't the woman looked familiar? It took all Cordelia's efforts to reassure Granger that the woman had been a stranger.

Early that summer Bill Paisley pointed out that Lovejoy's had grown and its financial structure was antiquated. He showed Cordelia that there would be many advantages to turning it into a stock company. As sole owner, Cordelia would hold all the stock at first: It would be hers to sell or give as she chose. She liked the idea, so Bill and Marty began to work out the details of the conversion, which would take weeks. She told Granger what was going on, and in his vague way he seemed to approve: Fine, fine, as long as he personally didn't have to bother with the details.

Through the summer and into the fall of 1905 there was much activity next door at 125 East Thirty-sixth Street. Workmen came and went at the narrow brownstone, which was only half as wide as Cordelia's house. One day a coachman left a card for Cordelia: Mrs. Sara Delano Roosevelt of 200 Madison Avenue, a mansion diagonally across the street from Mr. Morgan's. At Cordelia's invitation Mrs. Roosevelt came to tea. She was a stout, forceful widow with bulldog jaw whose conversation was one long display of snobbery.

As a Hudson Valley aristocrat who understood New York bloodlines, Mrs. Roosevelt recognized that Cordelia had been a Dorfman before she married a low publisher and began dipping into trade herself. As a Delano, she had been nouveau compared to a Dorfman, but she had married a Roosevelt, and the Roosevelts had been living in New York almost as long as the Dorfmans.

Mrs. Roosevelt went on and on about the subject dearest to her, a son Franklin. Graduate of Harvard and now a student at Columbia Law School, Franklin recently had married one Eleanor, a distant cousin in the Roosevelt clan. Soon the young folk would return from their honeymoon in Europe, and Mama had bought this little house for them so that they could live close to her.

After Mrs. Roosevelt left, Cordelia remarked to Mary, "I feel sorry for the bride. She's victim of a disease that can fell any woman who hasn't the constitution of an ox. It's called mother-in-law."

The day the young Roosevelts moved into 125, Cordelia had Mary take over enough food for a sumptuous dinner. She need not have bothered, for, counting a part-time cleaning woman, Mama had provided the young couple with three servants. Franklin, without formal ado, bounced right over to thank Cordelia for the repast. He was a handsome young man, as effervescent a conversationalist as Granger could be when he chose. In the popular fiction of the time he would have been called "dashing," and Cordelia thought his eye somewhat roving.

Fifteen minutes later Eleanor rang the bell and came in shyly. At first Cordelia did not believe she could be the bride of handsome Franklin. Her figure and complexion were good enough, but she had a receding chin and protruding teeth. Worst of all, she carried her tall body with the awkwardness of an ungainly child. But then Cordelia realized that Eleanor's large eyes were lustrous and lovely, possibly the loveliest she ever had seen, and they sent out a curious appeal. Surely, Cordelia thought, she did not misread the message from Eleanor's eyes: *Help me, I'm lonely.*

Eleanor lingered after Franklin, who said he had to go see his Mama. Eleanor was a ninny, Cordelia realized, the product of a worthless education like that provided at Miss Troy's. She had done all the so-called right things, but didn't know how to do anything right. However, she was sweet natured and basically intelligent. If only she would overcome her shyness, she might do something interesting.

At last she confessed, "I'm not feeling well. I'm with it, you know."

"With what?" asked Cordelia.

Eleanor blushed and lowered her gaze. "With child."

"Oh, you're pregnant."

Eleanor nodded and her blush deepened.

"Well, congratulations." Cordelia had introduced her three children. "Children are a—uh—blessing."

"I hope so," Eleanor said. "I mean I know they are."

"Are you going to Doctor Prettyman?"

"No, Mama sent me uptown to Doctor Wade."

"Doctor Prettyman is awfully good—and he's handy here on Murray Hill."

"But Mama swears by Doctor Wade," Eleanor said.

The young Roosevelts were away a lot, especially after Franklin finished law school and went into an office downtown. They were often at Mama's house up the river at Hyde Park. Summers they spent at a cottage Mama provided on Campobello Island in the Bay of Fundy. But almost every day when both Cordelia and Eleanor were at home, Eleanor dropped in or asked Cordelia to come over. Cordelia kept trying to improve her younger friend. She gave her books to read and tried to interest her in cooking and sewing. Eleanor read avidly, but Mama put her foot down when it came to cooking and sewing and said that such things were "common and unnecessary."

Cordelia learned that Eleanor's problems had not begun with Mama Roosevelt. Her childhood had been miserably unhappy. Her mother, a beautiful woman, had despised her as ugly and called her "Granny." She had died when Eleanor was eight. Next her adored father, Elliot Roosevelt, brother of the Colonel Teddy who would become president, died after a long bout with alcohol. At ten Eleanor went to live on Fifty-seventh Street with her Gradmother Hall, who hated the Roosevelts and tried to cut her off from all contact with them. One bad experience had piled on another for Eleanor until she met Franklin. And even then Mama had tried to break them apart, saying that

Eleanor was unworthy of her darling Franklin. Of course Eleanor had deeply resented that. And she had resented as much the fact that Franklin listened to his mother's protests about her. Yet somehow love had triumphed over Mama, and now love had been brought to terms by marriage.

Cordelia decided to hold a small ceremony at 127 one afternoon in November for the signing of papers that would make a stock company of Lovejoy and Son. A uniformed Mary would serve sherry and biscuits, as happened in nearly all the current New York plays which had been imported from England. To this ceremony Cordelia invited all of the principals. After giving a great deal of thought to what she would do with the stock, she had decided not to offer a single share for sale. But when it came to *giving* shares to whom she pleased—that was something entirely different and a great pleasure to her.

Those invited to 127 at three o'clock on that raw autumn afternoon were Bill—who brought along a young lawyer aide to assist as notary and clerk—and Marty, Max, and Granger. Also present was Steve, who was happy to be there because he always liked ceremony and welcomed an afternoon off from school.

Cordelia, enjoying the occasion, said, "I'll play chairman."

"How can a lady do that?" asked Marty.

"Throw that man out," Cordelia said. "As it's been explained to me, now that we're becoming a stock company there's going to be a board of directors of five members that can be expanded in number later. So I propose, nominate, or whatever the word is, that the members be Mr. Paisley, Mr. Goldman, Mr. Gurland, Mr. Cantwell, and myself. I understand that my son Steven cannot serve until he comes of age."

As required by New York State law, the clerk read aloud the charter of the new stock company. Then Bill nominated Cordelia president and chairman of the board. All voted aye, though she thought Granger spoke inaudibly.

"I have an announcement on the division of shares," she said. "To my son Steve, who I hope will someday direct the fortunes of our company, I assign ten percent of the stock—to be in the care of a trusteeship with the approval of the board until he is of age. To Marty— Mr. Goldman—because he is forever faithful and as hardworking as a coolie—I give five percent of the stock of Lovejoy and Son. To Max—Mr. Gurland—I give the same amount of five percent for the same reasons. To Bill—Mr. Paisley—the same. And to Mr. Cantwell the same. The remaining seventy percent I'll keep in my own name for the time being. If—"

"Five percent?" Granger, livid, lurched to his feet. "Five percent for *me*? I who *made* this company and carried it single-handed for you through the lean years! *Five* percent?"

The clerk dropped his pen while everyone stared stunned at Granger.

"Five percent," he cried, "is the fee of a real-estate agent, not the rightful profit of a leader. And that's all I've been to you all these years, Cordelia—a real-estate agent, the cat's paw of all your selfish schemes! *Five* percent!" He made an ugly face. "Faw!"

Cordelia did not know what to say.

Granger, enraged, dashed from the room. Steve, curious, followed him at a cautious distance, watching him jam on his broad-brimmed hat, snatch up his cane, and storm out of the house without even slamming the door.

East along Thirty-sixth Street came the most splendid auto Steve ever had seen outside Lacy's big showroom on lower Broadway. He recognized it as a Peerless touring car, a new model of that very year. Its twin open leather seats were shiny black, its long engine hood the shape of controlled power. Four polished brass gas-lamps were forward to the driver, two bracketed above the dashboard and two close to the fenders. The steering wheel had an amber quality, but the truly wonderful thing about this magnificent car was that its entire body was painted a gleaming fire-engine red.

The driver, one Lyman Forsyte, later testified that he was proceeding at twelve miles per hour. Forsyte, the tennis pro at the Racquet Club, was coming from the squash court in the Morgan stables where he'd just given a lesson to Mr. Jack Morgan. A find athlete whose reactions were likened to lightning, Forsyte was distinguished by a superb guardsman's mustache. When driving his Peerless, he disdained goggles or duster, but always wore gloves of the finest kid.

Suddenly onto Forsyte's course lurched a pedestrian. Forsyte squeezed the rubber bulb of his horn: *wah-wah-wah*! But the sound served to infuriate rather than warn the rather odd-looking man loping across the street. Instead of turning from the auto, he turned *at* it, face contorted angrily and walking stick upraised. Forsyte slammed the brakes, but the Peerless was too close upon the man rushing at it to stop in time, so Forsyte swerved sharply to his right in an effort to avoid him. But he could not altogether. The man brought down a smart crack of his stick on the forward left lamp of the Peerless before the auto knocked him eight feet (as carefully measured by the police).

Cordelia ran into the street at the same instant, with the men following. Granger lay as still as an overturned statue. Beside him was his stick, broken in two like the sword of that memorialized Roman centurion who had died while trying to repel an onslaught by barbarians.

Steve, paying no attention to Granger, was tenderly rubbing a slight dent the cane had made in the lamp and had given himself over to ecstatic admiration of the smell, the color, the texture of the magnificent automobile.

Cordelia shook him frantically by a shoulder and cried, "How did it happen?"

"Mama"—Steve took his gaze off the Peerless reluctantly—"he *attacked* the auto. Honest he did."

"Hurry!" Cordelia told him. "Run fetch Doctor Prettyman."

Dr. Prettyman came running five minutes later from his office, but Granger was dead.

15

At first Cordelia was secretly relieved that now she didn't have to fire Granger. But then she felt guilty. Was she responsible for killing him? Certainly she did not think that young Forsyte had done it with his handsome Peerless; she attested to Forsyte's innocence when the district attorney's office wondered whether to file charges against him. Her sense of guilt did not last long, however.

Immediately she let it be known that she was looking for a new editor-in-chief because there was no one at Lovejoy's with enough experience for that position. Since Granger's office was grander than hers, she began to use it for interviewing the men who applied. One day she brought favorite snapshots of her three children from home and arranged them on the desk. Shortly thereafter she ordered the office refurbished, the furniture replaced, and, with all trace of Granger obliterated, she had her own desk and office.

It was only temporary, she explained to everyone, while the search continued for a new editor-in-chief. Meanwhile, she said, she was "only trying to help out." She was so convinced of this herself that everyone appeared to believe what she said. She promoted Runyon to senior editor, Jerry Newcomb to assistant editor, and hired Rita Vance, an English instructor at Barnard College, as a reader in Jerry's place. Her hiring of a woman reader caused raised brows.

"But it's only temporary," Cordelia kept saying. "Miss Vance wants some temporary practical training before returning to the academic world." Then she stilled all criticism by hinting that Miss Vance's father had powerful financial connections of importance to Lovejoy's. In fact, Rita Vance's father had died a pauper some time ago; Cordelia had hired her after they met at a lecture on contemporary poetry where she had been impressed by Rita's intelligence and good humor. "She's just the sort of modern young woman whose viewpoint we need around the company," Cordelia told Maude.

If slow about finding an editor-in-chief, Cordelia was indefatigable at functioning as one herself. She managed it by doing most of her reading at home afternoons and evenings. At first she sincerely thought she didn't want a full-time job because it would detract from her role as mother. Gradually, however, she saw that active children like hers who were in school and interested in dozens of things had only limited time for a mother. They needed her at odd, critical moments, and, as long as she was available then, she did not have to be perpetually underfoot.

Later all three said they felt Coredlia always was available when they needed her. She did a remarkable job of spreading herself between the office and 127 because she genuinely enjoyed being at home and seeing family, friends, and neighbors. One person in particular with whom she maintained her friendship was Eleanor Roosevelt.

The Roosevelts' first child, Anna, was born in May 1906. She was a sickly infant who cried interminably. Cordelia immediately saw that Eleanor was not an instinctively competent mother. To help her, she enlisted the aid of Dr. Prettyman and found a trained nurse, Blanche Spring. But neither Blanche nor Cordelia could overcome some of Eleanor's stubborn notions about the rearing of her firstborn.

If Eleanor and Mama Roosevelt agreed on a single thing, it was the healthful value of fresh air. They kept windows open in the coldest weather; sometimes Cordelia did not remove her overcoat when she visited 125 in winter. No wonder all the Roosevelts were forever having colds.

Cordelia and Blanche agreed that Eleanor was carrying her fresh-air theory too far when, in the fall of 1906, she had Mama's handyman fashion a little box which looked morbidly like an infant's coffin, cover it with chicken wire, and attach two guy wires to it. Into the box Eleanor bundled the sickly Anna, fastened the chicken wire over the top so she couldn't fall out, and lowered the box a couple of feet from a second-floor rear window. There Anna lay by the hour, screaming herself hoarse.

"Lord save us all!" Mary exclaimed to Cordelia. "I can't stand that child's screams another minute. She's freezing to death."

To Cordelia's and Blanche's protests, Eleanor answered stubbornly: "The fresh air is good for her."

"Well for heaven's sake," Cordelia cried, "at least put her on the ground! If that wire ever breaks—"

"It won't break." Eleanor pursed her lips tightly. "On the ground she'd be prey to cats and rats and—oh—all sorts of things."

Cordelia thought of a solution. Through the company production department she had a printer run off a letterhead: The Society for the Prevention of Cruelty to Children, 111 Broadway. Under it, in disguised hand, she wrote a letter addressed to Mrs. Franklin Delano Roosevelt that began, "Madame Roosevelt: Agents of our society have discovered that you . . ." and went on to threaten court action. Cordelia even thought of an appropriate name to sign the letter: Calder Peabody.

Next morning, after the postman delivered the mail,

Eleanor came running into 127 without bothering to ring the bell. "Cordelia! Cordelia!" Her face was white, her breath short. *"Court* action! The stigma! What can I do?"

"Stay calm," Cordelia told her. "Haul Anna into the house and never lower her out again. I'll turn this over to my lawyer to handle—discreetly. Franklin must never hear of this."

"Never, never!" Eleanor gasped.

When a son, James, was born to Eleanor in December 1907, he, like Anna, seemed prey to every known disease. Franklin was especially terrified that infantile paralysis might afflict his children, and his fears spread to Cordelia. Since flies were then believed to be carriers of the dreaded disease, she followed Franklin's example when he fortified 125 with extensive screening and kept a flyswatter handy in each room. Sometimes on late spring evenings before the Roosevelts went to spend the summer at Campobello, Cordelia would see Franklin prowling about his parlor and swatting at flies that had penetrated his screen defenses.

One afternoon when Blanche Spring had fallen ill, and another pair of servants had quit, and Anna and James were screaming their heads off, and Franklin was drinking at the Astor Bar with politicians instead of coming home as promised, and Mama had just stormed out of 125 with the announcement that Eleanor was a fool, Cordelia came in. Eleanor stood silently in the middle of the little kitchen, lustrous eyes filled with tears.

Cordelia, smelling something burning, turned to the stove and snatched off a pot. Trying to speak lightly, she said, "Eleanor, it helps to add water when you go to boil eggs."

Eleanor, controlling her trembling lips, said, "I am an ass."

"No, you're not," Cordelia said. "Mama is the ass around here. Have you ever thought it might be good to tell her so?"

"I have thought about it, Cordelia."

"Then why not do it?"

"Because it wouldn't help. Mama isn't really an ass. She just wants to control life. But so do I. When I was young I lived perpetually with horror. And I learned something important from the experience. That is—all the horrors came from a complete loss of self-control. That's why I try so hard never to lose it."

"I understand," Cordelia said. "But doesn't complete self-control lead to the subjugation of all desire? And can't that result in something bad instead of good?"

"I don't know." Eleanor spoke slowly. "That's looking far ahead. And a thing I learned about putting down the horrors is never to look too far ahead."

Nearly a year after Granger died, the position of editor-in-chief still had not been filled.

"Men have stopped applying for it," Cordelia said to Runyon. "I haven't had an applicant in two months. Can you tell me why?"

"Well," Runyon said.

"Do you think I'm setting too high standards for the job?"

"Well."

"Stop yessing me, Runyon, if you don't agree. I *am* setting too high standards. How long can we continue to function without an editor-in-chief?"

"Mrs. Lovejoy—"

"Time and again, Runyon, I've asked you to address me as Cordelia. It makes me feel I work here, too, instead of just flitting in and out."

"Cordelia, doesn't it occur to you that *you* have become the editor-in-chief?"

"That never was my intent. I just came in as a temporary."

"But you've made it permanent. Everybody in the trade knows it. That's why nobody applies anymore."

"Everybody knows it but me." She pondered for a while. "I sound like either a fool or a hypocrite, but I'm neither. Yes, I see what has happened. Maybe deep in that unconscious mind of mine, as discovered by Dr. Freud—"

"Take the job, Cordelia." Runyon grinned at her. "I just interviewed you and hired you. Make it official."

"Well," Cordelia said doubtfully.

She continued the fabrication that Lovejoy's had no editor-in-chief, but she stopped hunting for candidates. She was supremely happy in her work despite many problems and setbacks.

A major worry was Maude's failure to deliver her new novel. Maude was beginning to avoid her. Could she be having trouble with alcohol again? When Maude did not answer a note inviting her to lunch, Cordelia walked to the boardinghouse and asked to see her. Maude came downstairs; she was pale and distraught, but Cordelia could not smell liquor.

"It seems years since I saw you, Maude."

"More like decades." She looked close to tears. "I'm stuck, Cordelia, like somebody who fell into a cement pit and got solidified."

"Please, let me beg you again, may I see what you've written, even if it's only two pages?"

It was more than one hundred pages. Maude insisted that she read them immediately and tell her candidly what she thought. So Cordelia sat and read while Maude walked around the block a dozen times.

Cordelia believed she saw the trouble before reading far. In this new novel Maude was trying to be a philosopher; but she was a storyteller, not a philosopher.

Now, however, she was neglecting to tell a story, and that neglect was burdening her conscience.

When Maude returned, Cordelia gave her opinion. "I urge you to put this aside and write something else. What I'd like to see you write is a moving love story of about sixty thousand simple words using the same background as *Side Street*."

Maude began writing the next day, and six weeks later she brought Cordelia the manuscript of *Margaret, Margaret*. It became one of the most popular novels brought out in the succeeding publishing season by any American house. Highbrow critics hooted, but the public loved it. Cordelia thought that the most intelligent critique of it was a line appearing in the periodical *Review of Reviews*: "This novel is poppycock, but the poppy part makes it the most intoxicating reading in several recent months."

Margaret, Margaret was uncomplicated enough to appeal to readers such as Mary. As far as Cordelia could tell, it was the first novel Tim ever had read, and it turned him into an avid reader of simple fiction. In June 1907, she begged him:

"Tim, quit Hart's and come on my payroll."

"Quit now, Miz Cordelia? Ain't ye heard there's a business panic on?"

"I know, but we'll survive it. The point is Mary needs help around the house so she can have more time with Cora. And she has some trouble getting along with the laundresses and cleaning women we hire part time."

"She picks at 'em 'cause they ain't perfect," Tim said. "Well, this is one cleaning *man* she has to git along with. And I'll be with Cora a lot more."

"Good, then you're hired."

He and Mary were delighted with their new couple's salary of eighteen dollars a week and keep. As Mary said later, a trifle proudly, "Now yer average workin' man'd just resign his job at Hart's, but that was too dull for my Tim."

Tim was remembered in the legends of the store (which had only a few more years of existence) as the only employee who ever terrified the owner. He chose the morning after what he had determined would be his last pay envelope.

On that bright morning Mr. Hart, smoking the customary cigar, approached at the customary eight-fifteen precisely. Tim said, "Ready! Aim! Fire!" to the assistant doorman, who had no idea what he was talking about.

Mr. Hart stepped briskly into a compartment of the revolving door, prepared for Tim to turn it at exactly the right speed with his matchless timing. But that morning his timing was off: He was turning the door too fast. The glass partition behind Mr. Hart hit his heels and he cursed Tim, but no one could hear him because the door was turning faster, shooting him past his point of entrance into the store too fast for him to get out. He began running to keep up with the speed of Tim's turning. Faster and faster Tim turned the door, and faster and faster ran Mr. Hart. He tried to find something to tug against Tim's thrust, but there was nothing to grasp. By that time he was yammering with rage and terror and Tim was howling with laughter while the assistant doorman and a couple of clerks stood transfixed.

Gradually Tim slowed down the pace of his turning and at last he allowed Mr. Hart to stagger dizzily out of his compartment.

"Well, Mr. Hart," Tim said, "fast enough for ye this mornin'?"

"You!" gasped Mr. Hart. "You!" He came banking dizzily at Tim, like a Lackawanna train on the infamous Tunkhannock curve, his cigar somehow broken in two and ashes spilled on his waistcoat. But he never did complete his curving approach to Tim. His feet slipped from under him and he tipped over and lay on the floor, cigar still clamped between his teeth while he made sobbing sounds.

"Ye can't fire me, Mr. Hart," Tim said, " 'cause I just quit."

He flung off his braided cap and tore off his braided coat and might have taken off his trousers, too, if Mr. Hart had not long ago decided that it was too expensive for his doormen to wear braided pants. Then Tim danced through the revolving door and went skipping and laughing up Murray Hill to freedom.

Cordelia had both Tim and Mary spend the summer at Hasty's with the children, and she went out there as often as possible. She felt that Steve should have male companionship, and Tim was the man Steve liked above all others.

And in the fall of 1907 Cordelia did not worry about leaving the children in the couple's care when she decided to make a trip to England. No one from Lovejoy's had gone across the Atlantic in search of titles since Granger made his final trip in 1903.

"Can't say we've been suffering from this lack of English titles," Cordelia told Max.

"Matter of fact, we've gained," he said.

"But there are *English* books," she said, "and then there are English *books*. English *books* are written by superlative writers, and I wish we had a couple of 'em instead of our second-raters. I'd like to get Mr. Kipling, Mr. Hardy, Mr. Conrad, and Mr. Conan Doyle."

"Sure," Max said, "and while you're about it, why don't you sign up King Edward to write his memoirs? They'd make spicy reading."

Cordelia invited Maude along as a companion, offering to pay her way. She was eager to go, and insisted on paying her own passage: "I'm so prosperous that I'm threatening to become rich. Maybe I'll find some interesting material."

"If you try to write an *English* novel," Cordelia said, "I'll *beat* you. I want you to write another novel like *Margaret, Margaret.*"

"And call it *Mary, Mary?*"

"No, that's the title for the one after the next. The next you can call *Martha, Martha.*"

"I'm so fraid of repeating myself," Maude said.

"Please don't be. That's mainly all successful novelists do."

"Money isn't everything."

"No, but with a bit of luck it lasts longer than fame."

They sailed at the end of September aboard the *New York* of the American Line. Photographs still in existence attest that it must have been a gay departure from the Inman Line pier at Fourteenth Street. One, taken on deck by Steve, showed Cordelia and Maude with Eleanor Roosevelt, who came to see them off. All wore long black suits and ruffled white blouses. On Cordelia's head had settled a huge something that looked like a peacock; it was a hat, and she was clinging to it tenaciously even though the wind had not yet begun to blow hard. Another picture showed Mary, Tim, Cora, and Penny. (Eunice was not present because she had something more important to do at Miss Troy's School that day.) Mary, remarkably small, radiated energy. Tim, wearing a bowler and lean and fit as a welterweight, had a pugnacious look. Little Cora, an exquisitely beautiful child, made Penny beside her seem large and awkward as both gawked aloft at the three stacks of the old *New York*.

That voyage remained the most memorable to Cordelia of her many to Europe. The American-owned ship had been built on the Clyde and was very grand. Cordelia and Maude's suite on the promenade deck had patent fans which admitted fresh air but excluded the sea. Their private bath had hot running water and their beds closed up in the daytime as on a Pullman car. Huge meals were served at long tables in the dining saloon—a vast place fifty feet long and rising twenty-five feet to an arched glass roof with an oriel window at either end.

Soon after the *New York* passed beyond Sandy Hook she slammed into a North Atlantic storm. Maude and many others were quickly felled; Cordelia, unsinkable sailor, remained in the public rooms. At dinner almost the only survivor at her long table was a pleasant gentleman from New Bedford who was in the textile business and on a trip to Lancashire. After dinner he invited her to play chess. She did not know how, but accepted his offer of instruction. On the second day of instruction he made an improper suggestion that she come to his cabin. Of course she declined, but decided—as with Tranch's propositions—to be flattered rather than outraged. So they remained good friends for the remainder of the voyage.

Cordelia had written several publishers in advance, and at the suggestion of one she rented a flat for the three weeks of their stay instead of going to a hotel. A top floor of an Adelphi Terrace building of historic Adam architecture, its riverside site was delightful even though the weather misbehaved and fog obscured the Thames much of the time.

The dogmatic, indefatigable T. Fisher Unwin, whose company was housed in the same block of Adelphi, came to breakfast at seven A.M. the morning after they arrived—he insisted it was the only time he had free.

"Mrs. Lovejoy, you are a phenomenon unknown to the British Isles—a lady publisher. Pray what qualifies you to be a publisher?"

"Sheer gall, Mr. Unwin."

"I used to do some business with your Mr. Cantwell,

deceased. He had a good taste in literature. Let me inquire about yours. Is there a particular author in whom you're especially interested?"

"Thomas Hardy."

"I cannot deliver you Hardy. I can put you in touch with one who could deliver him *maybe*. Who else?"

"Rudyard Kipling."

"My dear lady, Kipling is a cliché No one delivers Kipling, not even Kipling."

"He doesn't answer my letters."

"You must not have made your offer high enough. Forget these currently prominent names, Mrs. Lovejoy. Think of prominent names of the future. I'm thinking of a young man, Somerset Maugham. He's mean and nasty—called me a hard old skinflint, but I'm used to abuse from authors. However, Maugham has great energy and greed, desirable characteristics in an author, like staying power in a racing colt. Forget good personality. An author with it usually lacks much else. Personally Maugham is a little stammerer, an effeminate backbiter, but on paper he conveys the grand manner of a wise and simple man."

"I'm very interested in Joseph Conrad," Cordelia said.

"He's spoken for in America, I think. But he's a hungry one, and I'll try to get you his address. Now there's something you must absolutely buy from me. I'm starting a series called *Story of the Nations* that's being highly praised here. . . ."

She did not want *Story of the Nations*, but she recognized horse-trading. She might have to take it in order to get to Hardy and Conrad.

Fond of mystery and detection fiction, Cordelia thought Sherlock Holmes one of the great creations of her time. Ever since Granger's death she had been trying to make a connection with his creator, the recently knighted A. Conan Doyle. It had been to no avail.

When she described to Arnold Bennett her difficulties in making contact with most of the literary great of England, he explained the problem: "It's because you're a woman, I think. Maybe you should just send them your photograph. When they see you're young and beautiful, they might relent. Also, there's a deceptive innocence about your eyes. Most Englishmen fear anything not completely masculine. Or you should sign your letters Cord Lovejoy instead of Cordelia. They might find it safe to answer a *man's* letters."

In any event, she continued to pursue Sir Arthur Conan Doyle after she arrived in England. But she might never have caught up with him if it had not been for the aid of John Galsworthy, who arranged for her to be included in a dinner party of a dozen people at Brown's honoring Doyle for something or other.

"I'll warn you," Galsworthy said, "you're going to be vastly disappointed."

"How could I be?" she exclaimed. "To *meet* Sir Arthur at dinner!"

"I don't know how you could be, Mrs. Lovejoy, but you *will* be."

She fussed over her dress and she and Maude worked on her coiffure for hours before the dinner party. She arrived too early; the only person in the private dining room was a plain, thin, tall young woman who stood awkwardly in a corner under the critical gaze of two waiters.

"Oh!" She reached out for Cordelia as one drowning for a life preserver. "Would you happen to be Mrs. Holmes? Oh!" She colored and clapped a hand to her mouth. "How could I say that? I mean Mrs. Doyle."

"No, I'm Cordelia Lovejoy. I come from New York."

"I'm Constance Hedges. From—it's unpronounceable and in Cornwall. Are you with the spiritualist society?"

"No, just a—visitor."

Constance glanced about nervously. "I'm not a spiritualist, either—and not at all rich. But glad to pay the twenty-pound spiritualist fee to meet Sir Arthur Conan Doyle."

So *this* was the occasion! She owed John Galsworthy twenty pounds for this kindness.

The rest arrived in a group, women outnumbering men. The most ordinary looking of the men—rotund and as ingratiatingly smiling as a shopkeeper—turned out to be Sir Arthur.

"How d'ye do, how d'ye do," he greeted Cordelia and Constance when they introduced themselves, then backed away before they had a chance to say more.

A woman spiritualist addressed them as if they were recruits in a revolutionary movement.

Constance said to Cordelia, "I *have* to get to him— Sir Arthur, I mean."

"Why?" Cordelia asked.

"I've written a detection novel. I've written three, but this last one is the problem. I want to ask him about it."

"Well," Cordelia said, "before the spiritualist leader locks us into our chairs, let's step over to him and— try."

They tried, but the leader interposed and said, "Later!"

"I'm beginning to see," Cordelia told Constance, "why so many men hate women."

It must have been one of the worst dinners Brown's ever served, but before they could start on the course of indigestion the leader harangued them more about spiritualism and Sir Arthur's growing interest in it.

Midway through dinner, which was served without

wine, Constance told Cordelia again, "I just *have* to speak to him about my novel. It's why I paid the dinner fee and came."

"Why don't you just walk around the table, lean over his shoulder, and start asking questions," Cordelia said. "He doesn't strike me as socially brilliant, but he does appear a kindly man."

Constance did as suggested and returned in a moment, tears of frustration in her eyes. "He said, 'Nnnyup, nnn, ser.' I guess his mouth was full. And the spiritualist next to him said, 'Later!' "

"I don't like that woman," Cordelia said. "I'm not fond of Sir Arthur. But let's not hold this against Sherlock Holmes."

"Never!" Constance said. "Great creations should not be held responsible for their creators."

They never did have the opportunity to exchange anything with Sir Arthur Conan Doyle, if in fact he was capable of conversation. When coffee was served, the spiritualist leader announced that everyone could go on to a wonderful seance where the fee would be five pounds.

Constance was close to tears again. "I don't have five pounds left."

"I don't, either," Cordelia said. "Let's get out of here and I'll drop you at your hotel."

"I don't have a hotel," Constance said. "I'm traveling—direct. I'll wait in Waterloo Station for the early-morning train."

Cordelia took her back to the flat on Adelphi Terrace where there was plenty of room for her to sleep the night. All that Constance had brought with her was a large knitting bag. And about the only thing the knitting bag contained was her latest manuscript, a mystery novel entitled *Six for Dinner*, which she'd had a vague idea of showing to Sir Arthur.

Constance showed it to Cordelia after learning with

great surprise that she was a publisher. Cordelia, glancing at the manuscript before breakfast next morning, was engaged at once. She continued to read it with a growing feeling of suspense until she finished around noon. *Six for Dinner,* the first novel by Constance Hedges to be published, was the first manuscript Cordelia bought on her trip to England. It introduced Inspector Stuart of Scotland Yard, who, in the course of twenty novels, would perform brilliant feats of detection before being killed off—and then, in response to public outcry, would be resuscitated by the author.

Next Cordelia bought the *Story of the Nations* series from Unwin. But that did not help her with the big names she hoped to land as authors for Lovejoy's. Mr. Kipling continued to ignore her letters. Mr. Conrad came to tea; he was an unpleasantly austere man with a trim Vandyke and threadbare cuffs on whom Cordelia was ready to lavish money, but he could not be seduced away from his commitment to another American publisher. Mr. Hardy was the most pleasant of all; he and his wife joined Cordelia and Maude for dinner in London, but he never made any response to her very best offer.

"So I'm left with uncertainties," Cordelia told Maude. "That nasty little Somerset Maugham, H. de Vere Stacpoole, H. G. Wells, John Galsworthy—people like that."

"I don't see anything uncertain about Mr. Galsworthy," Maude said. "He's a fine gentleman."

"Of that there's no question." Galsworthy had refused to take the twenty pounds Cordelia tried to press on him for enabling her to attend the Doyle dinner, explaining that the fee had been paid by a friend and that he had not wanted to attend himself. "But I think that John Galsworthy is basically a dramatist and that his novels will come to nothing."

The day they sailed home from Southampton on the

Philadelphia Cordelia felt deeply discouraged. "I think this has been a worthless trip."

"What about Constance?" asked Maude. "That's a very good novel you bought."

"I agree, but is one popular novel worth all this effort? And I'm afraid that mystery fiction is one of those passing fads that will soon fade away."

She would not have believed that by 1939 the hard-cover sales of Constance Hedges's mystery novels would have surpassed fifteen million copies in America or that she would be the most consistently popular novelist Lovejoy's ever published.

16

By the fall of 1908, when Eleanor Roosevelt was pregnant again, builders had completed twin adjoining houses at Forty-seven and Forty-nine East Sixty-fifth Street which Mama had ordered and Franklin had enthusiastically helped design. One house was for Mama and the other for Franklin and his growing family, but Mama would keep title to both.

Cordelia and Mary helped Eleanor pack, and on moving day Cordelia had her in for a farewell luncheon. After she saw her and her children off in one of Mama's carriages, she felt depressed. With sadness, not condescension, she thought that Eleanor would always try hard but never accomplish anything much. It seemed to be her fate with that handsome husband who was so fond of his tyrannical mother and that growing brood of noisy, ailing children.

Probably she and Eleanor never would see much of each other. That seemed to be the way with friendly city neighbors after one moved to another part of town. But Cordelia guessed wrong. She failed to reckon on one of Eleanor's strongest attributes: abiding loyalty. She had made a friend for life.

The Roosevelts' move from Murray Hill typified for Cordelia a world that was changing much too fast. All her life she had enjoyed change as representing progress and new adventures; but now she wanted everything to remain as it was.

When she celebrated her fortieth birthday in 1910, she suddenly felt that she had grown old, that life was all behind her. Now, she thought, there was no chance she would marry again, she had aged too much for romance. Tranch, reporting in a doleful letter that he had stopped writing and become reconciled with his dear wife Janet, apparently would be her last romantic experience. Occasionally Cordelia attended social occasions at Mrs. Fish's and elsewhere with middle-aged bachelors or widowers; some professed to be greatly attracted to her and two proposed marriage. However, she thought both eccentric and could not imagine living with either.

In 1910 Steve entered Exeter. It was the year Penny started at Vassar as a tall, scrawny freshman determined to become a great poet like Vachel Lindsay. In that same year Eunice finished at Miss Troy's, and, refusing Cordelia's offer of a college education, was sent abroad for three months with a wealthy young classmate whose mother served as chaperone.

Steve was to Cordelia the most mysterious of her children, and therefore the most interesting. He was passionately fond of mechanical things—and where did that bent come from? He never acted impatient with her, but rarely consulted with her, either. Already he seemed caught up in a man's world from which she was excluded. She was delighted to see how adept he was at managing things. A deft baseball infielder, he was athletic enough to be well accepted by his Exeter classmates. Tall and slender, he was too light for football, but such a clever organizer that he was made manager of the football team in his senior year. His grades were good, though not brilliant, and his teachers assured Cordelia he should have no trouble in being accepted by Yale, the college of his choice. But in Steve's opinion, the most exciting thing that happened at Exeter was when he and a classmate rebuilt an old, discarded Winton which they could make go twelve miles per hour. (After their juggernaut frightened a horse into running away with a local clergyman, the school adopted a rule that students could not have automobiles.)

Penny was totally different from Steve. Cordelia was pleased that she wanted to be a writer and glad she adored the work of Lindsay instead of some mauve romantic like Swinburne. But she was somewhat troubled by Penny's politics. They agreed wholeheartedly on women's suffrage: Women should indeed have a vote. From there on, however, Penny wandered into a bramblebush of socialism where Cordelia could not follow. Everyone equal no matter the attainment? Hang Mr. Morgan from the nearest lamppost? It was this brashness, this harshness of Penny's that was the most difficult for Cordelia to understand.

Eunice was a beauty who believed everything she had been told at Miss Troy's and was determined to follow those maxims for life. She had mapped out her future, step by step and stop by stop, like one of those travel guides by Baedeker. In 1911 she would be presented to society. In 1914, after spending two years in selecting a lifetime mate, she would marry him. And so forth. She was totally self-centered, utterly selfish. Being a beauty, she had no lack of beaus. The chief trouble with them was that they were uninteresting—but always rich. Eunice never caused her mother any worry, yet she was expensive. It was fortunate Cordelia could afford her until Eunice should find the man who would pay her bills.

Lovejoy's was enjoying great financial success, most of it based on Cordelia's decisions. She named Runyon editor-in-chief and took the title of president and publisher for herself, but everyone knew she was the one with the power of life or death over every manuscript the company published. Constance Hedges's mystery novels were selling fabulously. So were those by Maude.

Maude had found a successful formula that had great

appeal to young women readers and she agreed with Cordelia that she should not vary from it. She published two novels a year, one much like another, each telling of a young woman's romantic love affair and ending happily.

"You're doing it better and better," Cordelia told her one day when they were lunching at White's Uptown.

"Like the girl in the bordello," Maude said, "I can keep on doing it easily just as long as I don't think about it. What I think about as I grow older is money. Did I tell you that last week I started negotiating for a brownstone on East Thirty-fifth a block from you? It's only about half as wide as your house and they're asking nine thousand. Do you think it worth that?"

Cordelia thought so, but Maude said, "I'm trying to bring the price down."

Commerce, commerce. Ah, where was the idealism in publishing books?

Yet there was much idealism, and Cordelia shared it. With all the busy, practical ways of her mind there went the deeply rooted feeling that moral goodness and real truth were identical. Despite occasional qualms, she believed as Edward used to: American civilization—with frequent setbacks—was pursuing a sure road toward moral and material improvement. Escapist fiction by writers like Maude and Constance reaped large profits, but Cordelia was concerned with more than making money in the decade following 1910.

Like most others in responsible positions in publishing and the arts during those years, she was sure that personal life and public literature should reflect moral standards. She agreed whole-heartedly with the dean of American letters, William Dean Howells, when he wrote in *Criticism and Fiction*: "In the whole range of fiction we know of no *true* picture of life—that is, of human nature—which is not also a masterpiece of literature, full of divine and natural beauty."

Lovejoy's offered works of practical idealism in the vein of the political novels of Brand Whitlock and the American Winston Churchill. Though a later generation would find these novels bland, most readers at the time did not. Long after muckraking exposés like those of Lincoln Steffens ceased to have much of a reading audience, Cordelia continued to publish nonfiction on corrupt politics and corporate evils; such books gave her intense moral satisfaction and she did not care that they usually lost money because the mass of readers had grown weary with being told about social ills that no one seemed able to cure.

With similar moral earnestness she published volumes of verse by new American and British poets which invariably lost money. Not one of Cordelia's minor poets ever attained a majority.

"What's the matter with me?" she asked her friend and fellow publisher, J. D. Taylor, president of Bond's. "Is my judgment of poetry that bad?"

"Well, how about mine?" J. D. replied.

"But you've got what's-his-name—Gerald Zouten, the new white hope of literature."

J. D. mimicked a surreptitious look around the banquet room of the Astor where they were attending a dinner given by the board of the Metropolitan Museum. "I have news for you, Cordelia. Zouten sells as badly as every other new poet. And I'll bet you one Yankee dollah that by 1917 nobody knows who he is—was."

"Then why do you persist in publishing him?"

"I guess to atone for my sins in publishing such popular works as—well, I won't go into detail."

"I'm sure," Cordelia said, "we all want to publish literature. Isn't it a shame there's so little of it?"

Eunice proceeded on her prescribed course. In 1911 she was presented to society. In 1913 she was married to Bayard Newcomb in a lavish St. Bartholomew's ceremony. Her Uncle Nick gave her away. Cordelia did not like Bayard, who was three years older than Eunice and would inherit a railroad fortune: She thought him weak and not very bright. Bayard returned her dislike, though for what reasons Cordelia never could ascertain. Bayard was so well bred by way of ancient Virginia family and private tutoring that he rarely expressed how he felt about anything. When asked for an opinion, he usually replied: "Eeeen-yule," a sound most took to signify agreement with their own prejudices, whatever they might be. After a three-months' honeymoon in Europe, the young couple would take up residence in a marble palace far up Fifth Avenue provided by the bridegroom's father.

"One less inhabitant on Murray Hill," Eleanor Roosevelt told Cordelia at the reception. She was up from Washington where Franklin was serving as Assistant Secretary of the Navy. "Why is everybody moving uptown?"

"Let 'em go." Cordelia made it sound good riddance. "Do you really hate Washington as much as you say?"

"More," Eleanor replied. "Once Franklin gets over this notion he must serve the federal government, I hope never to see that dull little city again. I still think Murray Hill the best place in the world."

If Eunice's leaving Murray Hill meant one less resident, Nick's move meant one more. For years, almost since the days when it was a sheep meadow, Gramercy Park had been Nick's home except when unemployment had made him take refuge at Dorfman Manor. One day a wide crack suddenly appeared in all the ceilings of his flat which overlooked the Park. The cracks, when plastered over, only grew wider. Nick, panicking, took it as an ominous sign. He offered to move in with Cordelia to keep her company, but she would have none of his living under the same roof. So he found a flat on Lexington near Fortieth Street and began to talk about Murray Hill as if he had discovered a new continent.

Another important development in 1913, besides Eunice's marriage, was Steve's admission to Yale in the class of 1917. To celebrate his acceptance, Cordelia presented him with a two-seated touring car with yellow spoke wheels whose entire tonneau he quickly painted a Yale blue. Cordelia had hoped the gift would somehow draw them closer. First thing, he took her for a ride in the Flyer all around Central Park at breathtaking speeds of eighteen and nineteen miles per hour. After that he was so busy tinkering with his new toy that sometimes he did not have time to join Cordelia for dinner. In fact, the Flyer caused him to leave earlier than necessary for New Haven so that he could show it off to classmates. Cordelia preserved a postcard he mailed her from Stamford.

> Dear Mama,
>
> Roads awful muddy, but made Stamford in six hours! Staying here at the Griswold House to fix a busted gasket will make New Haven by tomorrow night.
>
> Lovingly,
> Steve

That winter Cordelia decided that in the summer of 1914 she would take Steve and Penny to Europe. But she had not reckoned on what would happen during the May preceding that summer. Unknown to her (he said he hadn't wanted to worry her), Steve had been taking flying lessons with an aging nut on the outskirts of New Haven who, when drunk, thought he was one of the Wright brothers. The airplane in which Steve crashed was a box-tailed biplane with motor and push-propeller aft of the pilot. When it suddenly dived into an elm, its motor piled onto Steve. By the best of fortune he was not killed or his back broken, but he fractured his right shoulder and arm and his left leg. He spent a fretful summer in casts on Murray Hill, having only one week at Hasty's before he went back to New Haven.

Cordelia had presumed that Penny would graduate from Vassar with the class of 1914. She was bright enough and got good grades in every course where she applied herself. As Cordelia figured it, Penny's problems began when, in her junior year, she decided she must work the rest of her way through college. Cordelia tried to explain to her that it was totally unnecessary, but there never was any point of trying to explain something to Penny that she didn't want to understand. By that time she had joined the masses and insisted she never should be better than anyone else. ("Well," Cordelia rejoined, "that doesn't mean you have to be *worse* than they are.") Refusing to take more money from Cordelia, Penny turned to self-support and became drab and scrawny. One of her chief jobs was washing dishes in a college kitchen with what one of her former friends described as local slatterns. This job gave Penny the golden opportunity to make up a line with which she shocked Mary and anyone else who would listen whenever she came home: "Up there in Poughkeepsie, what between dishes and douches, I'm in hot water all of the time." Cordelia hoped that wasn't literally true.

Then, as the Christmas holidays approached in Penny's senior year, the hired kitchen-help decided to throw a party and someone brought in a few quarts of cheap rye whisky. Penny had been contemptuous of liquor ever since she'd made herself sick nipping sherry when she was fourteen. But in her new mood, anything good enough for the masses was good enough for her. Though she could not tolerate alcohol, she drank a slug of rye anyway. If she'd just gone off somewhere and been sick, all would have been well. However, she turned belligerent. Arming herself with a meat cleaver, she went in search of an assistant dean she disliked. She was disarmed by a night watchman, but the scandal could not be suppressed. The founder of Vassar College had been a Christian gentleman, who, though he owned a brewery, had vowed that none of the young ladies in the seminary he endowed ever should drink anything stronger than tea. Penny was expelled. Summarily, as one of Cordelia's best-selling authors was fond of describing such situations.

Cordelia tried to be philosophical about it and said, "Penny has overdone it again." But secretly she was deeply disappointed. She had hoped that at least one Lovejoy woman would manage to graduate from a good college.

After Penny came home they held long discussions on what she should try next. Penny, favoring a literary career as poet and essayist, stayed home and wrote through winter and spring. The results distressed Cordelia. A typical poem began:

Trembling flower in the gray, crannied church wall
I pluck you frail root and snotty filth and all. . . .

"What you really object to are the words 'snotty filth,'" she told her mother. "You're just too hypocritical to come straight out and say so. Have you ever really *looked* at these little blossoms you see growing in the crumbling walls of old buildings?"

"Frankly, no," Cordelia said, "I simply haven't had the time."

"Well, if you'd take the *time* away from your office, Mo-ther, you'd find these little blossoms actually grow in a kind of mucous compost that—oh, why should I have to *explain*? I *told* you in this very long poem that may run to thousands of lines I'm launching an all-out attack on organized religion of every kind."

"Launch away, as far as I'm concerned," Cordelia said. "And I don't object to 'snotty filth' per se. What I find objectionable is that I think you're launching against Alfred, Lord Tennyson. It sounds as if you're doing a burlesque of him. And the dear old gentleman has been dead a long time. It seems naively late to rebel against the Victorians, who have already been polished off by the Edwardians."

That winter and spring Cordelia did at least manage to get some flesh on Penny's bones, with Mary's help, and have her spruce up her hair and dress. But in May, Penny decided to become a hermit at Hasty's. She announced she was going back to nature and would become a naturalist writer. The sage of Hastings, the John Muir of Long Island Sound.

In June she discovered a fellow naturalist. Or he discovered her. He was a brawny young fisherman named Alben Albright who could barely write his name and read a few words. Upon each other they lavished a passion that Penny found too eloquent even for poetry. He took her virginity. Though she did lose her childhood to him, maturity did not immediately ensue. Of course she loved him, this great, strong, laughing child of nature. They would marry and she would teach him to read and write well and they would go into the fish business and open a store in Hastings and all their children would be strong and wise and beautiful. However, she was surprised by how quickly their first child announced existence within her.

Penny went to Alben and said they must marry at once. He agreed, and they would discuss the details tomorrow after another night of lovemkaing. Next day Alben was gone. Though he had many kinfolk in the area, he never was seen in Hastings again.

It was early September. Dr. Prettyman had removed the last cast from Steve and he had just gone back to New Haven when Penny came home and told her mother.

Cordelia was stunned and angered until she realized, *This could have happened to me with Jay Spencer.* Youth never was prepared to pay the toll for the hazards of passion. A part of Cordelia—the part that was not silently keening over what had befallen her poor child—stepped back from the immediate sadness and had to admire Penny's calm forthrightness. Possibly it was Penny's manner that caused Cordelia's voice to sound so cool:

"What do you want to do, sweetheart?"

Penny spoke very slowly: "I would like to grow up, Mama. If that is ever possible."

"It is possible." Cordelia took Penny in her arms and kissed her and both cried for a while.

"I mean," Cordelia said, "do you want to have the child or—lose it?"

"It's all I've been thinking about," Penny answered calmly. "I want to lose it—now. I'll lose it anyway. Adoption or the orphanage or whatever. And I couldn't stand that, once my child had been born and I knew it was alive. And I don't want to keep it. If I'm ever going to grow up, I have to start being practical. And I can't think of anything more impractical than trying to start again with a fatherless child."

They went together to Dr. Prettyman, who examined Penny, verified that she was pregnant, and said calmly, "These things happen."

"Obviously," Cordelia said.

"But they shouldn't have to happen," Penny said. "Why don't you doctors invent a pill or something that would prevent women from becoming pregnant unless they want to?"

"That will never be done," Dr. Prettyman said. "But

if some madman managed it, it would so upset the laws of nature and mankind that the world would become an entirely different place. I think nature would strike back and exact a penalty from those who defied her laws."

"From what you say," Cordelia told him, "I guess you'd object to what Penny and I want done."

"No, I wouldn't," he said. "I know what you want done. It's illegal, but I approve of it being done. It's quite different, in my opinion, from a—a—some obliterating medicine that destroys the normal biological functions. It—well, as I said, these things happen. I know a capable gynecologist who will do what you want. He has two capable nurses. The asepsis in his office is as good as in the best hospital. It will cost you two hundred dollars—in cash. Penny runs a certain risk. Never forget that. If anything tragic happened, I would ask a gentleman's agreement—a *lady*'s agreement never to go to the police. Think it over for twenty-four hours. I can make an appointment for you if you still want to go ahead. If you do, there's one thing that's a bit—eerie unless you're prepared for the experience. The physician and his nurses wear masks."

That was true when Penny and Cordelia went to a house in Greenwich Village a few nights later. But Penny observed before the masked physician donned surgical gloves that on a finger he wore a large Masonic ring. Although he took the fetus from her safely, she ever after mistrusted the Order of Freemasonry.

Penny's abortion was one of those rare secrets Cordelia kept from Mary, as from everyone else. She knew that the news would be almost more than Mary could bear. Mary grew more devout while Tim became less so. They regretted having no more children after Cora. It seemed unnatural to them since both came of prolific families, yet it manifestly was God's will.

Mary's greatest wish in life was that Cora would become something better than a housemaid. And Cordelia was determined that Cora would. She was a bright child, stable emotionally and so cheerful that she seldom cried.

"Someone in this house," Cordelia told Mary, "*somebody* in this household of women has *got* to graduate from a red-blooded women's college. Eunice and Penny booted it. It's too late for you and me, Mary. That leaves Cora."

Mary's invariable reply to such remarks was, "Lord save us, Tim and me are savin' for it."

They could use that money in their old age, Cordelia thought. *She* was going to see to it that Cora received as good an education as she had offered Penny. She found herself taking greater interest in Cora's grades at the parochial school on Second Avenue than she used to in her own children's report cards. When Cora graduated from eighth grade at the head of her class, Cordelia was more pleased than when Steve managed to make it through another year at Yale. The nuns said Cora was eminenty qualified to enter St. Agnes's Parochial High School for Girls, but could her parents afford it? Cordelia insisted on paying the fees herself.

"You've got to plan for your old age," she told a portesting Mary and Tim. "How can you be so improvident as to spend your savings on your daughter's high-school education?"

Penny at last showed symptoms of maturity. In October 1914 she took a job teaching feebleminded children at a charity school in Greenwich Village and moved from Murray Hill to be near her work. The patience necessary to her teaching the retarded began to show in her general attitudes as Cordelia had thought it never would. Somehow she began to look prettier and younger when Cordelia expected her to look plainer and older. She was much taken up with good causes. One was women's suffrage, another pacifism.

Cordelia and most other Americans had a sense of unreality over the outbreak of war in Europe during the summer of 1914. It seemed incredible that those people over there actually were killing one another. It seemed certain that reason would quickly prevail and peace descend again. When it did not, Cordelia was instinctively for the cause of the Allies against the Germans. But it was *their* fight, not America's. She was delighted when President Woodrow Wilson said the United States never would become involved in the European war. Thank heaven for that and that Steve was safely at Yale.

Penny brought the war closer to Cordelia with her vehement pacifism. Not a week passed that she wasn't marching in a pacifist parade in some part of the city. Then she and two other young women, speaking militantly for peace without holding a permit for public assembly on Bank Street, were arrested, and Cordelia had to go downtown and bail them out.

Steve, reading about it in a newspaper, sent one of his rare postcards.

Dear Ma—

Good gosh old Penny sure has gone to war. I could save some money if you sent me one of those new laundry boxes and I sent my stuff home by rr exp evry wk.

Lovingly,
S

Cordelia, pondering the message, wondered if she shouldn't enroll Steve in a summer course in English next year instead of carrying out her plan to have him spend July and August working for the company.

She saw increasingly less of her children, and Eunice least of all. She even stopped inviting Bayard and her to Christmas dinner after Eunice let her know that Bayard found her custom of having the servants sit down to dinner that day "quaint and very middle class." Marriage to Bayard made Eunice more snobbish than ever. The world rotated round *her*. To her mind the worst thing about the European war was the inconvenience it caused them: They had planned to spend the winter on the Riviera after taking the waters at Baden-Baden. It was no wonder Eunice and Penny quarreled violently. One day they happened onto each other in the parlor at 127 and fell to snapping and snarling like two angry bitches. Cordelia didn't even try to break up their quarrel. She believed she no longer felt anger, sorrow, or pride over her children—only a kind of inevitability.

Steven frightened her half to death when on New Year's Day, 1915, after spending the holidays at home and being unusually solicitous of her, he said, "Mama, I want to talk to you about something serious."

Her first thought was that he'd got some girl in trouble. Well, no doubt it was a thing that could be bought out of. But what he said next stunned her momentarily speechless:

"Mama, I want to go to France and join the Foreign Legion."

When she found words they were a colorful oath of Colonel Bob's she had thought she'd forgotten: "Oh, Jesus H. Christ and General Sherman! No, Steve, *no!*"

"Please, Mama, listen to me."

But she would not listen. She stifled his notion as forcefully as a commissar putting down an insurrection. And as effectively, she thought. She just hoped she hadn't damaged his feelings too hard, for when he left for Yale there were tears in his eyes and he kissed her more tenderly than he had since childhood. She cried for ten minutes after he had gone. A week later she received the warmest letter he'd ever written her.

She did not hear from him again till late February. The letter was written from Toulouse in France where he was starting basic infantry training with the Foreign Legion.

Her cry was piercing. She actually turned faint and had to pitch into a chair. Mary sent Cora running for Dr. Prettyman. After he arrived in his quiet little electric car, he gave her a sedative.

Cordelia heard Mary, as at a great distance, babbling to him, "Stevey joined the Foreign Legion, Stevey joined the Foreign Legion! Where's that? Where is it, Doctor?"

In a moment he replied, "It's in a streak of insanity that seems to run in the Lovejoy family."

17

Cordelia, giving Steve up for dead. felt she must arrange affairs for her own death. Should she sell the
company? Neither Eunice nor Penny ever could run it.
Nevertheless, in the summer of 1915 she asked Penny if
she was remotely interested in publishing. To her surprise, Penny said she would *love* a job at Lovejoy's.

"A word of warning," Cordelia said.

"I know, Mama. I am *not* going to start as an editor,
but only a reader. And you're *not* going to pay me
more than I'm earning teaching. And just because I'm
the president's daughter I can*not* take off whenever I
please to attend a rally or something. And I will *not*
indulge my personal prejudices in verse, but remember
we're in a business firm and our purpose is to make
money. Mama, you forget that a long time ago I told
you I'd like to grow up."

Cordelia was pleased.

Penny was living then with a woman friend on the
south side of Washington Square. It was different there
from the elegant north side where Granger had lived.
On the south side the handsome brick houses of the
well-to-do had given way to the pressure of the tenements at their backs. During the nineteenth century
those tenements had been the center of the city's black
population, but early in the new century waves of Italian immigrants had forced out the black people. Now
the brick homes on the south side of the Square had
been turned into rooming houses with low rents which
young writers, artists, and political rebels could afford.

In those years the tide of migration to New York was

not from Europe alone; there was a trickle of would-be writers and artists from the hinterland of America. As Frank Norris wrote in *Blix*: "Of all the ambitions of the Great Unpublished, the one that is strongest, the most abiding, is the ambition to get to New York. For these, New York is the *point de départ*, the pedestal, the niche, the indispensable vantage ground."

Penny introduced Cordelia to Norris, who had a small front bedroom at No. 61, where she lived. S. S. McClure, the magazine genius, had discovered Norris's work in an obscure San Francisco periodical and invited him to come east and write for *McClure's Magazine*. Through Penny, Cordelia met others who lived or socialized on the Square. She became acquainted with Edna St. Vincent Millay, Willa Cather, Floyd Dell, Lincoln Steffens, Carl Van Vechten, Hutchins Hapgood, Walter Lippmann, Jo Davidson. They were names to remember, but there were dozens of other writers and artists whom she would not be able to recall a few years later.

One evening when she and Penny went to dinner, as they frequently did, at Polly's Restaurant, next door to the Washington Square Book Shop, Steffens and a handsome young man sat down at the long table with them. Steffens introduced his friend: the famous Jack Reed, who had recently returned from France where he had been covering the war for *The Masses*.

"Mrs. Lovejoy has a son in France serving with the Foreign Legion," Steffens told Reed.

Reed looked at her intently: "Why is he doing that?"

"I don't know," Cordelia said. "How do you ever explain youthful folly? My only consolation is to think of him as dead."

"Mama," Penny said, "I wish you would *please* stop saying that."

"That's how I feel," Cordelia went on steadfastly.

"That way I can stand it better when I receive the official notification."

Steffens looked distressed; he was such a kindly man it was a wonder he wrote such harsh words about villains in high places.

"I've read some of your reports in *The Masses*, Mr. Reed. I liked the way you ended each dispatch with the words 'This is not our war.' But I find it hard to accept your view this war is only a clash between 'traders,' as you call them, instead of a struggle for democracy and liberty."

"It's the way I see it," Reed said.

"I realize that. I appreciate your integrity. For all I know you may be right. But if you are, what a tragedy for all who die in the war and all who love them. Your way we can't dignify our grief with a touch of nobility."

"Has there ever been any nobility in war, Mrs. Love-joy?"

She grimaced. "Probably not. But how would you convince my son and my husband, who died over that Cuba nonsense, and *his* father, who—oh, what's the use?"

Hippolyte Havel, the chief cook and assistant waiter at Polly's and a confirmed anarchist, burst upon them and began pounding Reed, whom he adored, on the back. "What," he cried, "are you and Lincoln doing eating here with the bourgeois pig?" It was what he called all nonradicals.

"The appellations grow shorter," Cordelia said to Steffens. "Usually he calls me a bourgeois pig publisher. Why do I come here and pay to be insulted?"

"It's his spareribs," Steffens said. "They really are the best."

"That's what I'll have tonight, Hippolyte," Reed told him. "That's why I came here."

But Hippolyte said he had made a lamb stew that

was far better than his spareribs; Reed must have some. Reed said he didn't like lamb stew, but Hippolyte insisted he would change his mind after he tasted *this* stew.

"Mr. Lincoln?" Hippolyte asked Steffens.

"Do I really have a choice?" Steffens replied.

"Not really," Reed said.

"Two lamb stews," Hippolyte said. "Comrade Penny?"

"Oh, well."

"Three lamb stews." He turned to Cordelia. "Because you're with good friends of mine, bourgeois pig publisher, I'll make it four lamb stews."

"No, I'll have the spareribs," Cordelia said.

"Lamb stew!"

"Spareribs!"

They carried on like children while many in the restaurant stopped eating to watch the titanic struggle of wills. At last Hippolyte stormed back to the kitchen, and Steffens said, "I wonder what you'll get?"

"Spareribs," Cordelia said. "He knows I won't touch the lamb stew. But they won't be properly done spareribs."

Hippolyte brought three lamb stews and then a helping of spareribs for Cordelia. He watched Reed take a bite of the stew and asked him, "How is it, Comrade Jack?"

"Delicious, Hippolyte."

He returned to his kitchen, beaming, and Cordelia asked, "Honestly now, Mr. Reed, do you like the stew?"

"No. As I said, I loathe lamb stew, but can't bear to hurt Hippolyte's feelings. How are your spareribs?"

"Undone. As predicted."

"Mama," Penny said, "would you like some of mine? It's really good and I know you love lamb stew."

"Thanks, dear, but I wouldn't *think* of it. I'm having a principle for dinner."

"Say now"—Reed cast all a startled look—"are we acting out some kind of fable?"

"Not a fable," Steffens said. "More a kind of paradox."

"I'll tell you something." Reed swallowed with an expression of distaste. "Paradox is a word I really only understand under certain specific conditions."

Cordelia sawed at a string of meat. "G. K. Chesterton says it best. 'A paradox is truth standing on its head to draw attention to itself.'"

Not until that dinner did Penny realize how much she loved her mother. Almost anyone could accept despair with a bit of grace, but Cordelia took it with some wit. Penny knew that she was lonely and deeply depressed by her firm belief Steve would die in France. The certainty depressed Penny, too. She read Steve's letters to their mother—those half-witted scrawls that did not reflect his true intelligence. She also read some of Cordelia's letters to him—awkwardly formal words that lacked her usual expressive ease.

Penny wrote him herself, at great length and eloquently, saying she was still a pacifist at heart but had quit wearing her heart on her sleeve; out of respect for him, she no longer participated in peace parades and rallies. (And that was absolutely true.) Please, she begged Steve, try to write Mama something interesting about what you're doing and who your friends are and things like that.

Back came a beautiful letter, pleasing Cordelia as nothing had since he went away. Cordelia, nearly always perceptive, did not comprehend at first what Penny divined immediately: Steve, artful infantryman, had hired a literate comrade to write the letter and then recopied it in his own hand.

"Just read this," Cordelia said with wonder. "Steve has finally turned articulate. Do you suppose the pressure of combat has—well—matured him?"

When Penny wrote and told him how much Cordelia appreciated the letter, he finally replied near Christmas.

Dr P—

Glad Ma liked letter. Was writ by good pal Bert Hall. L's shud publsh him someday. His last job before joining Fr Leg was driving a Paris taxi not knowing a word of French. Joining Leg claimed to be professional soldier. Asked where, sed '5 yrs in Salvation Army.' Good man!

Hey old P you stay pasifist. Im one now but too late. This Joffre chap insane. Throws divisions at ironclad enemy positions like snowballs. That is Al Seeger's phrase not mine. Very bad in Artois in Sept. Objective our 2d Leg Rgt a farm called Navarin. German machinegun fire everywhere like hailstorms. That is my phrase, not as good as Al's. Awful casualties. I was lucky, Bert too. Maybe the censor will cut this. The hell with the censor. He can't read English. Cannot in fact read French either.

Say now Penny you tell Mama I transfered to Red Cross or something safe like that. YMCA. That's it! I transfer to YMCA. Between you and me am transfering to int'l air squadron called Lafayette Escadrille. Going down south & really learn to fly this time but dont tell Mama. A few of us finally figure out in our fat heads its safer in the air than on the ground but don't tell Mama.

Glad Mama liked the lit'y news Bert put in that letter about Al's poetry & dispatches to the Sun & all. Al best dam jolly poet ever did live. Would join int'l air squad with me but seems to prefer death to life so he's staying in 2nd Regt. I go now to YMCA!

Love,
S

Steve at the same time wrote a brief note to Cordelia that he was quitting the Foreign Legion to take a nice safe job with the YMCA. She did not believe it.

"And now I realize he didn't write that literate letter," she told Penny. "He got someone else to write it. How can he fool me so easily? What's this talk about the YMCA? What's he up to? If you know, Penny, I beg you to tell me."

Penny could not lie to her. She would find out eventually that Steve was leaving the infantry to fight in the air—and maybe never trust Penny again. So, as gently as possible, Penny told her of Steve's plan to join the Lafayette Escadrille.

Cordelia did not carry on about it. She simply said, "Since he's so determined to die, I suppose it doesn't matter much how he does it."

Penny had fallen in love with one Leonard Zukoff, who was working for his doctorate in psychology at Columbia. They lived together on Washington Square in order to make sure that they were strong enough to withstand the assaults bourgeois marriage would make on free love like theirs. Leonard, who was fond of analyzing everything, went on at length about Steve's letters.

All those abbreviations, misspellings, and violations of syntax were, Leonard said, symptoms of impatience and rebellion. He must not have written like that in school themes and papers; and Penny admitted that was so. "Then what is your brother rebelling against?" asked Leonard. "I will tell you. He is rebelling against your mother. Your mother is a very strong-willed woman. I can tell that from having dinner with her. She cuts her meat *against* the grain."

"Doctor Zukoff," Penny demanded, "are you analyzing my brother or my mother?"

"Both. You can't analyze one without the other. A widow like your mother had to have a strong will to survive and prosper. That publishing house became like God to her—both the Creator and the Created. Her son—her adored son—she wants him to share . . . I have mentioned the work of Dr. Sigmund Freud to you."

"You have mentioned little else to me. Lenny, are you trying to say that Mama wants Steve to become the head of Lovejoy's and he doesn't want to?"

"I'm leading up to that," Leonard said. "Why do you always rush the point so?"

One day in April 1916 Cordelia's secretary, Lucille Birch, said that John Speer was in the reception room wanting to make an appointment. Cordelia, delighted, had him shown in at once.

"Good heavens, John, you haven't changed a bit." It was true: the same blue eyes with only a trace of lines in the fair skin and a touch of gray in his curly black hair.

He cast her a kind of surprised look. "Nor you, Cordelia. Success becomes you. And the farther up Madison you move, the handsomer your offices become. Edward used to mention the top of Murray Hill. Looks like you've made it."

"Not quite. A new office building is starting up two blocks north. Whoever takes the top floors of that will really be on top of Murray Hill. Are you still at Bacon's in Boston?"

He'd left there long ago and become production manager at Greene Brothers, then comptroller at Leacock's in Philadelphia. A year ago Haney and March, in New York, had made him executive director of its education department, but now, as she probably had heard, Balcomb's was absorbing Haney and March, and Balcomb's had its own education director. So he had come looking for a job. She felt the vague disappointment she always did in old friends who never came around to say hello until they wanted a favor.

"Publishing," John said, "seems more and more an itinerant trade. Like apple-knocking in the fruit belt."

"Colonel Bob used to say it always was." As Cordelia talked, she pondered what John had been doing. Did such a diversity of jobs spell talent or a knockabout nature? Well, he used to be talented, all right. But what was he these many years later?

"Cordelia, how would you like to start an education department at Lovejoy's?"

She was caught by surprise, but did not show it. She had been considering the field and investigating it for a couple of years. Over a long period of time few ventures had been more profitable for Lovejoy's than the Blackwell readers Cordelia had acquired. That might have served as a solid basis for a textbook department, but somehow she never had found the time to try to develop it.

"I don't think so, John," she answered. "The education field seems already overcrowded."

"Overcrowded with deadwood," he said. "This war—I hate to say it, but I know we'll get into it—this war will change everything. The publishing house that comes out with newer, better texts after the war is going to make a fortune."

"Better texts of what?"

"In the physical sciences and the social sciences. Forget English literature—alas. The shelves are already groaning with anthologies of literature. But a new generation of teachers is clamoring for better texts in physics, chemistry, biology, in sociology, and in something they're beginning to call modern civilization."

Cordella smiled. "Is that what it is called now? John, are you talking about college texts or public school texts? The whole area simply appalls me. There's this business of acceptance. How do you get an institution or a school system or a state to accept your work? I've heard dark tales about money under the table and all that. I want no part of it."

"That's grossly exaggerated," John said. "I'm cynical about human nature, but there's general honesty among educators. Stuffy sometimes, yes. Stupid, maybe occasionally, But—"

"Here's the sort of problem I see," Cordelia said. "I would not *think*, for instance, of publishing a text on biology that didn't discuss and espouse the theory of evolution. But what state in the Bible Belt would accept that book? What Roman Catholic parochial school or college would allow it in a classroom?"

"There's a new day coming," John said.

"And am I to lose my money trying to bring it on? John, which way do you want to go? College? Or public schools? You can't go both."

"College. It will cost you about three hundred thousand before things turn around—and then it's profit all the way. Public schools would cost at least half million to start—and you might lose your shirt. I want about a week to work up a study for you. First I wanted to see if you are interested."

"But I'm really not," she said.

"But I think you might become so."

"John, why do you suddenly bring this to me *now*?"

"Because, Cordelia, *now* I'm unemployed."

"Are you still married?"

"Yes." For the first time he did not meet her gaze. Why was that? "No children. We live in Brooklyn. Cordelia, even if you're not interested in a college-textbook department, can I interest you in having lunch? Do you have a date?"

She did, but Lucille could break it for her. Suddenly she loved the idea of having lunch with John Speer.

That night Cordelia had a rare nightmare and awakened herself with an odd cry. Orienting herself, she realized she had cried out the word "Apple-knocker!"

Itinerant laborer, apple-picker, following the crops and reaping the harvests that the farmers had grown and tended. Apple-knocker! It applied to John Speer. She wished she did not like him so much, for he was no different from all the employees who had come and gone at the company. Away back, when she had wanted him to return to Lovejoy's and help her, he had refused. But now that he needed work he was on her doorstep. Apple-knocker!

It seemed in the nature of publishing that many of its people changed jobs often. For some it was the only way to get ahead. Runyon was rare in that he'd risen to editor-in-chief of the house in which he'd taken his first job out of college. No other oldtimers remained except for Li'l Abe and Bill Paisley, whose role as company counsel was only part-time work. Max Gurland had retired and—of all surprising things—was trying farming in New Jersey. Marty was gone—and Cordelia grievously missed him as comptroller. She had offered him several thousand a year more to stay, and possibly he expressed the feelings of many who left when he told her: "It's not just the money. It's the boredom of the day after day. And then you think of the adventure of a new move." Severense, a new house, had offered Marty a big chunk of stock. Then Severense went broke, and Marty disappeared in the direction of Minneapolis, too proud to come round and ask for his old job back.

Lovejoy's employed more women than any other

publishing house in the country. There were two associate editors, one male, one female, both of them inhouse promotions from readers. Of the three readers, two were women. The chief of the copy department was a woman. Among major publishing houses, Lovejoy's had one of the first full-time publicity directors—a woman. But the advertising director was a man. On the other hand, the art director—and Lovejoy's was the very first house to have a full-time art director—was a woman. A gruff male named McNamarra, who succeeded Marty as comptroller, would hire only men clerks, claiming that women were poor at figures. The sales manager and everyone in his department were men—a situation Cordelia expected never would change.

She scarcely ever fired anyone. If she wanted to be rid of someone, she made work so unpleasant that the employee resigned. The employee Cordelia fired most often was a woman reader named Gertrude Nayton— or, as Cordelia often referred to her—"that goddamn Gertrude, always acting like a damn woman." Gertrude could walk along an empty corridor and fall flat on her face: the result, she maintained, of having weak ankles. Gertrude was a slow reader (Cordelia called her a backward one). Usually Cordelia fired Gertrude for rejecting a manuscript that turned out to be a best seller when published by another house. But then Cordelia would relent and hire her back because Gertrude was the sole support of aged parents. One time she fired Gertrude for staying away from work all day without following the prescribed rule of going to a public telephone and informing the company receptionist that she was sick. However, it turned out that Gertrude had gone to one of the newfangled public booths where she had somehow trapped herself and discovered she didn't have a nickel to make a call. You had to know Gertrude well to understand that she would stay there most of the day, too shy to make passersby aware of her plight. Cordelia, knowing her well, rehired her.

After Penny came to work as a reader, she made a suggestion that astonished Cordelia. Gertrude, Penny said, was perfect in her judgments of children's books. At the time the company did not have a juvenile department, but published five or six books a year for children which were carried on the regular trade lists. Gertrude had a passion for stories about chickens which could be illustrated in beautiful full colors, always with a basic red motif. She became fearless in her defense of a chicken story, with the result that Lovejoy's published more chicken stories than any house in the history of book publishing. And all of them sold well, indicating that the American reading public shared Gertrude's passion for Rhode Island Reds.

"Start a juvenile department and make Gertrude the editor," Penny told her mother. Cordelia tried it and found to her delight that the square peg finally fit into a square hole. She anticipated never having to fire Gertrude again—at least not until the public tired of chicken stories.

That was how matters stood in the company when John sent Cordelia his prospectus about the creation of a college-textbook department. In another few weeks some of the apple-knockers might depart, but they would be replaced by other itinerant workers. Action did not signify real movement, nor did movement mean true change. *Viva* Lovejoy's, where genius never lingered long enough for Cordelia to reward it amply!

But this proposal of John's was something different from the usual going and coming. It troubled her because it was so well done, so absolutely logical. John had left out nothing but his own salary. The clever man, leaving that trustingly to her! He proposed the initial preparation and publication of six textbooks, three in the physical sciences and three in the social. He had the specific subjects, citations of their need in current curricula, the professors who should write them and what their royalties should be, the professors who should edit the texts and what their fees should be. His estimates of the costs of the physical production of each book, projected a year and two into the future, were as sharp as the rest of his arguments.

Cordelia recognized it as a great idea in the vein of John's famous John Jacob Astor Edition. But it was not a quick turnover idea such as had characterized most of Lovejoy's financial successes. It was slow growth, involving capital investments that would not begin to reap their full harvest for many years. She gave Penny the prospectus and asked her opinion.

Early next morning Penny came into her office and said, "Mama, this is the best, most creative idea I've seen since coming to work here."

"Well," Cordelia said, "at least it's the most expensive." She phoned John and invited him to lunch next day.

She took him to White's, where a woman could go to lunch without the waiters treating her like an object of charity. "You underestimated the cost of your project," she told him.

"Do you mind," he said, "if I order a Manhattan cocktail? Have you ever tried one?"

"Of course. Once in a while I have one before dinner instead of sherry. But a Manhattan at *noon*?"

"Would you prefer, Cordelia, that we leave now and come back for dinner?"

She had to smile. "Two Manhattans, Gerald," she told the waiter. "This gentleman is trying to get me drunk." She looked at John. "You didn't count your salary in the prospectus. How much are you seeking?" He just shrugged. "How much were you earning at Haney and March?" she asked him.

"Twelve."

That was true. She had taken the trouble to find out. Why did people ever try to lie about their salaries in publishing? Didn't they realize that even bitter enemy publishers supplied the vital information to one another upon request? If John had lied to her by as much as five hundred dollars about his previous salary she would have scuttled his idea immediately.

"What makes me most dubious about the whole thing," she said, "is the prospect of war. You say you think it's coming. So do I. What a bad time to start a long-range college thing. All the young men go off to war and get killed. What then?"

"Everybody else goes to college and studies your books. You're not going into this to make a quick buck. You want to make a slow one. Something for your old age after all the fast dollars have been spent. When you start in college texts, don't think of the students now in college. Think of the students who are still only gleams in their fathers' eyes as they look at their mothers."

His rubbishy talk made her smile again. "Try it for the irony of the situation, Cordelia. Here I am, a child who never made it to eighth grade being an expert on college education. Think of my egotism. Mind if I have my letterhead printed John Speer, Ph.D.?"

"I wouldn't *think* of allowing such."

He did the most charming thing. Reaching out, he touched her hand and said, "I know you wouldn't. That's why I'd like to work for you."

She said something foolish: "Why did you wait so long to come propose this?"

He looked away. "As I said, I've been employed."

They talked on and on about the project. At the last minute she panicked and didn't want to do it. Throw away three hundred thousand dollars she'd slaved to earn? But she knew the crestfallen look that would come over John's handsome face if she refused. Somehow that seemed worse than throwing away the money.

She said, "You might as well begin on Monday. I think your starting salary should be thirteen thousand."

18

As soon as McNamarra learned that John was earning more than he was, he demanded a raise. When Cordelia refused, he quit and took a job at Bacon's. The pay was no more, but he was glad (he told everyone) that he'd had the chance to tell off that vicious Lovejoy woman. It left Cordelia short one vice-president (the other vice-president being Runyon), so she appointed John to that office. For comptroller she hired a hotheaded young Scotsman named MacLennon, who had been fired from Bacon's, among other companies. If one could win at the game of musical chairs, Cordelia did, for she hired MacLennon for far less than she'd been paying McNamarra.

John left at once on a tour of colleges and was gone for the remainder of the school year. When he returned, Cordelia asked if his wife disliked his long absence from home. He just shrugged. Later she was talking to Allyn Bacon, owner of Bacon publishers, who had come down from Boston to attend an awards dinner at the Waldorf. He congratulated her on hiring John: "A gem. In fact, a saint. How saintly you'd know if you knew his wife Veronica. A woman afflicted."

"I'm sorry. What's her affliction?"

"Religion. The Roman Catholic variety. John is a healthy agnostic, like me. Why he married Veronica I can't imagine. Well, she is, or used to be, a good-looking woman. But *obsessed* by her religion. They say in Boston that even the priests run from her when they see her coming. I think she married John with the idea of converting him to the Faith. But it hadn't worked last I knew. Guess their home is like an armed camp. One of those religious wars between them. The most savage kind, you know."

Cordelia met Veronica at the annual company picnic held at Hasty's in August. She was dark, handsome, statuesque, so reserved that she made everyone around her act shy. She kept her gloves on until it came time to eat the watermelon. Of course she declined to take part in the softball game between women and men. That year the women almost won. Penny knocked in the tie-breaking run, but Gertrude fell down rounding third base and was tagged out at the plate.

That year Cordelia paid for Mary, Tim, and Cora to take a vacation at Asbury Park the last week in August. Mary wanted to have a cousin come in to substitute at 127, but Cordelia refused. She hadn't spent an evening alone since childhood, and she looked forward to the solitude. Each afternoon she came home early, put on a light robe, sipped some iced Rhine wine, broiled herself a chop, and read for pleasure. First she would reread one of Sherlock Holmes's adventures, then intersperse the rereading of a chapter of *Bleak House*, next another Holmes adventure, and so on. Never falling asleep until midnight, she read the familiar stories as avidly as she had for the first time long ago. How sweet were the vices of iced wine, Holmes, and Dickens.

When two chemistry professors from Michigan showed up with their wives at Lovejoy's one afternoon, Cordelia didn't want them to interfere with her secret pleasures of the evening. John said he *had* to take them to dinner, and could she possibly come along? No, she said, take Penny. He reported back that Penny claimed a date.

"Then find somebody else, John. Try Gertrude."

"I *can't!*" He made a gesture of despair. "She might fall down or something. These professors are sort of stuffy and I *have* to lure 'em away from Balcomb's.

What's the matter with this company that the only attractive women in it are you and your daughter?"

"Flattery will get you nowhere, John." It occurred to her that neither of them had mentioned his wife, that he *couldn't* invite Veronica to dinner with those people any more than he could ask Gertrude. Relenting, she agreed to go.

They went to a French restaurant where the chemistry professors gorged sickeningly on snails and their wives carried on boringly about the social shortcomings of the university president's wife. At last, after dispatching the four back to their hotel by cab, John and Cordelia decided he would walk her the few blocks home. It was a warm, still evening, with muted voices and an occasional blare of gramophone music drifting from open windows.

When they reached 127, Cordelia said, "I'm going to have a cold root beer. Do you want one, or do you prefer the regular kind?"

"Make mine the regular kind." He followed her inside and on to the kitchen.

"Chip me some ice for my root beer," she told him. "I hate to chip ice. It flies all over the place and never comes out the right size. The pick's in that drawer."

As he leaned across to get it, his hand accidentally brushed her side. Suddenly everything was different. They paused, grew still, alertly examining past, present, and future. Cordelia imagined that she remembered everything John ever had said, every gesture, the fact that over the years they had not even shaken hands. There was something selective about him, as about her, that made indiscriminate handshaking unpleasant. The only previous time he had touched her was that day in White's when he had reached out a hand.

She found she had closed her eyes and drawn in her breath. But she would die of asphyxiation if she continued to hold her breath while studying the future. His lips moved softly against hers and her breath rushed out, leaving her body inhabited by a strange sensation. Their arms drew them together tightly, and she wondered if this strange feeling were something new or only a thing forgotten.

Deciding it was brand new, she buried her face against his neck and whispered, "Can you stay here tonight?"

The word failed him, he could only nod dumbly.

Now she fell prey to tremulousness. She felt as weak as someone very young or very old. She might have just stood there and trembled to death if he had not guided and supported her up the stairs. The lights remained on, the doors open, the ice melting in the sink.

When they entered her room, she formed a thought: *No stage directions, please*. But being the managerial sort, she could not resist one:

"John, are you prepared?"

"Christ, no!" He sounded plaintive. "Why should I be?"

Oh, glory hallelujah that this was as unexpected to him as to her! Why should he be prepared, indeed? In some cranny of her questioning mind she had wondered, since he seemed to enjoy being a traveling man, if maybe he plied the whorehouse circuit from Portland to Peoria. Those traveling old boys, like the children who espoused the cause of Baden-Powell's youth movement, were said always to Be Prepared. If John had answered that of course he was, she might have found the strength to stop her absurd shaking and tell him they must not go through with this. *Might* have. But probably not.

"Oh, the hell with it," she said.

They took and gave without stint. Never had she known such pleasure. Intuitively she had known he would be a wonderful lover, but how magnificent she never could have imagined.

At some cool hour of morning she came blissfully awake. John slept at her side like a child. Up Murray Hill came Harry Spink's milk wagon, the horse that seemed to walk in its sleep putting one foot softly ahead of another, the clank of Harry's milk cans and the rattle of his sterilized bottles irrepressible. The wagon stopped in front of 127, the horse uttering snoring sounds, and then Harry clanked around to the back of the house and put two quarts of milk and a pint of cream into the icebox through the outside hatch. She heard Harry close the back door and come around and close the front door, too. Then there was a pause while he scribbled and put in the mailbox a chastening note that she had neglected to close and lock her doors in a city filled with thieves. At last the horse gave a startled snort and walked on in its sleep.

John stirred, and within minutes they were loving each other again.

She cooked him a big breakfast and had her usual fruit and coffee. "I didn't know a grown man could drink so much milk," she told him. "Maybe Harry Spink knows what he's doing after all. I've been writing him notes all week to leave only one quart of milk, and he's been writing me back that's not enough."

The best thing about breakfast was that neither felt any need to try to explain what had happened. She washed the dishes while he dried them, and then they went to the office together.

Cordelia was in love as she never thought she could be, even in her wildest adolescent daydreams. Of course she did not intend it to show, but of course it did.

Penny was the first to see it. "It's really quite marvelous," she told Leonard.

"But can you tell if the man—what's his name— reciprocates the affection?" asked Leonard.

"It's perfectly obvious he does every time he looks at her—which is most of the time."

"That's extremely important," Leonard said. "How old is your mother now?"

"Forty-five. No, I guess it's forty-six. I don't remember. But I can't get over such *old people* falling in love."

"It's quite common," Leonard said. "There are instances of people in their sixties falling in love."

"That's sweet, but sort of sad, too." Tears came to Penny's eyes.

"Why are you weeping?" Leonard asked.

"I was thinking about people in their sixties falling in love and then—not being able to do it."

"Not being able to do what?"

"Make love."

He frowned. "Do you mean have sexual intercourse? Why don't you say what you mean instead of indulging in these middle class euphemisms? There is plenty of sound evidence that lots of people in their sixties have sexual intercourse. . . ."

Penny stopped listening to him and thought about her mother, knowing that Leonard still would be talking when she felt like listening again. He was.

"I don't want to think about it," she interrupted him.

"You don't want to think about what?"

"About my mother having sexual intercourse with any man but my father."

"That's the most immature thing you've ever said," Leonard exclaimed. "You're full of immaturities, but—"

"Shut up!" Penny cried. "My mother is *not* having sexual intercourse with John Speer! They love each other, but it's all very platonic and sad because he's married and Mother is the most honorable woman who ever lived and—"

She and Leonard quarreled long and loudly over the

matter, but of course Cordelia and John were having sexual intercourse, and of course Penny finally realized it. Being essentially honest, she admitted it to Leonard.

"I've been waiting for Mama to do something crazy," she told him. "I thought maybe she'd take up horseback riding again or fire Gertrude for the seventeenth time. Of course she's bought a whole new wardrobe—maybe two new wardrobes—and redone her hair. But today convinced me that she and John are—you know. He smokes cigarettes—Fatimas. Today I went in her office and there she sat smoking a cigarette—a Fatima. She stared at me with utter defiance, and I couldn't remember what I went in to see her about. I turned around and walked out and in the hall I ran into Gertrude. She was fuming. She said to me, 'You can smell the smoke everywhere.' She said, 'I object to women smoking on moral grounds.' I said, 'Pipe it down, Gertrude, you want to get fired again?' She just went on down the hall and had a loud coughing fit outside Mama's office."

"This cigarette-smoking is a very interesting symptom," Leonard said. "As I guess you know, smoking is an oral habit."

"Well, I wouldn't call it anal."

"Surprise, surprise," Leonard said, "some theoreticians do. But I think it's most significant that your mother has taken up an oral practice engaged in by what's-his-name and—"

"Now you listen here!" yelled Penny.

Their quarrel was dreadful.

What Cordelia finally did surprised everyone, but astonished Penny most of all. It happened just a week before President Wilson asked Congress for a declaration of War on April 2, 1917. Cordelia put 127 up for sale and bought a handsome Georgian mansion on Park Avenue near Fortieth Street at the very top of Murray Hill.

Not even the President telling a weeping audience

that "the world must be made safe for democracy"
quite surpassed Penny's surprise that her mother was
giving up their beloved home. How beloved had not occurred to Penny until she was about to lose it.

Immediately after the transaction closing the purchase of the new house, Cordelia took John there to
show him the mansion, and in each of its twenty rooms
he seized her in his arms and kissed her. So she was
breathless when they emerged onto Park Avenue that
afternoon.

It happened that at that moment Mrs. Stuyvesant
Fish was passing by slowly in her Pierce-Arrow with
chauffeur and footman riding in the open front seat.
Though Mrs. Fish was well enclosed by glass and wood,
she wore vestiges of pioneer automotive days—a scarf
over her head and large dark glasses. Since she had
grown deaf with aging and could not hear anything her
chauffeur and footman said beyond the partition of her
glass-and-wood cage, Mamie Fish imagined that they
could not hear her either. Having no faith in the speaking tube connecting them, she had improvised a mega-
phone through which she bellowed orders.

Now, seeing Cordelia and John coming out of the
house, she cried to her chauffeur through the mega-
phone: "Whoa! Stop! Stay! Halt!"

The chauffeur halted with such prompt obedience
that Mrs. Fish was almost flung onto the floor. She
beckoned Cordelia, who introduced John after the footman leaped out and rolled down the window. Cordelia
told her she had just purchased the mansion.

"Now, why," asked Mrs. Fish, "did you do that?"

"I was beginning to feel hemmed in where I live,"
Cordelia replied.

"People only feel hemmed in," said Mrs. Fish,
"when they're living with someone they don't love.
Could this handsome gentleman possibly be the one you
love?"

Cordelia did not hesitate: "Yes!"

"Abosolutely wonderful," Mrs. Fish said. "You both must come to a private tea at my house tomorrow at five o'clock. Mr. Speer, you come at five-fifteen so that Mrs. Lovejoy and I can gossip about you."

Cordelia was there promptly at five.

"Is he rich?" asked Mamie Fish.

"No. He works for wages as an official of my company."

"How really too bad," Mrs. Fish said. "What else is wrong with him?"

"He's married to a Roman Catholic woman who refuses to divorce him."

"How could you fall in love so foolishly? There are lots of well-off, single Protestants running around loose. I've introduced you to several over the years, but you persist in—Are you seeking a role in a Greek tragedy?"

"Not that I know of," Cordelia said. "It's just that I fell in love with John."

"Well, he is very sweet. He must bring you to dinner a week from Saturday here. Special guests only. It's to celebrate my retirement from society."

"Mamie, you can't. Your friends can't live without you. What are you going to do?"

"We're going up the valley. Stuyvesant says with some wisdom that Fishes belong up the river."

It was the most enjoyable dinner dance Cordelia ever attended. She found it hard to believe that the Fishes were retiring to the country, but they did—and Cordelia never saw Mamie Fish again.

Incredibly, Mary was beginning to get on her nerves. Mary was too much with her; she wanted more privacy. It was a chief reason for her buying the Park Avenue mansion. Besides, her money was piling up. Why shouldn't she spend some of it and realize that old ambition of Edward's? To live in a mansion on Murray

Hill now meant little to her, she thought. But why not try it, just for old times' sake?

What she truly wanted to do was live with John, married or not. Yet she never could do that unless Veronica died. John had asked for a divorce, but Veronica refused absolutely. They had been separated for months, and he lived in a hotel near the office.

John begged Veronica again, promising all kinds of money or anything else she wanted. He told Cordelia the results of that interview when they met at the Barclay Hotel in Philadelphia. John got drunk while castigating Veronica. For a moment Cordelia thought that he might, in his rage and frustration, try to jump out a window into Rittenhouse Square.

"That bitch!" he cried. "She has a detective agency on us. She's out to humiliate you any way she can!"

"John, let me go talk to her person-to-person."

"No! There's no person-to-person possible with that bitch. If you ever go to her, I'll never see you again."

"All right, all right, my name's not Veronica! So please don't talk to me the way you do to her. I say again, let's forget about Veronica and move under the same roof and live as if some priest or parson had mumbled his words over us."

But he would not because of what it would do to her reputation. In vain she insisted that she did not care. Though John was free of old-fashioned restraints, he could not bring himself to let them live together out of wedlock. No matter that many knew or suspected they were having an affair; he insisted that they maintain the appearance of convention.

The Park Avenue mansion was more expensive than Cordelia had anticipated. She paid a hundred and twenty-three thousand for it, then found she had to spend nearly fifteen thousand more for refurbishing. After that came the expensive task of furnishing it. A few times in the course of it all she had fits of crying, a new experience for her. The house was not ready to be occupied until September 1917. Meanwhile, the family that had purchased 127 for twenty-nine thousand brought suit to gain occupancy.

Meanwhile, too, there was the servant problem. A trained butler now was necessary, and Tim neither wanted nor was adaptable to the role. The task of chief housekeeper was too formidable for Mary, she refused to accept a secondary role under someone else. She quit. Cordelia, who had been wishing she would do that, suddenly found that she could not live without her. A compromise was worked out: Neither Mary nor Tim ever would be accountable to any servant in the house.

Cordelia planned a grand opening for her mansion, as if it were a new art gallery or Madison Square Garden. But nothing was ready on time, and so she postponed it. Somehow word of the postponement did not reach Penny, who came at the appointed six o'clock and brought Leonard.

Leonard had an owlish look, which new horn-rimmed glasses accentuated. When he stepped into the large foyer and looked about he showed disapproval. "How can you equate this place with the slums?" he asked Penny.

"Equate? Equate?" she snapped. "Why must you speak in Middle English?"

"I mean, think what only a fraction of the money put into this place would do for several dozen slum families."

Cordelia, pondering the furniture arrangement in the next room and hearing what he said, felt stricken. She came into the hall, surprising them, and said, "I know what you mean, Leonard. But I don't know whether the problem is one of human selfishness or social distribution. I'm incapable of giving all that I have to the poor. And if I were capable, I wouldn't know how to distribute it equitably."

Leonard, flustered, spoke shrilly: "I know what you mean, Mrs. Lovejoy. I was speaking only theoretically. I know that *I* am incapable of giving all *I* have to the poor."

Penny suddenly loathed him for being a social coward instead of sticking by his socialist guns. "What have *you* got, Leonard? A Chinese laundry ticket and car fare back to Washington Square."

"Please," Cordelia said to her. "Welcome anyway to you both. Welcome to the Castle of Otranto. I forgot to inform you that grand opening night has been postponed. But as Teddy Roosevelt used to say, 'We can rustle you up some grub.' "

The front doorbell chimed and the butler glided to answer it. Nick stepped in bearing a huge floral bouquet.

"You specified no evening dress," he said. "Because of the war, I take it."

"Oh my God, Nicky!" Cordelia kissed his cheek. "You got the invitation, but not the postponement. It's good to see you. And how sweet you are about the flowers. Here." She handed them to the butler, who took them with a look of revulsion and handled them as if the wrapping contained snakes. "Bring us champagne in the—" She waved vaguely out yonder.

The man departed, and she said to Penny, "I can't remember his name. Isn't that awful? Penny, what's his name?"

"I haven't the vaguest idea, Mama."

The doorbell chimed once more. All started to answer the door, and then, remembering, looked in the direction the butler had disappeared. He failed to issue from his lurking place, and the bell sounded again.

"Want me to get it?" Leonard asked.

"I will." Cordelia went to the door.

Leonard, aware at last of Penny's loathing, explained apologetically, "I was only trying to be helpful."

"Ass-kisser," Penny said.

Nick looked at her with utter astonishment, and then Cordelia let out a cry as Eunice stepped in. They touched cheeks formally; a coolness had existed between them since the end of 1916 when Cordelia had said, "Eunice, you're not on target date with your first-born. Wasn't this the year you planned to give birth?" It had been unnecessarily cruel, and Cordelia had regretted her remark ever since.

"Eunice, how nice! Is Bayard with you?"

"Obviously not, Mother." What a beauty she was, all done up in mink and smelling of some exotic perfume.

"Nobody much here tonight but family," Cordelia said. "Let me take that beautiful fur. There's a butler around here somewhere, but he only comes out when he feels like it."

"Uncle Nick!" Eunice kissed his cheek.

As she and Penny had not spoken to each other since their big pointless fight, Penny braced herself and said, "Hello, Eunice."

Eunice hesitated for a moment, then replied, "Hello," in a tiny voice.

"This is my friend Leonard Zukoff."

Silently Leonard bowed from the waist, as he had seen it done on the stage, and Eunice nodded vaguely to him.

Cordelia's neglect to inform the members of the family about the postponement pleased her now. Eunice and Penny seemed to be reconciled, and Nick was enchanted with her mansion. Too bad that John had to be out of town on business.

After Eunice had toured the house and had a sip of champagne, she said she had to run along. "Mother, may I speak to you a moment?" They went into the music room where Cordelia had left her wrap.

"Mother, what I have to say isn't very pleasant, but I must say it anyway. Everybody is gossiping about the fact you're having an affair with some employee of yours—a John Speer. Mother, for the sake of your reputation and that of the family, you must break it up."

Cordelia retreated a step. She took care not to say that everyone knew Bayard was absent from home for weeks at a time while having an affair with a woman who bred horses in Kentucky.

"Good night, Mother."

"Good night, Eunice."

Cordelia closed the door, determined not to weep.

After that evening Penny could not rekindle the love she had felt for Leonard. At first he was tearful about the rupture, but finally he bowed to logic: It was indeed fortunate that they had not entangled themselves in marriage and children.

Penny moved into the mansion, where Mary, Tim, and Cora lived in basement quarters. On moving day she thought that her mother would be there to welcome her, but Cordelia was at an education conference in Atlanta which John happened to be attending. Penny so detested her large, high-ceilinged room with private bath that she began to work late at the office.

For some reason the mansion was not popular with anyone. The first butler lasted only a week, the next but two. Some of the maids and cleaning women could not stick it even a day. Oddly, all the quarrelsome confusion filled Mary with glee until Tim became so depressed by it that he got drunk and fell down a flight of stairs, spraining his back. Adding to the discomfort was the fact that military bands were forever playing on Park Avenue just to the south of Grand Central Terminal in those months; seemingly not a platoon of draftees could debouch from a train without a blare of patriotic airs that rang deafeningly in the house.

Finally, a few evenings before Christmas 1917, Cordelia managed to hold a grand opening of minor proportions at her new house. Some people from Lovejoy's attended, as did several old friends such as Maude. Another was Eleanor Roosevelt, who happened to be in the city from Washington.

Eleanor had clipped and brought Cordelia an article in *The Washington Post* describing a day that a correspondent had spent behind the front with the Lafayette Escadrille. In it Captain Steven Lovejoy, who had shot down twelve enemy planes in combat, was prominently mentioned.

"Twelve!" Eleanor said. "And the war isn't over yet."

"I know." Cordelia felt close to tears. "That's the trouble. It isn't over yet."

"But you never told me," Eleanor said. "I had no idea he was such a hero."

"I didn't know, either," Cordelia said, "because he never told *me*."

In the past she had avoided reading anything about the famed international air squadron, feeling that the less she knew about it the less she would be inclined to worry about Steve. But this time she read the entire dispatch, then wished she had not. For, near its end, the correspondent quoted Captain Lovejoy as saying something that would haunt Cordelia to the end of her life:

"I wonder," he said, "if those of us lucky enough to come out of this alive will find everything that happens to us ever after just anticlimax."

When Cordelia bought her mansion, she had an ill-formed thought that John might live there some day. Fond of luxury, he admired "good taste"—what he called "class." His early accomplishments as a book designer indicated that he might have been a successful artist, but he'd given that up because he could make more money in other areas of publishing. He was much concerned with *things*: the proper oil shine on shoes, good broadcloth, the very best year of wine, even the precisely right design of cufflinks. Such a man deserved to live at the top of Murray Hill.

At first Cordelia had the notion that she could convert the top floor of her house into an apartment for John. Usually she did not have such delusions, and it took him a while to convince her that such an arrangement was impossible. It was all Vernoica would need to bring that alienation-of-affection suit she was always threatening against Cordelia.

Occasionally, however, Cordelia could easily prevail on him to spend a night in the bedroom next to hers. On such occasions they slept together in one room or the other, the visitor slipping out early before the servants were about, and then they would have breakfast together in the downstairs dining room. Even if sex had been impossible for them, Cordelia would have loved to curl in sleep with John the way a child likes to sleep with her toy animal. He was that precious to her.

Cordelia always explained away such overnight visits as the result of their working together late on some publishing project—or any other excuse that came to mind. The servants winked at such explanations, but quickly learned not to make caustic comments around Mary or Tim, who defended her fiercely—Tim a few times with his fists. They believed her explanations why John stayed overnight as firmly as they believed in the Virgin Birth, declaring they had known her too well for too many years to think otherwise. Their naive faith, while touching, irritated Cordelia. Why couldn't they understand that true morality did not involve a rigid standard of sexual conduct?

Cordelia thought that loving John was the greatest experience of her life. Yet in some ways it was the most enervating. Their passion seemed so insatiable that at times they could not keep it under control. One day when they had a luncheon appointment with a college dean, they never got there; on the way they were overwhelmed by desire and went to John's hotel suite for half an afternoon of pleasure. The delights of making love with John that Cordelia found in his hotel made her sometimes shudder at the cost of her mansion, which she had vaguely intended to be a palace of pleasure, but which turned out to be cold and lonely.

Of course their affair brought them enemies—jealous Pecksniffs, self-righteous moralists. There was tensions involved in their arrangements, like those of fugitives on the lam from the law. It became tedious to register under assumed Mr. and Mrs. names in strange cities. And then there was that private detective who sometimes trailed them in the pay of Veronica. John became acquainted with him and said he was a pleasant old fellow, a retired city policeman whose feet often hurt him and who had no more idea than they why Veronica would order them under surveillance for a couple of weeks, then take the detective off the case for three or four months. Probably, John said, the pattern was the result of the wide-ranging mood swings to which Veronica was prey. Of one thing he became certain: She would not file suit again Cordelia as long as he kept paying her the hundred and fifty a week she demanded.

Naturally they grew weary with the deceptions that few of their acquaintances any longer believed in. A few times they thought about breaking off their affair. Once they even tried to. However, passion could become a habit.

On the night of August 1, 1918, John spent the night at Cordelia's house. Early in the morning Cordelia, wearing only a robe, stepped from John's room to return to her own and came face to face with Mary. They did not say a word to each other, but Cordelia never forgot the look on her face before Mary wheeled and ran toward the stairs.

After breakfast Mary asked for a word with her.

They went into the music room where Mary, still not looking at her, said, "Tim and me will be leavin'."

"As you please," Cordelia replied.

"Maybe it'll take us till the end of the week to find a place."

"As you please, Mary."

What about Cora's sixteenth birthday, which was tomorrow? Cordelia had granted her the use of the house for a catered party to be attended by a crowd of her young friends.

Mary canceled the party.

Cordelia recalled, though she did not mention it, that she was also planning to pay for Cora's education at Bryn Mawr. Cora had only one more year at St. Agnes's, where she was first in her class, and last April had taken the college entrance exams a year early, achieving such high grades that she was assured of acceptance. Cora said she was looking forward eagerly to Bryn Mawr.

The Park Avenue mansion was large, and the McMahons could be as furtive as mice in it. During the next three days Cordelia did not catch even a glimpse of Mary, Tim, or Cora.

Then, late on Firday afternoon, she came home to pack a bag and catch a train for New Haven, where she had a rendezvous with John at the Taft Hotel. When she opened the door she was almost knocked down by the current butler, one Henri Montcalm, who was bolting out. In his worst accent Henri let her know he couldn't *stand* it a minute longer.

Cordelia became aware of a woman keening and another voice that rose and fell like a dog barking. Rushing downstairs to the McMahons' apartment, she found Mary stretched on the bed with hands clasped to her brow and wailing loudly while Tim paced and shouted incoherently. She thought Cora must be dead and added shrieks of questions to the din. It took her a while, so distraught was she, to make out the note that Tim thrust at her.

It was written in Cora's fine hand. Yesterday she had been joined in civil marriage to Private Jack Doyle, who had a week's furlough from Camp Dix before shipping to France. Cora would not be home tonight. She would not be home *ever* if her parents continued to treat her like a child.

Mary gave a honk of hysterical laughter. "Writ by a grown-up *sixteen*!" Tim cried out for a gun—an annulment. Cordelia, wishing that Cora at least had mentioned Bryn Mawr, thought she remembered Jack Doyle: a pleasant, blond youth who assisted in Carlson's Bakery down Lexington Avenue.

"No!" wailed Mary. "That's somebody else. This Doyle is black Irish handsome and vicious." Tim cried out for a gun again.

It took Cordelia most of the night and into the next day to calm them. Twice John phoned her anxiously from New Haven, but she never did get there. On Saturday evening, in order to divert Mary and Tim, she took them to dinner at White's and then to a musical comedy. On their way home by taxi she patted Mary's hand and said:

"Seems like we're doomed to no woman in this house ever getting a red-blooded college education."

As soon as she said it, she feared that Mary would start to cry again. However, the remark appeared to comfort her.

After that, the McMahons said no more about leaving. Nor did Cordelia ask John to stay overnight at her home again. But that was not just because of Mary and Tim.

On the following Tuesday Cordelia received a cablegram from Paris that Steve was coming home.

BOOK THREE

19

Steve Lovejoy knew how lucky he was that the wound in his right leg had brought him a medical discharge, but he did not look forward to what lay ahead.

Released from the Neuilly hospital in August, he obtained passage home quickly and arrived in New York on September 14, 1918. Since no one knew he was coming, there was no one to meet him at the North River pier except for a few reporters whom a French publicist had alerted. Because the French generally had been hospitable to him, he felt it only decent to talk up the cause of France with the reporters. Hoping they would not misquote him, he found that his worst fears came to pass. His picture was displayed on the front pages of the *Journal* and *World* and inside the *Times* and *Tribune*. There were headlines:

GREAT ACE RETURNS. . . . HOMING HERO SAYS WAR WILL END BEFORE CHRISTMAS. . . . URGES COOPERATION AND UNDERSTANDING WITH THE FRENCH. . . .

The newspaper photos showed a slender, six-foot, handsome young man with dark eyes, sandy hair, and a remarkably serious expression. When Cordelia saw him she realized that Edward must have looked like that before she knew him. But for a while she was too busy weeping over Steve to comprehend much of importance. He had not told her that he'd been hospitalized after being shot down and barely missing death in a fiery crash; it took her a time to understand that he was out of the war for keeps and could throw away his cane in a day or two. From the moment Cordelia crushed him in her arms, Steve sensed something different about her. It was not that she looked older, but that she seemed more a stranger. He did not like the thought.

At last a member of the family appreciated the Park Avenue mansion. Steve limped happily about it, upstairs and down, delighted with his big room and private bath and all the stuff that must have cost Mama a pot of dough. With her trailing behind, he climbed all the way up the topmost flight of stairs of the five-story house and they stepped out on the flat roof. He had with him the camera he'd brought home from France and took Cordelia's picture.

It is one of the oddest that exist of her: The eyes look almost haunted; friends often did not recognize her in it. Penny said Steve must be a lousy photographer. Actually he was an excellent one.

He refused to return to Yale and get his degree, saying, "College is for children," and seemed willing to go to work at Lovejoy's. Cordelia wanted him to assume direction of the company gradually—how slow or fast was up to him, but she said she wanted to cease an active role as soon as possible. (She thought she truly meant it.) As a move toward his assuming control, she gave him more stock, bringing his share to thirty percent.

"There's a two-year binder on it," she told him. "During that time you can't sell or give it away without my approval."

So she was not really giving it to him at all. He could not do what he wanted to with it: sell some and invest the proceeds in his friend Orlo Peterson's air company in Teterboro, New Jersey. But the worst thing was that she had a desk set up for him in her own big corner office, the idea apparently being for the pup to watch and learn the old dog's tricks.

He sought out Penny, the one he liked most since coming home. Among other things he enjoyed her pacifist ravings, which fit the thinking of any sensible man who had been unlucky or stupid enough to become a front-line infantryman or combat pilot.

"Just want to say good-bye." He shut the door of her tiny readers's office and sat down. "This I can't do."

"You mean the desk in Mama's office?"

He nodded.

"I tried to dissuade her, Stevey, but she wouldn't be. The Dutch they are a stubborn race. You have to out-Dutch her."

"Okay, I suppose I have to try. Penny, what do you make of Mama and this John Speer?"

She lost his gaze momentarily. "Oh, I think they're quite fond of each other. He's a nice man."

"Seems to be. But sort of—uh—unctious."

"Watch your language," Penny said. "You never wrote such words to Mama. I thought nobody could write as bad as you in those letters and cards."

"I was just relaxing," Steve said. "Very relaxing to write illiterate. Otherwise you build up these grammatical tensions in yourself. Very bad for young people to have grammatical tensions."

"Stevey, you're just full enough of shit to make a very successful publisher."

"Been meaning to talk to you about this," he said. "Mama wants me to become the big Boom-boom. Penny, I just don't want to. I want to borrow some money and start air-mail service between New York and Washington. Isn't that a wonderful idea? Think about it! You want to be the publisher? You're almost literate. I've tried to convince Mama I'm not."

"I wouldn't mind," Penny said. "But Mama would never hear of it. She's got the idea *you* are going to be the publisher, and once she gets an idea—"

"I know," Steve said. "You, too. Me, too. And look

at old Eunice! Very stupid, impossible family. All I want to do is make my living flying. But they're going to throw all this—these books at me."

He returned to Cordelia's office and told her it wouldn't work to keep his desk next to hers. She seemed to understand and was abjectly sorry. He realized that his most potent weapon with her was the implication he might quit—as long as he never said the word aloud. Where, she asked, would he like to start?

He chose the accounting department under MacLennon. Next to flying, business interested him most. Indeed, he was smart enough to see that in the current state of aviation a successful flier must be a good businessman. He liked Runyon well enough, but editorial work didn't interest him at all. Sales and promotion he'd investigate later if he managed to stick at all. Briefly he had scanned the editorial lists, glanced at a few books, and found nearly everything fluff. The only book he enjoyed and read to the end was an account of Himalayan exploration that had sold only a couple of thousand copies. Obviously he had no editorial talent. Maybe he would learn something in accounting.

The first thing he learned in that department was that MacLennon hated Speer. MacLennon hated everybody who earned anywhere near what he did. He must hate Steve, too, for Mama had settled a starting salary of two hundred a week on his inexperienced young head. Then MacLennon went too far by making some nasty innuendo about Speer and Mama, so Steve marked him down for earliest possible execution. Meanwhile he tried to learn some basic principles of accounting from MacLennon and others in the department, but couldn't seem to master the ideas. So he enrolled in an accounting night course at City College. And that, of course, would interfere with his love life.

If you could really call it that, it was named Ann Renshaw. She was one of those golden girls they used to make up stories about at Exeter and Yale. She had corresponded with her cousin Ernest, a paraplegic in the bed adjoining Steve's in Neuilly, and Ernie had told him to look her up after he came home.

Even if she hadn't lived in one of those marble castles on upper Fifth Avenue, she looked as if she should have. Golden hair, golden skin, quick and slender, a curving golden girl. Eunice with her predatory ways had served as a warning to Steve to beware of such women, but Ann turned out to be not at all expensive. She had done the socially correct things; but also, that very year she had graduated from Wellesley with honors. She was serious minded, like Penny rather than Eunice: women's suffrage and politics and the social injustice of all the downtrodden. However, she was so lithesomely lovely that she made it sound interesting. Her views surprised Steve, since she was the only living child of a coal heiress now dead and an aged father now retired who had spent much of his life in the diplomatic service and still was called Ambassador Renshaw.

Such a girl was certain to have hidden faults, so Steve began research into what they might be. He made the mistake of introducing her to Mama, who promptly swooned over her and who would (he knew) ever after compare all other girls he dated to the exquisite Ann Renshaw. They went to a couple of parties and he took her to shows and dancing at the Plaza and dinner in Chinatown and riding around town in the Star runabout which he was buying on time.

At last, on a golden October Sunday afternoon, he revealed his innermost secret by taking her across the Hudson on a Fourteenth Street ferry and driving to Teterboro Airport. It was where, he confessed to Ann, he spent all the time he could afford—but don't ever tell Mama. Ann promised not to, and Steve introduced her to Orlo Peterson, who had shot down nine over

France before losing his right foot and being discharged home. However, you couldn't ground a big, bold, laughing Swede like Orlo, who found that a wood-and-leather right foot was no problem when it came to kicking over an airplane rudder. At Teterboro he had put together a few fighter and trainer types from overseas which he offered for rides or instruction or rental to qualified pilots in order to defray the costs of the secret plane models of his own at which he was toiling.

When Steve offered to take Ann up for a ride in a French Salmson, a two-seater biplane he could rent from Orlo for fifteen dollars, she winced and was silent. Here was the hidden fault, the fatal flaw in this golden girl. She was scared to fly!

Then she spoke in a kind of finishing-school accent quite unlike her usual voice: "Oh, that would be very nice. But am I dressed right for it?"

He grinned at her. "You got clothes on, don't you? Come on, Orlo loans helmets and goggles."

The air was calm that day when they took off with Ann in the front cockpit. He gave her a nice, level, dull ride around Manhattan, banking sedately so that she could look down at her house on Fifth and his on Park, and then he brought them low over the Statue of Liberty and back to Teterboro.

She climbed out gracefully—the telling thing about a woman was how gracefully she climbed in and out of a cockpit—and pulled off her helmet and shook out her tawny hair. She never had looked so beautiful to him.

"Were you scared?" he asked her.

"At first I was scared senseless."

"But you weren't scared shitless," he said, "or you wouldn't have gone up at all. Right?"

Looking at him with an odd, serious expression, she said, "No, Steve, I wasn't scared—shitless."

Orlo invited him to take up his French Nieuport, a single-seater biplane fighter model, and entertain the large Sunday-afternoon crowd that had gathered in search of excitement. Steve took the plane up and played the show-off: loops, Immelmanns, spins, dives. Yes, he was showing off for Ann, who acted properly impressed after he landed. But he also did it for his own keen joy: Up there he felt a release and found pleasure such as never came to him in the offices of Lovejoy and Son.

By the end of October 1918, when everyone smart realized that peace was close, Steve still was searching for Ann's shortcomings. It seemed he had known her forever, and he wondered why he didn't start seeing someone else. Yet she was the only woman he wanted to be with.

He made a confession to her. In his haste to learn the basics of accounting he had not comprehended that the course in which he had enrolled at City College did not start until January. But he wanted to study accounting *now*. Ann, understanding, consulted her father. The Ambassador knew just the man who, for a fee, would come to Lovejoy's and tutor him on company time. This neat solution made a great impression on Steve.

On November third, the day an accountant named Harriman was to begin tutoring him, he received a letter under a Brooklyn address that drove all other thoughts from his mind.

Dear Captain Steven Lovejoy:

I've been meditating a letter to you for a long time since reading in the newspapers about your return to America. I introduce myself as the wife of John Speer, who lives separately from me. You know who he is all right. But what you may not know is that your mother has stolen this legal husband of mine from me. They have been carrying

on a sexual liaison for months—years. I have a
quite complete record of their meetings—dates,
times, places, supplied by the detection agency.
It's time the world heard about this. Before I make
the announcement, I think you and I should discuss the situation. I ask you immediately to telephone my home, listed in the directory, for an appointment.

> Faithfully yrs,
> Veronica Speer

Steve's neck chilled as he read the letter. The last
time he recalled feeling this way was when two German
fighters had camped on his tail and he could not shake
them loose.

He took the letter to John's office, put it on his desk,
and stood silently. As John read the letter, the color
drained from his face and his hands began to shake.
Looking up and fixing his gaze on some point beyond
Steve's left shoulder, he said:

"Steven—Steve—my wife is insane."

"That might be, Mr. Speer. But is what the woman
says true?"

John, ashen, finally locked his gaze with Steve's.
"You know, my young friend, that's really none of your
business."

"Probably you are right," Steve said, "except that I
find a menacing tone in your wife's letter. Is it black-
mail?"

John shrugged. "She's tried menacing me this way
before."

"Well," Steve said, "I won't be blackmailed. May I
leave this with you, sir, and will you take care of it?
After all, she is your wife."

"Steve—Steven," John said, "I tell you honestly,
there's not a damn thing I can do about this. Better to
ignore it."

"You mean," Steve said, "you refuse to do anything about it? All right, sir, I'll take care of it myself." Picking up the letter, he left.

He went into Penny's office and shut the door. "Question," he said. "Does Mama truly and honest to God love John Speer?"

"She truly and honest to God does," Penny said. "They'd marry in a minute if Speer's wife would give him a divorce."

"Why doesn't *he* get the divorce?"

"Because she'd contest it and bring up the whole business of Mama and him in the newspapers and ruin her reputation. I don't think she gives a damn about that, but John does and won't do it."

"One up for Speer—I guess. Penny, how rich is this family?"

"Gee, I don't know. I heard Bill Paisley say one time that Mama's worth a couple of million."

"Could I have a thousand, please?"

She raised her hands. "In my bag here I have one dollar and some change. It's my lunch money, but you're welcome to it. I'm overdrawn in my checking account again. Mama's given me company stock—not as much as she gave you, but I can't sell it or do anything except cash dividends, which unfortunately don't come for another three months."

"Poor little rich girl. Poor little rich boy. Thanks, Penny, I know you want to help."

He telephoned Stan Jayberg, a classmate at Yale who was almost as rich as a Gould, and said he wanted to borrow one thousand dollars in cash.

"Sure," Stan said. "You can pick it up here at my office right now, Stevey. Why haven't you been in touch? You're the only war hero I ever knew. Let's get together for lunch."

"Later."

He went to Stan's office and picked up the money.

Stan wrung his hand and wanted to discuss aerial combat. "What have you got in that briefcase? A bomb device of some kind? Stevey, you're the only interesting man I ever knew at Yale. Is it a bomb?"

"It's an empty briefcase." Steve opened it and showed him. "I carry it around to make people think I'm very serious. Some afternoons I go out of the office with it and sneak off to the motion pictures."

"Fascinating," Stan said. "You're the only man I ever knew who walks around with an empty briefcase."

Steve put the cash in twenties and tens in his briefcase and went home. In the hall he ran into Tim, who said, "That was a short day at the office, Steven."

"Have to go on special assignment," Steve replied. "Just stopped by to check out my laundry."

"Bet you're going to Teterboro," Tim said.

"Who told you about that, Timmy?"

"A bird flying by. Wish you'd take me up flying some time."

"You never asked me. Sure. Saturday morning at ten sharp. Tell Mama you're going to caddy for me. She thinks I play golf at Ridgewood Saturdays and Sundays. Very healthful sport, golf."

"Very!" Tim beamed at him. "Thankee so much. Can't wait till Saturday. Trouble is there ain't never been enough men around here."

Going to his room, Steve dug his .45 from a mess of junk on a closet shelf. It had been issued to him two years ago; he had cleaned it a couple of times, but never fired it. He never wore it when flying and hadn't known how to dispose of it when discharged. As a good soldier he'd known never to give *them* anything back of value when released, so he'd brought it home and forgotten about it until the letter had arrived in the morning mail. There was a small box of rounds somewhere. He found it under an old pair of skates. Loading the gun, he put it on safety and placed it in his briefcase, then called Veronica Speer.

"Yes?" she answered.

"Good afternoon, Mrs. Speer." He made his voice ring with confidence and good cheer. "This is Steven Lovejoy. I received your letter."

"Oh, yay-ass." She reflected uncertainty.

"I think you and I should talk. Is it all right if I come to your house at seven this evening?"

"Well, it's after dark then. I don't like to go out after dark."

"But you don't have to go out. I'll come to see you. I can't get there before seven o'clock."

"Well, all right." She hung up.

It was a long afternoon to kill. He took the elevated downtown and visited a couple of nickelodeons and drank a lot of coffee. Just before darkness fell, he started on foot across Brooklyn Bridge carrying his briefcase. In the fading light the East River was the color of quicksilver and the numerous church spires of Brooklyn stretched out like a forest. He made out an old lumber schooner coming upriver under full sail against the dark smudge of Governors Island. He paused and watched darkness swallow her, having a moment of pure joy at capturing something beautiful and making it irrevocably his own before pleasure vanished in the recollection of his mission.

He scouted the street of narrow row houses on Brooklyn Heights carefully and did not climb the steps to Veronica Speer's house until he was certain no one saw him in the darkness. To his surprise she was statuesquely lovely. Her patulous dark eyes brooded on him briefly, and then she led the way into a parlor furnished in turn-of-the-century style where the shades were tightly drawn. Her way of decorating had been to launch a massive attack on all spaces and surfaces of the parlor with such a mixture of materials and designs that Steve was reminded of a secondhand furniture shop. He felt stifled. Disguise everywhere. As in a rural Italian museum, the walls were covered with undistinguished religious art; she favored Madonnas and the infant Christ with halo. Most surprising was the number of electric lamps, as if she feared a visit by the Prince of Darkness.

Well, he thought grimly, her fear had been realized.

"Now what is it you want to talk to me about, Mrs. Speer?" he asked briskly.

She twisted her lips. "That ought to be apparent."

"First I want to know if we're alone in the house."

"Yes, of course." She eyed his briefcase. "Why should I want anybody listening in to what we say?"

"I don't know. I have to check on that."

"You have it on my oath as a devout Christian."

"Not being a Christian myself, your oath means nothing to me." Carrying his briefcase, he searched the house thoroughly with her following at a distance and protesting mildly.

In the front upstairs bedroom two shotguns were propped in corners. Steve broke them open and saw that they were loaded. "Now why would you want *two* loaded shotguns, Mrs. Speer?"

"For protection. I'm afraid of invaders. Always have been. John was away a lot and I asked him. He taught me how to load and shoot them. A woman alone can't be too careful in these times."

"I suppose not." Steve propped the loaded guns where he had found them.

They returned to the parlor and sat down again. "Now in your letter," Steve said, "I found a kind of menacing tone. As if you'd do something against me if I didn't do as you say and come here. What would you have done, Mrs. Speer?"

"I've decided to bring suit for alienation of affection against your mother. I've consulted a lawyer and he says I've collected all the evidence I need. He's sure I'll be awarded at least two hundred thousand."

"I see." Steve nodded gravely. "Then how do I enter into this? Why don't you just go ahead and sue?"

She lifted her head and stared about at her religious pictures. "I thought maybe we can arrange an out-of-court settlement to spare all the publicity."

"What sort of settlement?"

"Well, I have in mind something in the neighborhood of a thousand dollars a month for ten years."

"And after that what assurance you won't come back for more?"

"Oh, I'll sign papers to that effect."

"For a hundred and twenty thousand dollars are you willing to grant your husband an uncontested divorce so that he can marry my mother?"

"Oh, I can't do that." She looked surprised. "I'm a good Catholic and totally opposed to divorce. I can't be any party to such a thing. My husband and your mother have sinned, and they must pay a penalty for their sinning."

Steve breathed deeply. "So there's no compromise?"

"How can there be compromise when it comes to sin?" She kept eyeing the briefcase. "I reckon you know that yourself. Did you bring some money with you, Captain Lovejoy?"

"Yes." He opened the briefcase and let her see the packet of bills. "Happens to be just a thousand."

She was greedy. "Let me count it." Her dark eyes seemed to glitter and she stared forward. Then she found herself staring into the muzzle of Steve's .45.

"No, you won't count it." He was surprised by how calm he sounded. "Because I'm going to kill you, Mrs. Speer."

She let out a gasping wail and sank back in terror. Words came, disconnected, but he understood them.

"Of course I'll get away with it, Mrs. Speer. Life means nothing to me—my own as little as anyone else's. No one saw me come here. No one will see me leave. No one will hear the shot that ends your life. A .45 makes a loud noise, but let me show you something."

Slipping the safety off the gun, he wrapped a pillow about it and fired a shot into the floor. The report was louder than he'd thought it would be. The pillow simply distintegrated in feathers and the hole in the floor looked enormous.

"You see?" He picked up another pillow and began wrapping it carefully around the .45.

Veronica screamed piercingly and flung herself on the floor, kicking and beating and slobbering and finally losing control of her bladder. If Steve actually had thought he could kill her, he realized he could not do it now. But he had come here to *win*.

"Listen to me, Mrs. Speer! I'll spare your life under one condition."

Gradually she grew still and sobbed, "Anything!"

"You will allow your husband to get an uncontested divorce."

"Yes! Yes! Yes!"

"Then be sure you don't change your mind. Because if you do, I'll hunt you down and kill you!"

He left her on the floor and walked back across Brooklyn Bridge. Midway he paused, took the gun from his briefcase, and hurled it as far from him as he could into the river.

Next morning Steve went into John's office, shut the door, and sat down beside his desk.

"Mr. Speer—John, I talked with your wife last night.

She agrees not to contest it if you file for divorce so that you can marry my mother."

John stared at him incredulously. "Veronica—said—that?"

"Yes."

"I can't believe it. Oh, I don't mean to question your word, Steven, but she's been so adamant. What changed her mind?"

"I can be pretty convincing when I want to."

"What does she want in return?"

"Nothing. Well, I suppose a judge would award alimony, but nothing else that I know of. Why don't you go to Brooklyn Heights and talk to her yourself? Just one thing. You've got to *tell* her about the divorce. Not *ask* her."

"Yes, yes." John could not suppress his excitement. "If you'll excuse me, I'm going to telephone her."

"None of my business," Steve said, "but I wouldn't phone her. I'd just go there and—tell her."

"No, I must call her first." Steve sat there while John got her on the phone. "Veronica? This is John. We have something important to discuss. I'm coming over the river right now to talk to you."

As he put on his hat and coat he said, "Steven, I can't thank you enough for what you've done."

"Glad to be of help," Steve replied.

He had forgotten there was a board of directors meeting that morning. Cordelia had thought up the title of secretary of the company for him and put him on the board with John, Runyon, MacLennon, Bill, and herself.

"Where's John?" Cordelia asked when they met in the conference room at half past ten.

"He had an important meeting," Steve said. "Sends his regrets."

"An important meeting about what?" Cordelia asked.

Steve felt exasperated with her. "I don't know, Madame President."

"Oh." She looked at him a bit timidly.

Meetings of the board were farcical because no one ever put up real resistance to whatever Cordelia wanted done. The business was completed in half an hour, and Cordelia walked to Steve's office with him.

"About John," she said. "You don't know where he went?"

"Yes, Mother, I do know. He went to see his wife in Brooklyn."

She stopped dead in her tracks. "Now, why would he do that? He knows it's hopeless."

Steve turned from her, picked up his briefcase, and carried Stan Jayberg's thousand dollars back to him. Then they went to lunch together at the Racquet Club and proceeded to get high on an interesting concoction of rum and pineapple juice that Stan had discovered on a recent trip to the Caribbean.

When they left the club about half past two and Steve steeled himself to return to the office, a newsboy was hawking an extra of the *World*. Steve paid no attention; for as long as he could remember New York newspapers had been pushing extra editions about the most trivial things.

The police detective, recently promoted from street patrol, had no tact. He showed his badge to the receptionist and asked, "A John Speer work here?"

"Yes. He's not in just now."

"He certainly ain't," the detective said. "Who's head of this company?"

"Mrs. Lovejoy. She——" Somebody from the mail room took him directly to Cordelia.

"Mrs. Lovejoy? Shaughnessy, New York Homicide." He waved his badge at the ceiling. "I want some information about a man employed here, John Speer."

Cordelia turned white. "What about him? What's wrong?"

"Plenty," Shaughnessy said. "The investigation's just begun. But so far it looks this way. This morning Speer walked into his house on Brooklyn Heights and his wife fired into his chest with a shotgun. Then, with another gun, she fired into herself. Both DOA at Brooklyn Hospital."

"DOA?" Cordelia asked dully.

"That means dead on arrival."

20

Steve felt that he had murdered John Speer. His mother's stony grief so weighed him down with guilt that he wanted to tell someone, almost anyone, what had happened. Several times he came close to telling Penny, but with great effort he kept the secret that in his violent way he had prepared Veronica for her final violence against her husband and herself.

Cordelia did not break down, as she had after Edward died. Dr. Prettyman, who seemed to understand what had happened without being told specific details, said to Steve and Penny that it would be far better if she gave way to her grief.

When they took her home from the office that terrible afternoon, she did not speak until they sat down in one of the big rooms with her. Then she said, "It's as if two of us have died."

Two had, of course, but not the two Cordelia meant. She never mentioned Veronica's name; it was as if Veronica Speer had not existed.

Steve and Penny attended the memorial services for John, but Cordelia could not make herself go. They were totally unprepared for what happened when they came home from the church.

"Steve!" Cordelia paced toward him like an angry lioness. "I had a phone call while you were gone. Heard about your secretly flying at Teterboro every weekend. Why didn't you tell me?"

"I thought it would worry you, Mama. Who told you?"

"It doesn't matter. Just a happenstance. No friend of

yours betrayed you. But it seems such a dishonest, adolescent thing for you to do—pretending to play golf when you're out there flying."

His temper flared. "Dishonest? Adolescent? I don't think it's near as dishonest or adolescent as things that go on at the company all the time."

"What's wrong there? If you don't like the way things go, why don't you suggest improvements? You haven't offered me a single suggestion since you came there."

It was time to tell her. All these weeks he'd been trying to carry on as a dutiful son under the illusion he loved her. But now he thought he no longer did. She had become only a figure of authority to him, a willful woman growing old, a self-indulgent creature he pitied now because she had lost her lover.

He spoke slowly: "Mama, I don't want to go on there anymore. I quit."

She gazed at him for ten, fifteen seconds, eyes welling, and then her tears burst in a torrent and she brought her hands to her face, sobbing uncontrollably. It was awful, yet it was emotional release she needed. Steve found himself standing beside her, stroking her shoulder gently. He was able to control his tears, but not the sweat that beaded his brow as he and Penny stared agonizedly at each other.

"All right," Cordelia said at last. "All right! All right!" She breathed deeply. "I've made my decision. One month from now you're going to become the president of the company with absolute control over its destinies. I'm stepping down, and it's all yours, Steve. You're going to sink or swim, as I did. You're going to—to fly or crash. It's the only way it can be done."

He started to tell her that he didn't want it. But then he thought that under those terms he might like it very much.

"Mama," Penny said, "that's not fair. It's not fair to

Steve or you or the company or any of us. He has too much to learn. And he's just told you he doesn't want it at all."

"Then I'll sell it off," Cordelia said. "Because now I don't want the bother of it, either."

"That's at the moment, Mama. A couple of months from now you're going to feel differently."

"I'll take it," Steve said. "I'll try. Don't sell it off till I have a chance."

"All right," Cordelia said. "I think you'll learn faster if I'm not looking over your shoulder. Maude has asked me to take a trip to California with her, and I suddenly want to get out of this place as fast as possible."

"I need some time in sales," Steve said. "I want to get out on the road and travel with some of the men and learn about their problems."

"That," Cordelia said, "is the most sensible thing you've said."

Penny gave a troubled smile. "Since deciding to become president of Lovejoy's"

"Runyon is the only one we'll tell," Cordelia went on. "You'll learn a lot from him if you'll let him teach you."

In the following weeks Steve stayed away from Teterboro and worked harder than ever before, trying to learn everything he could, even sitting up into the morning hours for nights on end to pore over predictable manuscripts. Runyon and Penny were of the greatest help. MacLennon, Steve discovered, didn't have as natural a grasp of accounting as he himself.

The transition wasn't accomplished in a month. More than two months passed before Cordelia returned from California and said to Steve, "Now!"

The board of directors meeting of January 21, 1919, was called for noon, an unusual hour. Cordelia came in wearing a hat, as if she were going someplace, and said:

"This is the briefest meeting in our history. I announce my retirement from the company. And I announce that my son, Steven Lovejoy, is your new president."

All but Runyon looked shocked.

"Meeting's adjourned," Cordelia said. "We and everyone else working here will call it quits for the day and reconvene at the Astor Hotel where I've reserved private rooms for feasting and frivolity."

One Saturday afternoon early in April, when Steve was in danger of fleeing to Teterboro, he forced himself to walk far up Madison Avenue and then over to Central Park. He had a vague notion of admiring nature, but the air was damp and chilly, the spring not at all serious about burgeoning.

He bought a bag of peanuts and was eating some and tossing others into a flock of greedy pigeons when a woman said, "Where's your airplane?"

He looked around at Ann, whom he had not seen in months. "I quit that. What are you doing away off here by yourself?"

"Keeping the best company I know. Why did you quit flying?"

"I'm a slave to the office."

"Somebody told me. Congratulations, Mr. President. How's your lovely mother?"

"Not well. But not ill, really. Maybe she's got those postwar blues everybody's talking about."

They walked on together, circling around onto Fifth Avenue, and he said, "I'll buy you lunch."

She looked at her wristwatch. "Lunch at four fifteen? It's nearer time for dinner."

"Then come to dinner. I'm starved. Stayed over working at the office—we close at noon on Saturdays—and lost track of time."

"I have a better idea," Ann said. "Come to my house for early supper. Papa's in Washington, the cook's down with the grippe, and I'm going to make the only thing I know how—Swiss fondue."

Her father's house, built on her mother's coal money, was grander than Cordelia's, the point possibly being that Americans bought more coal than books. She took him into what she called her den, which was lined with hundreds of books, like his mother's den at home. He built a fire on the hearth while she found some marshmallows to roast and sherry to pour.

"What do you do all day?" he asked her. "Read these books?"

"Some of them." She mentioned charities in which she was engaged. "And I'm looking for a job."

"What sort of a job?"

"Something interesting. I've taught myself to type. For a few days I tried out as assistant to a man in advertising. But he and I didn't have the same idea about what my duties were. Not that kind of job."

"Want a job in publishing?"

She dropped the box of marshmallows. "Yes!" She knelt and groped for it. "My God, yes! Doing what? When?"

"Reading manuscripts. Report at nine on Monday, and don't be late. We insist on punctilio."

"Oh, my God, Steve!" Her face grew flushed, her eyes dilated. "You mean a job like Penny has?"

"Like Penny had. She's been promoted to associate editor."

"Wonderful! I think it's great you give women a chance at Lovejoy's."

"I wanted to make her editor-in-chief, but she wouldn't hear of it. Claimed not enough experience. We're losing our editor-in-chief, Runyon Fiske. He's a grand old guy—well, he's in his forties—and has been a tremendous help to me. He's going to become editor-in-chief at Balcomb's. Not for hatred of us or great love for them or for money—I offered to outraise anything they're offering him—but just because he feels a want of change."

"Did your mother want Penny to be editor-in-chief?"

"I don't know. She never said. That's an interesting thing about Mama these days. All her life she's had strong opinions about everything, and now she has no opinions at all. Or whatever she thinks she keeps to herself. I appreciate that."

"I'm glad you do. That's a rare quality in a mother. What editorial plans do you have?"

"None. Not a one, Ann. That's sort of sad. New president of distinguished old publishing house has no plans. All I know is that I want somebody young with new ideas to lead us editorially into these nineteen twenties that everybody says are going to be so fascinating. I've pretty well decided to try out a young guy named Jim Dangerfield as editor-in-chief. He's a senior editor at Smith and Fein. Supposed to be a great hand at fiction. Frankly, I don't give a damn about fiction personally. Think the last novel I voluntarily read to the end was *Treasure Island*—or maybe *Kidnapped*. I think those are the two best damn stories ever written. But obviously you can't have a guy with such bad judgment buying fiction. Obviously he must surround himself with experts at fiction and everything else while he concentrates on trying to make the crazy company pay off."

"Steve"—Ann hesitated—"do you like your job?"

"It isn't what I'd have picked. You know how I feel about flying. But the way it finally worked around, I didn't feel I really had much choice. And now I'm beginning to sort of like it."

Ann began work as a reader at Lovejoy's on Monday, and before long Penny announced to Steve that she had natural editorial aptitude. He was glad, but he wouldn't have cared if she'd had none. She had so many other attributes. He enjoyed being with her more than he ever had with any girl or woman; he could talk about anything, and she always understood.

Eventually he found himself telling her about Mama and John. He was surprised when tears came to her eyes, for he'd thought she never wept.

"How sad," she said, "going from everything to nothing all of a sudden. How does she stand it? You're good to stay with her, Steve."

"Up to a point," he said. "But then she'll have to go it alone. And so must I, without her. Right now I can divert her with questions about the workings of the company, but that can't go on forever."

"How did you feel about John?"

"That didn't matter. I knew my mother loved him and I wanted things to work out for her."

Suddenly he realized that she was the only person who would understand fully, and so he told her the grim secret he had been harboring for months.

Ann Renshaw and Steven Lovejoy were married at a high-noon ceremony in St. Thomas's Episcopal Church on Fifth Avenue September 24, 1919. Friends and relatives went on to a large reception at the Plaza Hotel. At the reception several gallant men remarked to the groom's mother that the bride was almost as pretty as she.

From the Plaza a smaller party progressed to the Renshaw house for more champagne and a chance for intimate conversation. There Bayard distinguished himself by collapsing dead drunk and being carried out by footmen. Loyally Eunice accompanied the body home, thus removing the need for Penny and herself to try labored conversation further.

"Two shot down from the Lovejoy side of the aisle," Cordelia told Ann. "How many left to go? Say, have I really told you how pleased I am about this marriage?"

"You have, Mother." Ann squeezed her hand.

"He's not perfect," Cordelia said of Steve, who stood with them, a silly champagne grin on his face. "But he's cool under fire, and that's what his Grandpa Lovejoy would have loved most about him. I truly believe, Ann, you won't be sorry. Now, while I have you two here and before you dash off, there's something I want to say. I gave you a little loot, some trade beads among all that boodle on display over there. But the real gift I've been saving till now to tell you about. When you come back from your trip, you're to move into the Park Avenue house. It's yours."

Ann was speechless. Steve, finding his voice, sounded like a piping child: "Good golly, Mama, where are *you* going to live?"

"Maybe you can spare me a room when I'm in town occasionally."

"Of course!" Ann exclaimed. "But good heavens, Mother—"

"Mama," asked Steve, "you going to live at Hasty's?"

"I don't think so, Stevey. I don't know yet. One thing about the house, Ann. You've met the McMahons—Mary and Tim, the finest friends and servants you'll ever find anywhere. They—well, they go with the house. Is that all right with you?"

"It's fine! How wonderful they'll stay on."

"But Mama," Steve said, "where are you going *now*?"

"To Europe for a while. I have passage on the *Mauretania* tomorrow."

Ambassador Renshaw had suggested the Homestead at Hot Springs, Virginia, as the place for Ann and Steve's honeymoon. The old gentleman remembered it as it had been around the turn of the century when his late wife and other fragile creatures strolled Lovers' Walk under their parasols, rode in tallyhos, and played euchre with friends on honeysuckle-shaded porches. The Ambassador had a railroad magnate friend who was pleased to put his private car at the disposal of bride and groom and have them wafted to Hot Springs. To Steve's later chagrin, he fell asleep soon after they boarded their car and did not waken till they were in the Shenandoah. Ann, fatigued by the rigors of the wedding, did not mind.

The Ambassador had seen to it that things were done right. Though it now was the age of the auto, there was a black coachman wearing old-fashioned livery who waited on the box of a high Brewster victoria to drive Ann and Steve from their railroad car to the sprawling hotel. They arrived at the cottage reserved for them just in time for breakfast. A black waiter glided from the hotel kitchen, the tray balanced on his head containing shirred eggs, Virginia ham broiled in champagne, mounds of fresh wild strawberries, platters of pecan and cinnamon rolls, a huge pot of coffee. He served them on their cottage porch, where they ate hungrily while gazing across clipped yew and broad copper beeches at vapor rising from the Pleasure Pool and at the flare of autumn leaves along a hillside. Everywhere they looked birds rose and settled like the nervous flight of butterflies.

"They're getting ready to leave their nests and fly south," Ann said.

"Love nests," Steve said.

She looked to him to instruct her after night fell. Though she had read books on the subject, there were a couple of matters that still puzzled her. One thing she did know, however: It only happened after dark.

When they'd had their fill of breakfast, she asked, "Want to go for a walk?"

He stared at her strangely; she did not understand that his look expressed lust. "First," he said, "we should change into our hiking costumes." He uttered an odd groaning sound.

"Full of breakfast?" she asked.

"Full of lechery," he said.

She grinned. "As long as you're not filled with regret." She honestly thought they were going for a hike, even after they were half undressed and he cupped her breasts. When he kissed her frantically, she began to giggle. Never had she heard herself giggle, yet neither had she ever felt so wildly excited.

Since the experience was new to her, she had no way of knowing if he was a great lover. Certainly, however, he was a persistent one. For a few days they retired from the world, and Ann was the happiest she ever had been. Steve said that he was, too.

Yet he grew restless long before she did. She was surprised to find that he did not enjoy reading, except for newspapers. The New York and Baltimore papers reached Hot Springs late on the day after publication, and Steven ordered copies of each delivered to their cottage. In reading them, he did not share her interest in the fate of the League of Nations nor did he even care about the bull stock-market. What got him excited was follow-up news on the non-stop flight of Alcock and Brown across the Atlantic.

"Now *that* is history," he told her. "In my opinion, dear, there never will be a League of Nations to equal the American League."

"The American League?" she asked.

"The American *Baseball* League. Have you been following the fortunes of George Ruth of the Boston Red Sox, known as the Babe? Twenty-nine home runs! Think of it! The Yankees will be smart to buy him no matter what they have to pay."

Ann liked to ride and drive her own carriage, though she did not know how to drive a car. Steve seemed to hate horses, but was willing to sit admiringly at her side and watch her handle a four-in-hand over the winding drives of the Homestead.

What really stirred his enthusiasm was a new Model T Ford, a high and hideous machine which had been bought by an assitant manager of the hotel. Steve immediately rented it for a day, but would not let the owner show him how to start, stop, or operate it.

"Let me find out for myself!" he exclaimed. "That's the fun. If I wreck it, I promise to buy you a new one, sir. Scout's honor!"

He spent half a warm morning sweating himself up before he learned the knack of starting the thing.

"Look, honey." He finally persuaded Ann to watch him. "You should learn this. Set the spark and throttle levers here under the wheel at positions of about ten minutes to three." He leaped out the righthand door since there was none on the left side and seized in his right hand the crank hanging from the front of the motor. "See this wire loop? This controls the choke. Put your left forefinger through it. Give a mighty crank with your right, but don't let go or it may kick back on you and bust your arm. Like this!" There was a gasping sound. "Don't be discouraged." He cranked again, and the motor roared. *"Voilà,* as we French say." He raced around to the running board, shouting, "Move spark and throttle to twenty mintes of two position." When he did that, the motor gasped and died. "Never be discouraged," he said cheerfully. "We'll start over again, and next time we'll set at twenty-*five* minutes of two. . . ."

After his victory over the Model T, which he pronounced the most difficult car he ever had learned to drive, Steve looked around for new worlds to conquer. But there seemed to be none in Hot Springs, Virginia.

One morning when they were eating breakfast on their porch, something high in the sky caught Steve's attention and he stepped out for a better view. Ann followed as he pointed and said, "Look there! That's a grander sight than all your ground birds."

A hawk soard slowly, wings not beating but tilting skillfully to take advantage of upward drafts of thermal air. She imagined she could feel her heart rising with the wheeling bird.

"It must be great," Steve said, "to be a hawk."

For the rest of the day he was moody and restless. Ann knew what he was thinking. Not once since John Speer died had he gone near an airplane. Did it mean that he never would fly again? She hoped so, but she had firmly resolved never to protest his flying. For whoever clipped the wings of a hawk would earn his eternal enmity.

At dinner that evening Steve suggested that they move on someplace else, but they could not decide where to go and next day agreed to return to New York.

Although the honeymoon did not last as long as planned, Ann enjoyed her job at Lovejoy's so much that she was glad to get back to it. Thank heaven Steve was not one of those old-fashioned males who insisted that his wife's proper place was at home. He, glad that she liked her job and was capable at it, said she could work forever as far as he was concerned.

One afternoon in the following July, Ann took time off to visit Dr. Prettyman. When he told her she was pregnant, she burst into tears.

"Now, now, Mrs. Lovejoy, this is a time for rejoicing."

"But, Doctor, it means I'll have to quit my job!"

"For a while, yes. But you remind me of your mother-in-law. Now *she* is a woman hard to keep at home for any length of time."

21

On Cordelia's first morning at sea following Steve and Ann's wedding she had a curiously vivid waking dream/thought. In it she was trying to persuade Maude to write a book about the aging experience and explaining to her that she would turn fifty herself next year. Then Maude replied as clearly as if she were there in the cabin with Cordelia: "A woman can say despondently, 'I'm fifty.' Or she can say jubilantly, 'I'm *only* fifty.' It makes all the difference in the rest of her life."

Well, not necessarily, Cordelia thought when she came wide awake and the words failed to ring as profoundly as they had in her dream. Nevertheless, it would read well in a book on aging if she could find the right author to do it. Then, however, she recalled that she no longer was an editor. She was a retired widow with a lot of stock in Standard Oil and Lovejoy and Son. And no one, except fortune-hunting men, gave a damn about well-off, fifty-year-old widows. If she could remember that and manage never to feel sorry for herself, she might navigate her remaining time without acting like an ass.

When she arrived at Brown's Hotel in London she was dismayed to find a cable from Penny reporting that Maude had died in her sleep of a thrombosis. When? Could her dream have coincided with Maude's death? For a moment she was tempted to return home, but realized that would be pointless. She had reached an age when death no longer should come as a surprise.

She stayed in London for a few days and found that

a retired American publisher was not as warmly received by the English publishing fraternity as one ready to buy books. She found, too, that the British had been enervated by their war, that the ranks of young men were sadly depleted and many of the survivors were shattered.

It seemed even more true when she went into the provinces: Women predominated, most men looked raffish or very old. She was Constance Hedge's guest in the Cotswolds at her big manor house called Dirknoire. The fiction was that it had been bought by her husband, Sir Hugh Hobden-Trent, an aging, pleasant potterer. But Hugh was broke; Constance had bought Dirknoire with money earned from her popular mystery stories and held title to it. The lovely countryside was heavily populated by tweedy women who passed much time discussing the eccentricities of the menfolk. Hounds, horses, and hunting were the chief pastimes, besides drinking, but walking was acceptable. Cordelia walked a great deal, up hills, down dales, climbing over stiles, following one path until it came to another. The land often was wrapped in mist, and in the mist sheep were like rocks that stirred. There was, indeed, a permeating smell of sheep that seemed to infect one's woolen clothing and made Cordelia wish that Constance would not serve so much mutton.

"What do they do here in winter?" she asked Constance.

"I wouldn't know," Constance replied. "Hugh and I winter on Majorca."

Constance wished she would stay forever, but Cordelia was bored witless after two weeks. She wondered what ever had made her think she'd like to buy a place and settle in the English countryside.

Determined that she could not go home because there was nothing to go back to, she forged ahead onto the Continent. She became clever in her travels, learning how to restrict her luggage and how to doctor herself when she felt ill and how to tell at a glance a good restaurant from a mediocre one. Deciding not to waste much time in cities like Paris and Rome, she explored interesting places off the main routes of travel.

She was, for example, one of the first American discovers of Cahors in the Lot Valley of France. From Cahors she explored the region called le Périgord, fascinated by its prehistoric caves, the Romanesque-Byzantine churches, the ancient bridges and buildings, and enjoyed the world's best *foie gras* and truffles with earthy dark wine. Next she lingered in Avignon and Arles, then passed on into Italy with scarcely a look at Monte Carlo.

Nearly everywhere she went she met solitary wanderers like herself, both women and men. Few wanted a lasting attachment. They were as various as human nature, but many shared one characteristic: They were waiting for a time, presently uncertain, when it would seem right to them to go home again.

Some, Cordelia believed, were trying—like herself—to forget a lost love. And, like herself, they never mentioned the one lost. It seemed that she could not forget John, and it did not help her to recall there had been a time when she could not forget Edward. Of course she still remembered him, but pain had gone out of the memory while the pain of missing John remained. She had been glad to leave New York because familiar places there recalled his voice, his face, his smile: She forever thought of him as in an adjoining room, as appearing in a doorway at any moment.

Maybe the healing power of travel lay in the unfamiliarity of foreign rooms and doorways. Yet you could travel to a distant planet and not escape the nocturnal dreams of one loved and lost forever.

* * *

Cordelia entered Italy by an old invaders' route, the Via Francigena, that Way of the Franks leading down across the Lombardy Plains, fording the Arno near Pisa, and rolling on to Rome. At Pisa she turned east into the spurs of the hills and fell captive to Tuscany, that wonderful land where white oxen plod on distant yellow lanes lined by slim black cypresses. She came to Firenze, immortal Florence, and began to lay plans never to leave it.

One morning she rented a car with driver, who took her to Siena for two days and a night of sightseeing. Since the driver spoke no English, and she no Italian, he was a poor guide; however, she fared well on her own until the next afternoon when it was time to return to Florence. The driver had passed out; although it must have happened often, it was the only time Cordelia saw an Italian dead drunk on wine.

So she decided to leave him and drive back to Florence herself. The auto was of vague foreign manufacture, but she drove an American car at home and didn't see why she could not drive in Italy. A man showed her what to do with the pedals and things, and off she went through a beautiful afternoon under a dusty blue sky.

Late in the afternoon she drove down the last inclines into the valley of the Arno, leaving the silver olive groves behind and entering the copper haze of Firenze where the cupolas and towers, the Cathedral and the Bell Tower and the Palazzo Vecchio rose red and buff and white in the declining sunlight. She passed through the Porta Romana, down the Via dei Serragli, and then across the Ponte alla Carraia into a deafening din of blocked traffic. Horns blared, people shouted, horses neighed, oxen tossed their heads like whitecaps on a restless sea, yet, despite the angry stir, all progress was frustrated.

Out of the mass of people and animals there suddenly emerged a man who looked like a giant to Cordelia. Everyone shrank back and took pains not to make derisive comment as he strode along, for, to Tuscan eyes, this man appeared in the tradition of northern conquerors that extended far back to days of chain mail and sweat-blackened boar's leather. He was very tall, had huge shoulders, and his red hair and beard made him seem to be in flames. Looking at Cordelia, he paused, leaned down, and peered into her little car, then said something in a foreign tongue.

"Non capisco," she replied, somewhat frightened.

"American," he said. "Yah, you American." His accent, she thought, was Scandinavian. "My auto broke down again. Goddamn Italian auto! It stops the street. It make the jam. I leave it and walk away. Goddamn Italian auto! Will you take me to my hotel?"

She felt angry with him. "I can't get through that jam."

"Turn around."

"I can't turn around in this."

He beckoned two youths who were staring at him. Though he sounded as ignorant of Italian as Cordelia, he made them understand what they were to do. With him in the middle and a youth on each side, they lifted the rear of Cordelia's car and swung it around. *"Grazie,"* he said to the youths, and then, with him walking ahead, Cordelia drove slowly through the traffic beginning to block the Ponte alla Carraia. When he climbed in with her, the car sagged under his weight.

"The Bristol," he told her.

"Give me directions," she replied.

He grinned at her. "You are a beautiful lady. What is your name?"

"Give me directions."

"I direct. There's more than one way to cross a river. Turn left there, beautiful young lady. What is your name?"

"I'm fifty years old, you old goat, and you're full of shit."

He roared with laughter. "My name is Eric Lief. What's yours?"

Recognizing his name, she asked, "Eric Lief, the Norwegian explorer?"

He puffed up. "Yah!"

"Lief, the explorer of the Arctic and Antarctic who always gets lost and never finds anything?"

He laughed even louder. "Yah! Yah! You're bright, too, besides pretty. What's your name, china doll?"

"Mona Lisa."

"Wheee-ooo!" He almost encircled her thigh with a huge hand.

"Take your hand off me, you son of a bitch, or I'll have that policeman there arrest you!"

"Wheee-ooo! That's no policeman." But he removed his hand.

"You mean to say you simply left your auto blocking all that traffic and walked away from it?"

"Yah. Not mine. Just a goddamn Italian auto I rent. The Italians not yet discover the goddamn wheel."

"What are you bellyaching about?" she replied. "You couldn't discover the goddamn Northwest Passage and there it was right under your nose."

"Wheee!" His rocking merriment almost threatened to overturn the little car. "Yah, true. Next time you come north with me and I keep you warm and we do Northwest Passage together."

When they drew up to the Bristol Hotel, she said, "Good-bye, Leif Ericson. Nice to meet the discoverer of Vinland."

"He discovered America," Eric said. "I prove it. No goddamn Italian like Columbus can find America."

"Since you seem to hate Italy and the Italians so much, what are you doing here?"

"Looking for sun. I been very cold in Greenland for many months. Come, I buy you apéritif."

"No thanks. Good-bye. My husband's waiting for me."

"You have no husband. Come!"

She went into the lounge of the Bristol with him to find out how he knew she did not have a husband.

"Simple," he said. "You wear no wedding ring. Brightest American ladies very dumb. I know. I lecture there all the time. What's your name?"

"Cordelia Lovejoy. Why do you lecture in America?"

"To get money to find the goddamn Northwest Passage."

"Who cares about that?"

"*I* care."

"Who wrote that book, *True North*, that was published under your name?"

"*I* wrote it."

"You couldn't have. It's a sensitive, perceptive book about the Arctic, and you're obviously a brute."

He protested loudly.

Cordelia agreed to have lunch with him the next day. When he called for her at her pensione, he still did not wear a tie and was as rumpled as yesterday.

"You like to walk?" he asked her. When she said she did, he replied, "Come."

She almost had to trot to keep up with him as they crossed the river by the Ponte Vecchio and went along the Lungarno Serristori to an ancient watchtower which Eric said had been built in the thirteenth century.

"You like to climb?" he asked her.

"What if I said no?"

"I carry you on my back."

No doubt he would have if she had not said she liked to climb.

They went up the hill which rose from the river by a

series of switchback paths that wound through beech, sycamore, and sweet cedar. Cordelia was breathing hard when they came out on a large, paved *piazzale* and turned to a magnificent view of the city and its folding hills.

"Why did you come to Florence?" Eric asked her.

She did not hesitate to tell him the truth because she believed she never would see him again and it was time she told somebody: "I'm trying to forget someone who died."

He nodded, his expression grave. "I understand that. Once I spent six months in an ice house in Greenland trying to forget somebody. I couldn't do it until I stopped trying."

They lunched at the *loggia* in the center of the *piazzale* and talked about Florence until he suddenly asked, "Why did you read my book?" She said she read a lot, then found herself explaining that she used to be a publisher. That interested him. Probably, she thought, he had another book that he wanted to peddle to another publisher because his first book had not sold well.

But it was not so: "I never write another book. One is enough—too much. I said all I know. Why say it again?"

"Why do you lecture again and again?"

"For money. I like to travel in the north, and lecturing is the only way I can do it to interest sponsors. Now I want to fly to the North Pole and back, and that cost much money. It's so impossible to do that I came to Italy to forget—not somebody, like you—an idea. It's an impossible idea. I can't fly. I try to learn, like I learned navigation years ago, but I can't fly good. Must be too old. Next year I'm sixty."

He looked ten or more years younger. "I don't see why anybody would want to fly over the North Pole," she said. "But I've stopped questioning why anybody wants to do anything. How much would it cost?"

"One hundred sixty-five thousand dollars. I can give you every detail." He grinned suddenly and made a panting sound. "Cordelia, you want to pay my way to the North Pole?"

"Oh, my goodness, I don't have that kind of money," she lied. "And if I did, I wouldn't waste it on that."

"That's what everybody says." He sounded doleful. "Governments, kings, millionaires—nobody wants to waste the money. So here we are in Florence, you trying to forget somebody and me trying to forget the North Pole. Let's forget and be happy."

There was a comfort in his company that she had not expected to find with any man ever again. Though he could act fierce when he thought someone was trying to take advantage, he was never a bully; he was, indeed, as gentle as John had been.

Perhaps he was married—perhaps not. They never mentioned their families. He had a house someplace on Oslo Fjord, but seldom was there. He was like the chieftain of some mysterious clan who was almost perpetually on a Viking voyage. If she could have had access to a good English-language library, she would have found his background explained in some reference work, but that would have spoiled the enjoyable mystery about him.

Eric was the most observant person she ever had known. He had been trained in some exact science, maybe geology or physics, and used its methods in all he observed. Far fonder of people than of glaciers, he knew much about such things as history, art, the social habits of Polynesians. Despite his bluster about Italians, he knew that they were as interesting as his beloved Eskimos.

He and Cordelia went everywhere in Florence together, and then one morning they bought a picnic lunch and drove to the hill town of San Gimignano. It was a morning of dazzling sunlight as they drove south from Florence to Poggibonsi and then up into the hills through fields scarlet with poppies. They crossed a dashing stream lined with silver birch and poplar, and suddenly the pencil-slim towers of San Gimignano came into view far up and ahead. Cordelia cried out at sight of them, and her pleasure delighted Eric.

History, history, he said, stopping the car at a widening in the road so that they could gaze in all directions. The poet Dante had trudged up this very road one day in 1300 in a worthy but futile effort to bring peace between the two great warring families of San Gimignano—the Salvucci and the Ardinghelli. Aye, Eric told her, there had been much fighting. The Sienese used to come out over Monte Maggio, that long gray ridge down there to the southeast that stood like a rampart before Siena. The Florentines would march down the Valley of the Elsa there and the two sides fought and fought till the valley ran with blood. The people of these hills and valleys suffered most from the fighting since it was their land that was fought over. They'd hole up on their fortified hilltops and try to stay neutral, but they could not.

Eric drove on to the high summit where a cold wind keened and the towers of San Gimignano rose, silent and mysterious, like a forest of tall dead pine. The road became a rutted track that crept along the crumbling walls of the town, as if seeking an entrance it could not find. At last they abandoned the car and went through a narrow gateway and began picking their way through alleys that twisted among the towers. At first San Gimignano appeared deserted, but it was not. There were three or four barberships, hens picking among the ruins, dogs barking, old women wearing black, an old man who wanted to sell them something, the tolling of the bell in the Church of San Agostino.

"Tell me more history," Cordelia said.

Well, in those thirteenth- and fourteenth-century wars, the Ardinghelli family was for Florence and the Salvucci for Siena. It was in that time that the families built these towers and walled themselves in, shooting arrows and pouring boiling oil down on their enemies. Every bit as savage as modern man, Eric said. Absolutely no glory in it, despite what the ancient tapestries tried to depict. Rape and pillaging and burning, the arrow in the groin, the sword thrust through the neck, besides the ordinary perpetual discomforts of foot blisters and saddle sores, phlegm and dysentery, heat and piercing cold. Imagine being an old knight forty-five years old up in yonder tower on guard duty, your teeth all gone except for a few that ached, your eyes dim with cataracts, your prostate gland a mess, a pain in your gut that you couldn't cure, the young men refusing to let you ride the best horses any longer after taking your falcon from you: nothing to look forward to but killing an enemy in the tower next door.

"It's nice to hear somebody put in a good word for the twentieth century for a change," Cordelia said.

"History soothes," Eric replied.

After climbing a tower and visiting the church, they left San Gimignano. In the lemon light of early afternoon they drove down the mountain to the stream. Leaving the car, they carried their lunch upstream to a birch grove. In its rustling warmth they ate their bread, cheese, and ham and drank their wine while they talked and laughed.

Eric, growing drowsy from wine and from recounting history, pillowed his head on Cordelia's lap while she sat with her back against a slender birch. She nodded off to sleep herself and was awakened by him kissing her.

His lips moved against hers, softly at first and then crushingly. Desire for him made her start to tremble.

His arms moved about her, and desire for him grew. Then they were lying side by side in the leaves. It was not his great strength but his extraordinary gentleness that made her forget everything that ever had happened to her before.

She slept. When she awakened at some time that didn't matter he was asleep on her arm, his head on her shoulder. She wanted him again, and her free hand moved up his leg flung across hers. Instantly he was awake, murmuring to her. She wished he'd say, "I love you." But he did not.

On their way back to Florence she asked, "By the way, who won that war between the Ardinghelli and Salvucci?"

"Officially the Ardinghelli won San Gimignano for Florence in 1353. But the war never really ended. After the military action was over the families hired artists from their favorite cities to contest with each other over who could paint the best pictures to decorate the walls of churches." Eric reached out and squeezed her hand. "Some things have a way of never ending."

She wished that could be true of their love affair, but she never lost sight of the fact that he was a Viking who must always voyage on. A couple of weeks later he said he was late for something unexplained he must do in Sweden.

When they parted, he said he would see her next year in New York. She doubted she ever would see him again. Somehow, though, that did not much matter.

She lingered another week in Florence, then decided it was time she left Italy. She considered going to Switzerland, but next day she made up her mind to leave Europe. Something had ended, and now she could go home again.

Steve and Ann met her at the pier when her ship arrived in New York.

"Mama," Steve said, "you look great. I never saw you look so happy. Europe really did something for you."

"History soothes," Cordelia replied.

Then she went to Hasty's to live for a while.

22

Penny became even more involved in pacifism after the war ended and peace reigned. She was a leader of an organization called Patriots for Peace whose motto was "It must never happen again" and who were dedicated to abolishing the armed forces of the United States. The "P4P's," as they called themselves in their literature, staked out arch enemies against whom they warred fiercely: all generals, admirals, and hawkish congressmen, but especially munitions makers. These latter were vaguely defined corporations and individuals; some were innocent of actually manufacturing arms but were judged guilty by the P4P's because they supplied material from which the lethal stuff was made.

In November 1921 the New York chapter of the P4P's celebrated the third anniversary of the signing of the Armistice by hiring a special train for a "march on Washington." There the hero of the peace movement, one Senator Singsen, was holding hearings to show how the munitions makers were plotting war. Singsen (there were other members of his Senate subcommittee, but his until then had been mainly a one-man show) was accused by enemies of hiring a hall to conduct the hearings. In truth the committee hearings were so popular that there was no room in the Capitol or the Congressional Office Building which could contain even a few of the hundreds of spectators who wanted to get in. In order to accommodate them, Singsen moved the hearings to a large building off the Mall at the foot of Capitol Hill. It was known as a "temporary" because it had been built for the use of the War Department during the recent war and was called the Old Munitions Building. Singsen saw no irony in conducting his hearings against munitions makers in a structure so named, but then the ironical always did evade the senator.

In the same prevailing mood of moral earnestness the P4P's saw no irony in debouching from their special train at Union Station with military orderliness and marching in step by companies to the Old Munitions Building. Penny was one of the grand marshals of their parade and thrilled to the pacifist song to which they marched in time, singing words like "peace" which rhymed with words like "release" while the music was "Marching through Georgia." Not all of the marchers could crowd into the Old Munitions Building auditorium, but by prearranged plan Penny was one who did, while others deployed outside, chanting pacifist songs and booing a platoon of nervous Capitol policemen who had been assembled to keep the peace.

The first witness called was the president of the United Traction Corporation of New York, Israel Epstein. Penny did not recognize the name, so thoroughly had the traumas of maturity healed the traumas of childhood, and there was nothing about his appearance to recall the youth who used to go through the streets of Murray Hill with his father. He was a large man, already balding, nose generous, demeanor smiling—avuncular, not handsome. After being summoned to the stand and being sworn in by the clerk, he was asked by Singsen (as is many a condemned man before sentence is passed on him) if he had anything to say.

Izzy did not read a prepared statement, as was expected, but said, "Senator, I merely want to say that I'm as honestly in favor of peace as any other American citizen and don't know why I have been called a warmonger. I learned to hate and fear war as a private soldier who went all the way in the war with the First Division."

Senator Dickburn, a southerner who had been trying to upstage Senator Singsen, leaned forward and said, "The First Division, eh? You must know that song—" Then he sang in his mellifluous Baptist-choir voice:

> *The First Division went over the top,*
> *Parlez-vous—*
> *The First Division went over the top,*
> *Parlez-vous—*

"Yeah!" cried Izzy, grinning, and joined Dickburn in singing:

> *The First Division went over the top,*
> *They all returned but a Jew and a Wop,*
> *Hinkey-dinky parlez-vous!*

The Jews and those of Italian descent in the audience fell silent and watchful, but southerners who had come to see the fun laughed uproariously and remarked how well Dickburn had come out against Singsen. Izzy's voice cut through the babble:

"Very good, Senator! You in the First?" Dickburn, who never had served in the armed forces, pretended not to hear him while Singsen, scowling, rapped his gavel for order, and Izzy called out, "Well, Senator, here's one Jew from the First who *did* return."

Jews among the pacifists started to cheer, then remembered that Izzy was an enemy and fell into puzzled silence.

Dickburn, having seized an advantage over Singsen, refused to let it go, but leaned toward Izzy and pointed at him: "Then you admit, sir, that you are a Jew?"

"*Admit?*" cried Izzy. "You bet I'm a Jew, Senator, and I'm goddamn proud of it!"

In the pandemonium Penny was confused as to how she felt. She loved Jews as she loved Negroes and dogs in the pound and every other sufferer in the world. But that Jew there on the stand was an enemy of peace as described in P4P's literature and as targeted for today's demonstration. The fact he was a Jew must have nothing to do with how she felt or acted. Purge sentiment and deliver peace! But the fact he was a Jew was the cause of the pandemonium: Jews and those sympathetic to them cheering him while Jew-baiters jeered and cat-called.

Singsen, red-faced with rage at his upstaging, finally restored order and shook his gavel at Izzy. From the safe high ground of moral superiority he fired down at him wrathfully:

"The clerk will expunge this man's profanity from the record! I warn you, Epstein, if you take the name of the Christian Lord in vain one more time I'll find you in contempt of Congress and have you remanded to the District of Columbia jail!"

Izzy lowered his head meekly.

Grace Comstock, who sat next to Penny and was her second in what they called the Trojan Horse Plan, nudged her and asked, "Now?"

Penny, tense, shook her head.

Committee counsel began the routine questioning to establish Izzy's identity. Married? "Divorced," Izzy replied.

"Divorced?" Singsen and Dickburn uttered the word simultaneously and with the same inflection, so that Izzy must have known another point had been scored against him.

Grace nudged Penny again. "When?"

"In a minute," Penny whispered.

"I want to interrupt counsel at this point," Singsen said, "and cut through the red tape that so often obfuscates our governmental procedures. Come right out with it now, Epstein, and stop beating about the bush. How do you make your living?"

"I'm a junk man," Izzy replied.

Suddenly Penny remembered who he was. How could she have been so dumb? Izzy Epstein! If memory had an epidermis, layers of its skin peeled back.

"Come now, Epstein," Singsen was saying, "just where do you think all that scrap your company collects and sells ends up? You know perfectly well it goes into guns and bullets, sir. *Guns and bullets!* To murder the innocent young, to . . ."

The time had come to put the Trojan Horse Plan into operation. Summoning all her courage, and it took a good deal of it, Penny sprang to her feet and shrieked, "Murderer!" Gathering courage and conviction: "Rapist! Child molester!" Now Grace was on her feet too, shrieking imprecations while the two other women in the plan joined in.

The last Penny saw of Izzy before strong hands dragged her away, he had shrunk down in his chair and raised his arms as if to ward off blows.

If Penny had been born male, she might have become a professional boxer. She not only enjoyed combat, she was very strong. Furthermore, she hated policemen. The beefy men in uniform who dragged her toward a paddywagon outside the Old Munitions Building inflamed her. With a burst of strength and as quick as a cat she shook herself free and started running. The heavy feet were no match for her at running, and they were further impeded by enraged pacifists, both women and men, who flung themselves upon the police like suicide squads of infantrymen on barbed wire.

Back there it looked to her as if a dozen football games were being played at once outside the Old Munitions Building. Two policemen, younger and fleeter than the others, emerged from the scrimmage and came after Penny. She ran faster. Up ahead the Capitol dome looked cockeyed and the flag flew askew in a windy sky. To her right was a triad of copper beeches. Realizing that she could not run forever, she decided to try climbing for a change.

Leaping, she seized a low branch and pulled herself up. There never had been such a wonderful tree for climbing; too bad she hadn't found it when she was twelve. The branches continued on like a flight of convenient stairs. Pausing, she looked down at the two policemen, who stared up at her with total astonishment. One began groping around for a way to climb up, and she yelled down to him:

"Flatfoot, you try to climb this tree, I'm going to jump off it and commit suicide!"

He paused for consultation with his fellow officer, then one hoisted the other to a branch, and he began to climb cautiously.

"Flatfoot!" Penny cried. "You down there, you climb one branch higher an' I'll tell you what's gonna happen. I'm gonna rip off my skirt. Another branch after that I'm gonna tear off my petticoat. One rip off, my man, for every branch you climb. By the time you get to me, I'm gonna be stark naked, and I'm gonna say *you* tore off my clothes."

The policeman stopped climbing and gazed up at her earnestly. "Miss—ma'm—missus—I'm but doin' my duty. I'm under orders to arrest you for disturbin' the peace, so just come along an' I'll help get you out on bail."

"Never!"

A photographer had appeared and was sighting his camera up through the branches of the beech, like a hunter trying to get a shot at a treed possum, when the policeman on the ground began shouting to his comrade in the lower branches: "Harry, Harry, Harry, look! Here comes another! We got this one treed, come down and help me catch the other."

Penny stared, mystified, at Izzy running heavily from the direction of the Old Munitions Building with civilians rather than police streaming behind. To her further mystification, she did not recognize any of the pursuers as P4P's. What she did not realize was that idealism had become hopelessly entangled in prejudice.

Singsen had been compelled to adjourn the hearing after Penny and the others were dragged from the auditorium. A police lieutenant, recognizing the ugly mood of the audience, ordered a guard for Izzy so that he could get safely away from the building. Four policemen surrounded him and were jostling a way through the crowd when a man had yelled:

"Get the goddamn Jew junk dealer!"

The police didn't understand that the man was not a pacifist but a supporter of Senator Dickburn, the committee hawk who realized that his constituents wanted him to discredit Singsen and any Jews, niggers, pacifists, northern bankers, besides all New Yorkers, who appeared at the hearings. When Dickburn adherents tried to get at Izzy and the police fought to protect him, pacifists, thinking that the brutish police were attacking the innocent again, joined in the fray. Izzy, recognizing his enemies on the scene as southern rednecks rather than New York pacifists, contrived to escape by plowing his way through the crowd like a backfielder through a scrimmage line.

His enemies pursued because they wanted to batter this Jew bastard insensible while, far back, a few police chased the pursuers under the illusion they were pacifists. Izzy figured he could take on four or five of the enemy, but this score or more were too numerous for him. He was getting winded and the pursuers were closing the gap when the policeman dropped out of the tree where Penny had taken refuge. Already badly distraught, Izzy was almost completely unnerved by this business of policemen dropping out of trees. But then he recalled that, much as he had mistrusted the police since childhood, they now were supposed to be his friends. He veered toward the two under the tree, grateful for their protection from the savages.

Suddenly new alarm ravaged him as the two policemen spaced themselves with clubs raised at him. And seemingly from nowhere a photographer had materialized and was aiming a camera at him. Why did everyone think *he* was the enemy? He made a feint, but before he could start running again, the police seized him.

Penny, looking down from the tree, experienced one of her violent changes of emotion. Feeling that Izzy was being treated unfairly, she screamed out in his behalf. It took almost fifteen minutes for the police to talk her down from her tree.

A couple of days passed before a judge straightened out the confusion. Meanwhile, Penny was among four pacifists held on one thousand dollars bail each. Izzy, recognizing her as that child from Murray Hill, paid her bail with new hundred-dollar bills.

"I'm deeply grateful, Izzy," she told him. "I'll write you a check for this. I never thought to bring my checkbook along to Washington."

"Always bring a checkbook to Washington if you want to do business here." Izzy affected an accent called Jewish on the Keith-Orpheum Vaudeville Circuit. "But who's to worry? We'll go to my place for a bite of dinner. Am at the Raleigh Hotel. How's your mama? Your famous brother? How are *you*?"

"Fine, thank you. How are *you*? How's your papa?"

"Dead."

"Sorry."

"Don't be. He was a pain."

They climbed into a taxi, and she said, "If you'll drop me at Union Station, I'll take the next train back to New York."

"You can't leave," he said. "Under the terms of your bail you can't leave the District of Columbia before tomorrow's hearing. We'll have some dinner at the Raleigh."

In the corridor outside his suite he leaned over to unlock the door, glanced up at her, and came face to face with a strange reality. His legs bent weakly; his hair stood on end; icy flames enveloped him. He dropped the key and kissed her. She picked up the key and handed it to him, her eyes looking larger than chandeliers. The old God of Abraham and Isaac had finally rendered him a miracle after such a long time of fooling around.

"You might be Jewish, too?" he asked.

"Could be. Those old Dutch families that came over a long time ago, I always figured they had a lot of Jewish blood."

"God bless you." He kissed her again, and this time she kissed, too.

He had made love to many *shiksas*, but never to one as fabulous as Penny. She was a goddess, or at least she made him feel like a god. How could a snotty Murray Hill girl be so expert at screwing? Compensating, of course. But each took pains never to discuss what they might be compensating for.

Maybe he was compensating for having laid only one Jew in his life. Murial, his wife. His ex-wife, alimony two hundred a week, children none. How could you stay married to a woman who spelled her name Muriel with an *a*? Furthermore, she had a sister named Barbara who insisted her name was spelled Barbra. Their last name was Bamberg—good Jewish family. They convinced him before he walked out for keeps that he was not a good Jew. Gladly he would have denied his Jewishness to the world, but no one would let him, so he always went around confirming and defending it and screwing only *shiksas*.

It began for Penny and Izzy when she spent the night in his suite. In the morning a bellhop delivered *The*

Washington Post with breakfast, and they studied front-page photos of themselves: she treed; he being arrested.

"After this," she said of her picture, "nobody in publishing will ever give me a job—except at Lovejoy's."

"Not to worry," Izzy said. "You can do better working for me."

"I wouldn't work for a munitions maker if I was starving."

"Do you always eat toast in bed?"

"Whenever anybody'll serve it to me. I like the feel of the crumbs between the sheets."

He read the paper for a while. "It says here I spoke 'articulately.' That's an anti-Semitic way of saying I don't have a Jewish accent."

She said, "Why don't you shut up for even one minute about being a Jew? It's a bore." He raised himself on an elbow and gazed at her thoughtfully. She said, "And while you're up, get me some more coffee."

He climbed out of bed and refilled her cup. "You a Marxist?"

"Not anymore. Not after all the blood they're spilling in Russia in the name of social reform."

He started to discuss *Das Kapital*. At first she thought he was trying to show off, but he wasn't, he honestly wanted to discuss communist theory while lying in bed drinking coffee and smoking a strong cigar whose ashes dribbled onto his hairy chest. Personally, she'd never been able to read more than a dozen pages of *Das Kapital* because Karl Marx wrote so awkwardly.

Izzy had not made it beyond the sixth grade, but he'd read hundreds of books—such as Adam Smith's *Inquiry into the Nature and Causes of the Wealth of Nations* and Longfellow's *Hiawatha*—which nobody else had read and which he expected Penny to discuss intelligently with him. When she started to explain that Longfellow was a literary oaf, Izzy looked so crestfallen that she heard herself extolling *Evangeline*, another of Longfellow's works she had not read.

Izzy was helplessly transfixed between admiration of her body and the fact that she was an editor. It was so nice to meet a man with such well-rounded admiration of her that she quickly stopped trying to reform him out of the junk business. She felt she had not just met Izzy in Washington but had been reunited with him after long years of separation.

Now they allowed few interruptions, so as to satisfy their intense curiosity about each other and themselves. It took all kinds of pleasurable positions—standing, sitting, supine, in a bathtub, on a table, while looking out a window at a blank red-brick wall. What had begun in Washington continued in New York. Except for the hours Penny spent working at the office, she and Izzy were inseparable. She moved into his suite at the St. Regis where she chided him about his ostentatious lifestyle.

"I'm compensating for past poverty," he replied.

"Give all that thou hast to the poor," said she.

"I am," said he, "to my poor self."

Inevitably her family learned that she was living at the St. Regis with Izzy. Eunice (who else?) learned about it first and ran babbling to Mama and then to Ann and Steve. What most angered Eunice, who recently had become separated from Bayard, was the fact Penny was having an affair with a *Jew*.

Penny expected that Steve, good old rebel, would be sympathetic while Ann, good old snob, would be contemptuous. But it turned out the other way round. Steve invited her to lunch in the ladies' dining room at the Union League where, because of Prohibition, they served excellent martinis in coffee cups. When he took her to task about Izzy, she accused him of anti-Semitism. But Steve said his being a Jew had nothing to do with it: He just didn't have her class.

As a challenge to Ann, Penny invited her to tea at the St. Regis to meet Izzy. To her surprise, Ann accepted and for some reason brought along her and Steve's little Edward, who was always called Teddy and already was at the running-and-falling-down stage. They drank tea from a Russian samovar, Izzy imitated a horse to Teddy's delight, and Ann left Penny speechless by carrying on a literate dialogue with Izzy about Scott's Waverly novels. Ann showed her approval by inviting them to tea at the Park Avenue mansion one day when Steve had business in Chicago.

But Cordelia was the one who surprised Penny most of all. After returning from Europe she had quickly tired of living at Hasty's and had rented a narrow little brownstone on East Thirty-seventh in Murray Hill. There she occupied herself with charitable works and in being a doting grandmother to Teddy. She declined Penny's invitation to meet Izzy over tea at the St. Regis and prevailed on her to come to lunch alone. To Penny's consternation she absolutely refused to discuss Izzy. Such a lack of charity was so unlike her that Penny felt frightened.

It was then she realized how all these years she'd been clinging to Mama as one who could not swim clung to a life preserver. Unwilling to let go of her life preserver, she determined to rid herself of Izzy. And then she was equally frightened to discover that she could not let him go.

What was wrong? Together, she and Izzy had used all the four-letter words except love. They were very cautious about that—and must continue to be. Love was so unthinkable as to be unknowable. But of the two life preservers, she would take Izzy over Mama. When Cordelia invited her, but not Izzy, to Christmas dinner in 1922, Penny refused. (Causing Eunice to accept once she heard that Penny was not coming.)

It was a miserable Christmas for Penny, a day with

occasional showers of tears. Izzy's gifts of a rope of pearls and a mink coat did not help. How could she explain to him that she cared nothing about jewels and furs, that they made her feel like a kept whore?

Cordelia was not happy, either, that Christmas. She sat down to dinner with her family, but it was incomplete without Penny. She had thought she might miss Eric, but did not.

He had spent a week with her at Hasty's late in November and then gone to the Midwest on a lecture tour. She had been wrong in thinking she never would see him again after she left Europe. It was the second time they had been together since Florence: He would not think of passing through New York without letting her know. She had learned more about the facts of his life from his editor, Hal Wiggins, than she ever had from Eric himself. One of the most significant facts was that he was a confirmed bachelor with the reputation of not being very fond of women.

Yet certainly he was fond of her—as she of him. But love, no. Call it companionship: They enjoyed being together, though she rarely missed him after he went away. Such distances had developed among the members of the family that none except Mary and Tim knew Cordelia and Eric were friends. Presumably she could have spent a month with him at Hasty's and no one would have been any the wiser.

Come, now, she told herself that Christmas, try to be an honest with yourself as you used to take pride in being. For a long time you've been having an off-and-on affair with Eric while Penny has had a steady liaison with Izzy for more than a year. What right have you to act morally superior to her? In the view of the eternals an honest Norwegian explorer was no better than an honest Jewish junk man.

Even had Eric asked her, she would have refused to

marry him. Indeed she had decided never to try marriage again. Last August she had turned down a proposal from Marshal Barton, a widower and New York lawyer who had a country place near hers. They had known and liked each other for years, but she had decided not to see him again because his children objected strenuously to his remarrying. No doubt it was her last chance. So oil the wheelchair that would spin her off to some nursing home.

At dinner that Christmas, Teddy sat in a high chair between Ann and Steve, laughing and dawdling. Eunice, who refused to correct her nearsightedness with glasses, trailed her pearls in the lobster bisque. Nick, left jaw swollen from the removal of many teeth, carved the goose and the game birds because Steven claimed not to know how. Mary and Tim, who had left Ann and Steve to rejoin Cordelia as soon as she rented her brownstone, jumped up so often to fetch and carry that the special servants might as well not have been hired for the day. All of them needed Penny's happy laughter, Cordelia thought.

Something else troubled her as much. Company business was going badly; profits were down for the second year. Steve, she finally had to admit, was not directing well. But she didn't know how to help since he took any suggestion of hers as interference and refused to discuss business with her.

More troubling was her surmise that something was wrong between Steve and Ann. She sensed it, but did not know what the problem was. Several times Ann had seemed on the verge of confiding in her, then had not.

And look at Eunice heading into a nasty divorce fight in an effort to get money from the impossible Bayard. Nick, plagued with teeth and kidney problems, was always in low spirits. Even the once irrepressible Mary and Tim had come to the time of decay. He suffered from an intestinal ailment that puzzled Dr. Pettyman while she had become victim to complaining fits and both grieved that Cora so rarely came to see them with her infant daughter. Which left Teddy, overturning his milk cup, thumping his silver spoon, howling with glee at his foolish elders.

That day before the mince and pumpkin pies were served, Cordelia made a resolution. She must bring back Penny, not out of charity, but because she needed her.

Next day she telephoned her at the St. Regis. Izzy answered and sounded scared when he heard who was calling.

"Izzy," she said, "why don't you and Penny ever ask me to lunch?"

"Because we thought you wouldn't come. When can you? Name your day."

"What are you doing today, Izzy?"

She found him delightful. And it was pleasant for a change to see Penny subdued and empty of argument.

"Mama," Penny said at last, "a thing away back that you didn't understand. Even though we were just kids, I truly loved Izzy."

He rolled his eyes at Cordelia. "Such loyalty! It's moving."

"Not loyalty, Izzy," Cordelia said. "Obviously it's just a case of love at first sight."

23

Ann knew what was wrong with Steve, but did not know how to make things right. He was bored with publishing, he loathed his job. It affected his feeling for her, Teddy, the way they lived. Several times she was on the verge of discussing the problem with Cordelia, to whom she felt close, but she did not because his mother doted so on him and had ordained his role.

On New Year's morning 1923, after Ann and Steve had been up all night at a party and she was scrambling eggs for breakfast, she said to him, "Why don't you quit?"

"Can't." He had drunk too much and was very tired. "Mama has fixed my destiny. Can't break Mama's heart. Best friend a boy ever had."

"Honey, if you did quit, what would you do?"

"Now that," he said, "is the stupidest question I ever heard from a smart girl like you."

Of course he would spend all his time dabbling in aviation. Every Sunday, weather permitting, he went flying from Teterboro; and when weather grounded him, he tinkered with the airplane he had bought, or he gossiped with pilot friends. He and other men formed a club they called the Confederation of Air Bums. They held cross-country races, competed at stunt flying, and did just about anything childish that came to mind. Once in a while one of them would tumble out of the sky and kill himself, causing his comrades to hold a sad memorial service and get solemnly drunk. A suicide gang, crazy and wild. Or so Ann thought. But she never told Steve how she felt. Those Sundays of flying out of

Teterboro were what enabled him to endure the rest of the week.

Ann stayed home on Sundays and worried about him. Her father had died in the previous October, leaving her a couple of million, which appeared enough to support Steve and her for life if he quit Lovejoy's and did not blow money on airplanes. As an only child, she had thought that she'd like to have a lot of children, but now she had changed her mind. Teddy was wonderful, Teddy was enough. There was something about being married to a man who spun wildly through the air every Sunday that made a woman not want a houseful of children.

After Teddy went on the bottle, she had left him in a nurse's care and gone back to Lovejoy's as an associate editor. But the work, which she enjoyed, became unsatisfactory to her. Maybe it was because she was the president's wife, or maybe it was all Steve's fault.

He got along well with people in all departments of the company except editorial. But with editors and writers he quarreled like an Airedale with cats. Penny became so cautious about dealing with him in her editorial work that she kept short hours and did not accomplish much. Mainly because of Steve's attitude, Runyon quit and became editor-in-chief at McTeague's.

Then Osmund Fuller, who succeeded Runyon, resigned as editor-in-chief after Steve told Livy Harris, author of the best-selling *Over the Line*: "To be perfectly frank, Mr. Harris, I don't understand all the hoopla over your novel. I lasted two chapters and was bored to death."

Osmund, livid, asked Steve, "Why in the hell did you have to say a thing like that?"

"Because," Steve answered, "I think a little honesty around here is a refreshing thing. That is a lousy book."

"The public doesn't think so!" Osmund cried. "You just lost a best-selling author."

"No, I didn't. He has a three-book contract with us."

But Lovejoy's did lose Livy Harris. For his next submission he turned in a horror of a manuscript which he'd rented from a Columbia undergraduate for fifteen dollars, and two weeks later he submitted another atrocity which he'd rented for only ten dollars and which represented the third in his three-book contract. Then Harris moved to Perry and Halstead where his books eventually sold hundreds of thousands of copies under the chief editorship of Osmund Fuller.

While Cordelia was puzzled and saddened by what Steve had done, Ann was furious.

"You damn fool!" she cried. "What's the matter with you?"

Her anger amused him. "You turn very pretty when you get mad, baby. We don't need Harris. He's just another conceited prick writer. Besides, I think he's a pansy."

"That has nothing to do with it! All that matters is he tells interesting stories people want to read."

"Baby, you wanna be editor-in-chief for a while?"

"I'd love to. I simply don't have the experience, the savvy. But if I ever did become the big cheese around here I'd expect you to be the rat that destroyed me. What about Penny? Why don't you accept your mother's advice and give her a bigger editorial role?"

"Because I get along with her pretty well. And if she gets more editorial power, we're bound to quarrel because we don't see eye to eye on books. I'd like to have one sister left I like better than Eunice."

"Do you want to get rid of all the writers?" Ann demanded one day. "Would you like to publish books that have no authors?"

"I wouldn't mind getting rid of most of our present writers," he said. "I like that manuscript you had

me read by this young guy Preston. All that stuff about
the upper Amazon. Very crisp and exciting. Good title
might be *Up Shit Creek Without a Paddle*. I think people like to read stuff like that."

She agreed that Preston had an exciting true adventure to tell about his journey to the headwaters of the
Amazon. "But it needs a lot of work, Steve."

"Why? The trouble with you editors is you always
want to diddle writers. Are you all trying to prove you
exist? A writer like Preston should be given his own
head. Hell, he's an articulate man of action with a sharp
eye. What do you want to do to the poor bastard's manuscript?"

She tried to explain, but he didn't listen.

When Lovejoy's eventually published Preston's book
under the title *Going Yonder* in October 1924, the
noted critic A. Lionel Jones gave it a devastating review. He accused Preston, among other things, of showing total insensitivity to the poor Amazonians and cast
doubt on his veracity. When Steve read the review he
flew into a fury and called in the renowned literary lawyer Cyrus Goldstein, who agreed that, yes, this time—
as often before—Jones had gone too far by calling an
author a liar.

"And everything in this book really happened?" he
asked Steve.

"Everything. Preston has diaries, notes, witnesses."

Cyrus sighed. "You have grounds for a suit. But
what publisher is going to sue that bellwether critic A.
Lionel Jones?"

"Well, this publisher is," Steve said. "Not only that,
if I can find the son of a bitch, I'll horsewhip him
through the streets."

"Please," Cyrus said, "one suit at a time. Steven, this
is going to cost you a lot of money."

"My pleasure, Cyrus."

"And lose you a lot of critic friends."

"No critic ever has been or will be a friend of mine."

"I must explore compromises," Cyrus said.

"How much will that cost me?"

"Plenty. But not as much as a court action."

As a result, the publisher of Jones's review agreed, in order to avoid a suit, to let Steve take newspaper ads in which he could flagellate Jones within bounds of propriety. After spending two days and a night trying to compose appropriate invective and still failing to avoid libel, Steve hired the hack Jacques Pasquale to write the piece for him. Pasquale did it beautifully. Knowing that Jones was a failed novelist, he wrote a malicious review of his solitary, bad, out-of-print novel. Inflamed, Jones vowed publicly never to review another Lovejoy book. Three weeks later, however, he dropped dead of a massive heart attack and his successor quickly forgot there ever had been bad blood between Jones and Lovejoy's.

The morning Penny and Izzy read Steve's attack on Jones in the *Times* and *Tribune* Izzy asked, "Did he write this himself?"

"Probably not. But baby brother can afford to live vicariously."

She and Izzy had left the St. Regis and now lived in a large apartment on Murray Hill two blocks from Cordelia. That morning Penny had an appointment with Dr. Prettyman.

"Why," Izzy asked, "don't you take Mama's advice and talk to Steve about taking on more editorial responsibility?"

"Because I don't want to pick a fight with my only brother. I'm already fighting with my only sister." She put on her coat. "I'm leaving now to see Doctor Prettyman."

"Long as I can remember Murray Hill," Izzy said, "people have been praising Doctor Prettyman. Is there a Mrs. Prettyman?"

"I think so, but I'm not sure."

"Are there young Prettymans?"

"I think so, but I'm not sure."

"Why don't you ask?"

"Because, stupid, those aren't the sort of questions you ask Doctor Prettyman."

When she arrived at his office on Thirty-fourth Street—the same office he had occupied for thirty-eight years—and described her symptons, he told her to undress and called in his nurse. Sometimes he could be brutally frank, as when he told the nurse: "Adjust the stirrups, Miss Penny's legs are abnormally long."

After a time he said, "Miss Penny, you're pregnant."

Everything grew dim to her and when she could hear his voice again she said, "What did you say? I just fainted."

"You can't have fainted," Dr. Prettyman said. "Nobody faints while lying down. You heard what I said."

"But I can't be," Penny said weakly.

"Why not? This thing we have here is neither a tumor nor a baseball."

"Oh, my God, how wonderful!" Penny cried. "I've never been so happy in all my life! How old am I?"

"If you don't remember, I won't tell you," Dr. Prettyman said.

"I remember now. Doctor, I'm not too old to bear the child?"

"Of course not. Just last week I delivered a woman of twins who's ten years older than you."

Penny rushed home by taxi. Izzy had left for his office, which was four blocks distant on Fifth Avenue. She phoned him at once and said, "Come home immediately, something has happened."

"What?" he demanded.

"I can't tell you on the phone. Hurry!" She hung up.

He must have run all the way, for he came in panting and sweating.

"Lie down," she told him.

He looked at her dazedly. "Lie down where?"

"Anywhere. The floor."

"My God," he said, "I've never heard of such a passionate woman. At least let me get undressed."

"Lie down, stupid, because you're going to faint when you hear what I have to tell you and you can't faint lying on the floor."

He lay down, his bassetlike eyes gazing up at her reproachfully, and she said, "Doctor Prettyman tells me I'm two months pregnant."

Instead of passing out, he started to weep. Then he began to laugh. He lumbered to his feet and hugged and kissed her and might have fallen to the floor again if she hadn't supported him.

"Could you," he babbled, "now bring yourself to marry me?"

"Oh I suppose so," she said.

"I know I'm a—"

"Shut up, Izzy. Why didn't you ever ask me before? It was getting so I thought I'd have to ask you."

Two days later, attended by a joyous Cordelia and Ann, they rode downtown in Izzy's Packard, which was driven by a thug he seriously called his chauffuer. As the civil-court magistrate began the brief ceremony, Steve dashed in, shouting congratulations.

In the following months Mr. and Mrs. Irael Epstein held long discussions over what to call their son or daughter, and Penny had to steer Izzy away from some noxious literary names. His favorite poet was Alfred Tennyson—he would quote you long pages of *Locksley Hall* unless you stopped him—and he liked such names as Geraint and Enid in *Idylls of the King*.

They still had not settled on a name when a strapping son was born to them in New York Hospital on June 30, 1925. Suddenly Izzy had an inspiration, and

Penny was too weakened to put up strong resistance. He would be called Alfred Tennyson Epstein.

"Now that," Izzy crowed, "is one hell of a name!"

Everyone remarked on the great change in Izzy after he became a husband and father. Without one prompting word from Penny he quit the junk business, selling his company to a group of Chinese and investing most of the proceeds in the stock market. Subduing his tendency toward flamboyance, he stopped having business luncheons in speakeasies and taking Penny to night-clubs. He gave his flashy suits to the poor and wore dark pinstripes befitting a banker; he turned in his red Packarad in favor of a black Rolls; he rented Penny and himself napping space in the grand tier of the Metropolitan Opera House and often helped to sponsor concerts at Carneige Hall. In the handsome Murray Hill town house he bought for them on Thirty-eighth Street he began to collect rare books.

Old friends from his junk-dealing days faded away, but new friends did not take their places. At first Izzy thought it was because Christians shunned him as a Jew while Jews did not forgive his marrying a *shiksa*. But in time he saw that was not completely so. He did not make close new friends because he was in the process of building a fortune, as solitary and creative a pursuit as that of an artist or writer. His agora, his atelier, was the stock market, which he studied as carefully as he formerly had researched the processing of waste which Americans called junk.

In the market he was as conservative as his dark pinstripes: He did not go overboard on margin buying, he paid no attention to the blandishments of brokers, he kept spinning off profits into a mix of government bonds and real estate—not the quick-buck tenements of the slums, an investment morally repugnant to him, but midtown Manhattan office space. While the great bull stockmarket generated him capital, he was a bear at heart. He believed that prosperity, because of shaky economic conditions throughout the world, could not possibly soar on forever in the way that nearly everyone forecast. Any morning he expected to awaken to the flood on which he would float his personal ark. Twice he dropped almost altogether out of the market, but twice he returned in strength.

No one observed Izzy with more interest than Steve. From vague dislike of him Steve's feelings changed to vague admiration. Yet it seemed impossible for them to communicate well. Steve admitted that the fault was his, that he did not bend enough when he talked with Izzy. What he admired most was Izzy's having done what he wanted—quit the junk business for the stock market—while retaining a good relationship with his wife and child.

Steve knew that he made Ann unhappy. While he was having a grand time flying out of Teterboro, he knew that she was being miserable in New York. Yet what was he supposed to do? Whenever he forced himself to stay home on a Sunday and play the role of husband and father, he was bored. Teddy was too young to be interesting. And Ann's idea of Sunday fun was to read and exchange thoughts on what was read, then take a long walk and exchange thoughts on what they observed. What was the fun in that?

A few times Ann went to Teterboro with him to be companionable. But when she occasionally made a brief flight with him she insisted that Teddy stay on the ground. So she was afraid of flying. Did that mean he should stop doing what he loved more than anything? There was something wrong with their marriage. Penny and Izzy enjoyed each other's company all the time and never had conflicting interests. Look at Mama's friends Eleanor and Franklin Roosevelt: His promising political career, brought to national attention when he was the vice-presidential candidate on the losing Democratic ticket with Cox in 1920, had been struck down by infantile paralysis; yet he obviously found strength in his wife's devotion to him.

Steve thought that Ann seemed more devoted to the company than to him. Ann, like Mama, thought there was only one way to run a publishing house. Maybe it was typically feminine for them to think that a house must be run like a candy store: a dib here and a dab there, with virtue in diversification. His own wish was to publish fewer books and sell them in greater numbers through heavier advertising and promotion.

Toward that end he sold off the education department, which was beginning to make a little money after years of building. Mama fought ferociously to maintain that boondoggling idea of John Speer's, insisting that "the tide has turned, years of prosperity lie ahead." Steve triumphed, of course, but it took some doing. And when he sold off the juvenile department along with Gertrude Nayton and all her little red hens, Mama acted as if he'd torn off her right arm. Yes, there was a little money in juveniles, but not a lot. He tried to confuse Mama with talk about overhead, but she didn't confuse readily. She especially reminded him that he had just moved the company into new and more expensive quarters on Murray Hill.

The day in January 1926, when the company completed its move into the new quarters, Cordelia dropped by to take a look. With her was a big, aging man whose red beard and hair were whitening. She introduced him to Steve: Eric Lief.

"My God!" Steve exclaimed. "Eric Lief, the explorer?" Yah, said the giant. "Well my gosh, Mama, you never said you knew *him*." He wrung Eric's hand harder.

Cordelia's gaze became abstract. "I'm convinced," she said to Eric, "that after mothers turn fifty their children become totally unaware of them." To Steve: "Why were you carping to me the other day about expenses? These offices are preposterously large."

"Well, look around, Mama." He turned to Eric: "Would you like to write a book for Lovejoy's?"

"I already write a book," Eric said.

"I know. *True North* was one of the best."

"Now *that* is a compliment," Cordelia said. "Steve mainly hates books, Eric, so when he says one is good—Steve, who is that flapper there going down the hall?"

"That's no flapper, Mama, that's a new secretary who hopes to wiggle her butt into an editorial job. Mr. Lief—Eric, let me take you—and Mama—to lunch."

"Now, that's a change," Cordelia said. "You haven't taken Mama to lunch in six months. But the minute I show up with a retired Arctic explorer—"

"Not retired," Eric said. "I never retire. Just resting between expeditions."

Steve's face lighted up. "That's the old fight, Eric. Me, too. I'm just resting between expeditions."

They went to the Union League for lunch. From the way Steve questioned Eric about his plans Cordelia believed he wanted him to write another book. It pleased her until Eric began carrying on about his wish to fly to the North Pole.

At last she said, "Eric, you're really becoming a bore about that old idea."

"I don't think it's a bore," Steve said. "I think it's the most interesting idea I've heard of in about eighty-nine years. Eric, how much would such an expedition cost?"

Eric sighed. "Every year it gets more expensive. This year it cost a hundred and ninety-two thousand. That's in American dollars. Next year. . . ."

Steve's animated expression made Cordelia uneasy. Suddenly she was very glad that such a large sum of money was not available to him.

24

"No," Ann said to Steve. "I wouldn't think of doing such a thing."

"Please." He sounded to be half kidding.

"Throw away a hundred and ninety thousand on such an absurd idea? Do you know how many starving people that would feed? Do you realize what that would do in medical research?"

"But is it doing those things?" Steve asked. "Isn't it just sitting there gathering dust in the investment market? Pretty please, Li'l Orphan Annie. Loan Eric and me a hundred and fifty grand and I'll dig up the rest."

"No!" Maybe it was his sarcastic tone that made her look and sound so angry. "Do you mean to say you'd walk out of your job for several weeks to try to fly over the North *Pole*?"

"That's exactly what I mean." His voice sank almost to a whisper. "I know I won't get your cooperation, Ann, but I ask you one favor. Don't mention what I want to do to Mama."

She spoke the first cruel words she ever had uttered to him: "Are you going through your entire life trying not to let your mama know what you're doing?"

He blinked and answered slowly: "Well, she always finds out eventually, but I like to spare her as much grief as possible."

At Steve's suggestion they had had Eric to dinner that evening and did not include Cordelia. Once Eric realized that Steve was seriously interested in a polar flight, he understood that Cordelia should not be informed about it. The secrecy with which they laid their plans was what later astonished Ann and Cordelia most.

Eric had an option to charter a Norwegian whaling vessel in May with the plan of taking a group of amateur exploring-enthusiasts to the northeast coast of Greenland for three months. He had hoped to make some profit by charging each of the thirty or so interested people the sum of three thousand dollars. When Steve proposed that by charging each six thousand dollars they could be promised a part in a North Pole flight, Eric thought it a fine idea. But to their disappointment only three men would go along with the six thousand fee.

Next Steve tried his Yale friend Stan Jayberg, but Stan had just put backer's money into an Amazon expedition and claimed he had none left for the polar regions. For days on end Steve wrote letters and made phone calls to wealthy and prominent people, but everyone turned him down.

"It's my amateur standing," he told Eric ruefully. "They can't imagine a New York publisher knowing how to fly over the Pole."

"But what about my professional standing? I'm going to be the navigator."

Steve didn't have the heart to tell Eric that he had gained the reputation of being a hard-luck explorer who always started toward his goals either too late or with too little.

To Steve, even more than to Eric, it became unthinkable to abandon the effort. So he was elated one day in February to accomplish within a few minutes what he had been unable to do in the preceding weeks: A New York bank was glad to loan him one hundred and seventy-five thousand when he offered forty percent of his Lovejoy's stock as collateral. Of course Eric was ecstatic, as was Orlo Peterson, who was eager to take a vacation from Teterboro and go along as backup pilot.

At Orlo's urging they signed up a thin young man named Jake Ladelaw as chief mechanic of the expedition.

Steve, telling Ann he was going to Chicago on business, took the Twentieth Century with Jake. At a small airport outside the city they found the prize which Jake promised was waiting there. It was a trimotor plane built in Amsterdam by the famous German designer Anthony Fokker and it was fitted with Wright Whirlwind J-4B engines. Steve had hoped to get it for twenty thousand, but the owner held out for twenty-five.

Steve felt that he had no choice, for a plane like it was not available elsewhere and the Wright Whirlwinds were the best engines in the world. They were radial engines which looked like rimless wheels with fat spokes because their nine cylinders stood out from the hub where the crankshaft was housed. The outsides of the cylinders had fins which absorbed cooling air from the propeller wash—a great advantage in weight since they made the radiator, pump, and water jackets of liquid-cooled power plants unnecessary. The chief disadvantages of the engines were their head resistance and their low output of two hundred horsepower. Jake calculated that when the plane was fitted with skis, as it would be for the big flight, she would have a cruising speed of about sixty-four miles per hour.

"What are you going to name this baby?" Jake asked Steve.

"The *Cordelia Lovejoy*."

"That your wife's name?"

"My mother's."

"Won't maybe your wife be jealous?"

"I don't care. My mother has adventurer's blood. My wife doesn't."

The weather was so bad that it took Steve and Jake four days to fly the *Cordelia Lovejoy* from Chicago to

Teterboro. Along the way Steve sent telegrams home, explaining that he was delayed by business.

When he finally arrived, Ann asked him, "What kind of business were you doing in a place called Zanesville, Ohio?"

"Wanted to look over a new printing plant."

She believed him. And she believed that he had company business in Boston when he and Orlo went there and bought an old Dornier "Wal" duralumin flying boat which would serve as the backup plane. Both Orlo and Eric agreed on the worthiness of this model, which was called a Whale and had two Rolls-Royce engines mounted in tandem. To the chagrin of Steve and Orlo they got lost in a fog over Narragansett Bay and were hours late in reaching New York.

The expedition, as planned by Eric and Steve, was notable for its simplicity. On May first the whaler *Bergen* would put into New York and take on the dismantled *Cordelia Lovejoy* and the Dornier "Wal" and the American members of the expedition. On that day Steve and Eric would announce to the world the purpose of their expedition. Next day the *Bergen* would sail for Keelgin Inlet on the northeast coast of Greenland where it would arrive between June tenth and fifteenth, depending on ice conditions. Everyone would immediately stand to the task of making a runway and reassembling the *Cordelia Lovejoy*—a labor of five or six days, Eric estimated. Then the *Cordelia Lovejoy* would soar off the ice with Steve at the controls, Eric navigating, and Jake along as mechanic. The straight-line distance from Keelgin Inlet to the Pole and back totaled 1,586 statute miles. They figured that the round-trip flight, without favoring winds, would take 23.4 hours at sixty-three miles per hour. They would carry enough fuel to keep them aloft for 24.5 hours—the limit of their capacity. After the three returned from

the Pole and sent word of their triumph to a waiting
world, they would return to civilization. In the unlikely
event that anything went wrong with the Fokker and
they had to put down someplace, Orlo would come to
their aid with the Whale.

Like many projects conceived as simple, the Lief-
Lovejoy Polar Expedition soon became complicated.
Those involved in the proposed flight numbered fifteen
and did not include the thirty-two-man crew of the *Bergen*, who had no responsibilities except to their ship. It
was not enough men, Eric feared, to carve out a long
runway for the *Cordelia Lovejoy*.

"Those goddamn ship crewmen," Eric said. "I offer
extra wages for runway work, but only a few will do it.
They know the north and what hard work that is."

Then the three Americans who had agreed to pay six
thousand each to be among the fifteen members of the
expedition, realizing that they would be little more than
coolie labor, backed out. The day that happened Steve
was feeling deeply depressed as he and Ann arrived for
dinner at Cordelia's house.

He was mixing cocktails in the kitchen and talking to
Mary and Tim when Tim said, "There's nothin' ailin'
me that couldn't be fixed right with a change o' scene."

Mary thought his remark smacked of infidelity, but
Tim said, " 'Tis that there's nothin' of interest to do
anymore. I'm still strong as an ox. Fer instance, I likes
to shovel snow an' it don't even snow in New York anymore."

Steve stopped stirring the drinks and looked at him.

Mary took something into the dining room, and Tim
said, "Wot an empty life it's been, but don't tell Mary. I
mean drivin' them horsecars that niver went anywheres
except to the place where they started. Then twirlin' an'
twirlin' old man Hart's doors, but never—if ye understood wot I means, Steven—*steppin' through 'em.*"

"Timmy"—Steve poured him a nip of the Manhattans in a small glass—"would you like to go to the North Pole with me?"

Tim gaped at him. Mary came back to the kitchen, and he hid the forbidden glass behind his back. Mary went to the dining room again, and Tim said, "Steven, I've always known ye was sort o' crazy—It's the quality I most respects in ye—*but*—tell me more."

"All right, but you mustn't tell Mama or Mary. . . ."

When Mary returned to the kitchen, Tim was laughing and doing a jig. Mary said to him, " 'Tis odd how in your old age, Tim McMahon, just one little sip can turn you crazy."

"Old age?" cried Tim. "Crazy? *Madame* McMahon, ye'll soon see about *that*!"

It was apparent, however, that more strong backs than Tim's were needed. Steve told Eric, "We can't keep it secret any longer. I'm going to call *The New York Times*."

"And *advertise*?"

"No, offer them exclusive coverage. Send a reporter with us if they want to."

Eric agreed that was all right if the reporter was physically strong and the newspaper paid his way. "Cordelia is going to be very cross with you and me when she reads the *Times*," he added.

After a reporter interviewed Eric and Steve and a photographer took their pictures, Steve went straight home and told all to Ann. He expected anything but the way she reacted: She burst into wild laughter and finally walked out of the room. When he found her in their bedroom she was weeping.

"What a crazy way to act," he said.

She dried her eyes. "What a crazy man you are. Where did you get the money to do it?"

When he told her, she just stared at him silently. "Ann, will you tell Mama for me?"

"No, Steve, I won't tell Mama for you."

"Well," he said, "then I guess she'll just have to read about it in the *Times*."

Usually Cordelia read the *Times* and the *Tribune* with breakfast, but next morning she was so engrossed by an S.S. Van Dine mystery novel that she put aside the newspapers in order to finish it. Usually Mary did not read the *Times* or *Tribune*, but that morning she was looking at the front page of Cordelia's *Times* in the kitchen when a headline below the fold of the front page caught her attention.

PUBLISHER, EXPLORER
WILL ATTEMPT FLIGHT
ACROSS NORTH POLE

When Mary read Steve's name she cried out in dismay, but Cordelia was too absorbed in her mystery story to hear her in the dining room. Then Mary came to a paragraph that reported:

> Mr. Lovejoy and Dr. Lief said that there are still a few vacancies in expedition personnel that may be filled by men in sturdy health who can defray their own expenses. Mr. Lovejoy cited as an example a man he described as an affluent Irish businessman who has been active in the transportation and merchandising fields, Mr. Timothy McMahon of Dublin, who was not available for comment since, Mr. Lovejoy explained, he now is enroute to New York to join the expedition when it leaves on the *Bergen*. . . .

Now, realizing suddenly why Tim had been acting so strange and mysterious recently, Mary uttered a piercing scream that startled Cordelia out of her dining-room chair. If Tim had been at home, he would have come running, too, but he had gone out early to buy a fur hat.

When Cordelia had calmed herself sufficiently to pick up the telephone, she called Steve at home and spoke only one word: "*Why?*"

"Well, my gosh, Mama," he replied, "nobody's ever flown to the North Pole and back. Say, while I'm away, I hope you'll sort of keep an eye on the store and—"

She slammed the receiver, shaking with an odd mixture of grief, anger, dread, and frustration. At last, recalling that the *Times* said Eric was staying at the Wentworth Hotel (and she had thought he was in Norway) she called him there, uttering three words: "You lousy bastard!"

Cordelia, Ann, Mary—all were sufficiently recovered to wave the men farewell from a Brooklyn pier when the *Bergen* sailed for Greenland, not on May second as planned, but on May twelfth because the simplest things had become so complex.

Although Steve eventually was accused of mistakes and misjudgments by members of the expedition, no one ever criticized him for bringing Tim along. On a voyage marked by misunderstandings, jealousies, and bickering, Tim was liked by everyone. His constant good cheer lighted the general gloomy boredom as the *Bergen* wallowed northward through storms and ice floes. Even Carlin of the *Times*, a dour man who had been released from the city room to cover the expedition, became deeply fond of him.

It was slow going through the floes up the east coast of Greenland, but then the *Bergen* found open water. Despite the delayed start, the ship was off Keelgin Inlet by June twelfth and began ramming her way in through ice. To the eyes of the uninitiated like Steve and Tim, no land or inlet was visible: just a chaotic upheaval of ice stretching to a curiously flat horizon until a dab of black rock was like the revelation of a new continent. There *was* land under all the ice and snow.

Steve began to feel lucky after they walked ashore across ice six feet thick and he saw that the land slanted downward into the prevailing easterly winds. Immediately he set all hands, except the aviation experts, to shoveling and cutting and tramping out a half-mile runway down the slant while he and the experts reassembled the *Cordelia Lovejoy*. The weather held good, and three days after going ashore he and Orlo were ready for a trial run with the Fokker.

The plane roared down the runway, but just before Steve was about to lift her off, there was a popping sound and the craft began to vibrate wildly. They cut the engines, skidded to a halt, and saw how close they had come to disaster. A ski had broken and a landing gear strut was bent. With Jake they worked all night in the *Bergen's* machine shop making repairs while Eric helped them. His advice, as it had been from the beginning, was invaluable. When they started to rub wax on the new ski, Eric pointed out that the crystalline snow acted like sand and would quickly rub off the wax; he had them burn a mixture of pine tar and resin into the wood with a blowtorch.

It began to snow heavily, and two days passed before Steve and Orlo could make a trial run again. Again the *Cordelia Lovejoy* roared down the runway, and Steve pulled back the controls when she had gathered sufficient speed. Nothing happened. Frantically though he tugged, the Fokker would not lift off. Orlo cut the engines, but by that time the plane had gone off the end of the runway, bounded over ice hummocks, and skidded half over. They climbed out, badly shaken, and were relieved to find no critical breaks in the plane.

Everyone gathered and carried the plane back to the runway, then hauled it up the slant with ropes.

"Lighten, yes," Steve said to Orlo, "but can we lighten enough?"

Tim spoke up. "A couple o' hundred pounds no less, Steven." Then he revealed that he and several others had hidden stamped letters, packages, even a teddy bear away aft in the plane, their idea being that such things would be invaluable mementos after having been to the North Pole.

"But where the hell did you get the teddy bear?" Steve asked

"It belongs to Ted—your son. Remember how he used to play with it?"

"I guess so. But how did *you* get it, Timmy?"

"From Mrs. Ann."

"Well, I'll be damned!" Steve looked at him with wonder. "That's the first sign I've seen that Annie expects me to make it. Now that teddy bear flies with us for good luck."

They agreed to offload three hundred gallons of gasoline, but Eric was adamant in refusing Steve's urging to reduce their survival gear of pemmican, three pairs of snowshoes, a handsled, and three pairs of grass-filled canvas boots such as the Lapps wore on winter treks with their reindeer.

Eric had another wise suggestion: "Time goes fast. We don't try to test again. Do the thing itself. Start at midnight. Then the sun is closer to the horizon and the runway frozen harder."

Following his suggestion, they tried again with him, Steve, and Jake aboard, at twelve twenty-five A.M. on June twenty-seventh. This time the *Cordelia Lovejoy* skimmed off the end of the runway, the roar of her engines fading into a hum and then into silence.

* * *

Carlin of the *Times* was under order to file a daily story, no matter how trivial. Although he knew as an experienced newsman that many of his dispatches would not reach even the stage of overset type, he faithfully carried out orders. And for days he had kept ready a story about the takeoff for the Pole that required him only to fill in the precise time. During that early morning takeoff he stood at the top of the runway holding a red flag which he unfurled and waved wildly the moment the *Cordelia Lovejoy* lifted off. The radio operator of the *Bergen*, waiting with his watch synchronized with Carlin's, sprang to his key and started tapping out the story while Carlin ran and skidded across the ice to the vessel to add details.

When the airplane took off for the Pole it was eight twenty-five P.M. on June twenty-sixth in New York, and Carlin's swiftly transmitted story easily made the *Times* issue of June twenty-seventh. In the style of the newspaper in that age the lead was long and leisurely.

BY SPECIAL CORRESPONDENT OF THE NEW YORK TIMES

> Keelgin Inlet, Greenland, June 27—A three-engined airplane piloted by Steven Lovejoy, a World War ace, with Dr. Eric Lief, a Norwegian explorer, serving as navigator and Jacob Ladelaw as mechanic, took off from this bleak coast of northeastern Greenland at 12:25 A.M. this morning (8:25 P.M., June 26, New York Standard Time) in an effort to fly over the North Pole and return here. If successful, it would be an historic flight representing man's first conquest of the Pole by air. . . .

The story went on to explain that the flight was expected to take close to twenty-four hours and that the crew would make only three radio reports—midway to their destination, over the Pole, and midway through their return trip—because Ladelaw was the only licensed operator aboard and his other duties prohibited more frequent contacts with the base.

Cordelia had become friendly with the publisher of the *Times* when both served on a committee which was raising money for a charity, and he had kindly directed his office to keep her and Ann up with developments as they were received from Carlin. As they had arranged to do, Ann brought young Ted to Cordelia's house after the first report was received, and then they and Mary began a long night of waiting.

Ted quickly fell asleep, but the three women drank coffee and tried to reassure one another with remarks Cordelia knew were pointless. For instance, she heard herself saying for a third time: "The man at the *Times* emphasized to me there's no assurance Carlin's dispatches can get through quickly. There's a lot of static or interference in signals at those latitudes. That's what he said."

Ann looked at her calmly. "Yes, Mother."

Somehow Ann's calm manner began to irritate her as the hours crept by with no further call from the newspaper. Around five A.M., as light grew on Murray Hill and she fought tension and fatigue, she asked, "Ann, how can you act so calm?"

"Because I gave him up for dead when he went away."

"Oh, saints preserve us!" Mary exclaimed. "Never say such a thing!"

"I understand that." Cordelia spoke slowly. "It was the frame of mind I adopted about him during the war. But it seems impossible for me to do again."

Around eight A.M. the telephone began to ring as calls came from well-meaning friends and acquaintances and even strangers, all curious and offering best wishes. There even came a call from Eunice in Florida and from Nick, who was vacationing on Cape Cod. In mid-morning Cordelia decided her telephone service was blocked by incoming calls, and all of them except Mary moved to Steve's office at the company headquarters, after they were joined by Penny and Izzy.

"Sorry," Ann said when they went into Steve's office, "but I can't take it here. Look at that pile of unanswered mail! I simply can't take it."

They crowded into Penny's office where their fatigue and tension grew. In midafternoon a solemn-sounding editor called them from the *Times* and said Carlin reported no word from the *Cordelia Lovejoy* in the sixteen hours after she took off.

The headline on page one next day read:

AMERICAN-NORWEGIAN POLAR PLANE
OVERDUE; BELIEVED DOWN IN ARCTIC

Fresh word came that afternoon while they waited exhaustedly in Steve's office.

"Mrs. Lovejoy?" the solemn editor asked. "No word yet about your son and the other members of the crew. But Carlin has filed a fresh story. Orlo Peterson took off in the backup airplane on a search mission. There was some difficulty getting the flying boat into open water. One of those trying to fend it off the ice shelf was Timothy McMahon. He slipped into the water and was drowned before he could be rescued. We understand that you know his wife."

Cordelia wept as she told the others in hushed tones. "I'll go home and tell Mary."

Ann and Penny said they would go with her.

"You know"—Cordelia's voice turned harsh—"it's always been the same. It's not just what Steve does to himself, but how what he does affects others."

* * *

After the *Cordelia Lovejoy* gained altitude and they left Keelgin behind, Eric set their course for the Pole. All realized that the chief burden of the flight was on Steve, for they could easily drift if his concentration wavered from the plotted course. Jake or Eric could relieve him at the controls for a few minutes so that he could stretch or go to the latrine pot aft, but he could not be spared to snatch even a five-minute nap. In order to keep himself alertly awake he had asked Dr. Prettyman to prescribe caffein tablets which he tried out on himself and found effective for up to thirty hours.

As navigational aid Eric had a sextant, altimeter, two magnetic compasses, and a sun compass, with two chronometers to assure accuracy of his readings. At the start, flying at three thousand feet, they had a favoring wind. Eric computed their ground speed at 71.5 miles per hour, far better than they had anticipated. Steve could not suppress his elation; it seemed so easy that it was incomprehensible dozens of fliers hadn't tried it before.

"Admiral Peary should see us now!" he shouted above the drone of the engines.

Perhaps he should not have said that; maybe he had roused the ghost of the man who had tried it afoot. For the words were barely out of his mouth when Jake exclaimed and pointed to oil gushing from the starboard engine. Steve throttled it instantly and they continued on the other two engines at a groundspeed of sixty. Soon he started the starboard again, but the leak was so bad that he cut the engine entirely.

Damn his last moment of happiness, they would have to turn back. "Can't make it on two," he said.

Eric and Jake cursed, but agreed. Even had they not, it would have made no difference; they abided by the rule that Steve, as pilot, had absolute word on the worthiness of the aircraft for continued flight. He banked the *Cordelia Lovejoy* around, and Eric had just set their return course when the port engine died. There was no discernible reason. Steve surmised that its crankshaft had broken, yet that seemed incredible for the most reliable engine model of the time. Incredible or not, they were losing speed and altitude as they labored along on the single main engine.

"Lighten her," Steve said.

Eric and Jake finally got the door lashed open and began jetissoning cans of reserve fuel, tumbling them out as fast as they could. Still they continued to lose altitude slowly. As far as Steve could scan in every direction there was nothing but ice floes with here and there a patch of open black water. Nowhere could he see a smooth ice stretch on which to set down the plane. Shouting at Jake until he got his attention, he told him to send an SOS to Keelgin and give their position as about fifty miles north of the base.

Steve believed he heard Jake behind him, tapping out the message on 500 kilocycles, the frequency used by ships at sea, but he was too much occupied to glance around because the plane was beginning to buck in air pockets and settle faster. Far to portside he suddenly glimpsed a large floe whose ice looked smoother than most. Giving the remaining engine full throttle, he pointed for it. At first it seemed they could not make it, and then it seemed they might as the nose continued to sink.

Sweat streamed down Steve's face as he felt he was physically forcing the *Cordelia Lovejoy* to reach that floe. They made it, by what looked from the cockpit like inches. But then, to Steve's horror, he saw the floe was not the glassy ice he had thought. It was a mass of slush and low hummocks on which the landing skis jounced, skidded, and broke. There was a sound like ripping fabric and something dealt Steve a mighty sock on the jaw that sent him spinning over and over.

The ripping sound, he finally realized, was of flames. The *Cordelia Lovejoy* blazed, but somehow he was at a distance from it, sprawling on the ice with his left leg strangely bent and hurting under him. Eric and Jake were nowhere in sight. The flames roared higher, and suddenly the blazing debris burned through the ice and sank into the Arctic Ocean with a great hissing sound. It was, Steve thought dazedly, the sound with which the public greeted a horrendous failure.

25

Cordelia was stricken by the dread that she had destroyed Steve because she had introduced him to Eric. If she never had involved herself with that Scandinavian child, her own child still would be alive. Was there some kind of curse on her that brought death to the men she loved?

Yet she had not loved Eric as she had Edward and John. He had been mainly a big toy that entertained her in moments of childishness and she did not mourn his passing from her life. If by some unlikely chance he were to return from the Arctic, she would not want to see him, for he was the agent of Steve's death—and of Tim's, too.

Mary, after a first wild outburst, bore her grief as stoically as Cordelia and Ann tried to bear theirs. She was aided by the faith taught by her church, a faith that Cordelia and Ann lacked, and her grief had none of the guilt that marked Cordelia's.

Cordelia thought she was past being shocked by anything involving Steve's death. But then, two weeks after the *Cordelia Lovejoy* disappeared, she learned from the bank that it had loaned Steve the money to finance the expedition. She felt stunned at hearing that he had offered his precious Lovejoy's stock to pay for that insanity near the North Pole.

Immediately after she learned what he had done she walked to Ann's house on the hottest day of summer. The oppressive heat that gripped New York was of no consequence to her as she walked swiftly and thought about the foolish way Steve had financed his biggest folly. Children were begging and stealing chips from horsedrawn ice carts on the side streets of Murray Hill; ice-cream pushcart vendors had invaded the staid stretch of Park Avenue; the skirts of passing flappers had reached a new high that summer—but Cordelia was unmindful of anything except what Steve had done.

"Did you know where he got the money?" she asked Ann after telling her what she'd heard from the bank.

"Yes, Mother. I thought you did, too."

Cordelia rubbed her forehead. "I must be getting dotty. I never asked, but imagined he got some from you and probably some from other sources. I felt so overwhelmed by *what* he was doing that I never thought to ask *how*."

Ann's hand clenched. "He asked me for financial support, but I refused to give him any. It wasn't I cared that much about the money, I just wanted to try to stop him from killing himself."

"I understand," Cordelia said. "I see—and I truly understand, Ann—how that Lovejoy's stock doesn't mean to you what it does to me. Probably you see its market value more objectively than I do. Probably I'm being a sentimental fool, but I don't want the bank— any bank or other corporation—owning a single share of Lovejoy's. Call that ridiculous if you want to. But Lovejoy's is *family*. Lovejoy's is *people*. Lovejoy's is *publishing books*, which is something that banks and their like never will really understand. A long time ago I knew Jack Morgan slightly, but I never really understood how financiers like the Morgans operated till one day I read—well, it doesn't matter. The point is that I don't want that bank owning any of our stock and trying to put a hand into what we're doing. I'm going to pay off Steve's debt."

"No," Ann said, "I'm going to do that. It's no financial problem at all for me. I simply had not thought about what you describe to me now. I completely agree

with you. Lovejoy's *is* family, and I know enough about
the workings of large corporations to see that—"

"No," Cordelia said. "*I* am going to do it because—"

They were bickering on when a maid stepped into
the room and said to Ann, "Mrs. Lovejoy, a man from
the New York *Times* would like to speak to you on the
phone."

Cordelia, hurrying after Ann, watched and listened
tensely as she spoke into the phone: "Yes. . . .
Yes. . . . Yes. . . ." Suddenly tears dimmed her
eyes, and she told Cordelia: "Steve has been found.
He's in wretched condition, but he's alive. The sole survivor. Orlo Peterson rescued him."

Only a successful man received a hero's welcome
home. Steve's return went mainly unnoticed except for
a brief story in the *Times* on August tenth. Off Newfoundland the *Bergen* transferred him to a U.S. Coast
Guard cutter, which brought him into Boston where
Ann, Cordelia, Penny, and Izzy were waiting at the
pier.

Since he could not walk, sailors carried him down the
gangway on a stretcher. He was wasted thin, but it was
the remote, withdrawn expression on his pale face that
troubled the members of the family most. They had expected some quip from him. All he said, however, was,
"I booted it," then looked away from them.

They took him to Massachusetts General Hospital in
Boston where orthopedic specialists awaited his arrival.
He left leg had some rare infection that apparently resulted from gangrene; he was in constant excruciating
pain; two specialists recommended immediate amputation.

"No," Steve said.

"My friend," one specialist said, "if it isn't done,
you're probably going to die."

"Okay," Steve said. "Wish I had something more

original to say than that I've got to die sometime, so why not now? But since I know only clichés, old man, I'll say that you can take my life but not my leg."

"He's going to be all right," Ann said to Cordelia. "Whenever he talks like that he's rated high in the hundred-yard dash."

"Thanks, Li'l Orphan Annie." Steve looked at the specialist. "I guess in your line you don't have much time to read the funny papers. But my wife here is the original for that strip. See, she was born an orphan—well, practically—and grew up horribly poor. Then she married me for my money and. . . ."

"He's all better," Cordelia said. "We might as well take him home tomorrow, bum leg and all."

Three weeks passed, however, before he could be moved home to New York with his painful leg still attached to his torso.

His most recent editor-in-chief, Davis Whitcomb, came to see him soon after he arrived home and said, "Steven, I expect you to do something memorable about your experience."

Steve looked at Ann, who sat on the other side of his wheelchair. "I never understand this guy Whitcomb. What does he mean by something memorable about my experience?"

She looked as embarrassed as Davis suddenly became. "I think, dear, what Mr. Whitcomb—Davis—has in mind is that you'll write a book about your experiences."

Davis nodded vigorously, and Steve said, "Oh, shit, d'you mean that besides enduring this thing I got to write a book about it, too?"

"It could be a moving, significant book," Davis said.

"I've heard constipated people say the same thing about a good bowel movement," Steve said. "Okay, old Davis, I'll do it. But under one condition. I want an advance of a hundred and seventy-five thousand."

Davis, speechless, stared at him.

"I mean that's about the amount my wife paid to bail me out with the bank people. That's what it cost me—I mean her—to get me out of this f-f-f-foolish thing."

"Steven," Davis said, "Mr. Lovejoy—sir, you're speaking of company—of your money, Steven, when you—"

"This may be hard for anybody to believe," Steve said, "but I've always been on the side of the authors—the good ones, not the frauds. I don't think they get enough money and I think the company gets too much. I mean, we in the company practically live off the royalties we owe authors and wait six months to pay 'em. I figured this all out when I was squatting on that goddamn ice floe. So an author has earned ten grand in royalties during a six-month period, but we have his money and invest it and get about three hundred bucks. But the author doesn't get ten thousand three hundred for us using his money. What he gets is only the ten grand. That's cheating of the first order, Whitcomb."

"Mr. Lovejoy." Davis looked helplessly at Ann. "Mrs. Lovejoy."

"What Steve is saying—" she began.

"What I'm saying," Steve went on, "is that here the Lovejoys are livin' high on the hog in a Park Avenue mansion and maybe away down south there's some poor son of a bitch of a genius of a writer livin' like a shrimper in the swamps. But—"

"What Steve is trying to say, Davis," Ann interrupted, "is that he doesn't want to write a book about his experience."

"Right! Right! Hear, hear!" Steve said. "The thing about my wife, Whitcomb, is that she understands me. So I'll never have the excuse that she didn't when she decides to leave me. You're goddamn right I don't want to write that book. *But I am going to!* The hell with an advance, I'll rook it out of the publisher later."

Suddenly tears came to his eyes. He had not shed a tear since coming back, and Ann believed it was good he at last was showing some emotion.

"I want to write a book about Timmy and old Eric and Jake. I'd like to put into words the way Orlo Peterson really is. But can I do it without sounding like a sentimental fool? I don't know. I can only try."

"Yes," Davis said. He was looking around for the exit because he wanted to get out of there. "Yes, yes. I think it could be a great book." His eyes found the way out and he got to his feet.

Ann took him all the way to the last door that opened onto the afternoon heat of the city. When she returned, Steve said, "That guy is another one of the frauds. Am I going to have to fire him, too?"

"Not yet," she said. "Wait until he has molested your book before sending him to jail. Steve, do you really want to write it?"

"No, but God help me I'd like to try."

"If there's any way I can help—"

"Honey." He stretched out a hand. "You've practically got to write the goddamn thing for me."

They kissed, tenderly, then passionately, as they had not in a long time.

They went to Hasty's, taking Ted with them. Steve, who was beginning to hobble about, spent hours staring at a blank writing pad while he lighted one cigarette after another. Three days later he told Ann:

"No use. Can't do it. Listen to this first sentence. 'There I sat up to my ass in slush and snow while the airplane I'd named after my mother, the plane that was supposed to take me and my two companions to the North Pole, burned through an ice floe and sank into the Arctic Ocean.' What do you think of that?"

"Don't like it. You sound like a would-be Bob Benchley writing for *College Humor*."

"Correct," Steve said. "Honest woman. Even when I take the word 'ass' out, the sentence has no integrity. Let's take the boat out and fish."

"All right. So you don't want to try to write it after all?"

"Yes, I do, but I don't know how to begin."

"Don't begin at the beginning."

"Okay. Let's talk."

"When you were there on that floe, alone and in pain and expecting to die, what did you think about?"

"Not about you or Teddy or Mama. I didn't want to think about anything that would remind me of my loneliness and pain and coming death. I was like the guy I read about in the paper who watched Tom Mix movies all the time to try to forget he was dying of cancer. The way I tried to distract myself was to trace through each step of the workings of an internal combustion engine. You want to hear what they are?"

"No, and neither does any reader, so you can skip that."

Mornings they went fishing together and in the afternoon and evening they talked while Ann made notes. After a few days she read him a section that she said he had "talked" to her. It concerned the hard life of Tim McMahon and how wonderful he had felt upon joining a polar expedition after years of struggling for a survival that lacked significance to him.

Steve caught fire from the Tim episode and began to write, himself, about Eric and Jake. He and Ann stopped making trips into the city and sent Ted to the Hastings one-room school. Once or twice a week they talked by phone to Cordelia, who had resumed going to the office every day as she filled in for Steve. A rather typical conversation between them went like this:

"Hello, Mama, how's things at the store?"

"Very busy, Steve. An interesting problem came up on Monday. We received a manuscript from an agent on how to dance the Charleston. You know how that's all the rage now. Davis puffed up and said it's beneath the dignity of the house to publish a *manual* on dancing. He has a point, of course. But it occurred to me to have the manuscript revised and call it something like *Waltzing into the Charleston.* My idea is to have it heavily illustrated with photos. We'll get some pretty young floozy and some handsome chorus boy. Give it a little story line, sort of. So you see, it will tell the eager reader how to dance the Charleston, but not let on that it's telling her."

"Okay, Mama. A manual, but *not* a manual. Not a manual, *but* a manual. Just have a good time and make us pots of money. Bye-bye, Mama."

Hanging up, he said to Ann, "She's having the time of her life. She loves that Mad Ave action as I never will. It's amazing how she keeps up with the times. I don't really give a damn what's happening out there in Americaland, but I know that millions of girls and women wearing knee-length skirts and horizontally-striped sweaters are learning to dance the Charleston— or wanting to. Some day I'll bet they remember these times as when the art of publicity finally was perfected. The age of ballyhoo. That's what it is."

And it was. Out there, distant from Hasty's, a strong publicity campaign had made *The Private Life of Helen of Troy* by John Erskine the leading best-seller. Clever publicity had created a Florida land boom in which people were paying as much as five thousand dollars for an acre of swampwater—and it took a hurricane that fall to deflate the boom. Publicity turned a heavyweight championship fight between Gene Tunney and Jack Dempsey into a national event that received more newspaper coverage than had the dull inauguration of Calvin Coolidge.

But the acme of the con game called ballyhoo was achieved that year when Paramount Pictures set out to promote *Son of the Shiek*, starring Rudolf Valentino, who had died of a septic appendix after finishing the film. Paramount arranged for its dead star to lie in state in a New York undertaker's large establishment while shills whipped up riotous crowds to mob the place. Valentino's co-star Pola Negri, the Polish actress noted for temptress roles, told reporters that she and Valentino had been "engaged," then fainted publicly a few times. A burial extravaganza worthy of a European monarch did not end the Valentino ballyhoo, however. Several weeks later Valentino's divorced second wife, actress Natacha Rambova, arrived from Europe and told reporters that through a spiritualist medium she had been in touch with Rudolf in the Great Beyond: There, she learned, he was launching a new movie career by playing bit roles with the idea of working himself up to star status.

In November of that year Eunice was sitting on the sand in Palm Beach, Florida, broke and lonely. She also was cold, for it was cloudy and windy, one of those raw November days such as the Florida publicity people claimed did not exist. Nevertheless, she had taken off her robe and wore only her daringly short bathing suit.

She knew that her body was beautiful; she knew she looked at least ten years younger than the age of thirty-five she would reach next month. Her beauty was her last asset now that she and Bayard were divorced and he was bankrupt. No alimony. Not much of anything. Last week she had received another two-hundred-dollar check from Mama, who wrote in a note, "Please, Eunice, don't you think it's time you found gainful employment?"

She was staying with one of the lesser members of the Fish clan, but her welcome had worn out and she knew she must move on within a couple of days.

Though she had yet to find a job that could support her comfortably, she continued to look for the man who would. There was a possibility, she believed, in a new house guest who had arrived last night.

His name was Jim Perlow, and he was young, attractive, unmarried. The only question about him—and the most important to Eunice—was his income. He was a special writer for William Randolph Hearst's chain of newspapers. How much did such a man earn?

Eunice had a low opinion of writers, especially newspaper writers, but she also felt desperate. She must have lost her magic, for hours of studying herself in the mirror had convinced her that she had not lost her beauty. Or maybe she was just down on her luck. For more than a year she had been seeking a supportive man in the haunts of friends and acquaintances throughout the country. Nothing had worked out, however. A few love affairs had not led to anything more substantial. What had happened to her famous luck?

That morning she sat shivering on the beach, refusing to put on her robe in the hope that Perlow would come along and see how lovely she was. At last he did. Obviously he was practical besides being slightly handsome: Instead of exposing himself to the cold, he wore gray flannels and a jacket.

At first Eunice failed to give Perlow her provocative smile, for she had become absorbed in an article in an issue of the Chicago *Herald and Examiner*. It concerned Natacha Rambova having communicated with the great Valentino beyond the grave. As one adventuress reading about another, Eunice understood what Natacha was after and was fascinated by the cleverness of her approach.

"What's so interesting in the *Examiner*, Eunice?" Jim Perlow smiled down at her.

Eunice flashed her provocative smile and had an inspiration. What she needed to improve her luck was a big, interesting and convincing lie.

"I was reading about that divorced wife of Valentino's communicating with him in the spirit world."

"Hot air," Perlow said. "Anything for publicity. Rambova was an actress in Europe and now she'd like to work in Hollywood. There are two ways to work in Hollywood these days. Get yourself a lot of publicity or get yourself into bed with a producer."

"I think she's hot air too," Eunice said. "But I do believe there's such a thing as having supernatural—uh—powers of—uh—vision. I think I have them. Did you know my brother tried to fly to the North Pole?"

"Didn't know he was your brother till last night after dinner somebody told me. I didn't know you were one of the Murray Hill *publishing* Lovejoys. What about your brother?"

"When he was missing in the Arctic"—Eunice spoke with great care—"I *saw* him on the ice. I *felt* he was only about fifty miles from his base. I told Mama—our mother—and she—she believed me because she knows how often I've seen and forecast things before that turned out just as I said. So she—Mama—our mother had a message sent. They had given up and were about to come home, but they—the backup pilot—took one last look and found my brother Steve."

Perlow had sunk onto his heels and was staring at her with an expression that made Eunice enchanted with her lie. Why hadn't she thought of something like this before? In order to find security again she must be not only beautiful but *interesting*.

"What else," Perlow asked, "have you prophesied?"

"Well, let me see. I saw that Tunney was going to beat Dempsey in Philadelphia in September."

"Did you put any money on the bout?"

"Oh no, I never gamble. I feel that if I ever try to make money on my—my powers, I'll lose them."

"How are you on the stock market?"

Eunice was beginning to see what fun a big lie could be: all you had to do to make it succeed was to keep making it bigger. "I'm nothing much on the stock market. The things I *see* have to involve *people*. For instance, before I divorced my husband I knew he was being unfaithful to me. I knew with who and when and where. I could *see* them. And it turned out I was absolutely right."

Perlow inched closer to her. "Eunice, do you think this power of yours could be taught to others?"

She hesitated, then remembered that the trick about a lie was to keep making it bigger. "Oh, I think it might."

"Honey," Jim Perlow said, "come on back to the house. I want to have a good talk with you and make some notes."

Late that afternoon Eunice phoned Cordelia at Lovejoy's—collect, of course.

"Mama, I'm finally going to earn some money—a lot of money."

"Well, glory hallelujah," Cordelia said. "The unbelievable has come to pass. Knowing that you're a highly moral person, Eunice, I suppose this is all honorable."

Eunice made her tone stuffy. "You know perfectly well it is, Mother. You remember my ability to prophesy things?"

"No, dear, I can't say that I do."

"But of course you do. You remember how I knew that Steve was still alive when everybody else had given him up for dead?"

"You may have imparted that idea to others, Eunice, but never to me."

"Mother! My situation is desperate!"

Their conversation grew lengthy and cost Cordelia many more dollars before she came to a realization:

She did not really understand what Eunice was talking about, but she must act with understanding and loyally support her daughter when a writer for Mr. Hearst called and asked her to verify some things that were presently incomprehensible.

"Please, Mother, my *career* is at stake."

Jim Perlow called Cordelia at home that evening. She thought that they must do a lot of drinking in Palm Beach to pass away the cold autumns because she had decided that Eunice was somewhat squiffed that afternoon and this Perlow fellow clearly was smashed this evening and in the background as he talked were sounds of revelry. She confirmed that her daughter Eunice was indeed a woman of great insights and felt that she had been a loyal mother when she hung up.

"I think they're having a bacchanalia in Palm Beach," she told Mary. "Wouldn't it be fun to attend one?"

"What's a bacchanalia?" asked Mary.

"If you don't know," Cordelia said, "I don't think you'd enjoy one very much."

Mary, faithful reader of the *Journal*, was the one who reported Jim Perlow's feature on Eunice to Cordelia. Such, indeed, was Mary's faith in the veracity of the Hearst press that she asked Cordelia somewhat accusingly: "Why didn't you ever tell me that Eunice knew from a dream Steve was still alive and had you make them look some more for him?"

Cordelia, who had no idea what she was talking about, read the story and became indignant. She phoned Palm Beach, but Eunice had moved on to the home of another friend on Sea Island. Calling there, Cordelia learned she had switched plans and gone to Chicago. What, she asked Mary, should she do? Mary, who still half-believed Eunice had supernatural powers since it had been reported so in the *Journal*, offered sound advice: "Forget it."

Next day she was aghast to find that yesterday's non-sense about Eunice was only the first in a series. The new episode involved her having predicted the outcome of the Tunney-Dempsey fight. The series ran on, each succeeding installment getting longer and, as Mary said, "juicier." Apparently the subject appealed to readers of the newspaper, for each day it was more prominently displayed until there it was on page one, complete with photos of Cordelia's beautiful daughter.

MURRAY HILL HEIRESS WITH
MYSTIC INSIGHT DREAMED ABOUT
HUBBY'S INFIDELITY—SUED HIM

Beauty Explains How All Women
Can Tell if Husbands Unfaithful

Cordelia didn't know whether she was amused or angry. "I can't call the *Journal* and say my daughter's a liar," she told Mary. "And my thought is so embarrassingly trite that I hate to express it. But, honestly, what will people say?"

To her surprise she discovered that no one said anything. The Lovejoys and their friends did not read the *Journal*; or any who did were too snobbish to admit it; or any who heard of it were too kind to confront her with such embarrassments.

Steve, in one of his phone calls from Hasty's, asked her, "Mama, what's this shit in the *Journal* about Eunice?"

"Please," Cordelia replied, "I'm tired of the way you overuse that vulgar word, Steve."

He snickered. "You mean the word *Journal*? I didn't read it, but the guy who came to clean the well showed Ann a piece on the front page about old Eunice and the guy she used to be married to. Ann laughed her head off. I didn't read it because I don't want to look at a newspaper till I finish this book. The title Ann and I like best right now is *Strange Flight*. How does that grab you?"

"Nice," Cordelia said. "I like it very much. Are you and Teddy and Ann coming in for Christmas?"

"No, all of you are supposed to come out here for a change. Ann will talk to you about it. . . ."

In the first week of the New Year Cordelia received a telephone call from Eunice: "Mother—Mama—Jim and I are in town together. Did I tell you we're engaged? You've got to meet him. Can you have us to dinner tomorrow night?"

The moment she greeted Jim, Cordelia understood why Eunice was attracted to him. She doubted that they loved each other; she doubted that either was capable of loving more than self. But apparently that didn't make much difference anymore in a world where everyone struggled for "success."

Jim, ambitious, wanted to be more than a special writer for the Hearst chain of newspapers; he wanted to write books. After dinner, while sipping brandy with his coffee, he explained to Cordelia that he was offering her the opportunity of her publishing career. Next week he would send her the manuscript of a book entitled *Getting into Eternity* by Eunice Lovejoy as told to Jim Perlow that would make all of them a lot of money. It concerned, of course, Eunice's experiences as a prophetess and explained *how you too can be a seer*. Jim and Eunice would split the royalties.

"Mama," Eunice told her urgently, "you understand this is my new career."

"Indeed I understand," Cordelia said.

The following week she read Perlow's manuscript with a feeling of numbness. Yes, it might make a lot of money because it would appeal to the gullible in everyone. And would anyone except herself and Eunice see that it was a pack of lies?

She returned the manuscript to Perlow with a courteous letter explaining that the subject was too close to the heart of the Lovejoy family for the company to be able to publish it. Eunice phoned her, screaming wrathfully at her rejection of the manuscript and saying that they never would see each other again because of this wanton act.

"You wait, Mother," hollered Eunice, "Jim and I are going to publish this somewhere else and make a fortune from it."

"I have no doubt you will," Cordelia said as Eunice hung up.

The new house of Portas and Finester published *Getting into Eternity* the following August, a month before Lovejoy's brought out *Strange Flight*. The few who reviewed the book about Eunice hooted at it; *Strange Flight*, however, brought dozens of laudatory reviews even though the author had spent years doing his best to antagonize the critics. Yet the marketplace did not reflect the critical views: *Getting into Eternity* sold more than sixty thousand copies whereas *Strange Flight* sold fewer than twelve thousand before the author-publisher directed that it go out of print.

26

Strange Flight was not a best seller, Cordelia reasoned, because it concerned failure rather than success. However, sales never were her measure of a book's worthiness. She was very proud of *Strange Flight* because it revealed what she long had believed: Steve, in his difficult way, had all the integrity of his father. And she was equally proud of Ann for possessing the literary artistry to shape that blunt honesty of Steve's into a moving and sometimes humorous narrative about a group of ill-prepared men who undertook a daring venture and failed at it.

When Cordelia returned the reins of publisher to a reluctant Steve in the spring of 1927, she was glad that Ann was willing to serve as a senior editor. Penny had left her job late in 1926 to give birth to a daughter, Isabel. Then, just as she was about to return to work, she found that she was pregnant again and remained away to have another daughter, Marian, who was born in December 1928. Penny, obviously enjoying home and motherhood, kept talking about returning to work yet made no move to do so.

Public enthusiasm for flying and airplanes already was widespread when Charles Lindbergh's transatlantic flight in 1927 fanned it to a higher pitch. Cordelia encouraged several books on the subject during Steve's absence. After he returned he was able, because of experience and contacts, to acquire authors who had earned distinction in aviation. Using an advertising slogan that Ann had thought up—"Fly high with Lovejoy's"—the house began to be noted for its books on the subject.

Steve and Ann, preoccupied in early September 1929 with the preparation of books about a Canadian bush flier who believed in God, and an air history of the World War, paid no attention to the stock market until Cordelia phoned Ann one day and said, "Izzy's gotten out."

Her first alarmed thought was that he and Penny had broken up. "Out of what, Mother?"

"The stock market. I've been following his investment suggestions for more than a year and haven't regretted it. Nicky says he's crazy to get out now. Nicky's going in deeper on margin. I suppose he should know. After all, he's been a pro at this game for years longer than Izzy."

"Then you're following Uncle Nick's advice?"

"I don't know yet what I'm going to do. But I think you and Steve should talk to Izzy about your investments. Of course he's a little upset these days. He always gets upset when Penny's pregnant. Did you know she is again?"

"She told me."

"Whenever she gets pregnant she goes around telling everybody. I'm thinking of lettering her a big sign to carry around Murray Hill: I Am Pregnant Again. She said to me, 'Mama, why am I pregnant all the time now after years of never being?' I said to her I don't know. I said it was a subject she could discuss better with Izzy. Anyhow, you know how Izzy acted when she was carrying Al, and then Isabel, and then Marian, and now—Ann, you call Izzy."

Ann did, that same afternoon. "Am I interrupting at a bad time, Izzy?"

"No, I need an interruption. Am all needles and pins. I'm reading this best seller *All Quiet on the West-*

ern Front. This man Remarque is a good writer. He knows what it's all about."

"Izzy, Mother says you've got out of the stock market and I should ask your advice."

"I'm not the big advice brain, Ann. I just follow the lead of my betters. Wise men say the market has gone too high, and who am I to disagree? Away last year Eugene Meyer asked, 'What will happen when they forget to bid?' Bernard Baruch was uneasy even the year before that when the Federal Reserve Board lowered the discount rate to oblige the Bank of England—which thereupon pumped still more brokers' loan money into Wall Street. Do you know Joseph P. Kennedy? One smart man with ice water in his veins. He's out. He said, 'Only a fool holds out for the top dollar.' So who is Israel Epstein, Junior, to think he's smarter than such men?"

"I suppose you're right, Izzy. Offhand I'm not sure now what my broker has in my portfolio, but—well, I remember he bought me a lot of Radio stock."

"Radio?" Izzy said. "Let me consult my horoscope chart that is practically here right in front of me. As of noon today Radio was 505 on the board. The date I use for comparative purposes is a basic comparative date Dow-Jones uses. March third, nineteen twenty-eight. That is what we'll call our Get Dizzy With Izzy date. On that date stocks were at an all-time dizzy height. On that date Radio was ninety-four and a half, and I've adjusted that price to take account of split-ups subsequent to that date. Think of it, Ann! How dizzy a height can you reach? *Five hundred five!*"

"I follow you. But what should I do with the money if I sell?"

"Ann, sweetheart, there's something called cash. My papa used to love it. And there's something called a safe deposit vault in every bank. It's a very convenient place for the storage of cash. There comes a time when money gets tired, and there's nothing better for it than a nice rest in a vault."

"Thank you, Izzy. Go back to reading your book and give my love to Penny."

Next Ann phoned her money manager and ordered him to sell all her common-stock holdings, put the cash into a safe deposit vault, and give her a strict accounting. The man whined, howled, and argued, but she was adamant and he had to follow her instructions.

When she told what she had done, Cordelia said, "My word, Ann, that seems awfully drastic. What does Steve think?"

"Steve doesn't think. He never thinks about money until he's running out of it."

"Well, I guess I should talk to Izzy. But when you see profits go as high as they have on the stock market, don't you wonder if they might not go a little higher? I guess, though, that's being greedy. Yes, I'd better talk to Izzy. Have you read what Cassandra has to say about the stock market?"

"You mean Eunice?"

"Alas, yes, I mean my darling daughter Eunice. By the way, she *is* speaking to me once more."

Eunice was prosperous again. At precisely what point Jim Perlow ceased to believe in her powers of prophecy and she began to believe in them herself was uncertain, but it resulted in a fight and separation. Then the Hearst organization began to syndicate a column signed by Eunice and called "Cassandra" in which she prophesied the course of events six times a week; on the seventh day the public was allowed to rest and guess what would happen next.

"Cassandra" was the result of the commercially successful book Jim had written for her. Eunice's pay for the column, three hundred a week, became mere pin money after she entered into a lucrative marriage with a

dentist named Mervin Osgood who gave up practice
once he made it big in California real estate. Mervin
worshipped what he called "class," but had none—only
lots of money. Eunice, worshipping money, was glad to
trade her classy reputation for some after Mervin guar-
anteed her fifty thousand a year "living money."

So the syndicated column "Cassandra" became subsidiary and minor after Eunice and Mervin were married. However, it was a source of major satisfaction to
both when it gained them access to Hollywood "society." This Eunice achieved by directing her ghost-
writer to prophesy such things as "Gloria Swanson will
sound as elegant on screen as she looks in person
thanks to the suave tutoring of veteran stage actress
Laura Hope Crews." Until the Depression set in,
Eunice's series of ghost writers periodically rebelled and
quit over the paltry wages of seventy a week she paid;
after the economy collapsed, she could hire them for
forty-five a week.

Gradually, without anybody paying much attention,
"Cassandra" became a typical fan column of screen and
stage, sprinkled with gossip and popular names. Only
occasionally was there a prophetic word on national affairs, as when "Cassandra" forecast that Alfred E.
Smith would soundly beat Herbert Hoover in the 1928
Presidential elections.

On October 23, 1929, "Cassandra," writing in the
Journal and a couple of hundred other American newspapers, took a look at the economy and pronounced it
"healthier than it's ever been since the days of George
Washington. . . . If you have any money handy, buy,
buy, buy almost any common stock and I prophesy
you'll become wealthy. If you particularly buy Radio, I
prophesy   that   you'll   become   particularly
wealthy. . . ."

Cordelia, happening to read the column that day in
Mary's copy of the *Journal*, remarked on it when she

picked up Ann at the office at noon the next day, Thursday, October 24, to take her to lunch.

"Eunice makes me nervous when she gets into those realms of prophecy," Cordelia said. "Reminds me of the time she prophesied that the Supreme Court was going to repeal the Eighteenth Amendment. I wrote her, reminding her that the Court cannot do that, only the Congress can, but she never answered my letter."

Cordelia had decided that for lunch they should try Wingate's, a new restaurant on Forty-second Street, where she had telephoned for a reservation. However, they never got there.

As they strolled up Madison Avenue they saw a throng of people, mostly men, overflowing the branch office which the brokerage firm of Harris, Upham had opened at the corner of Fortieth Street. Ann asked a man what was going on.

He rolled his eyes. "The worst stock-market crash in history, that's all!"

Moments later they saw Izzy coming through the crowd with the huge mastiff that he and Penny had bought and named King Arthur, but could not seem to tame. Izzy had the illusion that it was he who often walked the dog around Murray Hill, but actually King Arthur walked him.

Ann said to Cordelia, "I never ask you, did you follow Izzy's advice?"

"God help me, no. I followed the expert advice of my financial genius brother. Did you follow Izzy's?"

Ann nodded.

"Izzy," Cordelia called out to him, "is it as bad as they say?"

"Worse." He started to tip his bowler to them, then thought better of it and clung to King Arthur's chain leash with both hands. "Whoa, halt, damnable dog!" But the mastiff plowed straight on. Izzy, a strong man, dug in his heels, but King Arthur seemed stronger.

They began to follow him, and Cordelia asked, "Izzy, have you ever tried taking a hitch around a lamppost with that monster?"

"Don't want to break a lamppost," Izzy said over his shoulder.

"Izzy, what do you mean worse than bad?" asked Ann.

"Just that. Both of you come on home and have a sandwich with Penny and me. We'll watch the ticker in my office."

"Let's," Cordelia said. "I've suddenly lost my appetite."

They followed along as Izzy continued his tug-of-war with King Arthur. "Sometimes," he called over a shoulder, "this moronic monster insists on going around by Thirty-seventh Street and sort of sneaking up on the house from the other side. If he does, I'll see you at home."

"How is Standard Oil doing?" cried Cordelia.

"Terrible!" Then Izzy was lost to them as King Arthur dragged him across Thirty-eighth while motorists stopped and blasted their horns at him.

They all sat in Izzy's comfortable home office, their sandwiches barely tasted, while they drank cup after cup of coffee and the stock and bond tickers hammered out messages of doom. The selling was so massive while prices plummeted that Cordelia asked where could the torrent of selling orders be coming from.

"It's not short selling," Izzy said. "I figure it's forced selling—the dumping on the market of hundreds of thousands of shares by poor bastards whose margins are exhausted or about to be. This whole prosperous market isn't some noble and powerful structure like everybody pretends. It's just a hollow shell, riddled and weakened with speculative credit. Like a building taken over by termites. Now it's collapsing under its own weight."

"I heard you," Cordelia said. "I'm going to phone Nick and tell him to sell everything." But she could not get her call through.

"How's your margin?" Izzy asked.

"Nil."

"Well, then, you'll be all right in time if you just hang onto your paper."

She made a wry face. "Sure, I figure the value will all be restored along about 1987 so I can enjoy it in my old age."

"Maybe," Ann said, "things won't turn out as bad as they seem now."

"Maybe," Izzy said, "they have a way of turning out even worse."

He was right, Ann thought. She would gladly give away all that profit she had made from selling her stocks before the crash if only she could get Steve back on track.

It happened suddenly, early in September. Like an alcoholic who resumed drinking, Steve went back to flying after having sworn off it for three years. One sip—one flight again with Orolo at Teterboro—and he was back to the habit.

What he tried sincerely to explain to Ann and what he failed to do—or she failed to understand—was how fed up he was with publishing. He knew how indebted he was to her for shaping *Strange Flight* into a publishable book, but he never let on how bitterly disappointed he was at its poor sales while the crap Perlow had written for Eunice sold like ice in the Sahara. He felt that something similar was happening with other books in which he was involved at Lovejoy's. For some unfathomable reason it seemed that the better a book was, the worse it sold—and the worse it was, the better it sold.

Yet everyone insisted that he be a publisher, which was beginning to seem a bit unfair. There was no one to talk to about it. In a curious way that none of the women would remotely understand, he missed Tim. Over the years they had seen things the same way, as no one in the family had. For a while he had been paralyzed by the feeling he had killed Tim. But eventually he had taken heart from the realization that Tim had died doing something that gave him pride.

Five minutes of flying with Orlo changed everything for Steve. In bright September sunlight, at five thousand feet above New York, he felt that he recovered his perspective. Madison Avenue no longer was the center of his life: It was just a barely discernible street on a small island in the conglomeration of land masses and bodies of water called New York City.

"Let's do a loop!" he yelled exuberantly to Orlo.

Orlo made one of those shoulder gestures that meant in the expansive sign language of open-cockpit fliers: Why not? And then they did a loop, followed by a barrel roll.

That happened on a Saturday. On Sunday, Steve went back to Teterboro for three hours more of flying. He realized he had lost some of his skill. His left leg, as a result of the injury and two subsequent operations, had been severely weakened. Orlo never had been hampered in flying by his war amputation, but for some reason Steve was troubled by his injury. What should a game leg have to do with flying? Maybe the real trouble was that he was growing older. On Monday, instead of going to the office, he went back to Teterboro to try to overcome his imperfection and believed he was improving.

When he arrived home about six o'clock, Ann asked him, "Where have you been all day?"

Looking her square in the eye, he lied, "Public Library." He could not tell if she believed him.

Next day he slept late, and when he went down to breakfast Ann had left for the office. Ted was at the table, however, eating cornflakes and reading yesterday's comic strips. He said he had the day off from school, but Steve did not listen to the reason because he was preoccupied wondering if he could get away with taking another day off and going to Teterboro. It really was a hell of a note, he thought, when your wife worked under the same roof and could check up on your going and coming. Why had all freedom been taken from him?

Ted was talking, but Steve did not hear him—and then he suddenly was ashamed that he never listened to this altogether delightful son. Now the words Ted had just spoken played back to him:

"Dad, do you ever miss flying?"

Steve blinked and felt he never had seen him clearly before. "Yeah, sometimes."

"Aren't you ever going to fly again?"

Steve put down his coffee cup. "Yes, I am."

"When, Dad? Whenever you do, will you take me up with you? I've never been up in an airplane and it sure would make me feel good to fly with you."

For a moment Steve feared that tears would rush to his eyes. *My God, this is my son!* Why did he think that Ted was exclusively Ann's child? Just because he had her blond, handsome looks didn't mean that she owned him.

"Ted, you want to come flying with me today?"

"Yes!" He almost oveturned his cereal bowl in his excitement to get started.

Steve rented an old Curtiss Jenny because it still was the safest, most reliable plane on the field. It was so slow and yet so light that in an emergency he could pancake it down almost anyplace. Before they took off Steve went over the controls carefully with Ted, explaining everything. Fortunately it was a clear, almost windless day; after they were airborne and climbed to three thousand feet the metropolitan area stretched out like a relief map. Ted was ecstatic. Turning around in the front cockpit, he made gestures to stunt it, but Steve shook his head. They flew sedately around the city and out over Long Island and back across the Palisades, banking as cautiously as an old lady getting out of bed. When they approached Teterboro and Steve pointed down, Ted shook his head violently.

Steve had an idea. Since they had plenty of fuel and the weather was perfect, he flew west to Route 23 and then followed it north over the lovely rolling hills and twisting valleys of northwestern New Jersey to a well-kept little field where he had landed a couple of times in his old days of cross-country flying. The little field was deserted when they glided in and landed, but within minutes a half-dozen boys came running. He gave them fifty cents to watch the Jenny while he and Ted walked a mile into the little town of Sussex.

Ted talked excitedly about the flight all the way to the Sussex Hotel, which stood on a knoll in the center of the village. There they ate and drank their way into silence with an enormous midday dinner of steak two inches thick, sweetcorn, tomatoes, blueberry pie topped with ice cream, and a huge pitcher of iced lemonade.

Ted, breaking the silence suddenly, said, "Mom doesn't like flying much, does she?"

"Not much, apparently."

"Will she get her dander up when she hears you took me flying?"

Steve shrugged. "I suppose so."

"Dad, is it better if we don't say anything about this today?"

"No," Steve said, "I'm not going to be the one to teach you dishonesty. Better we tell her when we get home and take the consequences."

"All right. Will you teach me to fly?"

"When you're older if you still want to. But you may lose interest in it. Lots of people do."

Ann was home when they came in shortly after six o'clock.

"Ma," Ted said, "I just had the greatest day of my life. . . ." He continued to talk about their outing most of the way through dinner.

Ann listened, uttering no word of protest, but she was more silent than Steve remembered her being.

That night after they went to bed she said, "I can't stop it, but I'm sorry you started it."

"Why?"

"Because it's so dangerous. I'm afraid it will infect him the way it did you. He's the only child we have and I dread to spend the rest of my life worrying about him."

Steve, rather than being angry, felt weary and defeated. He did not say anything.

"When are you going back to the office?" she asked.

"Tomorrow."

He returned to work and stopped flying for a while. Whenever Ted begged to be taken up for a ride, he said he was too busy at work to spare the time.

27

As times turned worse, a giant grew near the foot of Murray Hill. It was the Empire State Building, raising its 102 stories from the corner of Fifth Avenue and Thirty-fourth Street. Izzy likened it to a tombstone memorializing the deepening depression, for by April, 1930, only twenty-eight percent of its office space was rented. Nevertheless, its chief promoters, John J. Raskob and unsuccessful Presidential candidate Alfred E. Smith, kept trying to breathe life into it.

That April Eleanor Roosevelt corralled a few Lovejoys into going to the top of the Empire State in some kind of promotional tour. Cordelia had turned Democrat and worked hard to help elect Franklin Governor of New York. ("Deliver me Murray Hill," he told her dryly, "and you'll have delivered a chief bastion of Republicanism.") She and all her family greatly admired the way Franklin, with Eleanor's help, had struggled against the effects of infantile paralysis and worked his way back into politics. However, Cordelia was sometimes distressed by Eleanor's commercialism; she didn't think the First Lady of New York State should, as but one example, endorse Simmons mattresses, even though she understood that Franklin's mother still controlled the family purse strings and Eleanor sometimes was desperate for money. In any event, they remained close, and when the Rosevelts' good friend Al Smith wanted Eleanor to help promote his towering tombstone, she asked Cordelia to gather up some family and hurry them to the top of the Empire State.

Today no one remembers the precise nature of that

1931 publicity gimmick, but a wonderful photograph is preserved of the group in the observation tower. Al Smith stands, wearing brown derby and gray chesterfield, the invariable half-smoked cigar in a corner of his mouth, his countenance somewhat tired and uneasy, as if his tombstone weighs heavily. Next to him stands Eleanor, revealing her unfortunate teeth in a wide grin and wearing an incredible hat twenty years out of style which actually belonged to her mother-in-law because she had lost her own hat on a train coming down from Albany. (Cordelia always remembered that and wondered how on earth a governor's wife could lose her hat in an enclosed train.) Cordelia is next to Eleanor, wearing a smart cloche and mink stole. (She was always pleased when anyone remarked that she could not possibly be nearing her sixtieth birthday in this picture.) Ann is beside her, equally well groomed and very lovely. (Some asked, "Who's the beautiful blonde?") Next to her is a middle-aged man who no one ever could remember as having been there. Then comes a tall, white-haired, distinguished man who looks like a retired general. He is Nick, unemployed and unemployable, but sufficiently recovered from disaster to want to go everywhere that Cordelia goes. Penny is not present because she was home waiting to deliver her third daughter, Nora. Neither Izzy nor Steve is there. But the children are. Whatever faults they later displayed, they are handsome kids. Edward Renshaw Lovejoy is lean, blond, good-looking even at age nine. His young cousin Alfred Tennyson Epstein, known to all as Al, is handsome in a darker way and stands a bit apart from the others, as if to show he already has a mind of his own. His baby sisters, Isabel and Marian, are two dark, gorgeous little gems holding hands.

After that picture was taken, Cordelia stepped to the rampart and gazed down at the long afternoon shadow the Empire State cast across Murray Hill. "How little it looks," she said. "You can't see that there's a hill at all, just a few little blocks of buildings. So I guess we've come to the ultimate—the very top of Murray Hill."

She had addressed Ann on her right, but Al Smith answered on her left.

"When I was a kid in the slums I remember how we talked about someday getting to the top of Murray Hill." He took his cigar out of his mouth and grinned wryly. "So here we are, top of Murray Hill and mortgaged way up to our eyeballs."

The times were indeed hard and would grow worse. Although many were unemployed, like Nick, their numbers would increase into the millions.

Nick lost his job along with most other employees of New York brokerage houses immediately after the final collapse of the Big Bull market on November 13, 1929. On that day, for example, Radio stock—which only a few weeks previously had been at 505 and was so highly touted by "Cassandra" and just about everybody else—sank to 28. Nick, like numerous others, had bought heavily on margin and was wiped out financially. Cordelia never had seen him cry, but he wept bitterly when he appeared at her house on November fourteenth. She took him in to live with her, and before many days passed he began to make a rapid recovery emotionally and complain about the ways she did things.

Cordelia fared better than Nick in the crash since she had not bought on margin. After November thirteenth the paper value of her public common stock, which did not include her private stock in Lovejoy's, was down from more than a half million to about seventy thousand dollars.

But owners of common stock were not the only people hard hit. Mary kept the McMahons' life savings of slightly more than ten thousand dollars in a savings bank which closed its doors. When the bank finally reopened and paid off its depositors what it could, she received less than three thousand. The equanimity with which she took the situation amazed Cordelia.

"Easy come—easy go," Mary said. "No Irish was born to be rich. Those English bankers wouldn't tell you if your coattails was on fire."

"Praise to you, Mrs. McMahon," Cordelia said. "I'll make you the model for my own attitude. The way I'm going to look at it, I'm being punished for my greed."

"Me, too," Mary said. "Why should the McMahons ever have needed a savings bank account when so many Irish are starving? 'Tis a judgment on Tim an' me for not having given enough to the poor."

Ann, Izzy, and Penny were richer than ever because they had sold out in time and, at Izzy's urging, soon turned their cash into federal bonds.

Money was not what worried Cordelia in the spring of 1930, however. The sales of Lovejoy's books, like those of all houses, were beginning to slip badly and employee cutbacks appeared inevitable. "Economic doomsday is coming," she told Ann while discussing company affairs. "I remember the Panic of Ninety-three, and this time I think it'll be worse."

"Things already are worse," Ann said.

Cordelia did not think she referred to the economy or the growing problems of the company. She believed that Ann was worried about Steve, but she did not know how to begin to discuss it with her.

Steve kept trying to work hard and be a good publisher as he watched sales decline after the crash. For example, he bought a bad manuscript about cosmetology which he hired a ghost to repair in the expectation that it would sell well. When it flopped, making it appear that the depressed economy caused women not even to care about the healthful treatment of their skin and hair, Steve saw one more reason for giving up. He did not announce his despair, he simply began to stay away from the office for a day or two at a time and resumed flying. Probably Ann knew that he was, but she did not ask and he felt she would not interfere unless he started taking Ted on joyrides—which he did not.

One day in May 1930 he drove to a small airfield on Long Island where a man advertised an almost new Avro Avion plane for sale. When he arrived, another prospective buyer was putting the Avro through complicated maneuvers while the owner watched from the ground.

"Crazy pilot," Steve said to the man as they gazed up. "Shouldn't do an Immelmann at two thousand feet unless somebody's chasing you."

After a while the pilot landed without bothering to come about into the light wind. When Steve and the owner started toward the plane, the pilot taxied it off to a corner of the field and sat there gunning the engine. Steve was completely exasperated by the time he reached the sleek little plane. The pilot, who did not remove his goggles and helmet, was a kid with a thin, freckled face.

"You punk!" Steve shouted. "You're wasting gas jazzing that engine."

The pilot cut the engine and demanded in a shrill young voice, "What did you say?"

"You punk! An Immelmann at eighteen hundred feet? Landing with the wind? Get out of that cockpit!"

"I want to tell you something," the punk said. "Screw you, mister!" He climbed out of the airplane, and Steve prepared to take a swing at him.

He was a tall, thin, agile kid, and when he pulled off his goggles and helmet, Steve saw that he was a woman with gray eyes and closely cropped brown hair.

The owner laughed, and Steve, beginning to smile, told the crazy woman pilot, "Show some respect for your betters."

"That I can do," she said. "But not for my elders."

Her name was Regina Faunce, she was twenty-four years old, and she had been flying since seventeen. As a pilot, she had owned two old Jenny biplanes and had had nine crackups, most of them her own fault. At eighteen she had left her native Wisconsin and wandered from coast to coast, supporting her love of flying after her small patrimony ran out with such jobs as waitress, secretary, air acrobat, saleswoman, and teacher of English grammar—about which subject her notions were hazy.

At first Steve did not like her, but she exasperated him enough to make him pay attention. Women fliers fascinated him. He had the illusion he understood most of them thoroughly, but Regina puzzled him. She was a very good pilot when she concentrated on it, yet she had odd lapses and became a careless one. Her not bothering to land into the wind the day they met was an example of her careless ways. She argued that the field was large enough and the wind so light that it didn't make any difference. In reply Steve argued that a pilot invariably should follow commonsense safety rules, no matter the conditions, so that they became habitual.

She and he continued their argument in a restaurant where he took her for dinner. She ate like someone starving—two dozen clams and a whole broiled lobster with all the trimmings. Later he realized she simply did not get enough to eat on her salary of twenty a week as receptionist for a Garden City dentist. She was almost broke and had no hope of buying the little Avro Avion she coveted. Next day he bought it for twenty-two hundred and based it at Curtiss Field, not far from the boarding house where she lived. Of course he let her fly his plane; it would have been inhuman to do otherwise for one who loved to fly as much as she. In gratitude she never cheated him about her flying time, but kept a meticulous record of it and gave him every penny she could afford toward fuel and hangar costs.

If surprised that he didn't seek some personal favor, she did not show it. In those first days he felt no special physical attraction to her. She was a gamine, a tomboy, a thin girl. In appearance, though not in professional skill, she reminded Steve somewhat of his friend Charles Lindbergh.

In August a wealthy Bostonian named Edith Winthrop Clarke, a champion of greater equality for women, wrote Steve, inviting him to join her in underwriting a transatlantic flight in which a woman pilot was to be a member of the crew. Humanely Mrs. Clarke did not want to announce a prize and start unseemly competition among ill-prepared people who might lose their lives in the effort. In her dignified way she simply wanted a woman to fly across the Atlantic and thereby demonstrate it was not something that only a man could do. Mrs. Clarke had heard of a much-used tri-engined Fokker which was for sale at a Boston airport. She had found a qualified man pilot and a competent navigator-radio operator who were eager to undertake the flight, but the appropriate woman pilot was lacking. Her first choice, a widely known aviatrix, was currently hospitalized with fourteen broken bones and probably never would fly again. It had turned out that Mrs. Clarke's second choice simply would not do: She was a boisterous soul who had got drunk at the Copley Plaza and said something obscene to the president of a Boston bank.

Steve was fascinated by the idea. Apart from his personal enthusiasm for any daring aviation venture, he thought of it as a good publishing project: A book by the first woman to fly the Atlantic surely would be a best seller and bring Lovejoy's out of the doldrums.

Reggie was the perfect candidate. Whatever her short-comings as a pilot, she was not boisterous and did not drink or smoke. Another important asset was her fresh, clean-cut looks that gave her distinction in a world of pretty women; her photograph would enhance the dust jacket of a book.

When he broached the subject to her, Reggie burst into tears of joy and gave him a bear hug. Steve thought her affection for him was somewhat like Ted's.

Mrs. Clarke figured that his share in the venture would be fifteen thousand dollars, but he knew that would climb to twenty or twenty-five. Both agreed that secrecy was of the utmost importance in order that others not try to race them to the goal. Steve did not tell anyone, not even Ann. Especially not Ann since he had begun to feel alienated from her. She did not even know that Reggie existed because he did not know how to explain their relationship. Ann might think he was caught up with some floozy on Long Island, and that simply was not so, there was nothing going between them. Hating flying as she did, Ann would not believe how much it meant to him to find a young woman who loved flying as much as he.

The night before he was to take Reggie up to Boston by train to meet Mrs. Clarke, he told Ann, "I'm going to Boston tomorrow to see Edith Winthrop Clarke—you met her once—about an aviation book. I may be gone a couple of days."

"When you get back," Ann said, "I won't be at the office. I'm quitting."

He was dismayed, but he couldn't argue her into staying and finally accepted her statement that the staff must be cut and she, not needing the salary, chose to be the first to go.

Still he was left with the problem of raising the necessary money for the flight. He could not write off the money as an advance against royalties for an untitled book by an unknown author without raising questions from Cordelia and other members of the board of directors who had begun to keep a close eye on the company accounts. And certainly he would not go to Ann for the money. So he was forced to offer his personal stock to a bank again since he had no cash of his own. To his relief, a bank was glad to loan him twenty thousand.

Regina and Mrs. Clarke liked each other immediately.

"But you must stop calling her Reggie," Mrs. Clarke told Steve in her solemn way. "The newspapermen will pick it up when they hear what's happening and that will cheapen the whole thing. Regina is your name, my dear, and you must insist on everyone calling you that. Be queenly. And never, never chew gum."

Steve phoned Ann and said his book project was going to take longer than he had expected. Then he threw himself enthusiastically into the effort. Crosson, the chief pilot, and Weaver, the navigator-radioman, worked no harder than he. The Fokker, which they named *American Eagle*, was jacked up and welders fitted pontoons in place of its wheels. Steve fretted over the starboard engine, but no replacement was available, and—possibly disguising a multitude of weaknesses— the plane's seventy-two-foot wings were painted bright gold.

One night Crosson fell ill with food poisoning and asked Steve whether he could substitute as pilot if he didn't recover in time. Steve's heart leaped at the idea: Of course he could pilot the plane and would love to do it. But then he realized he must not. His name was well enough known that it would become *his* flight—not Reggie's.

Crosson recovered from his food poisoning, but Boston Harbor did not emerge from its dense fog. They turned the secrecy into a kind of game, coming and going as surreptitiously as spies from the old boathouse where *American Eagle* was hidden. Reggie was keeping a diary of events. Crosson and Weaver said her entries were amusing, but Steve did not want to read them for fear he might not find them so.

At last the weather cleared. There was a last-minute scramble. Reggie wore her old flying togs and, a few minutes before she boarded the plane, Mrs. Clarke thrust on her a coonskin coat for warmth. In a small knapsack she carried an extra notebook and pencils, a half-dozen handkerchiefs, a comb, toothbrush, toothpaste, and a tube of cold cream. Her spare clothing was stuffed into a duffel bag with that of the men.

As the big boathouse doors were opened, Reggie said, "Well——" It was a time for words more memorable, but none came from her. She pecked Steve on the cheek, the first time she had kissed him. Then she looked dubiously at Mrs. Clarke, but that patrician old face must have seemed too formidable, for she just nodded and hopped into the plane.

Steve, Mrs. Clarke, her chauffeur, and several mechanics went out of the boathouse and watched *Eagle* churn a long wake down the harbor into the wind. The engines screamed and Steve's arms seemed to ache from the effort of trying to lift her off himself, but no space appeared between pontoons and water. Crosson brought her around and taxied back. Silently those on shore watched the port open and Regina and Weaver jettison seven of their eight five-gallon cans of emergency gasoline.

Once more Crosson gunned his engines. When *Eagle* diminished to sparrow size far down the harbor, she began to lift off and soon was lost to view. Steve had a feeling of emptiness and desolation such as he never had known, not even the day when he'd left Mama knowing that he was going to enlist in the Foreign Legion.

Was he sending Reggie to her death? She did not seem a woman to him, only a vulnerable child who loved to be a bird and fly. Their companionship had not seemed to be anything much—a lot of long silences broken by irritable remarks—yet now he missed her unbearably. The trouble was that she, as well as the two men flying with her, was only a happy amateur, whereas Lindbergh had been a meticulous professional who had worked out every detail of his venture. My God, Reggie even had neglected to take on board a hamper of egg-salad sandwiches prepared by Mrs. Clarke's cook!

Mrs. Clarke had her chauffeur drop Steve at South Station, and New Haven Railroad service never had seemed as pokey as the train which bore him home to New York. He had been gone almost two weeks, and it had been almost a week since he had found the time to call Ann. What was he going to tell her? And then it came over him that there no longer was any need for secrecy, that he could tell her the truth.

He walked into the Park Avenue mansion a few minutes after seven in the evening. Ted, who was listening to *Amos 'n' Andy* on the radio, rushed to him, grinning. "Dad, now we know where you've been!"

Steve gave him a hug. "What do you mean?"

Ann came into the room, gazing at him gravely. "Lowell Thomas just told us on his evening news broadcast. He—"

"A young American woman, Regina Faunce, flying the Atlantic!" Ted cried. "With two men companions. Soon as we heard, Dad, we *knew* you were in on it!"

"Where does Lowell Thomas place her now?"

"They made it from Boston to Halifax," Ted said, "and now they're going on to Newfoundland. Dad, please tell us all about it."

"In a few minutes. First I want to get out of these filthy clothes. I think we're going to have to burn 'em.

Then I want a hot shower and a tall glass of Scotch and
ice and top it off with a big dinner. I haven't been hungry for days, and now all of a sudden I'm starving."

Ann did not go to their bedroom with him, and then
he discovered that she had moved her clothing out of
her closets into another room. "Hey, what's this all
about?" he asked her.

She answered levelly: "I could ask you the same,
buster. What's it all about when a husband takes off for
a couple of weeks and doesn't tell his wife where he
is?"

"Hey, honey, sit down here while I finish dressing.
Let's get something straight. There's nothing between
me and Reggie Faunce. She merely likes to fly and *I*
like to fly and. . . ."

He was so persuasive that she moved back to their
room that evening. They kept on the radios scattered
throughout the big house to catch fresh news bulletins
about the course of Reggie's flight, and at Steve's
suggestion Ted stayed up as late as he wished.

"I suspect Mrs. Clarke of leaking the story to the
press," he told them, "and I'll bet she suspects me.
Whoever did it, I'm glad. The more public furor, the
better the publicity for the book. And that's my chief
interest in this—a book that really sells, for a change."

Next morning, while they were eating breakfast,
there was a radio report that *American Eagle* had taken
off into the emptiness of the North Atlantic. Steve went
to the office that day, but nothing interested him there.
Friends on the *Tribune* promised to keep him informed,
but hours crept by with no word.

All that night he prowled the mansion, turning on
radios and twisting the dial from one station to another
in hope of some solid information. Everyone reported
the airplane overdue in Europe and missing over the
Atlantic. About five o'clock the following morning as
Steve sat smoking cigarettes and agonizing over having

killed Règgie, a man on the lobster trick at the *Tribune* phoned. The Associated Press had positive word that *American Eagle* still was at Trepassey Bay in Newfoundland, socked in by fog.

Ann recognized her rival long before Steve even realized she had one. The recognition came to her that night Regina was believed missing and she lay awake and listened to Steve pacing through the house. Well, she had read and heard about such things. Somehow she had been so vain that she'd thought it never would happen to her. But now that it had happened, she'd do battle for Steve as gamely and shrewdly as she knew how.

It was very hard, however, to fight an international heroine who had flown across the Atlantic in twenty hours and forty minutes on a bottle of sarsaparilla and a ham sandwich. A heroine who, running out of gas on the coast of Wales, which she mistook for the coast of Ireland, had leaned out of her airplane and held this colloquy with the skipper of a fishing boat:

"Do you be wantin' something?" asked he.

"We've come from America," said she.

"Well, we wish ye welcome, I'm sure. . . ."

A heroine who, at the first of endless news conferences, established her reputation in Burry Port, Wales, with this colloquy with a man from the *Times* of London:

"Do you know Lindbergh?"

"No, sir, I've never met the gentleman."

"Did you know everybody's already calling you Lady Lindbergh?"

"I'm glad to be taken for a lady."

"No, I mean—don't you know you look like Lindbergh?"

"I'm sure," she replied, "I don't look like anyone but myself. Especially right now."

Then the *Times* man, already a devoted admirer, informed his readers:

> Smiling, she ran a hand through her mop of curls and looked down at her wrinkled flying clothing.

Reggie did everything possible to have Crosson and Weaver share the spotlight with her. She tried to emphasize that she had handled *Eagle*'s controls for only about an hour of the long flight. Her protests, though heard, were rarely recorded. The public had discovered a heroine and did not want her fame diminished. Crosson and Weaver faded from recognition.

Ann met her the day she returned by ship with her flight companions and there was a festive tickertape parade up Broadway. What surprised Ann most was how plain Reggie was. What surprised Ann next was how modest and decent she was. And what surprised Ann the most—and would forever—was how much she liked Regina Faunce.

Since Reggie turned to Steve as to the father she lacked, perhaps it was natural for her to treat Ann as a mother. In the endlessly surprising events of those days Ann found herself enjoying the role. There was no question about Reggie needing help. She was totally unprepared for the fame, with attendant demands, requests, annoyances, and need for quick decisions, that burst upon her. But Ann never was sure whether Reggie truly savored the fame or merely tried to endure it as graciously as possible.

Steve ceased nearly all company business in order to devote himself to handling her affairs. In the theatrical world he would have been called her manager. Lovejoy's offices, someone said, became less like a publishing house than a booking agency. Everyone was running around doing chores for the star, Miss Faunce. Much against Davis Whitcomb's will, Steve turned him into a kind of assistant in handling Reggie's affairs. Davis found himself, instead of functioning as editor-in-chief, writing letters and talking on the phone at all hours of day and night to people in places like Kansas City and El Paso about receptions, parades, endorsements, and other outlandish things until he was thoroughly sick of it. One morning, when he found himself talking on the phone to a man in Maine about Reggie's endorsing a brand of canned rabbit meat, he finally exploded. Slamming the phone, he cried to his secretary, "I quit!" Steve did not try to dissuade him.

Cordelia understood what was happening. After she met Reggie she signaled Ann in every possible way, short of coming right out and saying so, that Steve was heading into serious trouble. Ann pretended not to understand what Cordelia meant because she had an old-fashioned notion that a woman whose marriage was in peril somehow maintained a stronger position by feigning ignorance that anything was wrong.

The time had come—indeed, the time had passed—for Reggie to start writing her book. All she had was a ten-cent notebook half filled with penciled scrawls, many of them cryptic, about her observations while flying the Atlantic.

"You've got to take her in hand," Steve told Ann.

"Take her in hand?"

"Take her to Hasty's. It's quiet there. I'll pop in and out."

"And just what am I supposed to do with Miz Reggie at Hasty's?"

"Help her write her book. If you concentrate on it, you can do it in about two weeks."

Ann was aghast. "But I'm not a writer. I don't even think I'm a very good editor."

"Yes you are. You practically wrote my book for me. And Reggie trusts you. I tried Hendricks with her. He's supposed to be the best ghost in the business, the one who got what's-her-name—that actress—to confess all about her love life in whatchamacallit."

"What I like about publishers," Ann said, "is how articulate they are."

"Reggie froze up on Hendricks. Said he was a conceited egotist who wanted her to describe things that never happened. But she has absolute confidence in you. Ted can stay with Mama at her house while you're away. You and Reggie get cracking out to Hasty's this afternoon. I'll drive out this evening."

Once they were in the quiet of the rambling old house, Ann opened the notebook at random and read aloud to Regina:

" '18:25. It gets dark early out here. Down below the ocean looks like eleph's back.' Reggie, what's an eleph's back?"

"An elephant's back. I never was on an elephant, but that's how it looked to me down there—all gray and waves moving like muscles under the skin. That was right after we left Trepassey Bay and night was coming on."

Thus *Transatlantic* by Regina Faunce begins:

> *Night was falling fast, and far below the airplane the rushing waves of the North Atlantic looked like an elephant's back. . . .*

Reggie always had the impression that she had written the book herself. Ann, who had suggested that it be written in flashbacks to Reggie's past life from ongoing moments in the flight across the Atlantic, felt that she contributed some. Steve congratulated Reggie on a superior writing job and thanked Ann for helping her. Naturally Ann was pleased by Reggie's dedication:

> *To Ann Lovejoy*
> *with gratitude and affection*

28

Transatlantic, published by Lovejoy's in April 1931, had an initial large sale considering the depressed state of the book market. Following a big and expensive publication party at the Astor, Reggie, fed up with fame, went off somewhere with a woman friend in order to enjoy a bit of privacy. Even Steve didn't know where she had gone.

"Not letting me know where to reach her really makes me sore," he fumed to Cordelia when she appeared at the office for a board-of-directors meeting.

"Why does it, Doctor Frankenstein?" Cordelia's voice lashed out, angry and sarcastic. "Must the monster you created report to you every hour?"

He was astonished. "Well, my gosh, Mama, what are you mad about?"

"I'm not mad, I'm furious!" she cried so shrilly that he hastened to shut his office door. "You've turned this place into a flying circus. It's Reggie, Reggie, Reggie from dawn to dark around here. You are *not* attending to business, Steven!"

"Now listen, Mama!" His voice rose too. "Tell me anybody else who brought as successful a book as Reggie's to Lovejoy's. Look at all my other aviation books that sold well. But we can't promote Reggie's book if the author is going to hide someplace."

Cordelia's eyes filled with tears; her shoulders slumped and her voice sank. "You foolish, foolish boy! I don't care if you ruin this company. I just don't want you to destroy yourself and your wonderful wife and son."

She left, closing the door on his protests, and walked home across Murray Hill. When she went in the house, the phone was ringing. It was Steve's secretary asking if she'd forgotten the board meeting.

"I didn't forget," she said. "I just won't be there."

What was the point in her going? Steve now was the one who made the decisions while the rest of them were mere rubber stamps. For she had given away her control of the company. Steve now owned fifty-five percent of its stock, Penny twenty-five, and another five was split between young Ted and Al. Which left Cordelia with only fifteen percent of her own.

Christmas of 1931 at Cordelia's house began tensely. The trouble was with Ann and Steve: No one could thaw the chill that had come between them. Also, Cordelia missed Mary, who for the first time ever did not sit down to dinner with the family, since she had gone to Camden to spend the holiday with Cora, Jack, and their three young children. Then, too, Nick was subdued because he had sprained an arm on Christmas Eve when he fell while tiptoeing downstairs to hang his stocking from the mantel along with those Cordelia had hung for her grandchildren. (Dr. Prettyman, summoned from home about eleven P.M. and looking sleepy and not very cheerful when he arrived, insisted it was a sprain, not a break, though he would take X-rays the day after Christmas in order to make sure.) Cordelia realized that Ted was old enough to have stopped believing in Santa Claus, but it bothered her that Al, only six years old, claimed *never* to have believed. However, his two young sisters, thought not yet baby Nora, had devout faith in the old Christmas gentleman.

The Epstein children had insisted that their King Arthur be invited to Christmas dinner, too. The huge mastiff sat on the floor at Cordelia's left hand, head well above table level, expression grave as he drooled and snuffled and eyed the food of which he was not allowed to partake. After sitting politely through the long dinner, he strolled to the door, and Isabel yelled that he had to go to the bathroom. Izzy groaned, and Al told his father that he would walk the dog for a change. "Izzy," Cordelia exclaimed, "you're not going to let a little boy walk that stubborn monster!"

Izzy kept groaning and saying he was too full of dinner to move and Al might as well learn right now that the damn beast was insane. Al picked up the leash, but neglected to snap it on King Arthur as they went out. Cordelia, going to a widow to watch them, let out a cry that brought all hurrying. Al was walking up the street with King Arthur, unleased, at his heels. When Al stopped, King Arthur stopped. When he trotted, so did the dog.

As Izzy watched them, he made baffled, moaning sounds. Penny, grabbing her coat, said she was going to try it: "You've no idea how ridiculous you and that dog have looked for nearly two years now," she told Izzy. Going outside, she had the same success with King Arthur, unleashed, that Al had had.

Cordelia, suddenly wanting to give it a try, exercised a mother-in-law's prerogative by slipping on a coat and making Izzy wait. King Arthur performed nobly for her. In that part of the performance where she trotted and King Arthur trotted behind her, she happened to be passing the town house of the snobbish Mr. and Mrs. Havelock Greene. Seeing them both, curtain drawn apart and gaping out at her unabashedly, she could not think what to do except wave a hand as she jogged past.

Still Izzy had to wait his turn. Ted went next. Then Ann. Nick was forbidden to go for fear he might fall down and sprain his other arm. King Arthur was having the time of his life; not since country vacation days at Hasty's had he had such good exercise.

At last it was Izzy's turn. He stepped out of the house first, smiling. King Arthur trotted past him and bounded up Thirty-eighth Street toward Park Avenue. Izzy ran after him. When seen next, King Arthur had rounded the block and was gamboling up the street from the opposite direction. Izzy, face red and breath short, still was in pursuit but had fallen a long distance behind.

Amid their shouts of laughter, Penny gasped, "I swear that clever dog is grinning." Izzy was too breathless to say anything when he came in. Just to make sure that King Arthur had not forgotten how to be obedient, Al took him out again, and the dog performed perfectly.

Izzy, finally recovering breath, said, "I'll tell you what's wrong with that goddamn dog—he's anti-Semitic!"

"It doesn't matter," Cordelia said, kissing him, "because *I* love you, Izzy."

Suddenly she looked around for Steve. But he had disappeared during their merriment, and she had not missed him till now.

All of the adults who ate heartily and had fun at Cordelia's that Christmas Day were mindful of how fortunate they were. Unemployment throughout the country was approaching the twelve-million mark, and no one could keep accurate track of the numbers of unemployed in New York City.

That day eighty-five thousand scant meals were served the homeless and unemployed at nearly ninety breadlines which had been organized by religious and charitable organizations, by several individuals, and a few corporations. Bread, soup, and coffee, or stew and bread, were the standard fare. Cordelia, Ann, Izzy, and Penny made weekly contributions of money to organizations supporting breadlines. But one thing they and other people of goodwill in New York could not help was the rise of squatters' villages inhabited by men and women who could not afford a roof.

One doctor of philosophy in physics camped for eight months in Morningside Park near Columbia University before being ousted. Sometimes it seemed that a college degree was certain to lead to unemployment. Cordelia, receiving a letter and the doctoral thesis of one Martin Hogate on Edgar Allan Poe which was delivered to her door by the author because he could not afford postage saw that Hogate was a talented writer. He lived in a squatters' colony called Hoover Village at Seventy-fourth Street and Riverside Drive, he explained in his covering letter, and picked up his mail at the address of a friend who could afford a furnished room. At that point in world history there seemed no need for another study of Poe, but Hogate's was so well done and interesting that Cordelia took a double-decker Riverside Drive bus up to Hoover Village.

She was so unprepared for what she found there that she nearly turned around and took another bus back downtown. Shanties put together from discarded boards, packing cases, sheets of corrugated tin, and strips of tar paper were jumbled together from the Drive down to the Hudson River. Thin and shabbily dressed men, and women, and children, many in tatters, were cooking afternoon meals in buckets over open fires while a cold wind keened out of the north. It seemed to Cordelia that every one of them turned and stared at her with a strange look that expressed—what? Not malice or envy because she had unthinkingly worn a warm sable coat to face their rags, but—but—injured incomprehension. That was it! The faces of these people expressed a surprised and hurt feeling that anything so incredible could have happened to them in America the beautiful, land of the free and the brave.

Cordelia spoke to a thin-faced woman wearing a

man's patched jacket, but could not look her in the eye:
"I'm trying to find a Martin Hogate who lives around
here."

"That'd be Hogate the poet," a man said.

"Poet Hogate!" another cried.

The cry was taken up down the rows of shanties, not
in scorn or derision, but with a kind of merriment. This
Hogate obviously was well liked in his village and the
people were pleased, or at least entertained, that a
sable-coated dame had come looking for him.

"Ho, Hogate!" a man shouted. "A visitor, brother
poet!"

He was a tall man with an old-looking young face
who had to bend almost double to make his way out of
a hut. He wore a wool shirt and overalls, his hair was
long and unkempt, and he peered at Cordelia through
glasses that seemed as thick as milk-bottle bottoms.

"I am Martin Hogate," he said in a high, reedy
voice. "You must be Mrs. Lovejoy."

"Yes, I am. How d'you do, Mr. Hogate."

He shook her hand. "I've done better at other times.
Is it a good sign that you're not carrying my manuscript
with you?"

"A very good sign." Cordelia had an inspiration.
"Would it be a good idea if we walked over to one of
the cafeterias on Broadway to talk about your book?"

Hogate nodded enthusiastically. "A very good idea.
Would it be agreeable if I take along my friend Jackie
Jones, who could stand a decent cup of coffee for a
change?"

Jackie turned out to be a woman wearing a tattered
overcoat. She was no longer young, but there was buoy-
ancy in her step and her smile did not appear forced.

As they started out of the shantytown, Cordelia
glanced up at the home of Charles M. Schwab, the steel
tycoon, which covered the block between Seventy-third
and Seventy-fourth Streets and was one of the most pa-

latial mansions in the world. She felt startled, then embarrassed, as if she had come upon a crude obscenity in an unlikely place.

"Marty," said Jackie, "quote Mrs. Lovejoy your poem on Charlie Schwab's mansion. It doesn't rhyme, Mrs. Lovejoy."

"It even lacks iambic pentameter," Hogate said. "Lift up your eyes, citizens of Hoover Village, and gaze upon the wonders of C. M. Schwab's riverside mansion, worth eight million bucks and bought with the blood of hunkies earning eight a week. Want to buy a piece of it, citizen? Seventy-five rooms. Forty baths. Two subbasements below a basement and in the subsub a vault. For storing Charlie's gold? Not so. For storing Charlie's beef, if he wants to. An inhabitant of Hoover Village, presently on vacation from his accountant's job, figures it this way. That vault can hold twenty tons of beef. And that, fellow Villagers, is enough to feed a family of five for eighty years. But who wants to? Not Charlie Schwab. He just has it there to point out to friends what it could do *if* he wanted it to. . . ."

"Marty," Jackie said, "I still think you ought to make it rhyme."

"Ask Mrs. Lovejoy," Hogate said. "She's my new editor—I hope."

"It shoudn't rhyme," Cordelia said. "That would turn it into propaganda for some pet scheme to—uh—adjust the imbalance."

Hogate's eyes gleamed at her through his thick glasses. "If I had any doubts about letting you become my editor, Mrs. Lovejoy, they have vanished."

She paid him an advance of one thousand dollars against royalties for his work on Poe, which after its publication was acclaimed by authorities but sold poorly. At Jackie's insistence the amount was paid at the rate of twenty-five a week for forty weeks, which enabled them to eat well and live comfortably in a furnished room. They hoped that after forty weeks the Depression would have ended and Hogate could find a teaching job again. But after forty weeks the Depression was worse than ever. Even Franklin Roosevelt, the new President and one already experienced in miracles, had not yet been able to turn the tide for the citizens of the Hoover Villages that scarred the land.

Hogate's work on Poe made Cordelia wonder if it was futile to publish good books in such bad times. Of course it was not, she told herself, but she wished that a publisher somehow could address himself incisively to the economic crisis and help the millions caught up in it. There was no way, however. A publisher's works could only hope to describe a situation—not reform it.

Cordelia's disgust with Steve grew deeper. He did not even seem to realize there was a Depression as he went carelessly along. His folly of 1933 was to help organize a transcontinental air race for women which was meant to star Reggie. He borrowed thousands of dollars from someplace and stayed away from the office for weeks before the race finally was completed—and Reggie came in second.

"But second place is better than third," he told Cordelia. "And it's put her so much in the public eye again that I'm going to start her on a countrywide lecture tour to start a new promotion campaign for *Transatlantic.*"

"Steve," Cordelia said, "listen to me. Please. *Transatlantic* is an *old* book. You can't promote it now and expect more than very slight results. You're wasting your time."

As usual, however, he did not listen to her. The lecture and autographing tour must begin, and he would go the first week of it with her.

Reggie had a strange capacity to swing Steve from depression to euphoria and back again. His emotional infidelity to Ann had become total.

The physical event that occurred between Steve and Reggie in an Atlanta hotel room seemed incidental. It was a rabbity event, quick, surprising, and not very satisfying to either. The most satisfactory thing about it to Steve was the way Reggie squealed in a kind of panic while it was happening. It made him feel he finally had established ascendency over this elusive gamine.

Afterwards he went alone to one of those "clubs" where a guest could buy liquor in a dry town, and downed a couple of bourbons. Then he returned to Reggie's room and awakened her.

"Listen," he said, "I want you to marry me."

She sat up in bed, tousled and looking frightened, while she clutched a sheet to her thin, naked chest. "I don't want to," she said.

"But I want you to. I'm divorcing Ann."

"You shouldn't do that, Steve. She's a nice person."

"Who said she isn't? But I don't love her anymore. I love you."

"But I don't want to get married ever to anybody."

"You'll change your mind after I divorce Ann." He sounded threatening.

Hurrying back to New York, he found Ann at home repotting plants.

"I'm sorry about this," he told her, "but I want a divorce."

Her expression did not change, but her gloved hands grew still. "So you can marry Reggie?"

"Yes."

She did not hesitate. "That's all right with me. But I'll have custody of Ted."

"We'll see about that," he said.

"No, we won't see about it. That is settled. You won't miss him. You never have. When are you leaving for Nevada to establish six months' residence?"

He looked alarmed. "I can't give up all my responsibilities and live in Nevada for six months. You have to do that."

"*Have* to, Steve? I'll just do what my lawyer tells me to."

"Look, Ann, there's just one favor I ask of you. Will you explain all this to Mama? I don't want to see her right now."

Cordelia took the news calmly. "I'm just surprised it didn't happen sooner. I'm sorry—terribly sorry—that it happened at all. But since it has, what can I do to help you?"

"I'm going to establish residence in Reno to get a divorce. I'd like Ted to finish out his year at Public School Eighteen down on Thirty-first Street. He adores you. May he stay with you for a couple of months before he joins me in Reno in June?"

"I'd love it. He's more than welcome. Something surprising comes over me, Ann. Here we sit talking about the—mechanics of the thing and neither of us has any emotion. It's as if—as if Steve no longer exists as a—a person."

"He no longer does to me," Ann said. "I'm sorry, but that's true. It took a long time for him to die in my mind—a lot of time and a lot of secret tears. But then he did die—died right in front of my eyes while we sat and talked together about meaningless things. I don't love him anymore. I won't miss him. Haven't missed him for a long time."

Cordelia enjoyed having Ted live with her after Ann went to Nevada. Both she and Ann had blind faith in a well-off boy like Ted attending public school with less fortunate children, theorizing that democracy led to moral improvement. After a few weeks of living with her grandson, however, Cordelia decided that most theories about rearing children were nonsense.

For example, she'd felt for a long time that Steve's

shortcomings were a result of his lacking a father's direction and companionship during his formative years. She also feared that Steve's failure to be a companionable father would result in Ted's personality being affected. But Ted taught her that such theories were not necessarily sound. She saw that maybe the most important thing in growing up was to learn how to accept being a stranger. (Later it would be called being "alienated.") Ted, like all the young, was lonely—and for much more than his absent mother and distracted father. But he had a cocker spaniel and plenty to eat and a bed and he liked to run the streets of Murray Hill in search of fun. In the process he digested his loneliness and grew. Perhaps it wasn't that simple, Cordelia thought, but neither could growing up be as complicated as many maintained.

She took care not to dote on Ted as she had on his father when young, with the result that she learned something herself about digesting loneliness.

All too soon the school year ended and Ted left for Reno to join Ann. Then Cordelia had little to do but face up to the unpleasant facts presented by Steve.

Colonel Bob used to say, "There's a lot of momentum in a publishing house. It's like the charge of an infantry regiment. Long after the heart's gone out of everybody and just before everybody turns and runs, all the people are still steamin' along."

Colonel Bob would have seen what Cordelia did: that Lovejoy's was running on momentum and thus running down. She tried to make Steve see it, but he would not. Even before his divorce from Ann was complete and he was married to Reggie by a justice of the peace in Elkton, Maryland, he had become only a part-time publisher. His main work was promoting Reggie; "guiding" was what he called it.

When she told him that she wanted to make a solo
flight across the Atlantic, he acted surprised. Why, Cordelia wondered, should he be? Heroics have a way of
demanding more heroics. Cordelia, knowing Reggie,
believed that she had long wanted to be the first woman
to fly the Atlantic alone, that possibly she had married
Steve because she knew he would back her effort. This
he did enthusiastically, spending eighteen thousand to
buy her a new single-engine Lockhead and equipping it
with auxiliary fuel-tanks to enable a thirty-two-
hundred-mile range. Not having that amount of money,
he borrowed from a bank again.

Reggie took off alone from Long Island with great
fanfare. Somewhere over Newfoundland she became
lost in fog. Steve had made her study navigation for
three months before the flight, but either her training
failed or her navigational aids failed because she apparently flew in circles. Then, for some mysterious reason,
her engine failed and she plopped into a choppy sea on
the Grand Banks. But her tiny life raft didn't fail, and
neither did her luck. Like the youth in Kipling's *Cap-
tains Courageous,* she was picked up by a fishing
schooner. Unfortunately the tiny vessel was not
equipped with radio, and four days went by before it
could pass her to a larger ship which did have radio
communications.

For three days the world had been mourning the
death of Regina Faunce. Steve was so distraught that he
chartered a plane he could not afford to go look for her
in person while Cordelia had Dr. Prettyman looking for
the best psychiatric institution in which to incarcerate
him. Word that Reggie had been found was accepted as
joyfully everywhere as if she had succeeded in her flight
across the Atlantic. Eleanor and Franklin Roosevelt
had her and Steve come for the weekend at the White
House, where they proved to be so charming and popular that they stayed a week. By that time Cordelia had

stopped reading accounts about her famous daughter-in-law and was devoting herself to worrying about Lovejoy's.

The editor-in-chief on whom Steve relied to run things during his many absences was a nice young man and failed poet named Maurice Treadway. He was competent enough, but saw in his responsibilities the opportunity to develop works of literary merit, such as—he said—Lovejoy's rarely had published before. The trouble was that Treadway's ideas of literary quality were on a collision course with the economic depression and the decline in book purchases. The public appetite for "escapist" fiction was greater than ever as people tried to forget the sad facts of unemployment and poverty. And there was a good deal of critical concern with "proletarian" fiction, which was not a new theme but the old one of mankind the victim and society the culprit. With their work falling somewhere between these general fields of interest, Treadway's authors, none a genius, found a very small reading audience.

"Treadway has got to go," Penny agreed when Cordelia fumed to her. "I remember when I was in the avant garde myself. Guess there's nothing like motherhood to put you in the rearguard. How does he take your complaints?"

"As just an old woman meddling."

"What does Steve say?"

"When his show is on the road, he doesn't answer my letters. When his show is in town for a few days, he says, 'Yes, yes, Mama, I'll see what I can do about it.' "

"But he can read a sales report," Penny said. "I had Izzy make a graph of these reports we get at the directors meetings. Over the past ten months the sales look like the stock market decline in twenty-nine. I'll show Steve the graph."

However, Steve seemed too busy with the preparation of Reggie's new book about her mishap to pay much attention to graphs or anything else. He talked sales of one hundred thousand or more for the book which was ghosted for Reggie, and then, when advance orders from bookstores totaled less than thirty thousand, he rushed about frantically, demanding greater zeal from the sales force. He was dismayed when the book began to receive unfavorable and lukewarm reviews.

Cordelia ordered him and Penny to her house for lunch. She thrust a glass of sherry on him, and, when he began to revile reviewers and Lovejoy's sales department, she interrupted:

"For once, Stevey, listen to me. Regina's book is not very good. The *Times* review says it all, and I quote verbatim: 'Everyone now knows it is possible to fly across the Atlantic Ocean or fall into it. What most thoughtful people wish to know is the nature of one who wants to make the effort. This Regina Faunce fails to reveal herself to us in her new book. In that respect the book is a great disappointment.' "

"So," said Steve, "must Beowulf now explain himself to the world?"

Momentarily Cordelia was surprised that he had heard of Beowulf. "Yes. Deeds alone no longer are enough. Explanations are the order of the day."

"My God, Mama, take a great fighter like Jack Dempsey. Would you expect him to try to explain himself—why he fought and how he felt while fighting? *He could not do it.* No great person of action can do it. They're just not that reflective. And it's unfair to judge them that way."

"But unfortunately," Cordelia said, "that's the way judgments are passed in the world of books. Serious book readers want to receive deeper insights into people and events than they glean from daily journalism."

He looked at Penny. "You think the same?"

"Yes, Stevey. If you're going to gamble in the book casino, you have to accept the roll of the dice. There's another thing about the sales of Reggie's book that Mama didn't mention. I think people take aviation much more for granted than they did a few years ago. Some of the thrill and excitement have gone out of flying."

"Listen, Penny"—Steve put down his glass—"the thrill and excitement will *never* go out of flying."

If she had not admitted it before, Cordelia knew then that he was not meant to be a book publisher. He had been doing the wrong thing ever since he'd left the Lafayette Escadrille. But it was too late for him to change now. So she tried to make him understand what was going wrong at the company and how he must pay more attention to business.

As first he sincerely tried. But he hadn't got much further than firing Treadway and hiring another editor-in-chief even less competent, when Reggie claimed his attention again. She had entered another complex women's transcontinental air race having all kinds of incredible complications that took Steve's full time to straighten out before she completed the course and placed first.

During Franklin's first term Cordelia was invited to White House dinners twice, but never at the same time as Reggie and Steve. She ceased to see Reggie altogether. On the rare occasions when Reggie was in the city, she never invited Cordelia to the mansion—and was not invited to Cordelia's. Each time Cordelia passed the mansion, she looked at it with dismay. While nowhere near as large as Charles Schwab's on Riverside Drive, it nevertheless seemed an anachronism in the hard times. She could not recall it bringing her any pleasure except when she had been able to give it to Ann and Steve. Why had she ever coveted and bought it?

She frequently saw Ann, who after the divorce had moved into a Fifth Avenue apartment and taken a job as the public relations director of a medical research foundation. Ted had become quiet and reflective, completely unlike his father in youth. He was attending St. Mark's, and whenever he came to New York he enjoyed visiting Cordelia. In their long, rambling talks she took care never to imply that some day he might be interested in book publishing.

29

Suddenly Reggie convinced Steve that she must be the first person to fly solo from California to Hawaii.

At first he was not enthusiastic about it, though he did not ask, as Cordelia did, "What will that accomplish for the human race in these troubled times?"

Understanding the mind of the adventurer, Steve knew that such responses were silly to one who wanted to make a venture. But he did tell Reggie before giving in to her wish, "You know, hon, you could kill yourself doing a stunt like that."

"She certainly could," Cordelia said to him when she heard about it. "You've told me time and again you won't let her try the Atlantic another time despite all her pleading to. What's better about the Pacific?"

"It's a different ocean, Mama. It'll change her luck."

"You people are incredible," Cordelia said. "If she flies the Atlantic she has the whole continent of Europe to aim at. But if she flies west in the Pacific she has to hit that teeny-weeny little point of Hawaii. And from all I can gather, navigation is not exactly Miz Reggie's forte."

"Why do you hate her so?" Steve cried angrily. "She's never done anything against you."

"Or anything for me or anybody else, far as I can see," Cordelia replied, causing Steve to storm out of the house.

Since Reggie must have the best plane available for this and future flights, Steve decided to buy a new twin-engine, all-metal monoplane with retractable landing gear whose Wasp engine generated eleven hundred horsepower and promised a cruising range of forty-five hundred miles. This airplane cost fifty thousand dollars.

In order to raise that amount of money, Steve put the Park Avenue mansion up for sale—then decided he'd better call Cordelia and tell her about it. "Reggie and I are really hotel people anyway," he explained.

"I suppose so," Cordelia said. "Just bed and board, eh? Well, why are you telling me about it, Steve? It's yours. And that mansion seems to have brought the Lovejoys so much unhappiness, I suppose the sooner the family's rid of it the better."

Yet she did regret its going up for sale. At dusk that evening she walked alone up the Avenue and paused to look at it. She thought of Edward and their simple beginning at the foot of the hill. When tears came to her eyes, she said aloud, "Sentimental old fool!" and marched firmly home.

The real-estate market was so depressed that Steve could get only twenty-four thousand dollars for the mansion. He had to go to the bank for the rest of the money to pay for the new airplane, putting up shares of Lovejoy's stock as collateral. Since he had not yet paid off the principal of his previous loan, which had defrayed Reggie's Atlantic mishap, he had to pay nine instead of eight percent interest on the new loan.

"All of a sudden," Penny told Cordelia, "Izzy and I are viewing Reggie's flight through bookkeepers' eyes. Hey, Mama, maybe there's a book in that. Columbus, Captain Cook, and all the rest as seen by their bookkeepers."

"How can you be so lighthearted about it?" Cordelia sounded sad. "Didn't you see last month's sales report?"

Penny gazed at her. "Mama, can we help a little?"

"Of course not!" Cordelia spoke with asperity. "I'm doing fine."

But she was not. Was it the fate of all Dorfmans to

die poor? Lovejoy's dividends were sharply reduced because of the decline in profits. Cordelia's other investments were paying poorly, too. She was living off savings—and living them up fast.

Sometimes her house reminded her of a hospital. Nick was up and down with ailments that so puzzled Dr. Prettyman that he finally told Cordelia, "Your brother's ailments can only be diagnosed in his own mind." (One of those Dr. Prettyman statements that Cordelia thought about for days.) Mary fell victim to arthritis, and there were times when she could not attend to her own needs.

Though Cordelia was vigorous enough to run her small hospital, she wondered about the day when she might fall ill herself. With Ann's help she found a remarkable black couple, Washington and Dolley Jones, who had become unemployed and were glad to work in Cordelia's house for food, comfortable living quarters, and twenty dollars a week. By the time Cordelia realized she could not afford them, they had become such fast friends that she would not part with them. When she decided to sell Hasty's for six thousand in order to help make ends meet, Izzy would not let her. He said he would pay the two hundred dollars annual taxes because some day that two-hundred-acre property would be worth a lot of money. Of course she continued to pay the taxes herself. Yet it was no wonder that her vision of life began to seem that of a bookkeeper.

The decline of the company was not accelerated by Steve alone, though his carelessness was the chief cause. Many events besides the Depression were conspiring to destroy Lovejoy's. It acquired a bad reputation with writers and agents because of a lack of advertising and promotion. First-rate editors did not want to work there because of its stigma of failure. Its bread-and-butter writers faded away.

For two weeks Steve was so busy helping Reggie prepare for the flight that Cordelia never heard from him. The first she knew he had left town was when one of the mail-room boys delivered a note from him.

Dear Mama—

Am flying with Reggie this morning to S.F., then will hop the *President Pierce* to Honolulu so as to complete arrangements there and greet her when she flies in two weeks from now. You take care of the candy store while I'm away.

Luv,
S

As soon as she read the note, Cordelia phoned his office. His secretary, a young woman who disliked Cordelia as much as Cordelia detested her, displayed customary rudeness in saying that Steve had gone. Cordelia put on a hat and steamed to the office. Why she decided to wear a hat on a warm June day she wasn't sure, but probably she was experiencing something akin to the feelings of a soldier who wore a helmet into battle.

First thing she fired the secretary. When the young woman questioned her authority to do so, Cordelia bundled together most of the things on the secretary's desk and tossed them into the hall. This so unnerved the woman that she fled the premises. Then Cordelia phoned an employment agency and said she wanted a secretary, never mind how many words she typed a minute, who must be at least forty-five years old and have extensive experience in dealing with a husband and children. They sent her Henrietta Pardue, who confessed to being forty-nine, typing only thirty words a minute, and having an unemployed husband and four grown children of whom she was weary. Cordelia hired her and was forever glad she did.

Next she called in Lloyd Hammer, the current comptroller, who was terrified of her. She kept him at her desk straight through the lunch hour going over the company books. It was then she discovered that Steve had been borrowing more and more money from the bank without the authorization of the directors and that the total of the indebtedness meant the bank owned about fifteen percent of the company stock.

"Why didn't you report this to the board?" she asked Hammer.

"Because Mr. Lovejoy said he'd fire me if I did."

"Apparently, Hammer, you're one of those individuals who cannot win. Because now you *are* fired. If you're not out of these offices in ten minutes I'll start criminal proceedings against you."

He fled, and she phoned Penny. "Get over here! And bring Izzy."

"Mama, what's—"

"Fire! Fire! Fire! Bring Izzy!" She hung up. "Mrs. Pardue—Henrietta—I want you to type up pink slips giving two weeks notice to all the editorial employees."

"Yes, ma'm. Have you got a list of their names?"

"I'm not sure who they all are. Dig around and find out."

"Mrs. Lovejoy, you're firing all of them?"

"Yes. I can tell by the way they react if any are worth keeping."

Penny and Izzy appeared, greatly alarmed. When she told them what Steve had done, Izzy started to swear. Pointing at Penny, Cordelia said, "You are coming back to work here as a senior editor."

Penny began to glow. "Oh, Mama, I'd love that. I'm so sick and tired of sitting around the house I don't know what to do."

"Izzy," Cordelia said, "I want you to become president of Lovejoy's."

He looked startled. "Me? What do I know about books?"

"You can quote Tennyson, can't you? But the books you have to know about are the account books."

"But this company already has a president, and it's illegal for a corporation to have two presidents."

"This company already has a vice-president," Cordelia said. "His name is Steven Lovejoy. There has just been a meeting of the board of directors and it is so decided."

"Illegal again," Izzy said. "The bank owns—"

"How much will it cost to recover that stock from the bank?"

"More than the amount Steve borrowed. The bank might like to have an interest in a publishing house." He figured on a sheet of paper for a while. "Maybe a hundred grand. Maybe seventy-five after we circulate the rumor that the company's going bankrupt. Where do we get that amount of money?"

"From you, dummy," Penny said. "Didn't you just say you'd like to be the president of a publishing house? Privileges like that don't come free, my lad. You've got to pay up to be a publisher."

"I didn't just say I want to be president of this place."

"Not just now you didn't, but about a year ago you were moaning to me about it being a lot nicer in your obituary to read that you were the president of a publishing house instead of the owner of some empty office buildings. Izzy, here's your big chance. Are you going to muff it?"

He began to grin. "You two dear ladies could make a fortune in the junk business."

"What else do you call the publishing business? Mama, I'm not too bright at figures. Let me get this straight. I have about twenty-five percent of the stock.

After Izzy buys back those collateral shares of Steve's, that'll give us about forty percent. You have fifteen. We have guardian voting rights on that two or three percent of Al's. Yes, that comes out all right as long as the three of us hang together. But how is Steve going to feel? More exactly I mean how are you going to feel about the way he feels?"

"I am going to feel sorry for him." Cordelia spoke slowly and distinctly. "I already am. But my mind is made up and I'm not changing it again. Steve has already destroyed a fine marriage. He's well on the way to destroying this publishing house, but we're going to try to prevent it. The one thing neither I nor anybody else can stop is if he decides to destroy himself. I won't even try."

It is 2,393 statute miles from San Francisco to Honolulu, a course no one had flown in either direction at the time Reggie decided to try it. Navigation-wise it could have been easier to fly from Hawaii to the mainland, but to an adventurer like Reggie difficulty meant daring—and daring was the point of attempting the difficult. Besides, she had been stung, ever since her plunge into the North Atlantic, by criticism that she was a poor navigator, and she was eager to demonstrate that she was a good one.

In theory at least, early July, the time she and Steve had selected for her to make the flight, offered the favoring winds of the northeast trades circling around a stable high-pressure area in the North Pacific that would give an aviator helpful tail winds in flying from the continent to the islands. But experienced ocean navigators warned there also was danger in the northeasterlies: When blowing very strong they tended to drive a craft southwestward into the tropical lows.

Fourteen changes in compass course must be made

during the flight, and Reggie's flying chart, thirty inches long by eight inches wide, was divided into sections—one for each hour of flight time. She had two altimeters installed, for she blamed a faulty altimeter for that fiasco over Newfoundland. The plane was equipped with a long-distance two-way radiophone, its antenna rolling out through a hole in the cockpit floor and arching back under the fuselage. Giving her call signals, KHAQQ, she was to report by voice on 3105 kilocycles at a quarter before and a quarter after each hour to a Coast Guard cutter standing off Oahu in Hawaii. The cutter was stationed and cooperating with Reggie at the specific instruction of the President, for he and Eleanor took deep personal interest in the flight. The cutter would send her weather reports and homing signals on the hour and half hour. Reggie also had a telegraphic key with which she could send and receive on 500 kilocycles, the frequency used by ships at sea.

Every detail except one was completed by the time Steve took ship for the five-day voyage to Honolulu: They could not settle on a name for the Lockheed Electra.

"Just call it *Number One*," Steve told her. "That's what you'll always be to me."

Reggie seemed unusually taut and complained of sleeping poorly. He wished there was some way he could relax her, but realized his restless nature never had made his presence restful to anyone. The night before he sailed on the *President Pierce*, however, Reggie slept soundly, curled against him like a kitten while he barely dozed. His feeling for her was so tender, his awe so great at what she was undertaking that it would have seemed like sacrilege to him if he had tried to make love to her.

The day after he sailed, Reggie had an inspiration that made one more story for the clamoring reporters in

San Francisco who kept after her day and night. The airplane was named *Eleanor Roosevelt*.

At one A.M. on a clear Thursday morning, when perfect weather was reported at her destination, Wheeler Field near Honolulu, Reggie waved to a crowd of reporters and well-wishers. Under a bright spotlight the watchers thought they could distinguish every curl of her tousled hair, and some wondered why she looked so grave and lacked her usual smile. Wearing warm flying clothes and an inflatable rubber vest, with a hatchet and sheath knife at her waist, she appeared to one reporter "to look like a strange visitor from another planet." The hatchet and knife were for use in the event of a forced landing. The weight of the wing tanks would drag the plane under quickly if she had to come down at sea, and it was her hope to climb out of the cockpit, crawl along the fuselage, and chop a way through the fabric-covered wood to free a small inflatable raft.

When Steve described this contingency to Lindbergh, the famous aviator had said, "There should be a better way." But neither he nor Steve nor Reggie could think of one. The raft contained a rocket pistol and sealed rations that should keep her alive for two weeks.

The *Eleanor Roosevelt* roared down a dimly lighted runway and lifted off easily into the darkness, for it did not have a full load of fuel—all agreed that was unnecessary and more of a hazard than a help considering the distance involved.

With an expected average ground speed of 140 miles per hour, Reggie was anticipated to make it to Wheeler Field in about seventeen hours. At one fifteen A.M., San Francisco time, a coast guard cutter about one hundred miles off the California coast heard Reggie's voice reporting cheerfully and replied in kind, but her signal apparently was too weak to reach the cutter off Oahu. About an hour later a freighter bound for Japan reported by key that the watch had heard the *Eleanor*

Roosevelt passing west overhead. The freighter added, in answer to a coast guard query, that the northeasterly had freshened to eighteen knots. This information, with the warning to take it into account in her navigation, was passed on to Reggie in the next homing message. She did not answer.

Steve was in the communications center at Wheeler Field with a group of army, navy, and coast guard officers, waiting to greet Reggie when she arrived and able to listen to communications between the cutter and the *Eleanor Roosevelt*. He began to pace nervously as KHAQQ remained silent while the coast guard broadcast reports and signals as scheduled and begged Reggie to answer.

At last, to the great joy of Steve and everyone else, they heard her voice. She came through faintly a few more times, but not on scheduled hours. It became apparent that the plane's receiver was not picking up the cutter's messages. Yet weren't the key messages on 500 kilocycles getting through? Steve, disheveled and sweating profusely, demanded to know. Naturally no one could tell. As one signalman said, "It's like we're dealing with an amateur."

Once Steve gripped an army air corps captain by the shoulder and cried, "It's the goddamn northeasterlies—up to twenty-three knots now! Did she get word of that? She's being driven off course!"

The captain cast him a shocked look and said, "But sir, *none* of us know if she's receiving."

At five P.M. Honolulu time, when Reggie had been in flight for eighteen hours, the cutter keyed a string of homing signals. Suddenly Reggie's voice broke in: "I am receiving your signals, but unable to get a minimum." She meant that she could not get a compass bearing. "Please take a bearing on me and answer with voice on thirty-one zero five."

Everyone calculated that she should have been over Oahu by then even if she had not maintained her projected ground speed. But neither from any ship in the vicinity nor from Oahu, where all listeners had been alerted by the Honolulu commercial station KGU, was there any word of sighting a plane in the bright sky.

Again and again the cutter broadcast: "Will you please come in and answer on thirty-one zero five! We are transmitting constantly, too, on five hundred kilocycles. Can you answer on key? We do not have you on thirty-one zero five. Please answer on thirty-one zero five! Go ahead, KHAQQ!"

Suddenly, at five-forty-five P.M., Reggie's voice came loud, clear—and frenzied: "I am in a line of position one fifty-eight—twenty-seven. Will repeat this message in five minutes. Wait! Listen! I am running north and south!"

All listened tensely for her next broadcast, but nothing came. Repeatedly, by voice and key, they begged her to reply. But Regina Faunce's voice never was heard again.

The prevailing opinion of navy and coast guard men was that Reggie had drifted to the southwest and overshot her mark through carelessness or faulty navigation or communications equipment and that she died after her plane ran out of fuel and plunged into the sea.

It is almost impossible to kill a legend, however. Since Reggie had become a legend to many, there were some who insisted that she had not died. Steve was the most stubborn of those who believed she still was alive.

At the direction of the President there was an intensive air and sea hunt for her in which Steve took part, flying a search plane himself for a while and then transferring to various ships. Officers and men began to refer to him as "crazy Lovejoy" as a result of his unend-

ing, intense talk about Reggie and the way he would
stand by the hour on a bridge scanning the sea with
binoculars and exclaiming that a distant whitecap might
be a bit of wreckage.

Every skipper wanted this touchy, wild-talking nut
off his ship, but all knew of his pull with the White
House, so none would think of imperiling a career by
antagonizing him. It took a serious-faced young lieutenant (who later would become a distinguished admiral)
to accomplish the improbable by getting Steve to ask to
be returned to the mainland. With sinister purpose and
paranoid logic the lieutenant convinced Steve that if he
returned to San Francisco and offered a reward for information leading to Reggie's recovery he might obtain
a vital clue from some merchant seaman whose ship
had been in the area when she disappeared.

First thing after landing in San Francisco Steve
phoned Cordelia. He sounded so ebullient that at first
she thought Reggie had been found, but then she understood that he simply was asking her to send money
so that she *could* be found.

Cordelia stalled. The afternoon newspapers carried
banner headlines about Steve's return to San Francisco
with clues that Regina still was alive. When she read
reports of his news conference, Cordelia saw that he
was saying wild and contradictory things. She phoned
Dr. Prettyman.

"I've practiced everything but psychiatry," he told
her. "But I can refer you to a good psychiatrist. First
fetch the poor boy home."

Izzy went with her to San Francisco where they
found Steve in a hotel suite with a little leech who
claimed to be a public-relations man and a drunken
sailor who claimed to have seen Reggie on a Pacific
atoll from a passing ship. At first Steve seemed barely
to recognize Cordelia, but when she took him in her
arms and kissed him, he broke down and wept. Offer-

ing no resistance to going home with her and Izzy, he slept exhaustedly in a compartment most of the way across the continent.

On a gray morning as the train approached New York, Steve broke a long silence: "Mama, do you think Ann would be willing to see me?"

"I imagine so, Steve, but she left New York last month."

"Where did she go?" He sounded alarmed.

"She's living in Paris. She has a job there that interests her, I'm not sure just what it is. Ted is with her. He hated St. Mark's and is going to school in Europe."

Steve broke into tears.

30

Cordelia intended to be editor-in-chief only a few weeks until she could find a good replacement, for she felt that in her sixties she was too old for the job. Ironically she needed the annual eighteen thousand salary to make ends meet. Her house was more crowded than ever, and she could not have managed without the help of Dolley and Washington Jones.

Steve was her chief worry. Once he saw that Izzy had taken over business management of the company, he never went back to Lovejoy's. He did not act hurt or angry, only relieved that his career in publishing had ended. He stopped speaking of Reggie; indeed there were days when he didn't speak at all. He lost all interest in aviation and never mentioned it. Rejecting the attention of a psychiatrist and refusing to look for employment, he wandered about the city like an insatiable tourist. It became apparent soon to Cordelia that he had an alcohol problem. After he discovered Delaney's Bar on Third Avenue, he passed long winter afternoons there, sipping beer and staring vacantly out the front window. Precisely at six almost every evening Washington would walk down Murray Hill and fetch him home for dinner.

There were days when Mary's arthritis was so bad that she could not get out of bed. She suffered her pain stoically, but fussed sometimes that after all these years of serving Cordelia she must now be the one served. She often spoke of going to live with Cora and Jack in

Camden, but that was impossible: Jack was out of work, Cora toiling nights in a diner, their house filled with children.

In February 1937, the eldest Doyle daughter, Sara, came to visit her grandmother. Whatever she lacked in worldly goods she more than made up in an inheritance of good looks. Her black hair, blue eyes, fair skin, and tall, lovely body made her a stunning beauty. "Aieee," mourned Mary to Cordelia, "with those Doyle looks she's headed straight for hell."

"Nonsense," said Cordelia, who thought Sara beautiful. "She's bright as polished silver and strong as steel. We can't send her to Wellesley just now, but we can help realize her ambition to study nursing. I'm going to phone Dr. Prettyman and find out how you go about that."

Thus it happened that Sara became a student nurse at Bellevue and lived at Cordelia's, sleeping on a cot in her grandmother's room and helping the household in every way she could. Perhaps her greatest help was in cheering Nick, who had dark moods over the state of his liver. (Dr. Prettyman insisted the trouble was with his gall bladder, but Nick would not hear of an operation.)

Late one afternoon when Cordelia came home, Steve told her, "Mama, I'm turning into a rummy."

She lowered her gaze and did not answer.

"I don't like the way I am," he went on. "Would you trust me to lay off the bottle if I went out to Hasty's and lived by myself? To start off, I'll paint the house."

"Yes," she said slowly, "the house needs paint. It would be very nice if you'd like to do that, Steve."

Almost a month later he phoned and invited her out to see what he'd done. She drove there in her Dodge sedan on Sunday. The house was a dazzle of white paint with handsome gray trim. Inside, the rooms were as clean and orderly as the footlocker of a soldier who wanted to pass inspection. Cordelia fought back tears and kissed him.

"Mama, I want to show you something else I'm proud of." He drove them to a Sunoco service station. "The guy I work for here six days a week is named Dan Zinke. He moved up from Sag Harbor not long ago and never heard of the Lovejoys. Sunday is my day off." They climbed out of the car, and a red-faced, heavy man shambled to them.

"Dan," Steve said, "I'd like you to meet my mother, Mrs. Lovejoy."

"Mrs. Lovejoy," Dan said cordially, "pleased to meet you. I want to tell you, your son can strip a motor better than anybody I ever knew."

Lovejoy's paid no dividends in 1937. Sales were the lowest in decades, and Izzy did not have the ready capital to play sugar daddy indefinitely. He, Penny, and Cordelia were tempted to sell out when the house of Braismith and Sons offered to buy the company for one million exactly. But then all agreed that if Braismith thought it worth a million, it potentially should be worth much more to them.

The editorial department consisted of Cordelia, Penny, and young Phil Federicci. Phil was the only one Cordelia reinstated after firing the entire department, because he was the only one who protested. The rest merely fled like a flock of frightened birds, screeching that she was a capricious, crazy old woman, but Phil came into her office and argued:

"Why fire me, Mrs. Lovejoy? I've put seven of the best years of my life into this place because I want to be a book editor. I started in the mail room and sweated it out in production, and now after I've read about two manuscripts, you suddenly fire me. Why?"

Cordelia smiled at him. "Well, then, stay awhile till I

see if you have more sense than those who left. Are you the one graduated from—"

"Boys' High of Brooklyn. Then straight into your mail room."

"Congratulations. It'll be a relief to have somebody around here who didn't go to Harvard."

Once she grumped to Penny, "Most undistinguished editorial department in the country. Not one of us with a college degree."

"You forget about Izzy," Penny replied. "He has a diploma for taking a three-month correspondence course in 1916 with something called the Washburn School of Finance."

Cordelia was glad she'd kept Phil. His first achievement was to buy and help rewrite a first novel by a former high-school classmate about a group of Italian-Americans who were constructing a New York office building. Phil gave it the title *Jesus Skyscraper*, and it was the first novel from Lovejoy's in a long time that both sold and was reviewed well.

Literary agents noted the fine promotion job the house did with the book and began to send it more manuscripts. One sent to Cordelia was a picaresque novel about an eighteenth-century adventurer that was nearly two thousand manuscript pages written in a lush prose Cordelia described as "overripe and fruity," and had been turned down by thirteen publishers. But it had a lot of well-described action and enough explicit sex that Bible Belt preachers would enhance its sales by ranting against it.

"We can tone down the sex a bit," Cordelia said.

"Why?" asked Phil.

"Good question," said Penny. "Don't put on the brakes, Mama. This year a kept woman, next year the whorehouse."

Vander's Folly, published in June 1938, remained a

best seller through Christmas of 1939. Li'l Abe, Love-
joy's oldest employee and manager of its Long Island
City warehouse, could not keep the book in stock until
Izzy personally stepped into the production process.
Thanks mainly to that novel, the company paid some
dividends in 1938 and much larger ones in 1939.

That was the year Cordelia stepped down to senior
editor and Penny became editor-in-chief while Phil
moved up to senior editor. Steve sold his remaining
stock to Izzy, who reorganized the board of directors
with a greater diversity of membership and became its
chairman while continuing to serve as president. Steve
put the money in a bank; he seemed perfectly content
to live alone frugally in Northport and work in Zinke's
Service Station.

Cordelia corresponded occasionally with Eunice in
Los Angeles. The Hearst chain had abandoned "Cassandra" and Eunice implied that times were hard, but
Cordelia was pleased to see she did not complain or beg
for money as she used to.

Gradually at first—and then suddenly—life never
had seemed better to Cordelia. Mary began getting
about more; Sara graduated from nursing school and
took a job at University Hospital; Nick, tiring of his
symptoms, stopped describing them. Dr. Prettyman
kept threatening to retire, but did not. (A favorite question among the folk of Murray Hill was: "How old is
Dr. Prettyman *really*?") Cordelia gave Dolley and
Washington money for a month's vacation in Louisiana,
and, after they returned, decided to take a vacation herself.

On June 7, 1939, she sailed for France aboard the
Normandie.

Ann and Ted's long absence was the only cloud on
the otherwise bright family horizon that spring. Cordelia decided it was provincial to be concerned because

Ann had chosen to make her home and raise her child outside the United States. Nevertheless, she didn't like it, mainly because she missed them so keenly. They had kept in touch those years with frequent letters. Ted had attended a preparatory school in Switzerland, then another in France. The nature of Ann's work with some kind of foundation was vague to Cordelia; all she knew was that it required a lot of travel.

Ted came to Le Havre to meet her, and at first she didn't recognize him: a tall, slender, handsome youth of eighteen wearing a blazer of rich blue. He walked quickly and gracefully with hands clasped behind him, like some blond European princeling; stewards, with their canny instinct for breeding, leaped to assist him.

"Grandma!" The princeling turned into a grinning, gangling American youth who opened his arms wide.

"Well, merciful heavens!" she exclaimed and started to cry as he crushed her to him. "How tall are you anyway—six four?"

"Two. Grandma, the most extraordinary thing happened yesterday. I was accepted to enter Harvard in September."

"Harvard?" She was elated. "Not Montclair State Teachers? Congratulations, Ted. How's your mama? Want to see the first-class dining room on this tub? It's monstrous. A hundred yards long, three stories high, looks to be lined with diamonds."

After they boarded the boat train for Paris, Ted said, "Mother is awful sorry, Grandma, but she suddenly had to go to Berlin on business. She's been looking forward so to your visit. She'll try to be back day after tomorrow. You and I can do some sightseeing if you like." Suddenly he asked about his father. "How did he take Reggie's disappearance?"

"Hard at first, but now he never mentions her. Do you ever hear from him?"

"Every time I write him. Which isn't very often. He

never *says* anything in his letters. He always asks about Mother, but has written her only once after she sent condolences about Reggie."

Occasionally Cordelia enjoyed a fantasy in which Steve and Ann were reunited and Ted found the father he had lacked, then always concluded, *Beware of your fantasies lest you enact them.*

Two days later, when Ann returned from Germany to her large, comfortable apartment in Neuilly looking very tired, she greeted Cordelia warmly. While still attractive, she had aged considerably and showed a purposefulness unlike her former easy-going manner.

A friend of hers, Dr. Karl Rathenau, came to dinner that evening. Ann had explained that he was a physician, a Jewish refugee from Nazi Germany who was practicing medicine in Paris. He turned out to be a pleasant man nearing sixty who spoke excellent English. After he arrived, however, he and Ann talked in rapid French at such length that Ted finally broke in:

"Mother, stop being cryptic in front of Grandma. She'd be interested to know what you're doing. Name somebody you can trust more."

"I'm sorry," Ann said to Cordelia. "Secrecy is becoming habitual with me. Tell me, do you hear much in the States about Nazi persecution of the Jews?"

"It depends on what publication you read. And there's a lot of talk about how hard it is to separate truth from propaganda."

"Even the worst you hear is true," Ann said. "The Nazis intend to exterminate the Jews of Europe and many other people with them. Just night before last I took a deposition from a double agent who inspected the Dachau camp in his capacity as a Nazi functionary. He was so revolted by what he experienced there he wonders if he'll ever sleep again. I'll read you some of it tomorrow, I'm too weary tonight."

Karl explained that Ann was one of a group of dedicated humanitarians in several countries who for a long time had been helping as many as possible escape from Germany. "She saved my life. But my wife was arrested and sent to a camp. So was our daughter—and her husband—and my wife's parents. You've heard of *Kristallnacht*—Crystal Night—last November?"

"Not that I remember."

"The world should be better informed about these things. Early in November a Jewish patient of mine—a French citizen living in Germany—said I must get out of the country. But where could my wife and I go? We had no money in any country, and you cannot get a visa to anyplace unless you have money there that guarantees you won't become—" He couldn't think of the English word. "My friend said, 'Let me take care of that.' He said, 'Any day or night soon someone will call you about your French lessons. Do as that person says.'

"My practice in Berlin had become nothing. My wife and I were living in a furnished room. Our daughter had gone with my wife's parents. At ten o'clock in the evening last November eleventh the phone rang and a woman said, 'Come immediately for your French lesson.' The woman was Ann. My wife and I went to the apartment she told us about. We were barely inside when Crystal Night began. It was awful. Crazy, howling mobs of Nazis breaking the windows of all the houses and stores owned by Jews. I heard later the Gestapo went to arrest me at our furnished room, but we were gone. That night they arrested most of the Jewish men in Berlin who still were free. Ann moved us around every night to stay with friends of hers in different embassies.

"By day we'd sit in parks so as not to be found in any house. The Gestapo was running in and out of every building in Berlin, it seemed, hunting Jews and arresting them. Ann thought of a clever idea when they began to catch Jews in the streets and parks. She had us hide in police stations. We would sit in a police station reading a book, as if we had an appointment and were waiting. Sometimes we'd move from office to office. It is not a part of the German mentality to think that a person they want to arrest would be sitting in a police station. One day when we got very hungry, my wife slipped out to buy us a loaf of bread. She never came back. She was arrested and sent away."

Karl struggled for self-control, but could not continue.

Ted said, "Mother and Karl and many others are still trying to get people out of Germany."

"You've done your part," Cordelia told Ann. "This is very dangerous. You should stop now, my dear. Come home."

"Not yet," Ann said. "This trip into Germany was my last. They know now what I'm doing and are looking for me. But there are many other helpful things I can do to aid the cause. You see, Mother, for the first time in my life I feel I'm doing something important. For me to do anything else now would seem—unimportant."

Cordelia pondered how unimportant her own life seemed in this turbulent world. She felt she was just a little old lady who had scrabbled for a living nearly all her days on Murray Hill. What was noble about that?

Next day Ann read Cordelia parts of the deposition she had taken from the anonymous German who was working secretly for their humanitarian cause.

"My assignment took me to the Dachau Camp. SS men and women guarding prisoners frequently beat them with cudgels and set dogs upon them. Under my very eyes I saw a woman prisoner torn to bits by dogs while guards laughed—and I was powerless to help her. . . .

"In that month of April there were eight thousand prisoners at Dachau and only one tap of water, which

was unfit for drinking. Prisoners were drinking from
filthy puddles and trying to wash their clothes in them.
I don't know what they do in summer. Even in spring
many were dying of thirst because their ration is only
half a cup of herbal tea twice a day. . . .

"A chief cause of epidemic and death is the fact that
prisoners are given food in large red mess tins which
are merely rinsed in cold water after each meal. As
nearly all are ill and lack the strength to get to the filthy
latrine trench during the night, they use these cans for
defecating. Next morning the cans are collected and
taken to a trash heap where they are rinsed in cold water and used for food again. . . .

"The dead or those near death from any cause anywhere in the camp are stacked in the yard of Block
Twenty-five. You see stacks of corpses there, and from
time to time a hand or head stirs among the bodies,
trying to free itself. In the yeard are rats as big as cats
running around and gnawing the corpses and attacking
the dying who lack the strength to fight them off. . . ."

It was a beautiful June morning in Neuilly, with sunlight shafting through courtyard plane trees onto a spar-
kling little fountain while Ann read to Cordelia from
her shorthand notes. That afternoon Ted was taking
Cordelia to the Louvre to see a special showing of
Rembrandt's work and that evening they were going
to the Follies. Yet suddenly, considering the terrible
events happening in Europe, it seemed criminal for a
tourist to enjoy oneself there.

Ann was certain Hitler would invade Poland that
summer and Britain would honor its promise to aid the
Poles, thus starting a general European war. Cordelia
had not been in Paris a week when Ann suggested that
she make ship reservations home for Ted and herself.

"But not for you?"

"I'm not going back to the States yet. I have important things to do, even after war starts. That monstrous

Nazi movement must be destroyed. Whatever little bit I can do to help makes my life worthwhile. There's nothing back in the States for me. Paris—Europe—has become like home."

"And when war comes?" asked Cordelia.

"I have the protection of the French Army, the strongest army in the world."

"Who was it said don't put your faith in strong armies?"

"I don't know. Probably somebody like Napoleon."

Ann made Cordelia believe in her cause. There was no telling how much of her personal fortune Ann had spent in it; among other expenditures, she had set up bank accounts for numerous German Jews in the United States, England, France, and Portugal so that they could obtain visas. Since that method of escape was scarcely possible any longer, Ann and her associates felt that their next chief effort should be toward general anti-Nazi propaganda.

Cordelia welcomed the idea of Lovejoy's publishing a book on Nazi criminality against the Jews. Ann had the writer for her: Charles Cook, a correspondent for an American news syndicate who had been banished from Germany a few months previously and now was based in Paris. Cook, rabidly opposed to the Nazis, felt that his syndicate had been cutting and underplaying his stories about conditions in Germany and was eager to write a book based on his own knowledge and the wealth of material Ann's group could supply him. In person he was an unprepossessing little man. Never having had much money, Charlie Cook was delighted with the five-thousand-dollar advance Cordelia offered; she, having little experience with fast-writing newsmen, was astonished by his promise to deliver an eighty-thousand-word manuscript in two months.

Ann accompanied Cordelia and Ted to Le Havre when they sailed June twenty-eighth on the *Ile de*

France. On the way Cordelia extracted a promise from her:

"If it's at all possible, I'll see you both on Murray Hill at Christmas."

As the ship put out, they waved to her till she became indistinguishable. Ted, fighting tears, said, "Mother should have been a lawyer. She's always using qualifying clauses like 'if it's at all possible.'"

Steve was at North River Pier Eighty-eight to meet them. He scarcely could believe the tall stranger was his son. Cordelia, for her part, scarcely could believe that Steve had come to greet them.

"Wonderful!" Steve kept wringing Ted's hand. "Mama said in her postcard you've been accepted at Harvard. Son, that's the greatest."

"Thank you." What did you call a father who was a stranger? Ted made a swift decision: "Pa."

It sounded right to them both.

"Listen"—Steve rested a hand on Ted's shoulder—"take a lesson from the lark, meaning me, Pa the Lark, and don't foul it up. College, I mean. Are you still as good at Latin as Ann used to say? How is she?"

He had driven his old Packard to the pier to pick them up. No one remembered precisely what was said, but somewhere between Eleventh Avenue and Cordelia's house everyone agreed it would be a good idea if Ted stayed with his father on Long Island for a while. After they unloaded Cordelia's luggage and said hello to Mary, Nick, and the Joneses, Steve and Ted drove on to Hasty's. As they were crossing Queensboro Bridge, Steve asked, "What did you miss most about America?"

"Talking American. I don't mean English, I mean American."

"That's funny." Steve glanced at him. "It's what I missed most when I did that stupid thing and quit Yale and—well, as the old army sergeants used to tell recruits, 'Don't do as I do, just do as I say.' When you get to Cambridge—Well, listen to Pa the Lark."

Much to the disgust of Dan Zinke ("You don't get mechanical talent like that anymore"), Steve took the summer off from the garage to be with his son. What resulted, really, was a fast friendship such as neither Steve nor Ted had known before and never would again.

Steve, concerned that Ted did not know how to drive, quickly taught him and showed him how to solve the basic mysteries of an auto motor. He went on to teach him how to use tools, tie knots, and a score of other practical things. They talked incessantly, never in attempted profundities, but with a desire to sort out information that might someday become profoundly valuable to each. Thus Steve talking:

"One of the most valuable things I learned in the Foreign Legion is how to be a clever malingerer. This is important for a man to know in a time of wars, like our times. It can save your life. For instance, put a pinhead bit of castor-oil bean in your eye and bandage the eye overnight. Result: acute conjunctivitis and one month in the hospital. Smoke tobacco impregnated with quinine and you'll develop a fever. If you cut yourself with a penknife and put a little tartar from your teeth in the wound, you'll develop an abscess good for one month in the hospital. Thread a hair on a needle and draw it through your flesh and you'll develop an abscess good for *two* months in the hospital. See, it's important to study cowardice. I mean, there are so many people these days looking for young men to die as heroes in their causes that sometimes the only way to survive is be a coward."

Naturally Steve could teach Ted much more than Ted could him. But Ted did tell him what terrible things were happening in Europe and what Ann was trying to do about them. Steve never tired of hearing about her and constantly thought up new questions to ask. Ted came to believe that his father still loved his mother, but Steve never said so, he never was confessional in the course of their relationship. The nearest he came was one morning when they were going fishing before daylight and stopped in a diner for coffee; a group of old fishing hands suddenly fell silent and stared at them. After they left the diner Steve said, "Those old crows have heard I'm a dead celebrity, the failed scion of a wealthy—ho, ho—New York publishing family. Ever notice how fond crows are of picking at dead cats?"

On September third, as they were about to leave on a clamming expedition to the south shore, the radio brought the lugubrious voice of British Prime Minister Neville Chamberlain announcing that a state of war existed with Germany. They went clamming anyway. But all day they were unusually silent and uncommunicative. When they returned home, they learned by radio that France had joined the war.

Steve finally spoke: "I want Ann—your mother—to come home."

"So do I," Ted said, "but just how do you manage that?"

"Think I'll phone her and tell her to come home."

Ted smiled. "Oh, sure, Pa, anything you say." He told him the Paris number.

Steve went to the phone and said to the operator, "This is Harry Hopkins calling from the home of Steven Lovejoy. I want you to get me a clear wire to the White House. My service identity number is three-BK. Got that? Three-Baker-King. While you're clearing that, put through a call to Paris, France, for me. The number is . . ." He gave Ann's. "Well, young lady, then put on your supervisor." He stared gravely at Ted. "Hello, supervisor, this is Harry Hopkins—I'm glad you recognize my voice. On the Paris call, give the chief overseas operator my White House identity number, three-Baker-King. Thank you, young lady, you're most helpful. Let me make a note of your name, we can use intelligence like yours in Washington these days."

He hung up, and he and Ted did not speak for lengthy minutes. At last the phone rang, and Ann came on: "Steve! The operator said Harry *Hopkins* was calling."

"Well—honey, one last favor, please, for old Stevey. As soon as the banks open in the morning, collect plenty of dough and take the express to Madrid. Then board the midnight to Lisbon. There I want you to get on any neutral ship sailing to the Western Hemisphere. Please Ann."

"Oh, Steve, I don't know what to say. I don't know how to explain to you what I have to do and—"

"Please listen to me, honey." Tears started to his eyes. "I love you and miss you and want you to come home just as fast as you can so I can spend the rest of my life trying to make up to you—here, talk to Ted."

Ann sounded stunned, which was how Ted felt. Their conversation was brief and incoherent before an overseas operator broke in to say that their time was up. Ted said good-bye and stared at his father, who sat in a big wingback chair looking crumpled and shrunken.

After a while the phone rang again. "Don't answer it," Steve said. "There's nobody at the White House I want to talk to."

Ted had to report in Cambridge on September eighteenth, and Steve decided to drive him there after they said good-bye to Cordelia and the uncles, aunts, and cousins on Murray Hill.

As they made their way toward the Merritt Parkway late in the afternoon, Steve said, "So many hellos and good-byes. In the bad old days when I was in the book business a writer said to me one time he was tired of these novels where it's all how-d'you-do and farewell. But I've decided those are the most realistic stories after all. Life is nothing much more than hello, hello—laugh a little, cry a little—good-bye, good-bye."

When Ted left his father in Cambridge, he felt as bereft as when he'd said good-bye to his mother at Le Havre. He wrote Steve once but received no reply. Instead of going to New York for the brief Thanksgiving holiday, he went skiing in New Hampshire with a couple of classmates. Returning to Cambridge, he found a letter addressed in his father's hand and postmarked Lisbon early in the month.

Sur les Dômes, France
10/29/39

Dear Ted old buddy,

As I told you, do what I say, not what I do. With a leer at sanity, wish to report have once more joined Foreign Legion. What other mil. org. in this crazy world would accept a 45-yr-old recruit? If you reach 45 and are turned down by a nursing home, remember the Legion will welcome you.

Sailed to Lisbon on Panamanian ship. Didn't know what would find here in France. Held pleasant negotiations with your mother in Neuilly. A fine woman, but stubborn. *She will not come home!* So me for military service close to her as possible. Find that the French Army was designed by Victor Herbert. If, as hoped, Germany Army designed by Rudolf Friml, war will have a happy ending, all marching off arm in arm to music of *Babes in Toyland*. This isn't just the Phony War, as the American correspondents call it; is one big fantasy.

However, since am tired of being American auto mechanic and yearn for the Big Picture once more, nowhere for me to go but *la Légion Etrangère*. The French won't let the true old professional Legion out of Algiers and into this fantasy on the Western Front because it's so honeycombed with Nazis. But the French always have tried to accommodate nuts like me who for some insane reason wish to participate in their wars.

So here I am in a newly formed Legion in continental France composed of a few French draftees and many maladjusted foreigners, including a large contingent of Polish Jews who seem to speak no French and arrived here under circumstances that mystify everybody. Anyhow we are all defying language barriers and studying the military arts in high spirits, possibly thanks to a lack of commissioned officers. You can imagine the desperate military plight of this nation when you hear that an old relic like me, who can't remember very well the small French I ever did know, is a sergeant and practically running our motor company. We appear to be in a cranny of the Maginot Line, not too snug in our tents in the fall rains and must report the lice are back, just as a quarter century ago and all the centuries before that. A comrade who has shrewdly decided to desert will run this out to Portugal for me.

Now you be a good boy, just like you always have been. Study hard and mind your own business. War is like cancer; has a way of becoming generalized, then terminal. You stay out of this one, please. If the old men close in on you and try to make you become a hero, I forgot to tell you one sure way to fox em. Attach a dried-out wine cork to the heel of your left foot (better not to do it to the right foot) and jump up and down on it hard a few times. Very painful, they say, but it does things to the foot bones that make you unable

to march. So no military service. Can't be as painful as being killed.

One other favor, buddy. Would you please try
to explain all this to your grandmother. She's a
great woman and I love her as much as she loves
you, but I've just run out of ways of trying to explain myself to her.

Luv,
Pa

Ted and Cordelia received occasional letters from
Steve and Ann through the winter and spring. It was
apparent that other letters had gone astray, that both
felt constrained by fear of censorship or spying, that
few of the letters Ted and Cordelia wrote ever reached
them.

"It's like trying to holler over a wall a mile high,"
Ted said.

In January, Lovejoy's published *Death Knell*, Charlie Cook's book about Nazi atrocities. To the disappointment of all, it did not sell well, falling victim to
American anti-Semitism and wide-spread reluctance to
ponder what actually was happening in Europe for fear
of becoming involved in that foreign illness.

"The book is a sort of victim of Ted's mile-high
wall," Cordelia told Izzy. "How can you breach it?"

"By going to war against the enemy," Izzy said, "and
beating them soundly. Then people will buy millions of
books about what happened. They mostly want to read
about victories."

"Please, no," Cordelia said. "I seem to have spent
my whole life at war or on the brink of it."

"There's no other way but war, Mama. You can only
beat a maniac like Hitler at his own game."

On June 5, 1940, the day Ted began his year-end
examinations at Harvard, the Germans opened their of-
fensive against the French on the Somme line. On June

fourteenth, the day he returned to Cordelia's house in New York, the Germans entered Paris and marched triumphantly down the Champs-Elysées. For days Cordelia, Penny, and Izzy ignored business at Lovejoy's while they, Ted, and the Epstein children camped within earshot of radios which reported rumors. Cordelia and Izzy employed every possible contact in an effort to find out what had become of Ann and Steve; Cordelia even importuned Eleanor Roosevelt, who had someone in the State Department put to work on the case of the missing Lovejoys. Ted was reluctant to leave for the summer-camp counselor's job he had obtained in Vermont, but Cordelia prevailed on him to go and try to take his mind off worrying.

Word finally came early in September after Ted returned from camp. The source was not the State Department, but Charlie Cook, who had survived incredible adventures during the fall of Belgium and then the fall of France. As the author of *Death Knell* and many anti-Nazi articles, he was high on the SS list of persons to be shot on sight. But with his customary luck Charlie had made his way into Spain and boarded a ship laden with repatriates which sailed from Barcelona. As soon as he reached New York, he phoned Cordelia and came to her home. He looked ten years older than he had in Paris; his voice and hands were tremulous from fatigue and tension. Ted poured him a large glass of Scotch, as if that would help him tell what he knew. But for once Charlie seemed unable to put a lead on a story.

"The only time I saw Steve was near the end of April. He was on leave from his outfit for a few days and staying with Ann at her apartment. They were very happy. You must remember that.

"Then I went up to Saint-Quentin with the French Seventh Army to do a few stories about how brilliantly the French would hold after the fall of Belgium and Holland. I'd just filed my final story on the impregnable Maginot Line when the Germans came whizzing through it. From then on it was confusion and run-run for me all the way to Barcelona.

"As I said, I didn't see Steve more than that one time for a few minutes, but I heard about him from another correspondent, Van Colby of Scripps-Howard, who caromed off some action on the Somme before going on the run with me. He was with Steve a couple of days before he linked up with me. Recognized him as Regina Faunce's husband and thought it would make a good story back home if only he had some place to file it. Personally I never wrote anything about Steve because he asked me not to; said his name was Lovejoy again, not Mr. Faunce.

"Anyhow, Steve was a member of something the Legion called Group Ninety-seven—or Crazy Group Ninety-seven. It was made up of drivers of Steve's motor transport company and some unhorsed cavalrymen and a few hardy infantrymen who liked the idea of riding instead of marching. These men were given some old armored cars so shoddy that a respectable bank wouldn't transport its money in them. They were sent to the Somme area in May with the mission of reconnaissance. Then heavy German armor came through. Van Colby was on the spot and saw it. Outgunned and out-armored, though not outmaneuvered, those guys raced their light vehicles among the German heavy tanks sort of like boys with peashooters in a herd of elephants. They were three squadrons at fist. But by next day they were little more than one.

"Van Colby hid in a church belfry and watched what happened that next day. Another column of heavy armor was coming through, and the remnants of light cars launched a suicidal attack against it. Within minutes half of the Legion vehicles were knocked out and blazing. But the survivors did not break off and withdraw. Steve was one of the survivors. They regrouped and hurled themselves at the heavies again. This time there were no survivors. After the Germans passed, Van identified Steve as one of the dead. . . .

"Ann? She was in Paris when it fell. Of course I wasn't there, but I heard what happened from— She asked me not to use her name. She was active in the same group as Ann and has gone underground in Spain.

"She—this woman—said that when the Germans entered Paris all was very quiet. No guns roaring. You could hear the droning of German tanks here and there, but the remarkable thing was the sound of horses' hoofs. Sort of a pastoral effect to the occupation. Despite the talk about German armor, they also had a lot of horse-drawn artillery, and those horses must have clopped all the way across France from the Ardennes.

"Now I quote this accurately. The woman became hysterical at first and cried, 'It's the end!' But Ann remained calm and said, 'It's only the end *here.*' They got in Ann's Peugeot and started south out of the city, then ran into noise and terror and confusion and roads blocked with traffic. It seems that every time a different political movement seizes Paris, which happens quite often, thousands of people have the notion they must escape to Tours.

"Ann and the woman had to abandon the car and try to continue on foot. When they came to a roadblock, the woman hid in a ditch, but the SS arrested Ann. Later the woman learned through the group that Ann was transported to a concentration camp in Germany in a railroad car packed with French Jews."

BOOK FOUR

31

Sara Doyle looked to be about five feet twelve and had an elegant manner that could freeze a man. Ted felt she didn't approve of him the first time he saw her at Cordelia's Christmas dinner in 1940. Of course they had exchanged remarks many times in the course of their coming and going from Cordelia's, but that Christmas was the first time Ted really *saw* her.

He was descending the stairs when she arrived from the apartment she shared with another nurse on Murray Hill. As she swung off her cape and he saw how lovely she was, she cast him a disapproving look that made him blanch. She must, he believed, be reading his lustful thoughts.

"Well, why are you both standing there?" Cordelia demanded.

"What?" asked Ted.

"The thing hanging over Sara's head, dummy, is mistletoe."

"Sorry, didn't see it." Sara moved quickly.

"Why be sorry?" asked Cordelia. "Most girls like to be caught under the mistletoe."

"Seems to me," Mary said, coming into the hall, "the children are getting taller these days."

"Maybe not," Cordelia said. "Maybe we are getting shorter."

Ted, dwelling on Sara's beauty, wondered why she seemed to be contemptuous of him. After dinner Al and his sisters rushed off to see friends, and Cordelia told Sara and him, "Get some fresh air and walk King Arthur around."

Ted thought that Sara accompanied him reluctantly—could it be because she was more than a year older? When they were outside with the big mastiff obediently at their heels, he said, "You don't have to do this, Sara. You probably have a boyfriend or something you'd like to be with."

"No, I don't have a boyfriend or *something*. Are you trying to say you have a girl friend you'd like to go see?"

"No girl friend." They walked toward the East River, which that afternoon was as bright blue as the sky and Sara's eyes: cold, cold; brrr, brrr! Apparently she was not much of a talker, for she scarcely had spoken all day; but he had been reared in the old-fashioned tradition that a boy should keep a girl chattering, possibly on the theory that a woman liked to talk. "Grandma says you enjoy nursing. What's good about it?"

"Not the work itself, which isn't very inspiring. But it gives me independence and self-respect. Do you like Harvard?"

"No."

"Why not?"

"No independence. No self-respect. They like you to be a hasty pudding of a boy they can mold into some kind of snotty little elitist."

She glanced at him with sudden interest. "Why don't you quit?"

"Because of Grandma. She's very pleased that I'm going there. She's had so much bad luck with family that I—hate to disappoint her."

Sara's glacial reserve thawed a bit. "Your grandmother is a wonderful woman. What are you going to do when she wants you to go into the publishing house?"

"Then I'll resist, if it ever comes to that. I don't want to go into publishing. I like to read books, but I'm not interested in huckstering them. I like to read the *Times*, but does that mean I should become a reporter for it? I don't even know what a publisher is. Maybe a person who isn't afraid to make mistakes—and has enough money to cover those he makes."

"What do you want to do?"

He smiled. "When I grow up? I'm not sure. I think grow things."

"*Grow* things? What sort?"

"I'm not sure. Anything from lettuce to palm trees. For years I've kept plants in my room wherever I go to school. It's fun. At first it makes some guys think I'm a fairy. Sara, what do you want to do?"

At last she smiled, too. "When I grow up? I've been thinking I'm all grown up, but maybe I'm not. Maybe what I want is to grow some more."

They came to a crumbling old bulkhead at Thirty-fifth Street on the river where the keening northeast wind made even King Arthur blink. In the declining sunlight the river was turning from blue to quicksilver. On the opposite shore a tug came racing out of Newtown Creek, which separated Brooklyn from Queens, and Sara said:

"Can't you imagine how it was back in the Revolution when New York was falling to the British and all this was the most beautiful place on earth?"

She made him *see* those British troops rowing across the river from the Brooklyn shore yonder. They walked up First Avenue to Fortieth Street, which Sara figured was about the place the British landed and the Americans panicked and ran up a rutted road through the thickets of Murray Hill. She and Ted and King Arthur followed Fortieth under the Second Avenue elevated tracks and then under the Third Avenue elevated until they came to Lexington. It was just about here, Sara calculated, that Washington galloped up with drawn sword and tried to re-form his frightened men. But they were too scared to pause and carried Washington and his horse and a couple of aides, all howling curses and beating their swords at the rabble, along the road to the place where the Public Library now stood.

"Down there"—Sara pointed south a couple of blocks—"was the Murray farm. Remember? That's the place Mrs. Murray prevailed on General Howe to pause for cakes and wine. That enabled Washington and most of the American army to escape from the trap on Manhattan."

Ted was skeptical it had happened exactly that way, but Sara believed in it so strongly that he found it pleasant to believe so, too. He intended to buy her a drink at the Biltmore to show how sophisticated he was, but somehow they ended up having hot chocolate in a Fifth Avenue Schrafft's while King Arthur sat outside and gazed reproachfully at them through the window.

She agreed to go skating with him in Central Park next afternoon when she was off duty. The skating after dark was exhilarating, and then they went to dinner. By midnight, when he took Sara home, he was totally in love.

Never having experienced the illness so violently, he did not at first understand its attendant depression, jealousy, nervousness, egomania, dyspepsia. Later in the week when Sara said she could not go to a Broadway show with him because she had a date, Ted was in despair. He stalked darkened streets, hating the nameless lecherous intern who (he believed) had scraped together movie money with the design of getting Sara to bed. Of course he did not realize that his disease was apparent to others.

In the privacy of the back den, Cordelia asked Mary with feigned casualness, "Does Sara like Ted?"

Mary spoke casually, too: "I just don't know, Cordelia. She don't discuss her beaus with me." Cordelia made a sniffing sound and pretended to read a book. "But I imagine," Mary went on after a while, "he seems awful young to her. Just another college boy." Cordelia continued to look at her book as Mary asked, "Any notion what he thinks of her?"

Cordelia shrugged. "Just another pretty girl, I guess. A young man like Ted can't have lived in France the time he did and not—well—" She turned a page, then feigned surprise at Mary's outburst.

"Well, I say!" Mary cried. "Who does that young whippersnapper think he is? If he tries to *toy* with my Sara— She spoke most respectful of him to me, but just because he's young Mr. Rich Man and Sara—"

"Oh, simmer down, Mary." Cordelia had learned what she wanted to know. "Innocent young Ted is just as respectful of Sara as she of him."

"Did you say innocent?" asked Mary.

"I said innocent."

"But suppose, Cordelia, they took a real fancy to each other? Wouldn't that gall you? You know how you're always carrying on about a woman having a college education."

"Between you and me," Cordelia said, "I think Sara Doyle would make Edward Lovejoy the best wife he'll ever find."

"Oh, Lord save us! Catholic and all?"

"Catholic and all!"

Mary burst into tears, and Cordelia wept a bit, too, in her companionable way.

Sara and Ted, however, lacked the understanding of the two dear old friends. They did not quarrel, but simply drifted in different directions on tides of misunderstanding. She thought of him as displaying an admirable independence that he could afford because he was a rich playboy: If he were poor, he might enchant her. He thought of her as the most beautiful, desirable woman he ever had met: If only she were younger and more vulnerable, he would try to sleep with her.

* * *

Ted's constant concern about his mother had taught him to live with emotional stress. Was she dead or still alive? Dead, he hoped, knowing what he did about concentration camps. The members of the family did everything in their power to learn what had become of her, but to no avail. There was no way of proving she was anything but missing, as both Reggie and Steve also were listed. Although Ted was Ann's sole heir, he could not receive benefits from her considerably diminished estate for many years to come—at least seven. It troubled him to be dependent on Cordelia for most of his education and spending money, but the result was to make him thrifty and hardworking—far from the playboy Sara imagined.

The rest of that sophomore year at Harvard he tried to forget Sara, but found, instead, that he lived with the memory of her in much the way he did of his mother's. There was a measure of fortitude, but little satisfaction, to be found in such an emotional life.

He joined the Naval Reserve in order to maintain draft-deferment status as a college undergraduate. Cordelia approved, rationalizing that if war came (as she secretly felt inevitable), he would somehow be safer in the navy than in the army. Immediately after classes ended in June 1941, he put in four weeks of active duty, then accepted Cordelia's suggestion to come back to New York and work in Lovejoy's mail room "to become familiar with the business."

His cousin Al, just turned sixteen and home from Exeter, already was at work in the mail room. They were not close. Al was bright and bossy. Dark, strong, stocky, inches shorter, he was the most competitive youth Ted ever had known. It finally came over him that Al was jealous of Ted's being Cordelia's favorite, that *he* wanted to be the president and publisher of Lovejoy's someday. Well God bless him, let him be, what a relief, Ted thought. After that, Al's aggressiveness no longer bothered him.

He saw Sara only once, when she called on Mary one Sunday afternoon. They visited cordially. She was not aloof, but somewhat removed, as if thinking not of him but of other matters. By the time he made up his mind to ask her for a date, she had taken a month's leave from work and gone to Camden to care for her ill mother. When Ted returned to college, he thought he'd forgotten her.

Like every American of mature mind at the time, he never afterward forgot what he was doing the moment he heard the news of the sneak Japanese attack on Pearl Harbor. The radio brought the news on the Sunday afternoon of December seventh while he was studying for a history test on the Thirty Years War. Cordelia, putting a phone call through to him an hour later, sounded querulous:

"I was just changing my typewriter ribbon when Nicky came plunging down the stairs. He's going to break his neck on those stairs someday. He'd heard it on his radio, and I turned on mine. Ted, Nicky has turned awfully senile since you were home. Now he's very indignant at the Japanese. Plans to enlist in the cavalry tomorrow. Senile? Last night when I was carving roast ham for dinner, do you know what he said? 'I wonder how a roasted baby would taste.' That's what he said! Mary had to leave the table. Anyway, thought I'd report how a lot of senile men will stupidly try to enlist tomorrow. . . ."

Ted, while understanding her dread of losing yet another Lovejoy male to war, doubted that she understood how deeply he felt. He hated German Nazis with the passion ascribed to Appalachian mountaineers in blood feuds; he wanted personal vengeance, not just for what they had done to weaker peoples, but for their destruction of his mother and father. The Japanese, ever imitative of anything developed elsewhere that would work to their advantage, did not rouse much hatred in him. He had been waiting to get at the Germans personally, and the Japanese merely offered him the opportunity to do so. He tried to be calm. He completed his mid-year examinations, then quickly obtained transfer from the reserve to active duty. Given two weeks leave before reporting to Headquarters of the First Naval District in Boston, Ted went to New York in order to explain to his grandmother.

He came out of Grand Central Terminal carrying his B-4 bag and wearing uniform and greatcoat with its lonely ensign's stripe. It was dark, and wet January snow was falling as he waited to cross Forty-second Street. How could he hope to last out a war when he was such a coward about the simple act of telling his grandmother what he had done?

"Ted!" Sara stood beside him while a crowd of commuters broke around them. "The uniform! Does your grandmother know?"

"I'm on my way to tell her I went active, and I'm scared to death. Maybe a Scotch would help. Will you join me?"

"Love to." She had an armload of packages. "Yesterday was payday and today is mine off. So I'm sort of—well, a sailor on shore leave." Finding a bar on Lexington less crowded than others they had passed, they sat in a booth. "What happens to you now?" Her eyes were wide, alarmed.

"I have a few days off, then report to Boston. And then I guess I'll be sent to school somewhere."

"Honey, you sure you want to do this?"

Suddenly he wanted to reach out and stroke the face of this lovely woman who had called him what his mother and father used to call each other in the good years. But he merely gazed at her thoughtfully and said, "Yes, it's what I want to do, Sara."

She offered him a Camel. He did not smoke, but decided to start. He lighted their cigarettes, and she said, "Funny thing running into you this way, Ted. I've been debating whether to apply to the Navy—nursing. Seeing you makes up my mind. I will tomorrow."

"Don't, Sara. People need you where you are."

"Ho, ho, ho!" she said. "Do you know how silly that sounds? Don't you think I can feel as—patriotic as you? What do you want to do in the navy?"

"Be a flier, but I can't pass the eye exam. Can't line up the things the way you're supposed to in order to land. So I think I'll try for submarine school."

She put down her glass. "I like brave men. It's a romantic Celtic weakness. One time last fall I heard your grandmother and mine saying how you never seemed scared of anything. And I thought, 'Dear God, and the guy never asked me for another date!' But I'll tell you something about you and submarines. You're just plain crazy! Why would you even *think* of going to the bottom of the ocean to die?"

"Because I hear submarine officers are all going into Atlantic duty now. And that's where I want to be. I want to fight the goddamn Germans. I think fighting the Japanese is a waste of time till we've beaten the Nazis. In submarine service you're more likely really to fight instead of just sitting around."

Her expression was totally changed as she gazed at him; he didn't know how to describe it. "If you're bound to do it, Admiral, a word of advice. Break it slowly to your grandma. Tell her you're slated for a public-relations job in Boston."

"Good idea. Hadn't thought of it. The truth, but not the whole truth. Do they teach you that in nursing?"

"They teach you in life. A little hypocrisy helps—

unfortunately. For instance, I'm a bad Catholic, but Grandma thinks I'm a good one. Should I tell her I'm not?"

"Let's have another drink while we ponder that question."

He was not a practiced drinker, and neither was she. But she had the good sense to know she was not. It was she who said they must have something to eat and took them to a restaurant she knew near Thirty-fourth and Lexington which was called The Last Musketeer and was a bit larger than a phone booth. There, on the strength of his uniform and regardless of the talk of meat rationing, he was able to purchase them both a good steak for a price.

She had found another history of old Manhattan in the Public Library and was excited about it. "Ted, you want to know something fascinating? When Peter Cooper took apart his house—it was put together with pegs in the old Dutch style—and moved it to what's now Fourth Avenue and Twenty-eighth Street, there was a *clear, babbling stream* flowed near the house down to the East River."

He agreed that was interesting and inquired the year.

"It was eighteen thirty-eight. But you know something else absolutely fascinating? The stream flowed into the river near *the old Horatio Gates mansion.* And do you know where *that* was? *The present site of the Bellevue Hospital*—approximately. Isn't that wonderful?"

"Remarkable," he agreed. "But Horatio Gates—I'm trying to place him."

"You don't remember *him*?" She was amazed. "The hero of Saratoga, dummy. But then he fouled up the Battle of Camden. Remember? That's Camden, South Carolina, not New Jersey. After I read about it in this book, I checked on Gates in the Britannica. He didn't die till eighteen six!"

"Interesting." But more interesting, he thought, was that close to Sara in this quiet corner of the restaurant he could see completely through her blue eyes and find wonderful things hidden behind them.

"Something I've wanted to tell you," he said, "you smell like oranges."

She weighed the thought and seemed to find it not unpleasant.

"The point being"—he grinned at his devastating wit—"I'm very fond of orange juice."

"Maybe you should have some instead of that brandy."

Suddenly, incredibly, a clock behind the bar cuckooed midnight. He absolutely refused to believe it. But she absolutely refused to linger longer because she had to go on duty at eight o'clock in the morning.

"I'll see you home." His legs felt as wobbly as an old man's when he hauled himself to his feet. She wanted to see *him* home. "Over the hill to Grandmother's house we go? Never, Sara, on my honor as officer and gen'leman." Outside, the night air was not bracing. Then she remembered his B-4 bag and went back and got it for him. But the most confusing thing of all was that she and her roommate had moved into a basement apartment on East Thirty-fifth. When he brought her safely to the door, he took off his cap and leaned forward to kiss her a passionate good night. But he leaned too far and would have tipped over if she had not caught him. Then he leaned too far the other way and did tip over.

After one of those blessed lapses that enable humans to survive outrageous blows, he awakened on the couch in Sara's living room, clothed except for his jacket, which was hung neatly over the back of a chair. It was almost ten o'clock in the morning. When finally able to read the note Sara had written and placed under a Bromo Seltzer bottle, he decided she was the most thoughtful woman who ever had lived. Her roommate,

Eve Swan, was away on vacation, she wrote, then explained the contents of the refrigerator and an eccentricity of the shower, thanked him for a delightful evening, and assured him he would soon feel fit to face his grandmother.

With the aid of bromos he finally was able to shower, shave, dress, and fry a couple of eggs. The apartment fascinated him because it described so much about its tenant Sara: clean, orderly, comfortable, with many books, mainly concerned with American history, and numerous photos, mostly of Doyles, besides one grand old snapshot of Mary and Tim on the boardwalk at Asbury Park. (The photos of strangers obviously were Eve Swan's.) In early afternoon he went out to buy groceries, avoiding Mr. Columunicci's butcher shop on Third Avenue where he'd be recognized, and walked away down Third to buy baby lamb chops, a bottle of Châteauneuf-du-pape of a good vintage year, new potatoes, fresh asparagus, oranges and strawberries imported from Florida, besides French bread, pâté, a bouquet of chrysanthemums, and numerous other things.

Laden with bags, he was making his way across Thirty-fourth Street when he saw Washington Jones coming straight at him. Just in time, he believed, he raised his packages and camouflaged his face.

But Washington saw him and stopped himself from exclaiming, "Mr. Ted!" when he realized Ted did not want to be recognized. As Washington explained to Dolley when he returned home, "Couldn't help myself, just turned round and followed him. Guess where he went." "To Miss Sara's on Thirty-fourth?" "That's right." "Isn't it grand, they must have got secretly married." "Who said anything about marrying? It's his uniform stops me." "What uniform? . . ."

Their conversation, exchanged in whispers in the kitchen, reached Mary, who sometimes could not hear people shouting but could catch inaudible whispering three rooms distant. She swept into the kitchen, demanding, "What are you whispering about?" and frightened them speechless.

Nick, who had been playing with his stamp collection at the dining-room table, said, "I know what they said, but I'm keeping their confidence." This infuriated Mary, who reported to Cordelia when she came home that something was terribly wrong, she didn't know what, though Nick did.

Cordelia wasn't interested. She was concerned about a letter which had arrived in the mail addressed to Ensign Edward R. Lovejoy. Why Ensign? Did they make those ROTC boys ensigns so quickly? She held the envelope up to the light, but didn't quite dare to open it.

When Sara came home about four-thirty and found Ted there and saw what he had done, she started to cry. At first it was rather frightening: this tall, strong woman wearing nurse's white who never displayed emotion, scarcely a smile, standing there and weeping as at sight of a corpse.

"Don't tell me," he said, "you have a date. Will I have to eat all this myself?"

For some reason she wept harder. He had a notion of soothing her with a peck on the cheek, but somehow her hand got in the way, and he found himself nibbling at her fingertips, which tasted of orange and were delicious.

"Stop that!" she exclaimed and stopped crying. "That's the sexiest damn thing ever happened to me." Lifting his hand to her lips, she nibbled at his fingertips. "See what I mean?" He did see, but when he tried to kiss her lips, she ducked round him and went into the bedroom and shut the door.

"What did your grandmother say?" she asked through the closed door.

"Haven't seen her yet." Never having felt so excited, he tried to play cool. "Too busy being a housewife to-day."

"The chrysanthemums! I saw them. Edward—I'm going to start calling you Edward if you don't mind—you *arranged* them!" After a while she came out wearing skirt and sweater and examined his preparations in the little kitchenette. "Lord, oh, Lordy, as Evey would say, Edward, you're a better cook than I."

"No, I'm not. All I know to cook is here—except soufflés."

"Except soufflés!"

The phone rang, and he asked must she answer it. "Yes, because I'm positive it's Grandma and she'll ring it off the hook until I do." Sara sat down and listened patiently while he prowled about restlessly trying to contain his strange excitement. When he realized she was watching him, their gazes locked and did not part until she hung up.

"Dark days at the manor house," she said. "Madame your grandmother has a letter addressed to *Ensign* Lovejoy on Thirty-seventh Street and is deeply puzzled. She called Cambridge, but some dear friend of yours reports you're skiing in New Hampshire."

"Good old Mac!"

"And Madame my grandmother wants to know if *I* have heard from you. She mentions secrecy among the Joneses, insanity in Uncle Nick. But why should she ask if *I* have heard from you?"

"Beats me. Today I saw Washington, but he didn't see me."

She touched fingers to her forehead. "You saw *him*, but he didn't see *you*? Edward, could it be more in the national interest if you started teaching at cooks'-and-bakers' school and forgot about going to submarine school?"

"I trust Washington. He wouldn't squeal under torture."

"I know, but your grandmother has supernatural powers of gathering information."

"Do you want me to go right now and tell her?"

Sara stared at him. "My dear young friend, if you walk out that door now, it's locked to you forever. I mean—my God—I've went and captured myself a cook, a man who does *floral arrangements* and has dinner ready when I come home from a hard day at the office. I should let him go? Does that wine need chilling?"

"It's not the kind you chill."

She started to laugh. "Good old Sara Doyle. Can you ever take the shanties out of the Doyles after you take the Doyles out of the shanties? Honey, that's the best thing anybody ever said to me. 'It's not the kind you chill.' I'm going to engrave it on the wall there. You just proved I don't appreciate you rightly. Let's have a drink of warm wine."

She came to help him find the corkscrew. They touched, and it was like an explosion. Their lips opened hungrily to each other, their arms wound tightly as if to still the trembling of their bodies.

They undressed swiftly. If they were clumsy in their frenetic longing, their revelations were tender. Her mouth and hands, like his, expressed insatiable desire; her coital cries were like a bird's seeking sustenance. After the knocking of her heart against his began to slow somewhat, she spoke:

"I love you, Edward. Always will."

Five days passed, and then they rehearsed how he would tell Cordelia. First Sara phoned Mary and arranged to be invited to dinner; next he called Cordelia, pretending to have got off a train in New Haven to tell her he was on the way.

When he came into the house, Sara already was there. One glance at his uniform, and Cordelia's eyes filled with tears. Kissing her, he said, "It's all right, Grandma, I've got a nice soft job in public relations."

"Yeah, I'll bet," she said.

"Isn't that so?" he asked Sara. And then he forgot and added, "Honey."

Sara grimaced at his lapse, then had one of her own. "It's so, Cordelia. Edward has a public-relations job."

Cordelia dropped abruptly into a chair and stared with amazement from one to the other: "Honey? *Edward*?" Mary made honking sounds while Nick complained that the naval uniform wasn't what it used to be: too plain these days.

"Never mind the navy thing," Cordelia said. "What's this calling him *Edward*? Mind you, I like it. It's what I always called my—" She blinked hard, trying not to sound maudlin. "I guess it's that I wish I'd thought and called this darling boy Edward instead of Ted all these years."

Ted, seeing that his and Sara's act had fallen apart, said, "Grandma—Mary—Uncle Nick. Washington, come in here and bring Dolley. I have an announcement to make. Now hear this, all hands! Sara and I are engaged to be married just as soon as possible."

Sara gave him a stunned look. In all their loving, this was his first mention of marriage.

32

Edward Renshaw Lovejoy and Sara Agnes Doyle were joined in civil marriage at Cordelia's house on February 2, 1942. All the Epsteins attended, except for Al, who was away at school. So did all the Doyles, except Sara's eldest brother, John, who had been drafted four months before Pearl Harbor and now was in Iceland. A bevy of Sara's nurse friends, including Evey, were there. Evey, an enthusiastic photographer, took pictures of the event that survive to the present.

There was a good mob scene, as Cordelia characterized it, which Evey took while standing on a chair in the living room and shouting at everybody to go right on talking and drinking champagne, as if she weren't there at all. In that photo Mary is waving an arm to make some point: Cordelia said she was explaining that it would take a few weeks to make Ted fit for the proper Roman Catholic ceremony. Away off in the left corner of the picture the gray little man eating a piece of cake is Dr. Prettyman, who claimed never to attend social functions. One of Evey's best shots, taken from the bottom of the front steps, is of Ted and Sara stepping toward the limousine while the Epstein girls shower them with rice. Ted looks incredibly young and uncertain; Sara, holding him by a hand, radiates serenity and self-confidence. Ted, when he saw a print, said that one had to be entitled "Tarzan Takes a Mate."

They disappeared from the world for three days. (Actually they stayed at Hasty's.) Then Ted reported to Headquarters, First Naval District, and Sara went back to work. Her ardor for a naval career of her own dimmed after she realized that it would prevent her being with Ted while he was in the States. Within a couple of weeks he was sent to the submarine base at New London, Connecticut, and after another month qualified for underseas duty.

By that time Dr. Prettyman had confirmed Sara's belief that she was pregnant. (Cordelia had insisted she go to him.) "It will be easy for you, Mrs. Lovejoy," Dr. Prettyman said. "You seem well adapted to childbearing, like Mrs. Lovejoy—the first Mrs. Lovejoy—the very first Mrs. Lovejoy."

Sara went to New London, where she found a civilian nursing job and the Navy helped Ted find a one-room walk-up over a drugstore for them. He was promoted to lieutenant, j.g., and spent increasing amounts of time at sea until Cordelia said she'd never heard of a public-relations officer spending so much time away from a desk. By then she had become deeply interested in the prospect of being a great-grandmother, and, as she told Penny:

"I'm resigned to my fate that all Lovejoy males are suicidal. Besides, I'm sort of proud that Edward has the guts to want to be a submarine officer."

"For my part," Penny said, "I wish Izzy would act his age and stop trying to show guts."

Despite being fifty years old and thirty-five pounds overweight, Izzy kept applying for a commission in various branches of the armed forces. Every time he flunked a physical he'd go to Dr. Prettyman to find out, he said, what was *really* wrong with him. Dr. Prettyman's response always was the same.

"Please stop talking for just a few seconds, Mr. Epstein, so I can listen to your heart." Then he'd say: "It's just what I told you the last time. Your blood pressure is high and you're overweight. The medicine I prescribed for the pressure is no good because of the side effects on the kidneys. So that puts it up to you. If you would stop using salt and stop smoking and drinking and lose thirty-five pounds and take proper exercise and not get excited over anything, then—and only then, Mr. Epstein—will you be fit to give your life for your country."

Izzy always replied: "If I do all those things, Dr. Prettyman, the sacrifice won't be necessary because I'll already be dead."

Under Izzy's direction Lovejoy's was prospering again. Having foreseen paper shortages and rationing, he had stockpiled ahead; nevertheless, publication lists had to be cut back as the war progressed. Izzy was one of the first publishers to see importance in cheaply printed paperback books for distribution to the armed forces. There was little profit in it for the company, of course, but there was satisfaction in contributing to the war effort and encouraging young people to read books. A shortage of men editors posed problems for all publishers in those years; there simply were not enough experienced women available. ("The industry is paying the price of centuries of rule by men," Izzy pontificated in an interview.)

Penny, deciding that her daughters needed a full-time mother, had quit her editorial job in 1941. She declined to return to the office full-time a year later when Phil Federicci, who had been doing an excellent job as editor-in-chief, was seized by patriotism and became an Army intelligence officer. Cordelia no longer went to the office regularly, but, like Penny, continued to read manuscripts at home.

"Our judgments are not out of date," Cordelia said.

"Not yet, Mama," Penny replied. "But maybe soon. Just the other day I found myself having kind thoughts about Republican Senator Taft. *Me* sympathetic to a Republican?"

"I often get sentimental about Republicans," Cordelia said. "Last week, while reading Eleanor's newspaper column, I realized I was suddenly irritated with the Roosevelts. I laughed out loud to remember Alice Longworth's remark that Franklin is two-thirds blah and one-third Eleanor."

"Mama, would you accept a novel for publication that contains explicit descriptions of oral sex?"

"Never! Lovejoy's will not publish pornography!"

Penny grimaced. "Not yet, Mama. But maybe soon."

While both still were concerned about how the company fared, they now cared more about family and friends.

One day Eunice suddenly appeared in New York and spent two weeks with Cordelia and Penny, acting as if she always had adored her sister. Eunice had grown stout and her hair was colored from a bottle, but the really miraculous thing, Cordelia thought, was that she had turned jolly.

When Cordelia asked about her husband, Eunice said, "You mean Mervin?" and started to laugh. "Mama, how could everybody else make a killing in California real estate, but Mervin lose his shirt? He really is a dear, though, always cheerful, never downhearted." She laughed some more. "Last year he had to go back to practicing dentistry so we could eat regularly. Imagine a near-sighted man seventy-one years old who hasn't practiced in twenty years!" She gave a shriek of laughter. "Right off he filled somebody's *wrong tooth*!"

In November 1942, Sara returned to New York and was delivered of a healthy eight-pound girl named Catherine. Edward could not be notified because he was absent on patrol duty under radio blackout. Somehow this squawling great-granddaughter Cathy appealed more to Cordelia than any Lovejoy or Epstein infant in memory. She found herself utterly content to sit with the child by the hour.

Cathy helped to distract Cordelia—though not Sara—from worry over Edward. Weeks passed with no word from him. Finally Sara, going to New London to inquire, learned that he was safe but had been transferred to another base. Assured that she would hear from him soon, she closed out their little apartment and returned to Cordelia's. The two had accepted the idea his boat had been sent to Britain and that he was engaged in the Battle of the Atlantic when a long distance telephone call came for Sara one evening.

It was Edward, sounding disgusted. He was in San Diego and destined to fight the war in the Pacific.

Cordelia cared for Cathy while Sara flew to California and spent the off-duty hours of three weeks with him before his fleet-class submarine went on west.

In February 1943, when Sara had at last decided to go back to nursing at the hospital, Mary fell ill with pneumonia. Sara cared for her until she died in her sleep two weeks later.

At first Cordelia was inconsolable. "It's as if two of us have died," she kept saying. But then she began to recover, and her chief consolation seemed to be in Cathy. When Sara did return to the hospital, she knew that Cathy could not be in better hands than Cordelia's during her hours of absence.

Nick died suddenly of an embolus in June of that year, but Cordelia did not grieve as she had for Mary. Though she did not remark on it to anyone, he had become a trial from which she welcomed release.

Weeks would pass when there was no word from Edward, and then a half-dozen letters would arrive all at once. Sara sometimes wondered if she could have endured his absence without the distraction of her employment at the hospital. Though his letters conveyed his love for her and Cathy, he could not explain even a bit about what he was doing.

After Nick's funeral Cordelia said to Penny, "All this dying, all these wars. I can remember when I was young how nobody died and there never were any wars."

Penny was delighted that Al had been accepted at Harvard, and Cordelia tried to take delight in it, too. But she had grown a little weary with members of her family being accepted at good colleges and then dropping out of them. Nevertheless, she tried not to show her skepticism that Al ever would graduate. She tried to pay him lots of attention and not notice that he barely concealed his boredom with her.

A day they had thought might never arrive finally came on March 17, 1945. Lieutenant Commander Edward Renshaw Lovejoy telephoned his wife from San Francisco and reported that he was flying home. Cordelia felt so faint with joy that Penny and Izzy hurried over from their house to help revive her with what Penny described as a flagon of Scotch.

Edward not only had matured into a man; it was possible to see in his gaunt countenance how he would look if he lived to be old. He had done surprising things: been exec officer on one of the first American submarines to penetrate the Inland Sea; commanded his own fleet boat in the Battle of Leyte Gulf; won the Navy Cross; and at last was relieved of combat duty and returning to New London as a training officer after four weeks leave. If he wished, he could have a career in the navy after the war.

"Would you want that?" Penny asked.

He shook his head. "Never. I want out as soon as possible."

Then did he want to join the company? Cordelia stopped herself from blurting out the question.

Little Cathy was in such awe of this stranger who was her father that she wasn't sure she wanted to go with him and her mother on a vacation trip to a Blue Ridge resort which had remained open through the vicissitudes of war.

"You two run along and have a good time," Cordelia said. "Let Cathy stay with me."

"Thank you, Grandma," Edward said, "but I want Cathy to come with us. It's way past time I got acquainted with my lovely daughter."

After the three left, Cordelia never had felt so lonely. She sought the companionship she'd used to find in Penny, but Penny had turned into a doting mother and thus could be a bore at times. All she wanted to talk about was her darling daughters and Al, who, it began to appear, would actually graduate from Harvard under the speeded-up wartime curriculum.

Sometimes Penny appeared to have lost her sense of humor. "If only Al can get his second lieutenant's commission," she said.

Cordelia laughed, and Penny asked why. "Don't you remember when you used to be a pacifist?"

"I still am, for Al," Penny said. "Got it all figured out. When he's activated, he'll need about six months of training in a camp Stateside. By that time the war will be over, and he'll be safe."

"What does he want to do after that?" Cordelia tried to sound casual.

"He wants—" Penny hesitated. "Mama, he's fascinated with marketing books and wants to go into the company. He's bright, really. You can't say anything against him—except that he's young and inexperienced. How do you feel about what he wants to do?"

"That's grand." Cordelia knew it didn't matter how she felt. Izzy and Penny, between them, controlled more than sixty percent of the stock. But it was sweet of Penny to ask her opinion, for, in fact, the Epsteins had the power to do as they pleased.

"Mama," Penny said, "you're holding back something."

"Nothing much," Cordelia said. "It's just that—after Izzy wants to quit, either to retire or concentrate on his real-estate investments, I'd be happy to see Edward directing things. It's odd—after all my complaints about military things, I wouldn't at all mind seeing somebody like him in control. A man has to make all the lightning decisions that a submarine commander must so that his crew can stay alive is not—in my opinion—a bad man to have running any sort of business operation."

Penny gazed at her. Though not hostile, she no longer was the close ally she used to be, Cordelia realized. There should be some way they could resume their closeness, yet she could not take back what she had said—and there was no more implacable enemy than a doting mother who felt that her son's ascendency was threatened.

When Edward, Sara, and Cathy came back from Virginia, Cordelia was pleased to see that they were affectionate and devoted to one another. She did not ask Edward his plans, but would have given much if he would tell her that he wanted to join Lovejoy's after he got out of the navy. They moved to New London and stayed there until he was discharged in September. Now, Cordelia hoped, Edward would say he was ready to take a job with the company.

Instead, he announced that he was going to Europe in an effort to learn what had happened to his mother and father. Sara went with him, and Cathy stayed with Cordelia. Edward and Sara returned late in November 1945. They had pretty well established that Ann had died in Auschwitz prison camp late in 1942, but they had not found a trace of Steve's grave in France.

Cordelia no longer could wait to ask him the crucial question.

"Lovejoy's?" He looked at her almost compassionately, as if Lovejoy's were some incurable disease she suffered. "My interests are a long way off. Sara, Cathy, and I are settling in Ithaca, New York, while I take some agricultural courses at Cornell. No, Grandma, I'm sorry, publishing it not for me. But Al seems to like it."

Dr. Prettyman said, "Few people have the courage to live their lives all the way to the end. They get deflected by the climate or what some acquaintance is doing, things like that, and end up losing their purpose and being miserable."

He said that while giving Cordelia her 1946 physical examination close to her seventy-sixth birthday. "Oh, you're all right," he added afterwards, rather parenthetically. "Eat less salt. Salt is delicious, but it's poison."

Cordelia meditated on what he had said as she walked home from his office. There was no question, of course, what was the end of life: death. The question was when it would occur, and it was a very good thing that no one knew the answer to that. But she did know what Dr. Prettyman meant by purpose. It was the purpose of a physician to practice medicine, the purpose of a writer to write books, the purpose of a publisher to publish them, and, when they voluntarily ceased to do such things, they were not living their lives to the end.

In the past cold winter Dr. Prettyman had taken his wife to visit his friend Dr. Naismith, who had retired to Orlando, Florida, with the notion that he might do the same himself before another winter. But Dr. Naismith was so manifestly unhappy over having stopped living and gone to Florida that Dr. and Mrs. Prettyman fled back to Murray Hill within a few days. Similar things were forever befalling people Cordelia knew.

Eleanor Roosevelt came to dinner a week later, and Cordelia told her what Dr. Prettyman had said following his Florida experience.

"I think Doctor Prettyman left out something,"

Eleanor said. "A purpose can change." She flashed a grin almost like her Uncle Teddy's. "Sometimes my purposes change a dozen times a day. Doctor Pretty-man knows one thing, medicine, and practices it expertly. But one can have dozens of different purposes and fly from one to another like a bee in clover."

At the time Eleanor was happily pursuing dozens of purposes. Following Franklin's death she had been circulating in and out of Washington and New York while visiting and lecturing in distant parts of the country. She was concerned about the fledgling United Nations Organization and the administration of Harry Truman, among many other things she discussed with Cordelia that evening.

"And your children and grandchildren?" Cordelia asked. "How are they?"

Eleanor raised her hands with mixed despair and bafflement. "Of all the purposes we aging women may undertake, I think the most frustrating are our children and grandchildren."

Cordelia smiled. "No argument from me. But I know one purpose I wish I could inspire you with. I wish you'd retire from society for a few months and devote yourself to writing your autobiography. I mean tell *everything*, Eleanor, the way you used to tell me when we lived next door to each other on Thirty-sixth Street."

Eleanor fell silent for a long time, nibbling at food on her plate. Finally she looked up at Cordelia and said, "I'd like very much to do that."

"And I'd like very much for Lovejoy's to publish it," Cordelia said.

Eleanor smiled. "So would I. Book-wise I've stayed free of binding long-range commitments."

"Then will you sign a contract with us for your autobiography—maybe a work that will require two or three volumes? Would you like an advance against royalties?"

"No advance, thanks. Advances make me nervous. I like money, but I dislike being a hostage to fortune."

"Then can we talk about a contract?"

"No, Cordelia, you and I don't need a contract yet. We're too close friends to require one. When I'm ready, I'll write that book and you will publish it."

Next day Cordelia telephoned Izzy and told him what Eleanor had said. He was elated at the thought of acquiring her autobiography for Lovejoy's.

Reflecting on her conversation with Eleanor, Cordelia decided that she was in danger of absorbing herself too much in the lives of her children and grandchildren. As Eleanor had said, it could be frustrating. Cordelia's favorites, Edward, Sara, and Cathy, were living near Ithaca where Edward was studying agriculture, Sara was pregnant, and Cathy was enrolled in kindergarten: They were beyond her reach. Eunice was far away in Los Angeles. Penny and Izzy were nearby whenever she needed them; they were friendly, but busy at all kinds of things. Al was a second lieutenant at Fort Monmouth; he had no time at all for her whenever he came to town. Isabel was a twenty-year-old student at UCLA who had embraced life in California; she cared nothing about anyone on Murray Hill. Marian was a freshman at Bennington; she found Cordelia quaint. Nora at sixteen was the most dutiful of the Epstein children; once a week she paid a call on her grandmother and they made frantic efforts to communicate.

So, on analysis, it would be a waste of her time and theirs if she tried to devote herself to her relatives to the exclusion of other things. Dr. Prettyman's friend had quit practicing medicine before he was tired of it. So many writers stopped writing because of public indifference to their work when they should continue it for their private satisfaction. And publishers?

She must be judicious and not quit before that terminal unpleasantness called death ended all purpose.

Ever since she had decided to try to run the company herself, people had been complaining that she was interfering, a know-nothing, arrogant, ruthless, capricious, stupid, bluffing, a nasty bitch. But she had run the company, and she and her family had survived and finally prospered. Well, she no longer wanted to run it, she only sought a role that would bring some satisfaction and sense of purpose now lacking in her life.

By late afternoon she had a firm idea of what she wanted to do and invited Izzy to lunch at the Algonquin next day. There she led with a martini, followed by, "Izzy, do you think I'm a hopeless old bag at age seventy-six?" After he got through explaining that she certainly was not, it was time for a second martini. Just before coffee was served, Cordelia landed a job as editor of young adult books, which would be a new line for Lovejoy's and would be produced by the juvenile department, whose editor-in-chief was Grace Stevenson. Izzy agreed that Grace, fair minded and strong willed, was just the person to keep Cordelia in line and prevent her from getting grand delusions about her functions or being otherwise obnoxious.

All went well from the start. There was a market for young adult books in public and school libraries that Lovejoy's never had tapped. Cordelia's philosophy was made clear in a 1948 interview with *Publishers Weekly*.

Q—Mrs. Lovejoy, what is a young adult book?
A—Any book that won't embarrass you with either your children or your mother. I know it's old-fashioned of me to mention embarrassment, but many people do still get embarrassed over some things.
Q—Isn't the term *young adult* confusing?
A—Indeed it is. It's absurd. I'd prefer to call them family books. But *young adult* is a term publishers have adopted, and, publishing being the

most categorical—and maybe antediluvian—business in the world, it never will be changed.

Q—After your long and distinguished career as a publisher of adult books, what made you turn to *young* adult books?

A—Young man, do you imply that I'm into my second childhood? Seriously, it's a field new to me that I find challenging. I like most young people and I like the idea of young people reading books that will stimulate them.

Q—What is your criterion for good young adult fiction?

A—First and foremost, a good story that one wants to read to the end. What is the purpose of fiction for the majority of people of any age except to entertain? In out particular area of discussion, the subject matter must be of interest to young people. Do you realize how many downright dull books are published every year under the name of fiction? Anyway, I'm not talking about what some old hand like myself thinks younger people *should* read, but what they *want* to read—what is relevant to them in their everyday living. That includes many subjects. Love, for one, without explicit sex, which is for them to discover on their own. Action, for another thing, but without the sadism and masochism that's a creeping disease in much so-called adult fiction these days. . . .

It was Penny's idea to give Cordelia a surprise party on her eightieth birthday, July 19, 1950. Attendance at family gatherings had dwindled as the years passed, but Penny was determined that everyone come to this party.

Her chief worry was that Al and his wife of less than a year might fail to appear. She did not understand why Al made little effort to conceal dislike of his grandmother. When she pointed out that Cordelia always had been kind to him and asked what really was wrong, Al answered: "Mom, it's just time she got off the field. It's time she stayed on the sidelines and let somebody else play for a change." When Penny asked what difference that made to him personally, he simply replied, "Plenty, Mom, plenty."

Al's strong prejudices in ideas and people often puzzled Penny and Izzy. "How can the son of an old radical like you turn out to be such a conservative?" Izzy asked.

"Maybe that's the trouble," Penny replied dolefully. "Be anything, but not like your old lady."

Izzy said, "I can understand him being a Republican, but I don't understand a boy his age being so far to the right he makes little Tom Dewey look like a socialist."

Al's feelings were reflected by his wife Victoria, whom he called Foxy and whom Penny, Cordelia, and Izzy privately referred to as the Vixen. She was a darkly beautiful and bad-tempered creature who looked Jewish but was pure Saxon—the daughter and granddaughter, actually, of Methodist clergymen, who, rather than instilling a love of God in her, had given her a dread of penury. When Al met Foxy, she was hating her employment as a model and looking about for a prosperous marriage.

"What I wonder about their first date," Izzy said, "is who paid the check? Or did they just sit there into the small hours trying to outfumble each other for the check and finally compromise on marriage? Probably they'd heard that two can live cheaper than one."

Although Al was only twenty-five, his stinginess and love of money already were legendary. When, as a young child, he had hoarded most of his allowance, his parents had thought it cute. As he grew older, they commended his thrift. Eventually, however, they had

found themselves trying to teach him to spend money—
an effort as difficult as training a paraplegic to walk.

To hear Izzy talk, you'd think that he didn't love his
son. He did, actually; he just found much to criticize in
him. On one trait of Al's Izzy was wholly affirmative:
He was naturally a good businessman, as shrewd as his
father or his grandfather Epstein or his Grandmother
Lovejoy. During the three years since Al had been released from the army and gone to work for Lovejoy's
he had been a learner in the sales, accounting, promotion, and production departments; in each he had
showed that he drove a hard bargain whenever he
could.

"In the fall," Izzy said that summer before Cordelia's
birthday party, "I'm going to start him in editorial, and
then he'll really begin to hum."

"Hum," Penny said dubiously. "I wish he loved literature like he does ledgers. But then I know that love of
literature has never been a requirement of a successful
publisher. And that's what we want him to be, isn't it,
Izzy?"

He nodded vaguely. "Yeah, sure, I guess so. Have
you noticed how happy Ted is—and Sara too—just
growing things in the back country?"

"Of course I've noticed. But Al has never taken the
slightest interest in even a potted philodendron, let
alone all that scientific breeding Ted is into."

Al and Victoria did come to the party, which was
held at six in the evening at the Epsteins' house. Everybody came. Eunice and Mervin took a train from Los
Angeles. Edward and Sara, bringing Cathy and little
Eric, flew in from Oregon where Edward was working
in an experimental agricultural program; they checked
into the Waldorf, so as to surprise Cordelia. Penny even
coaxed Isabel all the way from California by the tactic
of paying her round-trip expenses and those of her boyfriend. Not a member of the family was missing. Dr.

Prettyman was there, though his wife couldn't make it because she'd broken a hip. Eleanor Roosevelt was one of the first to arrive. There were members of the staff of Lovejoy's, a few neighbors, and many of Cordelia's old friends in publishing. Penny forgot no one, not even Washington and Dolley, who had to wait until Cordelia had left her house before they could scamper to the Epsteins'.

The affair took on aspects of some elaborate military maneuver, with Penny the general in command exacting complete obedience from everyone. Everybody *was* there before six o'clock, even Dr. Prettyman, who was habitually tardy. All waited tensely. What if Cordelia failed to appear? In a last moment of anxiety Penny wished she had confided in her mother that there was going to be "a little surprise." But she had simply directed her: "Mama, please be there at six sharp to have dinner with Izzy and me."

Cordelia appeared as ordered, climbing the front steps as the Epsteins' huge grandfather clock boomed six. Suddenly the dead King Arthur's son, named Lancelot and every inch and ounce the mastiff that his father had been, threatened to spoil everything. Overwhelmed by the excitement of the occasion and the silent crowd in the house, he rushed to the screen door and made blood-curdling sounds, like those of the Hound of the Baskervilles, at Cordelia.

"Penny!" she called out somewhat querulously. "Does this damn dog mean to attack me?"

Izzy sprang into the hall, shouting imprecations at Lancelot, and began to wrestle with him. Lancelot struggled free and leaped through the screen, nearly knocking Cordelia down the steps, then raced up the street with the speed of a whippet.

"Well, I never!" Cordelia exclaimed. "Izzy, aren't you running after him?"

"No!" Izzy looked in a state of shock. "Come in, come in!"

As she stepped inside, lights came on and a swelling chorus sang "Happy Birthday." She wept, she laughed, she scarcely stopped talking during five hours of drinking champagne and eating an extraordinary buffet. Al and Victoria left early, with a courteous good night and happy birthday, but nearly everyone else lingered. Eventually Lancelot returned home, entering through the hole in the screen he had made in his exit and coming apologetically to Cordelia. She forgave him, and he remained her inseparable companion for the rest of the evening.

About eight o'clock Izzy tapped a spoon on a glass and quiet finally prevailed after cries of "Speech! Speech!" For once Izzy sounded subdued and looked older than his years as he began:

"I know some good mother-in-law jokes, but I'm not going to tell them."

In the adjoining room Dr. Prettyman called out: "Louder, please, Mr. Epstein, my hearing's not what it used to be."

"Is that you, Doctor Prettyman?" answered Izzy.

"Who else?"

"Is my mother-in-law near you?"

"Where else?" called Cordelia.

"Well, Mama, when Doctor Prettyman goes to eat the chicken livers, don't let him put a drop of salt on 'em. . . . Now, come on in here, Mama, so you can hear what I have to say."

The guests had been forbidden to bring presents, but many had contributed to the single gift of the occasion. It was a large book, handsomely bound in leather and embossed with gold leaf, entitled *The Book of Cordelia Lovejoy*. On its opening page was recorded in illumined script:

> *I was born Cordelia Dorfman July 19, 1870, on
> East Forty-eighth Street in New York City.*

There followed that photograph made by the man named Clarke of ten-year-old Cordelia holding a bucket of blackberries while wearing black stockings and a scowl. (Cordelia herself had been a chief though unwitting contributor to the book, for Penny had surreptitiously rifled her old scrapbooks and albums.)

Miraculously Penny had dug up rare old photos of Colonel Bob and Edward and the wedding party and the company's old Twenty-third Street quarters with several employees hanging out the windows. (Li'l Abe, who had been brought to the party in a wheelchair, whooped with delight when he identified himself.)

There was a photo, courtesy of the Bettmann Archive, of Mrs. Stuyvesant Fish in her overstuffed Fifth Avenue mansion. Under it was inscribed:

> *When I was twenty-nine years old and feeling
> destitute, Mrs. Stuyvesant Fish said to me, "Do
> what you want to in life, but make sure you do it
> better than anyone else."*

Next came a contribution from Eleanor Roosevelt of herself, Franklin, and their children Elliott and Anna sitting on the stoop of their house with Cordelia and Eunice. The inscription read:

> *I never knew a family less likely to live in the
> White House.*

Photos and inscriptions ran on for pages.

"And the best thing about it," Izzy said, "is the large number of blank pages yet to be filled."

At some unearthly hour of the next hot summer morning the jangling of the telephone at Cordelia's bedside brought her awake. She felt confused as, dragged from an already forgotten waking dream, she had the illusion of having died and then been reborn in a different time and place. She did not recognize the voice that seemed to come from *future* time with which she must take great pains to get acquainted.

"Mama, Izzy died a few minutes ago."

Of course she was hallucinating. Izzy was still a young and vigorous man while she herself was a very old and tired woman who had lived beyond her time and must now be listening through the distortions of a dream or a stroke.

"Mama"—it could not possibly be, and yet it was Penny—"it was so sudden. Doctor Prettyman was here in five minutes. He must sleep with his clothes on. There was nothing he could do. Oh Mama—" Penny's voice broke into millions of pieces.

33

"Grandma," Cathy said, "let's go to the top of the Empire State Building."

"When?" asked Cordelia.

"Right now," Cathy said. "Come on, Aunt Penny."

"I have never," Penny said, "been to the top of the Empire State."

"Well," Cordelia said, "There's nothing like new experiences at your time of life."

It was two days after Izzy's funeral, and all of his relatives, with the exception of Penny, Cordelia, and Cathy, had resumed their usual preoccupations. Isabel had gone back to California with her boyfriend, Marian back to her retail job in Boston, Nora to counseling at a music camp. Penny did not miss her daughters—the only one she missed was Izzy. Like Cordelia when Edward had died, she found no satisfaction in her children. At Cordelia's urging, Penny had left Lancelot in the care of servants and come to stay with her for a few days.

Cathy was there when Penny arrived. Edward and Sara had brought their children to New York for Cordelia's birthday—and stayed over for Izzy's funeral—on their way to an agricultural project in Texas where they were to live in a mobile home for two months before returning to Oregon.

The day after the funeral, a few hours before they were to leave, Cathy had announced, "I want to stay here with Grandma."

Cordelia had said, "Please let her. I don't know what

good I can do her, but she can do me a lot of good right now."

Edward and Sara had agreed to let Cathy stay and take her three-year-old brother Eric with them; there was nothing appealing about keeping a seven-year-old daughter in an anchored mobile for two months while the wind and the tumbleweed blew and Edward did whatever it was that he felt he must to learn further about a new hybrid grass.

Soon after Penny arrived at Cordelia's home, both realized they were in danger of depressing each other in their mourning over Izzy. But Cathy picked them up.

"Let's walk to the Empire State," she said.

"Let's take a taxi," Penny said.

"Can't afford a taxi," Cordelia said. "Have to walk."

"Can't afford?" Cathy looked surprised. "Papa gave me plenty of money before they left. I'll pay for the taxi if you're too tired to walk."

"Who's tired?" Cordelia asked.

"Not me," Penny said.

Cathy dashed and ambled ahead of them as they walked across Murray Hill. "What a beautiful child she is," Penny said. "Wish just one of mine had been that lovely."

"Oh, stop knocking your products," Cordelia said. "All of yours are beautiful, too. When is Al going back to work?"

"He already has—yesterday."

"When are you—we—the company going to announce that he's the new—uh—"

"The board will meet next Wednesday. Mama, when are you going back to work?"

"Soon as I've defused this bomb that ticks inside me. Have you thought of trying a job there yourself for a while?"

"I'd like to, but I won't. Al wouldn't like it. He wants this to be his show."

"I get your message," Cordelia said.

"No message, Mama. You know Al."

"No, Penny, I don't know Al. And, if it wouldn't sound rude of me to say so, I'm not sure I want to."

They took an elevator to the top of the Empire State and pointed out Murray Hill to Cathy. Ignoring its non-descript flatness from such a height and gazing with fascination at the curves of the East River, Cathy said, "Murray Hill is just beautiful."

"I wish my kids were that polite," Penny said to Cordelia.

"Let's go to the Statue of Liberty," Cathy said. "I've never been there, either."

"Neither have I," Penny said. "The trouble with the Statue of Liberty is that you can't take a taxi there."

"That doesn't matter, Aunt Penny. Grandma says we can't afford taxis anyway."

They took a subway, then a boat to the island, which teemed with children, and climbed up into the statue. Afterwards, as they rested on a bench, Cordelia wondered, "Why are children so fascinated by old Miss Liberty?"

"I don't know, Mama. But I used to know a psychologist who said where else can kids enter from the rear under the dress of such a huge woman figure and climb so high up her legs?"

"What does that mean?" asked Cathy, who they had thought was off buying popcorn.

"She is making an architectural reference with allegorical embellishments," Cordelia said.

"Grandma, and what does *that* mean?"

"Yes, Mama," Penny said, "I wish you'd try to express yourself more clearly."

They took a boat back to Manhattan and, to Cathy's delight, ate dinner in an automat and returned home so tired that Penny and Cordelia had their first sound sleep since Izzy died. Next day they took Cathy to

Coney Island, and the day after that Penny drove them and Lancelot to Hasty's where they spent three days swimming and loafing.

"All this land," Penny said, gazing across the woods and untilled fields which Cordelia owned. "Mama, if you divided it up into real-estate lots, you'd make a million."

"Who needs it? I've already got a million now that the stock market is healthy again. But someday I or you or somebody will sell it off because the taxes will get too high, and then there'll be another million or so that nobody really needs."

"I know," Penny said. "All we've got anymore is money."

"If we've got so much money," Cathy said, "why can't we afford to take taxis?"

Cathy had an infinite capacity to entertain herself; she never seemed lonely or out of sorts, but constantly expressed cheerful interest in her surroundings. Cordelia wished she could be the same.

The day after she attended the board-of-directors meeting at which Al, by unanimous vote, was named president and publisher of Lovejoy's, she decided to return to work. Cathy was ecstatic over being invited to go along and sit at a table in Cordelia's office and "play editor."

Cordelia admitted to a mood of disenchantment with her work that morning. The accumulated mail was depressing. The head of a school-library system in Oklahoma chastely chastised Lovejoy's for publishing a young adult novel in which someone said "damn." From a California town came a board-of-education letter reviling Lovejoy's for publishing a young adult biography of that notorious communist Karl Marx. Two authors whined about the low sales of their books. An agent sharply rebuked Cordelia for her slowness in responding to a manuscript. It all reminded her of a

crude yet apt remark that Edward had made more than
fifty years ago: "Some days publishing doesn't have as
much creative satisfaction as pissing in a snowbank."

She was working along at her problems when she became aware of someone looking at her from the doorway. She glanced up at Al, and was about to make
some pleasantry when she had a strange, intuitive sense
of warning. If pleasantries were to be exchanged, let
him make the first. Yet she knew none was forthcom-
ing. His dark face was somber and heavy with the
weight of bad news. While waiting for it to fall on her,
there flashed the realization that the way Al looked
now was how she herself must often have looked in past
years when about to fire some employee whose performance—or maybe whose mere presence—had dis-
pleased her.

She braced herself, determined to try to find some
wry humor in the fact that if age didn't swing much
weight it could at least turn some tables around.

Al's brooding gaze swept from her to Cathy, who
had grown very still and was looking at him oddly, as if
sensing something wrong.

"Hi, Cousin Al." Cathy's voice started out piping
and sank to a whisper.

He did not answer, but, barely nodding, turned and
disappeared.

"What," whispered Cathy, "is bugging Cousin Al?"

"Maybe his extreme youth, maybe my extreme age."

Cathy frowned reprovingly. "Grandma, sometimes
you say things awful hard to understand." Then, not
wishing to reprove her, she said, "Let's stop at our
work for a while and have a good laugh. I'm going to
tell you a joke." Cordelia did not listen, but chuckled
appreciatively when Cathy finished. "Now you tell me a
joke, Grandma. Don't you know any jokes?"

"Yes," Cordelia said after a pause. "There was the
boss of this company, and he came in to fire this em-

ployee. He said, 'You're fired!' And the employee said, 'You can't fire me because I just quit!' ''

Cathy gave a whoop of laughter. "Grandma, that's a *good* joke."

Cordelia put a yellow memo slip in her typewriter, dated it, and wrote:

> *To*: Alfred T. Epstein
> *From*: Cordelia Lovejoy
> I hereby resign as an editor and board member of this company, effective at once.

She put it in an envelope addressed "personal" to Al and said to Cathy, "We've had enough work for one day."

"This is a pretty short working day," Cathy said. "Papa wouldn't understand it at all. Some days he works twelve and fourteen hours."

"But his work is more interesting than ours," Cordelia said. "Bring along that picture book if you want to." Suddenly she realized there was not a single thing she wanted to take with her.

Pausing in the doorway of Grace Stevenson's office, she said, "So long, Grace."

Grace smiled at her. "Leaving for the day, Cordelia?"

"Yes, Cathy and I are going up to Central Park and eat hot dogs and look at the animals in the zoo."

"Be in tomorrow?"

"No, tomorrow we're going to the *Bronx* Zoo. I've come to the conclusion that animals are more interesting than humans."

"Funny thing," Grace said, "the sales of juvenile books bear that out as the absolute truth. If anybody looks for you, when will I say you'll be back?"

"Not this century," Cordelia said. "Next century I may change my mind. Take it easy."

* * *

Al scrawled "resignation accepted" on the bottom of Cordelia's memo and sent it back open-face so that everybody from the mail room on could read it and pass the word. Grace mailed it to Cordelia without comment.

Penny, greatly distraught, arrived a few minutes after the mailman delivered Grace's envelope. "I heard all about it!" she exclaimed. "Mama, you mustn't resign from the board."

"But I just did yesterday, honey, and I won't reconsider. At first I wondered why Grace sent me this, but now I know she—well—"

"Yes," Penny said, "Grace wants you to know what a—I'd call Al a son of a bitch except that wouldn't make me sound too good. Guess we should settle for just calling him a shit."

"Don't be too hard on him," Cordelia said. "Think what they used to call me when I was high in the saddle."

"Mama!" Penny cried. "If you try to act *big* about this, so help me I'll bop you."

Cordelia was not trying to put on a good face; she just felt unbelievably lighthearted over her release from Lovejoy's.

Penny said, "What Al has done is unforgivably rude and ridiculous."

"That's publishing," Cordelia said. "Unforgivably rude and ridiculous. Come along to the Bronx Zoo with Cathy and me."

"Would like to, but I have work to do. I'm going to the office and try to talk some sense into that little—"

"Better luck to you, Penny, than I had with Steve. Come to the zoo with us and see how happy more intelligent creatures can be."

"Sorry, no." Penny's eyes filled with tears. "Everybody at the company already hates Al—and it's going to get worse."

It did get worse. If, in fact, there were any way of keeping records of such things, Alfred T. Epstein might have proved to be the most disliked publisher in New York during the early years of his reign.

Personal greed, lack of feeling for others, fantastic egotism made him hated by associates, authors, agents, the general publishing community. Those who had been friends of his parents and Cordelia ran out of excuses for his behavior. Hard as everyone tried, none could find sensible reasons for his perversity.

He developed a hyenalike laugh that the big-game hunters who frequented publishers' parties learned to detect as the sound of Al feasting on some wounded or fallen literary lion. Indeed he seemed to take pleasure in putting down authors. Not only did he say it was a waste of money to advertise books in general, he told authors personally that it was a waste to advertise their specific works. Thus, when Lovejoy's attained a major book-club main selection after many years and gave a party for the author, Al told him that he didn't think his book was very good and was surprised the book club had been so stupid as to select it.

The author fled from him, spluttering, "That bastard would sell his own grandmother down the river."

"He already has," said the current head of publicity.

It was no wonder that Lovejoy's had numerous one-book authors, who passed on to greener pastures—or to the vacuum of the unpublished. Al did not much care. He said that writers were like weeds in a corn patch: chop down one, and two more would spring up in place.

A rival publisher, who disdained Al, referred to him as "that shotgun man who's scared to fire a rifle for fear he'll miss." What he meant was that Al expanded the company's lists, publishing twice as many books annually as Lovejoy's had before World War II, on the theory that the more one produced the better the averages that some would be commercially successful. The books, not as carefully selected and edited or as heavily promoted as in the days of Izzy, Penny, and Cordelia, suggested the scattershot effect of a shotgun: Fire away and you'll probably hit something.

In one area of publishing, however, Al did take careful aim at his targets. It involved books dealing with politicians and political subjects. When he took over direction of the company, American politics was charged with emotion. Politicians like Joseph McCarthy and Richard Nixon were taking advantage of Cold War tensions to further themselves by claiming that communist agents had gained power in government and other areas of American life; in every possible way they sought to discredit the Truman Democratic administration and the Roosevelt administration that had preceded it.

One morning, about six months after Al became president of Lovejoy's, Cordelia received a phone call from Eleanor Roosevelt. "Cordelia, remember that book we mentioned my writing a long time ago? Well, I've finished it and I'd like you to read it." Eleanor invited her to tea that afternoon.

Cordelia brought the manuscript home and sat up most of the night reading it. Before eight o'clock next morning she called Penny and told her what had happened. "She's really done a good job, Penny."

"Mama, did you make an offer?"

"Make an offer? Are you crazy? I'm not an employee of Lovejoy's. Haven't set foot inside the place or exchanged a single word with its president since I resigned."

Penny uttered a groan. "Oh, Mama, I know, I know. He's a churl. But maybe this will—It's a great coup to publish the autobiography of Eleanor Roosevelt. I think he'll be properly grateful to you and—well, things will get back together again."

"Back together? Doesn't he know where his grandmother lives? I'm listed in the phone book. My idea is for you to present it to him. He at least speaks to you."

Penny groaned again. *"Please,* Mama! Let me call him and we'll go together to see him, just as though nothing happened."

Cordelia meditated for a moment, then relented. "I never had any ambition to be Queen Lear."

When they went to Al's office, he greeted Cordelia cordially, even bussing her on a cheek and saying, "Long time no see," as if she had been in a foreign country.

"Grandma has some absolutely wonderful news for you," Penny said.

Then Cordelia told him. He had heavy brows that gradually drew as he listened, until they looked like a charcoal drawing of a crow in flight. After she finished, he said, "Is that the manuscript, Grandma?"

"Yes." She held it out to him, smiling.

"No, thanks," he said. "I don't want it. Lovejoy's will never publish anything by Eleanor Roosevelt. I think the Roosevelts have done more damage to American society than any family that ever lived. Lovejoy's will never be party to promoting the name of Roosevelt."

Cordelia and Penny were struck dumb.

Al went on, "I'm interested in nonfiction on politics and politicians. But I want to be very selective about it and do affirmative things about American government and this communist menace we face." He gave them his warmest smile. "Grandma, if you could land me the autobiography of Joe McCarthy—"

Penny gave a strangled cry. "Jesus H. Christ!"

His brows flew apart, as if that crow of the charcoal drawing had been shot. "Mama, what is—"

"You dumb, mean little bastard!" Penny shouted, swinging to her feet. "You're living proof of the need for birth control!" She raised her hands like talons and might have slashed his face with her nails if his big desk had not been between them. Unfortunately, he kept a rather clean desktop; but all that was on his desk she swept to the floor with both hands. Then she stormed out, nearly knocking down his frightened secretary as she went. Cordelia trotted behind, clutching Eleanor's manuscript to her breast.

When they reached the street and Cordelia had breath to speak, she said, "What am I going to tell Eleanor?"

"Tell her," Penny said, "that you and I will exert every influence we have in the book world to make sure she has the best publisher in existence at the most advantageous terms to her."

Penny might have flung herself in front of a taxi if Cordelia had not grabbed her by an arm. "Honey, what are you going to do now?"

"I'm going to my house and have a double Scotch. Come with me."

"It's only eleven o'clock in the morning."

"I don't give a damn if it's only six o'clock in the morning. You come with me. That is an order, Mama!"

After a Scotch, Cordelia found the courage to phone Eleanor. She said the manuscript was superb and then tried to explain that her grandson was an ass. Eleanor was very understanding, saying she knew how children and grandchildren could be complete asses. Of course she and her agent would appreciate any help Cordelia and Penny could be in finding a good publisher.

The two had another Scotch and agreed on who would be the best publisher for Eleanor's book. Cordelia called him, and, elated by the opportunity, he sent a messenger to pick up the manuscript.

Cordelia said they should have something to eat if they were going to have another drink. Penny said the cook was off today and there was nothing to eat but some old peanut brittle. Cordelia said she was afraid of cracking a tooth on peanut brittle, so they had another drink.

They began plotting to gain control of the company and unseat Al. For a while it was great fun, but then it became depressing. Because, no matter what allies they counted on, Al still would control fifty-two percent of the stock. Izzy, as well as Penny and Cordelia themselves, had planned it that way. Al had inherited the company while Izzy's large real-estate holdings had gone to Penny.

The entire course of Alfred T. Epstein's life might have been different if Foxy hadn't fallen in love with Alger Hiss. Foxy had never set eyes on Hiss, who had had a distinguished career in government until he and his wife Priscilla were accused of once having been communist spies by a *Time* magazine editor, Whittaker Chambers. Foxy had paid little attention to Hiss's two trials; it was not until later, after his conviction, that she read a book about the case and became convinced he was innocent.

When she told Al that Hiss was innocent, he said she had lost her mind. There was no doubt of his guilt, Al said, "and Whittaker Chambers is one of the great men of our time." (Later he wished he had put his money where his mouth was and tried to outbid another house for Chambers' memoirs.) Foxy persisted in believing Hiss innocent. She and Al were beginning to quarrel— at first over money. She liked money as much as he, but she didn't mind spending it, especially when she didn't have to earn it herself.

After he became president of Lovejoy's they continued to live in a small, inexpensive apartment on Murray Hill. Even though his salary increased to fifty thousand a year, he maintained they could not afford anything more plush. He complained about every penny she spent—for a Persian lamb coat (not even a mink!), for grocery bills, even over the fact she could have her hair done in a less expensive beauty shop. As time passed, this extraordinary stinginess of Al's weighed on Foxy more heavily than on his employees, who at least were free of tyranny on weekends. To her mind the worst thing about his lectures on thrift was that they were delivered in such cold, dispassionate terms, like a weary cleric reading from Holy Writ. It was so difficult to stir Al to passion, even in a double bed on a cold night.

Thus Foxy was interested to observe that she could make Al angry by insisting the convicted Alger Hiss was innocent of any crime. She never had been very fond of Penny until she learned that her mother-in-law felt the same about Hiss; and when she learned that Cordelia also was convinced of his innocence, Foxy adopted an entirely different view of her. As soon as Cordelia heard about Foxy's feelings she invited her and Penny to lunch and all had a wonderful time reviewing the case and assembling evidence that proved beyond doubt Hiss was innocent.

Penny said she and Al were going to a conservative-sponsored dinner next evening which would be addressed by Richard Nixon, the California Congressman who was credited with having done so much to bring about Hiss's trial on perjury charges.

"That dirty worm has smeared and jobbed everybody to advance himself," Penny said.

"Foxy, give him hell," Cordelia said.

Foxy did. In his after-dinner speech Nixon recapitulated the Hiss case and his own role in it for the edification of a couple of hundred of the political faithful. Questions were asked by admirers following the speech, and Foxy, quaking with fear, finally got one out in a squeaking voice:

"Sir, why are you so happy about convicting an innocent man?"

There were boos from the audience, and Nixon formed a condescending smile, shrugged, and said, "Next question?"

Al was enraged. When they got home, he paced wrathfully, to Foxy's intense delight. Finally he yelled, "You're in *love* with Alger Hiss!"

"Yes, I am!" she yelled back. "Al Epstein will never be the man that Al Hiss is. As soon as Al gets out of jail and both of us get our divorces we're moving to Ireland and—and walk the green fields together."

Al stared at her with an air of uncertainty. Then he sneered and asked, "On whose money?"

"On yours, you tightwad bastard! What a case I've built against you, Alfred Tennyson Epstein. When my lawyer gets through with you, you're going to be paying *ninety percent* of your salary in alimony! See these black-and-blue marks on my breasts, you sodomite?"

Al was aghast. He was not a sodomite and there were no black-and-blue marks on her breasts.

"Well," Foxy said, "there will be when I bare them for the jury!"

After that he became a little fearful of her, she was pleased to see, and stopped lecturing her on thrift. But maybe that was because he had hit on an ingenious scheme for saving money.

First he had the company rent a large, expensive apartment on Murray Hill for the announced purpose of entertaining authors, agents, and others who did business with Lovejoy's. Next he had the apartment handsomely furnished at company expense and then he and Foxy moved in as full-time tenants. Lovejoy's current comptroller suggested that the arrangement need not be reported to the Internal Revenue Service so long as he and Foxy maintained legal residence elsewhere. So Al listed Penny's house as their legal home and offered his mother some vague explanation to which she paid no attention.

Foxy was thoroughly content with the arrangement. She never had lived as well; she even had maid service at company expense and bought more steaks and lamb chops than she had been allowed to previously because part of the grocery bill went on the entertainment expenses paid by the company. Further, she enjoyed the entertaining that they actually did of authors, agents, and a select few top employees whom Al considered "loyal." Life might have gone on thus with some serenity if it had not been for the 1952 presidential elections.

Once Al's favorite candidate, conservative Senator Robert Taft, was out of the running, he had to go along with the Republican candidate, General Dwight D. Eisenhower, who had made a couple of shocking liberal remarks. But Al was encouraged somewhat when Eisenhower picked Richard Nixon to be his vice-presidential candidate. Of course Foxy was for the Democratic candidate, Governor Adlai E. Stevenson of Illinois. She had always considered herself a Republican, but four years as the wife of Republican Alfred T. Epstein had turned her into a confirmed Democrat. Naturally Al was outraged by her defection. He had a hunch she still was in love with the traitor Al Hiss, and when she began to poke fun at Nixon—the one who had seen through Hiss's perfidy—Al experienced strange emotions of jealousy. Sometimes when the television set was running late in the watches of the evening, they exchanged angry, bitter remarks that went beyond politics.

Their quarrel of the moment, coinciding with their political disagreement, involved ashtrays. There had been a dozen beautiful onyx trays in the original furnishing of the apartment which, mysteriously and one by one, disappeared. At first they suspected the maid and set a trap for her—but she was innocent. Next they wondered if Lovejoy's most popular novelist was a kleptomaniac, but then their suspicions shifted to the vice-president in charge of sales, and thence to a distinguished literary agent. Whoever was guilty, the ashtrays went—and they replaced them with a dozen more. When these too disappeared, Foxy was embarrassed to put more on the expense account, so she went to Altman's and put a dozen on her personal account.

The night Republican vice-presidential candidate Richard Nixon was to go on national television to try to explain why he had been receiving money from questionable sources, Al was reviewing the household bills. When he came to the ashtray item on Foxy's charge account at Altman's, he demanded an explanation. She explained, and he said:

"Take them back."

"Why? Can't we afford a few ashtrays?"

"So they can be stolen too? Foxy, take them back and buy some cheap ashtrays at Woolworth's."

"Take 'em back yourself and *you* go to Woolworth's."

At that moment Nixon came on the waiting TV screen and used his wife, children, and even his spaniel dog to humiliate himself and in that way to try to protect himself against the charges. Al's eyes filled with sympathetic tears for poor Richard Nixon, but Foxy hooted and jeered.

"Tricky Dicky!" she cried after he went off. "Ricardo the Prickardo! Remember the poor spaniel Checkers! What a low-down son of a bitch! Come now, old Alfred, can you offer any sensible defense for such a worm?"

Al, dashing moistness from his eyes, cried, "Victoria, you're an unfeeling bitch!" Inflated by rage, he seemed to float rather than rise from his chair. "Take the goddamn ashtrays back to Altman's!"

"Shove the goddamn ashtrays up your ass!" Foxy cried.

Al seized one of the ashtrays and dashed it on the floor. Possibly it was not really onyx, for it shattered, and a chip grazed Foxy's cheek. Quickly taking advantage, she clapped a hand to her right eye and screamed, "You *blinded* me!"

He started toward her, and then, almost fainting with horror at his viciousness, he fell back into his chair. By the time he had pulled himself together somewhat, Foxy was gone.

She'd had the presence to grab her bag and a coat as she fled. She started toward Penny's house, but then, recalling that Penny had flown to Chicago where Nora was in some kind of trouble, she almost ran to Cordelia's house.

Cordelia let her in and said, "Did you see that poor slob Nixon on television?"

"Yes! He's part to blame for—Grandma, can I stay with you while I'm getting my divorce?"

"Of course," Cordelia said. "What'll you have— Ovaltine or booze?"

"Booze." Then Foxy told her the absurd story. "I want to *murder* him."

"Naturally," Cordelia said. "But I have a better idea. You must frighten him to death. That way they can't prosecute you."

Cordelia sat up with her into the early morning hours listening to what was wrong with Al. He rang the doorbell around eight o'clock; after visiting East Side hospitals and awakening people everywhere, he had finally remembered Cordelia. She told him Foxy's eye would be all right but that she did not want to speak to him.

Al looked so wretched and was so incoherent with worry over her that Cordelia almost couldn't bring herself to say:

"This afternoon Foxy is seeing Lawyer Brown."

"Lawyer Brown, Lawyer Brown?" babbled Al. "Who's he?"

"An old retainer. Guess you've drifted so far from family you've forgotten him. Either he or Foxy will be in touch. Good-bye, Al."

Of course there was no Lawyer Brown, only Cordelia herself. After Foxy awakened and they were having coffee together, Cordelia asked, "Do you really want a divorce? If you do, I think you should. It's one of those modern conveniences, like improved plumbing, that just didn't exist when I was your age."

Foxy admitted she sort of loved Al, if only he'd stop acting so impossible.

"Then listen to old Lawyer Brown," Cordelia said. "I know he loves you by the way he acted when he burst in here. But we've got to make him sweat a bit, the way he makes everybody else sweat. You said last night you hate that company-sponsored apartment and want you and Al to have your own place. So you should refuse to go on living there. I think it's not only unwise, but unethical and probably illegal. So phone Al this afternoon and tell him Lawyer Brown says you can easily get five hundred a week support from him. Follow that up by saying Brown is shocked by the apartment arrangement and says it's illegal and he's reporting it to the Internal Revenue Service. And you must absolutely refuse to see Al."

He panicked when he heard the support figure and the news that the apartment was being reported to the IRS. Of course he didn't hire a lawyer, but sought advice from the company lawyer, Wade McLaughlin, to save a fee. Wade, who detested Al and was fond of Cordelia, phoned her and asked her what it was all about. She invited him to her house to discuss the situation with Lawyer Brown over a glass of sherry.

Wade, never consulted about the apartment arrangement, was irked by its illegality and fell in gladly with Cordelia's plan. The charade lasted only a couple of days before Al capitulated.

Lawyer Brown promised not to squeal to the IRS on Al's promise to abandon the company apartment and find an equally comfortable one for Foxy and himself on Murray Hill. Her promise to resume being Al's wife was predicated on his promise to curb, perhaps reform, his miserliness and stop delivering lectures on thrift. Then lawyers Brown and McLaughlin decided it would be a good idea to seal the bargain by Al's taking Foxy on a two-week vacation to Hawaii, first class all the way.

As Foxy told Cordelia, "We may not live happily ever after, but at least I'll get two weeks in Hawaii. Al's really being a good sport about it."

But she was a good sport, too. She never again mentioned the case of Alger Hiss to him.

34

Cordelia's strongest attachments, after Penny, were to Edward, Sara, and their children, Cathy, Eric, and David—especially to Cathy. So she was overjoyed when, in 1955, they left the Northwest and Edward bought a farm in the New York Finger Lakes region, where he devoted himself to hybrid experimentation with various fruits and vegetables.

His work as a plant scientist gave him complete satisfaction, and Sara said she wouldn't exchange country living for the softest life on Murray Hill. When Cordelia visited them for a couple of weeks in the summer of 1956, she saw that Cathy felt differently and was bored with rural living. She was very bright, an excellent student who found no stimulation in her regional school.

Edward and Sara said the only solution was to send her to boarding school, but they dreaded separation and believed a child should grow up with family. After a while Cordelia ventured a suggestion, somewhat timidly. Since there were many excellent day schools in Manhattan, would Cathy like to attend one and live with her?

"I'm really cautious about it," she said. "A very old woman like me and a very young person like Cathy can get on each other's nerves. I don't know that there's much we can communicate about. And I have a dread of being one of those awful creatures who wants to *mold* young people. I remember how I was taken over by cousins at about Cathy's age and how miserable I was with their trying to make me into something I didn't want to be."

"I like the idea," Sara said.

Edward agreed. "Of course it's up to Cathy. But it shouldn't be presented to her as something irrevocable. Tell her it's a temporary arrangement while she decides where she wants to go to boarding school. Then see what happens."

Cathy was ecstatic. She easily qualified for one of the best schools, and there certainly was no problem about money. At the outset Cordelia told her that she was not a policewoman, and if she ever had to be, then Cathy should plan to live elsewhere. She was old enough to know when to go to bed and not to oversleep in the morning; and if she didn't know, it was time she learned. They did not have to see more of one another than Cathy wished. Most of the time they would have breakfast and lunch separately. Cathy could bring home friends whenever she wanted to and go see friends as she pleased; it was up to her to balance fun and friendships with her studies. Every night that Cathy wished, Cordelia would enjoy her company at dinner, served at half past six.

As it turned out, she joined Cordelia for dinner almost every evening, and usually she was in the den at six o'clock with a soft drink when Cordelia had the preprandial double Manhattan which Dr. Prettyman had set as her grog ration for the day. During their long conversations Cordelia explored just what sort of woman Cathy might become. Beautiful, as she had forgotten she herself had been, but too high spirited to barter her beauty for any kind of gain. Though she had strong emotions, there were signs that she might be mainly motivated by her excellent mind. Most happily, she had no symptoms of snobbery and false pride.

Cordelia knew, of course, she was being overly optimistic about the maturing process, which always should be viewed with extreme pessimism. Just look at her three granddaughters by Penny! All had married and all divorced; none had made worthwhile use of the many opportunities their parents had offered. Look at Al, who had started out so tough and nasty and only now was beginning to level off. Look what a blah Eunice had become and what disasters had overtaken Steve. Apart from Penny, the only ones in the family who had survived happily were Edward and Sara—and they seemed to have managed it mainly by withdrawing from society and ceasing to engage in many of its battles. So why should she count on Cathy becoming anything worthy? Probably the best ever in this family had been Ann, who had paid the supreme price for her worthiness.

Don't, Cordelia kept telling herself, count on Cathy at all. And yet she did—she could not help it.

Of course Cathy could not make her young again, but she did remind her vividly of what it was like to be young. Cordelia had forgotten the anticipation one felt in youth. What would Cathy *be*?

For the first time in sixty years she hoped that a young member of the family would not become involved in book publishing. In that direction, she thought, lay unhappiness. Edward had been correct to shun it and go far afield as a plant scientist. Since Cathy received excellent grades in science (but then she got excellent grades in everything), how wonderful if she became a physician, a Dr. Prettywoman offering health and life to others—or a researcher who discovered something of benefit to humanity. However, her interest in science waned almost as quickly as it started and she showed increasing fascination with literature. Cordelia wanted to deplore that new direction of Cathy's interest; instead, she found herself pleased.

"Grandma, what writer would you have liked most to publish that you didn't?"

"Joseph Conrad. I met him once in London, but he was committed to another American house."

Cathy, who had recently discovered his work and loved it, asked, "What was he like?"

"I had an impression of a rather unpleasant man, but one of unquestioned genius. The only writer of real genius I ever met who was delightful socially was Thomas Hardy. But later unpleasant things were said about the poor man."

"What sort of things?"

"It doesn't matter. I think they were mainly spread by that nasty little Somerset Maugham, who liked to go around assassinating people. You can't generalize about writers any more than about publishers. Though Martha Foley—she's a woman who has done as much for American writers with her short-story collections as any living person—Martha says that as a group writers are probably the stupidest bunch of people on earth. Martha says no other group would be dumb enough to let themselves be used as badly as publishers use writers. She says when publishers aren't ignoring writers, they're insulting them. I think she has a point."

"But writers couldn't exist without publishers."

"As publishers couldn't exist without writers," Cordelia said. "Each lives off the gambles of the other."

Cordelia did not realize how deeply her talk of books, writers, and publishing interested Cathy. Nor did she fully realize how vital the child's companionship had become until Cathy graduated and left Murray Hill for Wellesley College.

Al would not have admitted to reforming himself because he did not seem to feel he ever had erred. Nevertheless, while still having spasms of penny-pinching, he grew more generous in spirit as time passed. He still had enemies, but they did not castigate him as they once had. He raised wages somewhat, began to listen to people more experienced than he, and found that employees stayed longer. Like everyone, he made mistakes. But he clearly was doing many right things because Lovejoy's made more money than ever and its paperback subsidiary, Planet Books, began to show a profit for the first time in years.

Al insisted that it was wise to free the company from strict family control. While he maintained a principal share, the stock went on the open market, at first as over-the-counter and later as an American Exchange listing. As its value was enhanced and dividends increased, Cordelia remarked to Penny:

"I used to be sure I'd die in poverty. Now I don't know how to spend all this money wisely. What am I to do with it?"

"If you don't want it, Mama, give it to the poor."

"No, I've never trusted the poor to spend wisely, either."

After years of despairing over Al, she was at last pleased by the way he was running the company. But she never expected him to say what he blurted out during Christmas dinner at her house in 1959.

"You know, Grandma, you were smart to quit work when you did. I hated to see you go, but now I'm glad to see how happy you are toodling around."

Cordelia and Penny looked at each other in astonishment; both knew it was as close as one of Al's proud nature could come to an apology.

Maybe fatherhood helped to mellow him, for a son, Robert, had been born to Foxy and him in 1955, and a daughter, Patricia, was born two years later. Foxy, who came to see Cordelia almost every week, said that Al wasted money on toys which were too mature for the children. Cordelia thought she was making a joke about the erstwhile tightwad, but motherhood had made Foxy more serious than ever: She truly felt Al was throwing away money.

Cordelia made Penny promise not to give a party for her ninetieth birthday in 1960. It would be too taxing for both her and relatives, who now included nine great-grandchildren: "There's no cause for those young ones to pay tribute to anybody who's lived to such an absurd age. Besides, sometimes I can't keep their names straight. Embarrassing to be caught with your senility showing like a slip hanging below your skirt."

Actually she showed no signs of senility and her physical health was excellent. She was slightly deaf and not as steady on her feet, but Dr. Prettyman pronounced her sound. "Basically, that is," he always added. "At our ages, Mrs. Lovejoy, there's no reason to brag. We should qualify a little. So I say basically."

At ninety-four he appeared basically sound himself. Though he had given up his practice at ninety-one after his wife died, he remained on Murray Hill, seeing a very few patients of long standing like Cordelia and entertaining himself with tropical fish, wood-carving, and books he'd never had time to read.

When he called on the afternoon of her ninetieth birthday and presented her with a small wood-carving, she told him, "Just last week I heard one of those big talkers on the television say, 'Who wants to live to ninety?' Nobody answered him, but if I'd been there I'd have said, 'Anybody who's eighty-nine.' "

For years Penny had been saying Cordelia should sell her house and move into an apartment, for the stairs seemed to get longer and the servant problem became serious after Dolley and Washington retired in 1957 and went back to Louisiana. Then the servant problem was resolved when the Joneses' youngest son, Sidney, was laid off by the Pullman Company and he and his wife, Olive, tried working as a couple for Cordelia: All went perfectly. But the stairs kept getting longer, so a few months after her ninetieth Cordelia sold the house and moved into a penthouse in a new

Murray Hill high-rise where the quarters were big enough for Sidney and Olive to live with her.

A few weeks later Penny, too, sold her house and took the penthouse next to Cordelia's. "This way," she said, "we can preserve our independence, but be close enough for mutual support when needed."

"You bet," Cordelia said. "Anytime you want to have a good fight, come on over. Well, I finally made it. This has got to be the top of Murray Hill—not counting the Empire State." From her bed, when the curtains were open, she could see the spire of the great building shining in the night sky. "I can't get over everything being right here on one floor. Why have I been climbing stairs all my life?"

"To get to the top," Penny said.

While Cordelia's world grew smaller, more rarefied, utterly secure, she did not rid herself of worries. Her chief concern was Cathy. What would become of her? Attractive, bright, and popular, she seemed destined to be the first Lovejoy woman ever to graduate from a first-rate college.

"But don't count on it," Cordelia told Penny. "Nothing ever is as good as it seems to those looking on. Cathy is too perfect to be real."

"Stop fretting, Mama. She's real enough. And she's going to graduate near the top of her class."

"But what will become of her then?"

"She'll probably do something unpredictable like Ted did after he got out of the navy."

"There have been too many unpredictables," Cordelia said. "I want something predictable for a change. Penny, am I sounding querulous?"

"A little, Mama."

"Then I'll shut up. But before I do, is there any news regarding that other thing I've been querulous about lately?"

"None that I know of."

That other matter was the fact a conglomerate was interested in buying Lovejoy's. It was not the first time a large corporation had expressed an interest in purchasing the company, but it was the first time Al had shown a wish to sell. When Cordelia heard of it she became deeply disturbed. She had thought she was finished with Lovejoy's forever and no longer cared what happened there. Alas, that was not so. She had heard and read a good deal about what bad things happened when a huge corporation absorbed an independent publishing house, and she carried on about it to Al until he became impatient with her.

"Grandma," he kept saying, "it depends on *what* corporation does the absorbing and *who* is in control of the company absorbed. This is a very good deal. I have absolute confidence in *them*. And absolute confidence in my ability to keep Lovejoy's free of objectionable interference."

Cordelia made a sniffing sound. "As the minnow said before it was swallowed by the shark."

"The value of your stock will almost double in a few years."

"A fat lot of good that'll do me. Al, what'll you do after they fire you?"

He smiled. "Reinvest my dividends and play golf."

"Play golf with who? Barnaby Fletcher says the men out at the Roaring Brook Club don't like to play with you because you cheat all the time."

He looked shocked. "Me *cheat*?"

The matter of Lovejoy's sale still was unresolved in June when Edward and Sara picked up Cordelia and Penny and drove them to Wellesley for Cathy's graduation.

After Cathy had her diploma safely in hand, Penny said, "Now see, Mama, how easily that graduation business went? We all know that none of mine ever made it all the way through, but a Lovejoy woman has finally graduated from a red-blooded college."

"As they say on the television," Cordelia said, "first down and ten to go. But what's she going to do now—complete a pass or fumble the ball?"

They found out soon after all five left Wellesley in Edward's car for New York.

"I've decided I want to try to find a job in book publishing," Cathy said. "I know you have to start at the very bottom for lousy wages and the main thing is that you know how to type and you've got to resign yourself to hunting and hunting because there are so many applicants and so few openings. Do you think I can find something eventually?"

"Oh my, oh my, oh my," Cordelia babbled while beaming at her. "Why, yes, I'd think so—in time, that is—wouldn't you, Penny?"

Late that night in New York, Cordelia and Penny had an argument. Cordelia thought Cathy should go to work for Lovejoy's; Penny thought that any other house would be preferable.

"Her name puts her at a disadvantage, Mama."

"No, her name is the finest there is. What is it these days that makes everybody pretend to be humble? They don't really mean it. They're just a bunch of Uriah Heeps. I'm proud of that company and proud of our name and proud that a great-granddaughter of mine named Lovejoy wants to carry on a fine tradition. Should she start as a reader?"

"Al started in the mail room."

"And there have been many times," Cordelia said, "when I wished he'd stayed there. So you think being a reader is too lofty a start for Cathy?"

"Yes. Remember she majored in English. And college English majors have a lot to unlearn when they start to wrestle with commercial words. Anyway, we're meddling. Cathy hasn't said where *she* wants to look for a job."

She told them at breakfast. "I'd like most of all to go to work for Lovejoy's, but I don't want to use any pull. I want to apply—anonymously."

"What will you say," Cordelia asked, "when they want to know your name?"

"Oh, I'll give my name, I'll just say I'm no relationship to the founding fathers."

"And what will you say," Penny asked, "when Al recognizes and greets you?"

"No problem," Cordelia said. "Al never recognizes and greets relatives within the precincts of his company."

"That's true," Penny said. "Cathy, he's as much against nepotism as you are. Now put on something sloppy, honey, and toddle over to Lovejoy's. You'll find the reception room jammed with supplicants—fellow Phi Betes and magna cums from the Ivy League and the Seven Sisters, all aspiring to be Maxwell Perkins. Ask for a woman named Frances Thorpe. She'll have you fill out an application and take a typing and vocabulary test. Then she'll say they're keeping your name on file and you'll never hear from her again."

After Cathy had gone job-hunting and Edward and Sara had left for home upstate, Cordelia asked Penny if she had talked to Al about the acquisition negotiations.

"I called, but he's tied up. I talked to Foxy. She can't figure what's going to happen. She's more against selling out than ever. But that doesn't mean our side will win. Wish I'd told Cathy not to mention it to Al. Did you see how upset she was when she heard about the selling-out possibility? I like her line that all big corporations are immoral, but I don't want her saying that to Al. He thrives on family opposition."

Cordelia went out on the penthouse terrace to tend

her geraniums. A chill west wind was blowing, but she could not find her sweater where she thought she'd left it. Since Sidney and Olive were away on vacation, she pondered what to cook for dinner for Cathy and herself. When she came inside to check over the refrigerator, she felt a bit tired and decided to lie down and rest for a few minutes. Cathy's voice awakened her. To her astonishment it was half past three.

"I'm sorry to wake you, Gradma. Didn't know you were napping."

"How did it go?" asked Cordelia.

"Just like Aunt Penny said. Only Mrs. Thorpe said there are no openings. Then I went on looking." She named three other publishing companies. "The same thing everywhere. But I liked Mrs. Thorpe better than the others. She seemed to like me, too. I think I got to her on one thing. I said I can work a switchboard."

"Can you really?"

"Sure. It's the only thing I learned in that stupid municipal government internship last summer."

"But *would* you work a switchboard?"

Cathy grinned. "To get my foot inside the door at Lovejoy's? You bet I would. Grandma, you sound as if you're getting a cold."

"Hay fever," Cordelia said. "There's no hay on Murray Hill anymore, but every summer I get hay fever. Think I'm allergic to geraniums. Think I'll stop growing the damn things. They don't take care of themselves like they're supposed to." She started to get up, but, feeling very tired, she settled back. "I'll rest a minute more, then get dinner. Honey, what do you want to eat?"

"Tuna-fish sandwiches. I can eat tuna-fish sandwiches three times a day for days on end. And sometimes have."

"I remember." Cordelia shivered and asked her to fetch the afghan from the chair yonder.

"I'll make the tuna sandwiches," Cathy said. "And we'll have a big mess of sliced tomatoes and iced tea and ice cream. There's chocolate ice cream in the freezer. I checked before breakfast. How does that sound?"

"Great. Thanks for getting dinner." She closed her eyes, then opened them. "Where's Penny?"

"She was going out of the building as I came in. Said she has a dinner date uptown. Grandma, are you all right?"

"I'm fine." However, she was freezing and could not stop her cursed shivering after Cathy went to the kitchen. At last she decided to call Dr. Prettyman; he would prescribe some medicine that Cathy would fetch from the drugstore and then she'd feel better. But she was shaking so badly that she could not fit her finger into the proper holes of the dial telephone. At last she made Cathy hear her in the kitchen.

Cathy dialed Dr. Prettyman. The phone rang and rang, but there was no answer. "Try Doctor Achilles." Cathy found his number, and the secretary said he was in office hours and of course he never made house calls, as Mrs. Lovejoy knew. Somehow Cathy was forceful enough to bring Achilles to the phone. After hearing the symptoms, he said:

"Cover Mrs. Lovejoy well with blankets, give her two aspirin, and have her drink all the fluids she can. There's a summer virus about."

"Tell him to shove his summer virus." Cordelia sounded very hoarse. "Cathy, please try Doctor Prettyman again."

But no one answered his phone.

"He must be out on his patio and can't hear it," Cordelia said. "Every summer he moves his tropical fish out to the patio. He covers the tank with a metal mesh to keep out cats and hummingbirds. Does that sound funny? I'm not out of my head, there really are hummingbirds on Murray Hill and they're crazy about tropical fish. Cathy, would you mind very much trotting down to Doctor Prettyman's and asking him to come up here and take a look at me?"

Cathy hurried to the small brownstone where Dr. Prettyman occupied the first floor. When she rang the bell, no one answered. Seeing that the door to his floor was slightly ajar, she pushed it open and called, "Doctor Prettyman!" Thinking that a voice answered, she stepped inside and called again. A sound came from the patio at the rear of the house.

Passing through the rooms, she realized it was the rasping cry of a catbird in the lone ironwood tree which shaded the small patio. What was a catbird doing in this gritty city place? As she stared up at it, the bird seemed to direct her attention downward to the slate where Dr. Prettyman lay dead.

Cathy called the police, and, after a squad car and a city ambulance arrived, she hurried back to Cordelia's.

"Did you bring Doctor Prettyman?" Cordelia whispered.

"He's out on call," Cathy said. "But I talked to him by phone and he wants to get you into University Hospital right away. He said a cold like yours could go to pneumonia and you'll have the best care at the hospital. Grandma, I'm calling the hospital and have them send an ambulance. I'll say Doctor Prettyman is ordering you a room there. Isn't that the way he always said to do it?"

"No!" Cordelia sat up suddenly, her expression strange, and cried, "I insist on speaking to Doctor Prettyman!" Then she fell back.

While Cathy was calling Dr. Achilles's office, Cordelia ceased to breathe and her face took on a ghostly pallor. Cathy tried mouth-to-mouth resuscitation, as her father and mother had taught her, but she could not restore Cordelia's breathing. When Dr. Achilles arrived, he said she had died instantly. The ambulance paramedic had said the same thing about Dr. Prettyman.

It could not all have happened so swiftly, Cathy thought dazedly, as she saw it was just five o'clock. Dr. Achilles was writing something when the telephone raised an unearthly clamor and Cathy answered it.

A woman said, "May I speak to Catherine Lovejoy, please."

"Speaking," Cathy whispered.

"Catherine, this is Mrs. Thorpe at Lovejoy's. Something has come up. Our regular switchboard operator will be away a few days because of serious family illness and our secondary is out sick. Would you like to take over the board tomorrow as a temporary?"

"Yes, ma'm." Cathy's voice was barely audible. "I'll be there."

Cordelia, ever managing things, had been very firm about what was to happen after breath had left her body.

"Into the incinerator with the corpus very fast. No music, no hearts and flowers, no speeches, no preacher, priest, or rabbi. I mean absolutely no bull and everybody get on with what they're doing."

But such simplicity of plans did not make the long night that followed any easier for Cathy, Penny, Al, and Foxy. There were messages to send, phone calls to make, memories to stifle. Al did as much as any of them with an air of preoccupation that seemed to shield him from grief. Once Cathy almost told him she was to man his switchboard tomorrow, but she did not. A couple of times she was tempted to beg him not to sell the company, if only as a gesture of love and respect for their dead grandmother, but she kept silent.

It seemed to her she had not slept at all when the alarm brought her to her feet at seven-thirty next morning. She had no appetite for breakfast and set out for the office shortly after eight o'clock, hoping that her anticipation of today would help her subdue the grief of yesterday. Good luck, Catherine Lovejoy! She must take care to do nothing that would bring bad luck today. As she swung onto Madison Avenue she carefully avoided all sidewalk cracks. She saw a tall window-washer's ladder leaning against a building ahead, and would not have walked under it for ten thousand dollars. If she had seen a black cat, she would have turned and run.

Mrs. Thorpe arrived early to show her the eccentricities of the switchboard. By nine o'clock, when people were beginning to arrive for work, she felt she was mastering the thing.

Mrs. Thorpe, seated beside her, looked up and said, "Good morning, Mr. Epstein."

Al did not reply as he stared at Cathy.

"This is Cathy Lovejoy, Mr. Epstein. No relation to your family, she tells me. She's filling in temporarily for Maureen. She applied yesterday for editorial, but I explained we have no openings."

"Good morning, Cathy." Al spoke gravely. "Can you type?"

"Good morning, Mr. Epstein. Yes, sir, I can do seventy a minute."

"Not bad. With a little bit of luck we may find you an editorial assistant's job in time."

He started on slowly, as if reluctant to face the big decision awaiting him. Then he halted, turned all the way around, and gave Cathy a kind of relieved smile.

Dell Bestsellers